The Crewel Wing

a novel

Erica-Lynn Huberty

Briar Press . New York

Briar Press, New York, United States

Published in the United States by Briar Press New York Publishing, New York, NY

THE CREWEL WING
First Paperback Edition: 30 April 2025

Cover Design: Blossom Haven Design
Front Image Detail: Birth Registry, Anonymous, English, 1865
Back Image: Page from Illuminated Sketchbook of Stephan Schriber, German, 1494
Frontispiece: 'Kennet' by William Morris, 1883
All Images Public Domain

AUTHOR PHOTO by
Bebe Huberty, Hampton Court Palace 2022

ISBN: 979-8-9923584-0-7 (trade paperback)

www.briarpressny.com

For Liam & Beatrix, my children
&
In loving remembrance of Hilary Mantel, my Izzie

PROLOGUE

1884 ~ 29th February
Hammpen Manor
Pettypoole, Oxfordshire

A boy who works in the village takes his usual route from his mother's remote cottage across the snowy, hardened fields. He trudges past a herd of sheep huddled in the wind, then climbs onto a wide, lengthy barrow and travels along it. The boy's name is Davie and he sings to himself as he goes along, his normally pale cheeks apple-red in the cold, his wool cap pulled over his brow.

There are bodies hidden in Pettypoole's barrows, and Davie knows this: hundreds of them are anyone's guess, in these burial grounds that were once called *burghs* in the Old Language. They were forged millennia ago by ancient peoples—likely the same hunters and gatherers that placed jutting stone monuments in confounding patterns around the whole of England. Nowadays, the barrows are nothing more than oblong hills, the bodies beneath mere bone and dust. In Spring, ewes stand atop them and graze until the grass is shorn to dirt.

But today, an uncharacteristic, rasping frost dominates all of Pettypoole. The village cobbles are slick with ice, dagger-shaped icicles clinging to the branches of beech and oak, and copper drains, in glinting deposits. The grassy fields beyond the village are frozen hard and sport a thin layer of new-fallen snow which the boy Davie walks upon.

The barrows sit on the high fields and wolds near the Roman Road and, strictly speaking, they belong to the estate of Hammpen Manor. Herders lease the land from his Lordship, and they and their families usually live in or very near the village, in cottages of golden limestone. Very pretty the village is, with its winding lanes and well-kept gardens, its views of the rolling hillsides. Some, like Davie's mother, might even call Pettypoole friendly (unlike his Lordship, 'bless him). Suffice to say, Pettypoole is not the sort of place where someone is led to slaughter unless that someone is, in fact, a sheep.

As he makes his way, Davie does a clumsy skip his mother has warned him many times not to do; because you never cut through Hammpen Manor, even if you are late for your employer, and you most certainly do not dance merrily on the place where the ancient dead are hidden (these particular dead perhaps slaughtered, perhaps just departed from illness or age).

He stumbles. He pitches forward. His hand, planted to break his fall, is gashed open. One cheek smacks to the ground and his straight, stringy hair flops across his forehead as his cap tips off. He is now face-to-face with someone else's eyes: open eyes, cloudy as scored marbles and slightly protruding.

Around the corpse the snow is sullied in blotchy, brown adhesions. Brown, but with a distinct tint of red. A shoulder swathed in a tattered, black Ulster juts from the crest of the shallow grave.

Likely it's the dead man's coat catching on the boy's boot and not the boy's skipping, which has caused him to fall. But he is too simple-minded to realize this.

PART I:
Dragon's Eggs

"The modern ownership of movables is reducing us again to a nomadic horde... others go farther still, and move outside humanity altogether."

E.M. Forster

ONE

1872 ~ Spring
Allswell
St. Allswell, Sussex

Claire and Meg reached the sea's edge at dawn, both wide awake even after their long journey. The shore was broad, the light bouncing off the high chalk cliffs and glimmering on the surface of the water. Pebbles and things that looked like small rocks, but which were not rocks, littered the beach. When plucked and held in their hands, the girls noticed, spine-like imprints hugged their worn undersides: the marks of creatures long ago made extinct. Little grey iridescent fish swam against the sisters' ankles and darted amongst the fossilized remains as they padded through the cold, clear water.

They wore matching blue dresses made of common calico which their mother had sewn. The tiny red rosebuds scattered about the fabric had faded to indiscernible blots with wear and age. Running into the sea up to their ankles, Claire and Meg felt the rocks cut into the soles of their feet. They ran out again, in more of a cautious hobble. The rocks were the intermittent size of cracked eggs, saucers, and the ball of Meg's nose, all locked together into a painful carpet. For an hour or more the two girls played along the shingle like this, running in and out of the shallows, having stuffed their black wool stockings into their boots and placed them several feet up from the tide.

Claire was the eldest, at eleven years of age. She was dark of hair and her skin was what they called olive — though she thought it looked more like a walnut's husk — and her faded brown apron was too short for her tall legs. The blue dress reached only her calves when it should have come to her ankles at her age.

Meghan — called Meg by all — was snow-white with pale freckles and was only six. Her brown apron grazed the hemline of her too-long dress, so that she and her older sister looked like someone had tried to pass them off as twins with little effect.

The sea was nearly flat but for the little ripples of waves and, as they looked out, it appeared vast. Claire imagined sliding into the surprisingly vivid turquoise water and swimming toward Spain. She wondered how long it would take before she reached hot sand and an even brighter, hotter sun.

Blinking against the thought, she reached down and took her sister's hand in a gesture that signified a sudden decision. Within seconds, she felt Meg pull away and run giggling from her. She always knows, thought Claire, when I need her to do what she is about to be told.

"Meg, we really ought to head back. Mother will worry. Meghan? Are you listen-ing?"

They'd have to trek across the marsh and up the mucky riverbank to get back to Allswell, Claire thought now, as that was the way they had come. She suddenly felt hesitant, almost afraid, as if going back from where they had come was too herculean a task for children.

She didn't know how to make Meg understand how vital it was that they do everything right and the importance of their new home. How to explain that the brick and flint house, with its somber slate roof and dark green pastures, was an unexpected gift, startling and immediately temper-altering. She wasn't certain she understood the full magnitude of it herself. But she felt it.

The house and farm called Allswell was situated two miles from the village of St. Allswell. From the center of the village the River Cuckmere followed the valley into the South Downs marshland and ended at the white chalk cliffs which towered above the beach where the girls now played.

Claire sighed and called for little Meg again, scanned the landscape, and found Meg wading in the muck and reeds at the river's edge. The river, she thought, was only slightly less dangerous than the sea's hidden currents. She put her own boots back on and brought Meg's to her. "Mother will wonder where we are, Meg. Come out of there. Now."

Mother had spent the morning rushing about the house. She had unpacked their belongings, swept out the rooms, and laundered the musty linen left in the wardrobes of her parent's old home. Her sister's old home. Now hers. It was almost too much to take in and believe. Laundering the linen had infused her with a nostalgic air beyond reason.

As the girls came into the garden, they found the linen hanging from a line stretched between two trees in the sun, and their mother in the kitchen looking slightly hysterical.

Her face was flushed, her expression rare and dazzling like the daylight itself. She'd hardly noticed the girls were gone. When they sloshed back in through the kitchen door, she gave only a quick glance up and said, "Is that seaweed?"

"It's mermaid hair." Meg held the mess up, a clump of coarse sand falling from it and hitting the floor stones with a thump.

"We might finish unpacking tomorrow," Claire suggested, realizing they'd tracked filth onto the newly swept floor. She studied her mother, trying to discern what was expected of her. Clean the mess, that was the first thought.

Meg looked up at Claire and whispered, "Why is Mummy so odd today?"

"Give me that, you little beast," Claire hissed, grabbing the clump of seaweed from Meg's hand and tossing it back out the door into the kitchen garden.

Meg glowered, then began to cry, her eyes glazing over with fury.

"Can I help, at least?" Claire asked Mother, ignoring Meg. She'd never seen Mother this excitable: she had hardly stopped moving since their arrival. If Claire hadn't been so giddy herself, she would have found it alarming indeed.

"All is perfectly well. No worries here," said Mother. "Meg, stop whinging, my love?"

At the window there was a tapping sound and when Claire looked, the face of a brown and white goat filled the frame. It nodded and chewed Meg's seaweed, then tapped the pane again with the nub of its horn. All the goats had come with the house.

A fortnight ago, the girls had overheard (telegram arrivals, shocked whispers) that they were to live at Allswell because Mother's sister was dead from tumors in her womb. Aunt Aileen, childless, left the property to her only living sibling whose children she had never even met. There were no brothers alive, no uncles, no male cousins. The whole farm had gone to Mother.

Included in the bequest was a herd of goats that could be milked and also shorn, their hair transformed into silky skeins that rivaled sheep's wool. Word of all this came when they were living on the outskirts of Leeds and they rode south for days in foul weather with their belongings piled into a carrier's cart. When they pulled into the village last night the air was crisp and dry. Stars littered a black sky. The church's steeple was just slightly blacker against it.

The house itself was not very large but it felt enormous to Claire and Meg. Downstairs was a sitting-room, kitchen, a little library for Father, and a narrow spiraling staircase at the top of which were two bedrooms.

The newel post on the twisty stairs was topped with an acorn the size of Meg's head, carved from oak. "Our room has chickadees," Meg had whispered to Claire last night, and Claire hoped she did not think the wallpaper was actually alive with birds.

"They have their own room," Claire had also noted of their parents in a shocked tone, "which used to be Mummy's parent's room; and Mummy says the fireplaces aren't even stopped-up. Our room was Aunt Aileen's and Mummy's when she was little."

The goat continued staring at them through the kitchen window, chewing slowly. It moved its vertical pupils toward the open door as though it contemplated walking round and entering it.

"I don't feel well," Meg declared.

"You need a lie-down is all." Claire gave the top of her head a little pat, as if to tamp down any vomit that might be planning to exit her.

"Here," said Mother to Claire, "open this if you want to be helpful." She pointed to a crate by the range.

"Where is Father?" Claire asked.

As if on-cue Father, his round cheeks flushed rosy above his full white beard, bounced into the room from the front of the house, stopped to kiss the top of Mother's head, then sprang out the back door into the garden. "Get back, beast!" they heard him roar at the goat.

All day, he had been bouncing in and out of the house, making proclamations about the "Extraordinary view of our fertile land!" and "The silken sheen of our beasts!" He was like some frantic White Rabbit: My pocket watch!

"Garden needs mowing," Mother called after him. She always looked so small and delicate next to Father, yet it was she who counted the items in the larder, silently calculating what must sustain them week to week. Would she still do this, now they lived here? Claire wondered anxiously.

Father swooped back into the kitchen. Taking hold of Mother's small waist, he lifted her off her feet. Her umber hair, like Claire's, bounced against her cheeks as he spun her in her pale yellow dress. She laughed and squealed until he put her down and left the kitchen again, this time hopping through the sitting room and bounding up the stairs in loud stomps.

Mother reached for another crate in which two cooking pots, four chipped plates and a half-bag of mealy flour had been nestled in hay. She leaned over and rummaged, then straightened up against her strangulating stays. She looked on the verge of some exultant collapse. "We certainly won't need these again!" she gasped breathlessly as she tossed aside the chipped plates.

Her voice quivered, as if hope and grief were conspiring to choke her. As she stacked the empty crate haphazardly atop another, it was not far-fetched to imagine her throwing both through the window crash-and-splinter.

Father breezed back in, having changed into new buckskin breeches, bottle-green waistcoat, and gum Wellingtons. It was the perfect gentleman farmer's attire, and Claire had never seen him dressed as such.

"When did you get those?"

He kissed Mother's cheek. "Sit, lass, sit. You will wear yourself out. Have a cuppa?"

"No time. Too much to do. Meg, put those in the pantry, love." She handed Meg three jars of preserved fruit. She turned to Claire. "We'll have to repair the old loom and sheer the herd this week."

She sounded, Claire thought, vaguely conspiratorial. "What room?"

"Loom." Mother handed Claire a large clump of packing hay. "Feed this to the goats. Meg, help your sister. Claire, wait!" She pulled her eldest daughter back by the shoulders and into a tight embrace, making her drop the hay.

Fiercely, Mother whispered in her ear, "There shan't be another move after this. No more soot-encrusted flats. No black smokestacks, and the choking city dust!" She hugged Claire tighter.

Claire nodded stiffly against her mother's grasp. On her forehead she thought she felt a drop of wet and was horrified to think Mother was crying. She wondered if Mother was speaking of their rooms in the old lady's house near Leeds or their rooms in London when she described soot-encrusted flats.

Claire thought—she worried—that Mother might be going mad, talking of places she and Aunt Aileen had lived long ago. But they had lived here at Allswell as children, hadn't they? Perhaps right up until Mother married Father. So perhaps Mother meant Claire and Meg when she spoke of transience.

It was all so confusing. Claire only remembered one dark little flat in London (and not much of it), and knew they had then lived at the old lady's house near Leeds for as long as… it had been a long time, hadn't it? Unless… unless they had lived in other places she had forgotten before London, when she was too young to remember, all of them cramped and dark and sooty?

"Go feed the goats now," said Mother, loosening her grasp. But she held onto Claire's cheeks a moment longer with trembling hands, staring at her through wide, glistening eyes.

In the afternoon haze, Claire watched as Mother stood in the garden wiping her wet hands on her apron and speaking to their neighbour whom they'd just met. Her hands were pink and raw, the yellow dress marked in patches with dust and ash. The rose-water scent that usually emanated from her was gone, replaced by salty perspiration and something more earthy and sour.

"I need a man to clean out the cowshed, Mr Bolton, do you have one?" Mother said.

The man nodded. "I can arrange it." His property bordered Allswell and it was not more than five minutes' walk from house to house. A widower, Bolton had a small herd of sheep of his own. He also, he told Mother, let four of his six shire ponies to other farmers and grew corn and cabbage as well.

"Did you know my parents, Mr Bolton? I lived here as a child."

"I did not, m'am, but I think my wife's family did. Evans was their name." He looked tall and gangly next to Mother. He wore a black, wide-brimmed hat and grave expression. His arms, under his canvas coat, were long but taut with muscle from labouring.

"Evans... of course," Mother murmured. "I did know them. And do you not have help of your own? On the farm?"

Bolton nodded. "I've a housekeeper who comes daily from the village since my wife left us to be with the Lord. But Will and I manage well enough, the two of us. I've got a herder, and during lambing extra men are hired. My son can help you," he said, "I'll send my herder with him."

"Thank you." Mother smiled. "Do you have him on your own? William, his name is?" She nodded at the boy standing politely away from them.

Claire watched and listened to the conversation from where she sat on the grass some feet away, thinking there was something in it she needed to understand. She thought that perhaps Mr Bolton's look was more solemn and intimidating than he meant it to be. His appearance was certainly an odd contrast to Father, who was busy dragging an upholstered armchair out from the house.

Father positioned the chair where he wanted it, the long seed-heavy tendrils of grass creating a fringed screen around its base. Sighing contentedly, he sat his large, soft frame down, leaned back with his pipe and newspaper, and kicked his shining new boots up on a stump. As if just noticing the people around him, he waved to Mr Bolton. "Another glorious day in the South Downs, is it not, neighbour?"

Mother continued, pretending not to hear him. "We are nearly out of feed, Mr Bolton, from what I can see. For both the horses and the goats. In the meantime, I've put the goats into the lower field, as it hasn't been mowed in some time anyway. I thought there had been a man helping my sister?"

"He left when she died, ma'am. Took off without saying." Mr Bolton removed his hat and looked down at it.

"I see. Took off with what, I wonder?" She crossed her arms in front of her.

Bolton smoothed the brim of his hat, then put it back on. "I'll help you anyway I can. But your husband will know all about planting, I expect."

"My husband is a business-man."

He glanced over at Father. "I see. Well… I've got a reliable bloke delivers feed, and his cousin knows how to work a field. Honest men, both. Plough only needs oil and a good sharpening, I'm sure. She always kept things in order, your sister did, until she became too poorly to manage. She was a fine woman." He nodded solemnly again and looked directly at Mother.

Something in his expression, and the way he held Mother's gaze, made Claire feel confused and sad all at once. Suddenly, Aunt Aileen was real—she'd existed, and only weeks ago—yet she'd never meet her now.

Next to her on the grass, Meg played with a small ginger cat she found in the barn, onto which she forced an old baby bonnet. "Stop that," Claire scolded, "she doesn't like it."

"He," replied Meg.

"Bring it back to the barn, its mother will be looking for it," she countered.

"No."

"A pint would do you good, would it not, Mr Bolton?" Father offered again, his full voice reverberating like a deep, sonorous bell.

Their neighbour nodded, though not particularly in assent, and half-raised a hand as if trying to stop Father from talking. His eyes were still on Mother, as if trying to ascertain something from her.

The boy, William, had inched his way not far from the girls

and sat himself down on the grass. He wore trousers that were too big for him, his arms and face browned from the sun, his hair dark. He gave the appearance of listening respectfully to his father but was more interested in the progress with the cat. He caught Claire's gaze, his dark brown eyes resting on hers. He winked and nodded toward Meg as she wrenched the bonnet over the cat's eyes. The humour in his face seemed older and more knowing than his age.

Claire stifled a laugh and Will smiled at her. He had a big smile, with white teeth that shone, and Claire felt interested in what he would do next.

"Are they going to live here, too?" Meg asked.

"What, Mr Bolton and his son? Live with us?" She rolled her eyes. She was continually amazed at how daft Meg was, even for a six-year-old.

"When are we leaving, Claire?" Meg tightened the ribbon under the cat's chin. It gave a low growl.

"What on earth, you dim monkey...? We're not leaving. We are home. And I said stop doing that to the cat."

Meg looked at Claire as if hearing her for the first time. "What do you mean home?"

"My dear Mr Bolton, are you certain you will not take a glass with me?" Father called from his comfortable chair. "The finest claret in the whole of Sussex, we have, if the ale does not suit you?"

But Mr Bolton just looked at him, expressionless. He nodded to Mother and gave a quick look to the boy who sprang up, unasked, and followed his father home.

TWO

1872 ~ Autumn
Allswell
St. Allswell, Sussex

The river wriggled and looped through the narrow valley. They followed it along the high bank until it ended, then skittered down onto the marshy lower bank. *Squish*. They could smell the sea, though it would be a few more minutes before they actually came upon it.

Will had joined the girls, having finished his chores quickly in the hope of being invited on an adventure, which the three had lately come to enjoy when their respective adults were otherwise occupied and failed to notice their absence.

The early October wind, stiff but not yet frigid, batted at their faces. Stretching his arms out to balance, Will led them along the bank to the beach. When he jumped down onto the shingle, he turned and looked at Claire as she stood a few feet above him. The wind had loosened Claire's hairpins.

"Help me down?" Her hands stretched out toward him, her fingers wiggling. Her dark wavy hair flittered wildly around her cheeks and neck.

He smiled up at her and said, "You look better this way." Then he held both her hands.

She jumped down, scowling, and kicked mud at him. But he merely smiled again. He was almost as tall as her, she saw now, though she was sure he wasn't just a few months ago.

When they reached the sea, their boots and woolen stockings were soaked through. The whole sky was a deep grey-green like Claire's eyes, with darker clouds punctuating the expanse. They watched the sun crack through a cloud, like a beak from an egg, and pierce the landscape with streaks of pale yellow.

"That's my dragon's stone," Meg said, intersecting Will's hand as they both reached down. They bumped heads. "Oww! Watch it!"

"It's not a dragon's stone," said Claire mundanely, "it's a fossil."

"It is a dragon's stone!"

"You know what Father says about all that."

"But Mummy says the dragon stones are for Aunt Aileen, so she can see what will happen next week."

Will looked quizzically at Claire. He rubbed his forehead where Meg's head had collided with it.

"Aunt Aileen is dead, Meg, you know that," Claire said in her best irritated School Marm Voice. "And there's no such thing as prophecy."

"But Mummy says!"

To quiet her, Will picked Meg up and spun her around, lifting her feet high off the ground. She screeched, her ginger-blond curls dancing on her chubby cheeks. He pretended he was going to throw her in the sea and Claire said, laughing hard, "I dare you! Oh, I dare you!"

The three walked together along the shingle, holding hands in a chain with Meg between Will and Claire. They walked up a steep path that would take them, eventually, to the top of the chalky cliff. At the base of the path, set just higher than the beach, was the old Admiral's cottage which had an unobstructed view of the sea. The Admiral was crouched in his tiny garden cutting dead stalks and scowling at the seedheads.

"Hello, Admiral," called Meg. Will and Claire waved in a friendly manner. It was best to stop him wondering what they were up to, even if they were up to nothing in particular, as the old man was known for his intolerance of children.

They hiked along the path to the top of the cliff where the grass was short and dark as moss, the chalky ground hard as cobble beneath it. High up, wind-blasted, they admired the sea below them with its white caps.

Will closed his eyes against the warmth of the sun, letting the gusts ruffle his thick, dark hair, and Claire watched him and noticed the skin on his face was no longer soft and his chin looked as though he'd had to shave recently. He asked, his eyes still closed, "What's a fowssal?"

"Something left over from times gone," Claire explained, watching his face tilted gently upward, his dark eyebrows drawing together in thought. "They are the bones of those creatures—the ones that came from the sea—when the Faeries and Jonah were still alive. Ammonites and such."

"The Faeries aren't dead, they're still alive, Mummy says so!" Meg shouted at her against the wind.

Will opened his eyes and looked thoughtfully out at the sea. He turned to Claire. "Where did you learn that?"

"Books. We have a book about old bones from the Royal Society and another about Indian gold, and one about Marie Antoinette who got her head cut off, and a Bible we're not allowed to read, though I have. And since that's all we've got I have read them all twice, 'cept the Bible."

"You can read?"

Claire laughed. "Of course, I can read. Can't you?" But her face fell when he just shrugged. "I'll teach you. It is easy enough."

Will gave her one of his big smiles, his hair lofting across his glittering eyes.

The girls arrived home later that evening, kicking off their sodden, sandy boots and leaving them on the stone porch step. They were late for supper, but only Mother was noticeably cross. She was in the sitting-room at her spinning wheel, Father in his armchair by the fire with his pipe. "Where have you been?" she asked, and without waiting for the answer she paused spinning to fetch the girls each a bowl of soup, then returned to the wheel.

Claire sat at her mother's feet, Meg next to her. She ate half her soup, gave the rest to Meg who had already devoured hers, then took out her own sewing from the basket. A handkerchief she was learning to embroider had been carefully folded around the needle. She unfolded it and proceeded to finish stitching a small rose she had begun earlier in the week.

Mother handed Meg a loose skein of wool. "Go and sit by the fire and wind this for me now, please."

"In the South Pacific, one can only eat coconuts from the Giraffe Palm," began Father, in the way he always began his tales. He'd been a great explorer when younger, before he met Mother. The girls knew that his father—their grandfather—owned land in Scotland where Father was born, and a house that had been built from a castle ruin which had views of the North Sea.

"And because they are, of course, the tallest of the palms," he continued, "it takes a skilled climber to retrieve them. Now one day, when I was living on the far-westerly island..."

Soon, Mother was no longer cross, and the girls were rapt. They listened to Father's tale, and after that he taught them all a sea shanty from his Adventurer Days.

"Now for the harmony!" He conducted, and the girls fell into a fit of laughter, Father joining them in it and eventually Mother, too (though she gave him a look that said *you're making them both silly*).

Father added another log and the fire blazed. A lamp was lit against the dark outside the panes, and the room became awash in warm amber light. Father related another story of surviving an ice storm in Reykjavik. A half-moon made its appearance in the window.

"Stop your spinning now, my love," Father said to his wife after a while.

"Almost done. Going to market tomorrow to fill three more orders."

"Come, sit by me." He patted the arm of his chair.

Mother smiled but shook her head.

"Five of the half-snowy-whites do not look well, of late," said Father thoughtfully. "Have you not noticed?"

"What do you mean? The bagots? They are in perfect health." The wheel spun the fleece and her fingers worked it into a line. The line grew thinner and thinner as it slid through her callused fingers.

"I am concerned, actually. They look quite poorly." Father shook his head, clucked his tongue. "Believe me, I know an old sickly goat when I see one. That one with the pink nose, it's gone brown with weeping, and her coat is not what it was."

Mother suddenly looked up, her foot stopped mid-air. The wheel spun nothing. Her fingers held the taut, unmoving thread. She gazed at Father in a way Claire thought was odd — slightly nervous, slightly something else she couldn't pinpoint — then she lowered her eyes.

Mother's foot pumped the pedal again, and she pulled the fleece and said mildly, "Look at our girls, they are worn out from their exploits today. It must be time for bed."

Father chuckled. "Did you have a good day, then, my little explorers?"

"We had a perfect day," said Meg. She had moved from the fire and rested her head on Claire's lap, playing with the edge of her skirt as Claire finished winding the skein. "Except when Claire kicked mud at Will after he told her she looks nice."

Claire huffed. "Lucky for you, I'm not a snitch." She gave Meg a little slap between her shoulder blades. Then she gave her a kiss and lifted her to carry her upstairs to bed.

"It's true," Meg called over her sister's shoulder, "I'm a snitch. Claire never tells."

Mother's eyes flickered in their direction, then returned to the thread turning over in her hand.

Father laughed. "Sweet dreams, my beautiful girls. Sweet dreams."

At the top of the stairs, Claire put Meg down and led her to their bedroom. They washed in the basin, plaited their hair, put their nightdresses and caps on, and climbed into bed. The bed was high and soft, the sheets always clean. No more soot-encrusted flats, Claire thought. She was beginning to understand what that meant.

THREE

1873 ~ Spring
Allswell
St. Allswell, Sussex

Eyes shut, Meg stretched her arm, flung it out and landed it on Claire's hip. She snored lightly. Claire's hand instinctually pushed her sister's arm from her, and in that moment there was a brief, vague sense of the waking world coming to the fore.

The sun had risen behind glum, inky clouds, morning refusing to rouse the girls punctually. The light in the room might have been dusk, not dawn. In fact, the whole of this spring was not like their first, which had been mild. Instead, the air was scowled with frost. The buds were late in opening, the landscape dull and spent.

Even so, they had wood and food, a roof that did not leak. They had goats and, though the nannies were not producing much milk in this weather, their thick coats had only grown thicker with the cold. More wool to spin, at least.

Claire felt herself finally waking and wondered why everything sounded so quiet. Perhaps it was late enough that

Mother had already let the herd out to nibble at the frosty grass. The herd, whose bells always jangled below their window and woke them if the sun did not.

The bells... there were none. Had she overslept, or just not heard them?

Claire's eyes fluttered open, and she stared at the faded chickadees perched limply on the walls around her. She listened carefully. She slowed her breathing to create total silence and strained to hear anything.

And then came an ungodly sound, coming from outside the glass panes of the window: a low, hoarse howl followed by a high-pitched keen. A human sound.

"What was that?" Meg sat upright, her nightcap askew. "Claire?" She looked at her with intense fear, in that preternatural way children have of transferring fright to the person nearest. Her little chest heaved, and her fingers immediately sought Claire's.

"Not to worry." Claire's heart was in her throat. "Come with me."

They pulled their dressing gowns on over their nightclothes, went down the stairs, and heard another cry. They ran outside in their bedcaps with plaits bouncing, their wool stockings slapping against the hard sand-and-pebble drive.

In front of the open shed doors stood Mother, both hands clamped on her mouth as if she was trying to smother the next sound clawing up her throat.

"But... Where are they?" Claire took a step toward the building's hollow void. "Where are the goats?"

The young grey horse, Stony, was in his stall chewing straw and staring at them, his door open and slapping gently on its hinges. He took a confused step toward Claire, who held her hands out and said, "Shhh."

Claire looked back at Mother who was moving only her head from side to side, shaking it in the negative. Her eyes were colossal, disbelieving orbs, her hands still over her mouth.

"Mummy? There's nothing to worry about, they have only wandered to one of the far pastures," Claire offered. Then, "But where is our mare?" Stolen, she almost answered herself aloud. But who would climb over their walls and stomp brazenly through their gates? Who would steal everything that would feed and clothe them, and pull their plough? Surely not Mr Bolton? Surely not Will!

Meg began to cry. "What's happened?"

"Mummy?" Claire approached her and touched her arm.

As if electricity had passed between them, Mother jolted into the present. She grabbed Claire's wrist and Stony's harness from its hook. She shrieked, "Put it on him!"

Hastily harnessing Stony, Claire then dragged the cart from its corner of the barn. Mother jumped upon the bench and wildly gestured for Claire and Meg to join her.

"Our coats?" asked Claire, meekly, handing Meg up to her mother. Mother tossed the one wool rug in the cart bed at them, and Claire wrapped it around Meg. They set off.

They sat atop the cart in their nightclothes, the girls' caps slipping back on their necks and exposing their frazzled plaits. They circled Allswell. They crossed every field a second time before leaving the property by a back gate and turning onto the bridle path.

"Look where you're going!" a man on horseback shouted at them as he passed. They were supposed to be on the coaching road. "I'll tell the magistrate if you don't turn round!" he threatened, pointing at Mother.

But Mother just stared straight ahead and clicked her tongue to make Stony quicken his step.

They rode into the village. On the small High Street, shopkeepers leaned out their doors to gape at the woman and her daughters crammed together on the bench in their bedclothes.

"What's this now?" whispered the butcher's wife to her husband. "Is she in her dressing gown?"

"Can I help you, Mrs Bietris?" asked the milliner, whose shop doubled as the Post. He wiped his hands on his leather apron and stepped forward as the cart passed as if considering stopping it.

Mother's eyes darted around the street and down the little alley between the shop and the pub, her cheeks flushed, her hair come undone and looking dark and wild around her pale face. With her two girls huddled against her, and villagers stopping to watch them, they appeared as if the forgotten segment of some mad parade.

"Do look away," admonished one woman to her husband, as they entered the tea shoppe and he turned back around to stare.

"But isn't that Miss Aileen's sister?" the man asked, sounding shocked.

They circled out of town and back onto the bridle path. From here they drove off it onto Mr Bolton's land, right through his cabbage field.

When he saw them approaching, Bolton emerged from his snug, well-kept stone farmhouse in his shirtsleeves and unbuttoned waistcoat. He was drying his hands on a cloth. Will, fifteen and as tall as his father, chopped wood at the side of the house. He stopped when he saw cart.

"Is everything all right, Mrs Bietris?" asked Mr Bolton.

"Have you seen Father?" It was Claire who spoke, knowing Mother could not bring herself to without sounding nonsensical.

Mr Bolton shook his head. Will did the same.

"Then, you haven't seen our goats, Mr Bolton?" Claire heard her own voice pitch higher.

At this, Will looked genuinely baffled. "What, the whole herd? Not really?" He looked to his father. "But how can that be?"

"Mrs Bietris..." Mr Bolton dropped the dishtowel and strode toward them.

As if in answer, Mother yanked Stony's harness and swiftly turned the cart around, tearing away from their neighbours and the dismay painted across their faces.

"Mrs Bietris!"

Mother smacked the reins against Stony's back and pushed him quickly up and over the adjoining field. She pushed him hard, then let him slow down. Claire could hear the horse's panting in time with her Mothers and she began to feel a throbbing at her own temples.

They continued to ride until Stony's gait grew uneven and hobbling. Claire was about to protest in the horse's defense when Mother veered them in the direction of an enormous, gnarled beech tree that stood in one pasture the herd always favoured. It was the place they were most likely to go if they should find their way home after wandering.

In the limbs of the beech was a hiding place where the girls liked to watch the beasts graze from above, at the end of a day, the sun low in the sky and painting the goat's fleece pink. The tree was Aileen's, Mother had always told them: their aunt's spirit still lived in trunk and bough though she no longer walked the earth. There were such things, Mother imparted, but they

29

must never be spoken about to Father: the dragon stones on the beach, the faerie houses in the hedges... Aunt Aileen's spirit, alive in the tree. These beliefs from her childhood, given freely to her by her parents who had come over from Ireland and farmed the land here by the Grace of God.

Mother drove the cart under the wide branches of the beech, as the light in the sky turned from pale lavender to a colourless twilight. For the sun never appeared today, it had stayed as hidden as the goats.

Stony stumbled a little, and Claire gently took the reins from her mother and said, "He is too tired."

Mother looked straight ahead at nothing, her eyes glazed, her cheeks flushed, her mouth straight. She put her arm around Claire and placed her head on her daughter's shoulders as if she was the child. And Claire gently guided the cart back to the barn.

Late that night, Father came home. Claire and Meg were already in bed, having never changed their nightdresses, though Claire had made them wash their feet and soak their stockings. They had left Mother in the sitting room, where she silently and mechanically wound the last skeins of wool left in her basket.

There was the clatter of Father's gig when he arrived, the sound of his horse snorting and a shuffle of footsteps on the drive. The bang of the door against the wall as it opened. Claire heard his reverberant, energetic voice. Her arm was wrapped tightly across Meg's shoulders as they lay wide awake but barely breathing in the dark.

"My love, it is a trade that will make us the wealthiest family in Sussex! Surely you can see that?"

Claire could not hear Mother, not really. A few words traveled up the stairs, but sense couldn't be made of them. The sound of Mother's voice—but not her words—bubbling here and there until, suddenly, there was a definite cry of, "For eight bushels of Dutch tulip bulbs!"

"Sweetheart, believe me when I tell you…" Father's voice was a syrupy baritone against Mother's high mad twitter. "Sit down, please," he begged. "The herd was old and feeble, good for nothing more than selling to the butcher, you know that as well as I…"

Some sort of choked wail sounded from Mother.

"…but do not say such things, dearest! I have thought only of you and the girls… And the mare—what need we of three horses? If you'll just sit with me, some brandy will dull the edge. Look, what a fine bottle I've brought you. Please, take this… Damn it, woman, listen to reason!"

Presently there was the crash of glass, then footsteps on the stairs, quick and sharp. A slam of the adjacent bedroom door. The chickadees, frozen in their blue flight patterns, shuddered and wept.

FOUR

1873 ~ Late Autumn
Allswell
St. Allswell, Sussex

The Dutch bulbs rotted in the sodden earth. Maggots sprouted from their soft bellies whilst fuzzy white spots of mold clung to their creviced husks. For a week, Father daily tended to them, digging them up, washing them, planting some of them again. A pile of the unsalvageable grew with each day. At the end of the week, Father took to his horse, returning two days later with a brightness in his eyes.

The following week it rained, and was cold, and when Father went out again for two days, Claire discovered no one had brought more wood in and the pile at the side of the house was too wet to light. So Mother took all the feather quilts and pillows and woolen blankets from their rooms and placed them before the stove in the kitchen, an idea which Meg thought was the basis for possibly the greatest night of her life.

The following week, Mr Bolton's housekeeper left pickled cabbage and a half-flank on the kitchen doorstep. She knocked on the door and when Mother opened it and saw her, the old woman curtsied, then walked away. Mouth open, eyes heavy with exhaustion and hunger, Mother watched the woman as she made her way over the stile and disappeared. It wasn't until then that she really saw the food on the step. She said, "Send it back" to no one in particular, and closed the door.

As she went back up to her room, Father called: "We cannot give the gift back, he will think us rude and ungrateful! Dearest? When my grapes are ready, he'll have all the wine he wants, I'll make a special present of it to him, yes? It will be the most sought-after vintage in all of Britain. And the season next we'll be ready for export to France."

Listlessly, from the top of the stairs, Mother muttered, "But why would you know more of grapes than tulips?" Then she shut her door.

The day after Christmas, Father went away for three days.

It was Boxing Day, and they were all meant to bring jams and cakes to the vicarage, for the poor. There was great tension in the house over this, as Mother refused to "give up what little we have" and then refused to stop pacing around the kitchen, placing two jars and a loaf into a basket, then taking them out again and returning them to the cupboard.

"God forgive us," she said, wiping her hand down her face and closing her eyes. She looked up at the ceiling and repeated, "Go maith Dia dúinn."

She retrieved the jam. Before it made it into the basket, it was back on the shelf.

Claire, anxiously watching from the stove where the kettle would soon boil, felt a drop in her stomach and a clenching in her throat as Mother begged God's forgiveness several times, in English and Irish. Each time, Claire's insides jolted as she imagined Father and the Vicar taking turns popping into the room, pointing accusingly, and bellowing at Mother. She did not know which man's wrath would worse. Either way, Mother would be doomed. Perhaps Claire and Meg would be too, as they were her daughters.

Eventually Mother abandoned the pull of the vicarage. Afternoon came and the sky darkened, and Mother made a fire in the hearth with dried wood she'd made the girls bring in days before. One must think ahead, Claire knew now. One must always think ahead as Mother does.

They drank tea soaked with yesterday's leaves and ate the nub leftover from the tiny roast Father had procured for Christmas dinner. No pudding, Mother had said last night, "I'll not give up flour for pudding." Father had made a face at this but said nothing. He'd given an uplifting toast instead, promising health and good fortune for his girls in the new year.

Claire and Meg made another nest of all their bedding in the sitting room where the fire blazed happily, and with the boughs they'd cut draped across the mantle, and the glistening gold and mercury glass balls that had been their grandparents' nestled in the greenery, the mood of the house lifted. It was a pretty room, a lovely house. My house, Mother had said to herself under her breath several times that week.

"This is our nest," said Meg, patting and shaping the blankets and creating a circle of pillows. "We are Christmas birds."

Mother smiled. "We are, my love. You are my baby birds."

Meg yawned and chose her place in the nest, and Mother lay down beside her and put her arm around her. "Go to sleep, Claire," she said, her voice low and tired.

"In a minute." Claire sat in Father's big chair, embroidering her linen square by the firelight. It was to be a pillow and put in a trunk for when she married. Mother had once said, "It will be for you, some years from now, and you'll be very glad of it" and Claire had heard Father say "dowery" once, in a sour manner, with Mother ignoring him.

It seemed somewhat mysterious, this trunk, these linen squares and petticoats, for the trunk itself did not yet exist, nor did most of the undergarments and bedlinens that were to be put in it, and she had only the slightest idea what marriage meant. She knew the Selkie's story, as Mother told the girls recently as they'd raked for whelk on the beach one afternoon, placing the snails in their up-turned aprons. In that story, there was a cap which the Selkie's husband had stolen so that he could marry her.

Claire focused on her satin stitches — of leaves and buds — and vaguely wondered if the Selkie's cap had been woolen or silk, woven or knitted. She could not remember.

A light knock on the window sounded and Claire turned, half-expecting one of their lost goats tapping its horn on the pane.

But of course, there was no goat. It was Will Bolton, cupping his hands around his face and peering at her from the dark outside. His breath fogged the pane and he raised his hand to her in greeting.

Claire looked at her mother and sister asleep by the fire. She rose quietly and placed her embroidery on the chair. She tip-toed to the window and motioned for Will to go around the back of the house to the kitchen.

It was freezing in the dark hallway as she went to meet him. She could feel the chill of the floorboards through her woolen stockings and gave a shudder. Colder still, when she unlatched the back door and let Will into the dark kitchen with a gust of icy, damp wind.

"Hullo," he whispered. He smiled. He wore a new dark grey wool waistcoat and jacket with his old canvas trousers, and a brown scarf wrapped around his neck. His ears and cheeks began to flush, and Claire realized the room did not feel as cold to him as to her.

"Is everything all right?" she asked in soft voice. "Why are you here?" She lit a single candle and set it on the scrubbed wood table. He sat on one side and she on the other.

"Thanks," he smiled again.

"I cannot offer you milk… we have none," she said. "Are you hungry?"

He shook his head. He had a pleasant, calm expression which suddenly made him seem older to Claire. "Everything is fine," he whispered reassuringly. "Happy Christmas."

"Happy Christmas," she whispered back. Was that why he was here? To wish her a Happy Christmas?

Will looked steadily at her across the table. Their hands were not far apart, and he tapped a little rhythm on the top of hers with his finger in one of his teasing gestures. She rolled her eyes at him, and he smiled again, his brown eyes looking very dark and warm in the candlelight.

He reached into his breast pocket and removed a small leather pouch which was a little smaller than his palm. He placed it on the table, then nudged it closer to her.

She frowned at him. *For me?* she mouthed, shrugging.

He nodded. He mouthed, *Happy Christmas* again.

Claire touched the leather. It was tanned and sewn with thread in a competent enough way to tell her the housekeeper had done it, not Will. She pulled open the little silk corded drawstring, which was worth as much as the whole pouch, she knew. Tilting the pouch into her hand, she felt a small but heavy object slide out. She caught it.

She looked at the tiny painted lead cat perched on a spool of thread. The spool was carved from wood with a few strands of real blue thread wrapped around it. The cat itself sat upright, lean and balanced perfectly. Its body was painted a light tan colour, a little lighter than the pouch he had come in, and its face and paws were dark, almost black. Its eyes were a dot each of bright, pale blue.

Claire pet the top of the cat's head with her finger, her mouth parting, her head racing. She looked up at Will, and saw he looked slightly anxious as his eyes caught hers.

"What do you think?" he whispered.

She pet the cat's head again, then turned the statuette over in her hand, examining the thread, and the beauty of it. "I love it," she whispered.

"It's one of those fancy cats, from Siam," he explained.

"I know." She nodded. She'd read about them in a book of drawings of different species of cats. "Ohhh…!" she exclaimed, then clamped her hand over her mouth and giggled.

Will nodded. It was one of the books she'd taught him to read by, a simple one with useful words and pictures to assist.

"Thank you." She smiled at him and their eyes locked onto each other in a strange, uncomfortable, but slightly thrilling manner; a little chill running down her neck to the base of her spine. "But I have nothing for you," she said, feeling suddenly horrible… Mother with the jam all over again.

Will just smiled and shook his head. "Think nothing of it."

He stood, settled his scarf tighter, and nodded to her. "I'd best be…"

"Of course. I'm sorry I can't give you anything to eat."

He almost laughed, and Claire wasn't sure what he meant by this, but then, as she stood and he walked passed her to the door, he reached out and quickly squeezed her shoulder as if to reassure her.

Then he was gone, back out into the dark December night.

Claire clutched the little cat on its spool of thread, pressing it against her heart.

Father arrived home with snow dusting his hat like the powdered sugar on their missing Christmas pudding. Claire and Meg ran out to meet him on the drive. Meg clung to his neck while he held her, walked and talked, announcing news of a new venture with Claire clinging to the edge of his coat.

"I tell you, girls, the deal I have made will clothe your mother in velvet and ermine for the rest of the winter." He lifted Claire, holding them both together in order to carry them inside. "Blasted grapes! Blasted fields!" he called out to the sitting room while stomping his boots. "This Sussex earth is not meant to grow anything at all. We shall finally have the life my girls deserve!"

Mother looked up from her sewing as if only just noticing him. She was, as usual lately, sitting quietly near the window, tilting her work into the dim natural light, as their candles had to be saved for the actual dark. "Our land is meant for goats and sheep. For gr-grazing..."

But she couldn't finish. She coughed instead, a hard tight cough as if a splinter of shale suddenly caught in her throat. She coughed again. And again. Her face turned a deep pink, a rabbit's eyes, then was drained of colour entirely. Claire rushed to her.

Father, too, ran over and pulled his handkerchief from his pocket, his boots still on and creating puddles on the rug.

Mother held the linen to her mouth, coughing and gasping while Father pat her back. When the fit was done, she closed her eyes and held the cloth tightly in her white-knuckled fist.

"Mummy, what is that?" Meg uncurled Mother's fingers with her own small hand.

The white handkerchief, with the B she'd embroidered for her husband with tendrils of ivy and thistle flowers growing out of the letter, was drenched red. A tendril of crimson spittle stretched from her bottom lip to the cuff of her dress, like the silk thread from a spider.

FIVE

1874 ~ Spring
Allswell
St. Allswell, Sussex

"Mother, are you awake?"

Claire knelt beside the four-poster. Her grandparent's bed, carved from pine and brought with them from County Wexford, where they had both been born. It was all they had had in the world, Mother had once said; everything else they created here, at Allswell.

The air in the room felt pleuritic and stale, and Mother's complexion was as dull as the greying sheets, as faded as the old drapes drawn closed. When had everything in this house lost its colour? If she had been wiser, more observant, Claire would have noticed Mother growing thin and sallow before the coughing had even started. Instead, she was shocked looking at her now.

"Is that you, Aileen?" Mother's voice was hoarse and deeper than her normal tone. She sounded so different to herself, that it unnerved Claire.

"No, it's me, Mother. It's Claire. Aunt Aileen is in the tree. *Beannaigh an bhiotáille de na crainn*," she said in the Old Tongue, the words secretly passed on to her when Father was not with them. "Remember, Mother?"

"Yes, 'bless her. Bless her soul. *Solas Mhic Dé ar a n-anam.* Mind the horses, then, in her place, so Papa won't know she is gone. She runs wild, sometimes, you know." A little smile.

"We have but one colt."

"Do we not have Ginger?"

"The mare is sold," Claire reminded her reluctantly.

Mother's breathing sounded a faint whistle on the intake. She reached up and pressed her fingers into her forehead as if it ached. "But what of the goats?" she asked. She pressed and rubbed, kneading the skin like dough.

Claire grabbed her hand, fearing she would scratch herself.

"The pain is worse, Claire."

"A head-ache? You're parched, is all. Let me get you water."

"No, that is not it."

"What do you mean?"

"It's my dreams," said Mother.

Though her mother had never given words to this particular idea, Claire understood. Dreams in sleep were one thing, but Mother also knew them in other forms. She had known Aileen's spirit inhabited Allswell since the day they arrived; she had even, perhaps, known what would happen to them here. Perhaps now she was just too weak to pretend otherwise. Was that possible?

"The goats, Claire," she asked again in that strange, hoarse voice.

"The goats are gone, remember? They were sick."

"Yes, he has lost them. And me. Where are your needles? You mustn't lose them."

Claire felt a pang of normalcy with the command and stood straight. "I have them, of course I have," she nodded vigorously. "And the floss we bought at market, and the muslin Mr Bolton's housekeeper gave us—let me get them. You shall help me, yes? We'll sit together, and I'll finish the crewelwork on the linen pillowcase."

Mother coughed, a wet choking sound as if she'd swallowed a cup of silt.

"Sit up, please, Mother, your cough is worse with lying down."

She strained and coughed more violently and the cough seemed to overtake her.

"Mummy, sit up, quickly!" Diving behind her, Claire angled her forward. A sharp gurgle, and a wine-red clot sprayed through Mother's fingers onto the bedspread.

Claire pulled the case off one of the feather pillows and started mopping the blood. "I think we should fetch the doctor." Her chest clenched and then heaved as she said this, as if it was an admission of something horrid she wouldn't be able to take back. She blotted her mother's face with the pillowcase, smearing grotesque rouge across her cheek. She rubbed and rubbed but there was too much blood and it smeared and stained everything.

Mother took Claire's hand in hers suddenly and kissed it over and over, and Claire could feel that her lips were cracked and scabbed as they left red streaks on her hand. "My dearest, my dearest. Make certain the nannies nurse the kids, or they will perish before winter!"

"Please, the goats are long gone, Mother... let me go! Mummy, please! Let me fetch the doctor."

"No, no, no, Papa will be home soon. He will. Stay with me. Do not leave me alone."

Silent, teeth clenched, Claire managed to wrest her hand away and rub the remains of the blood off Mother's cheek and neck. She threw the pillowcase across the room, and then the coverlet, replacing that with a tartan wool throw from the wardrobe.

Claire held Mother's hand until she felt her grip relax and saw her eyes flutter closed. Then she slid to the floor at the side of the bed again, onto her knees, never leaving to retrieve the sewing, or the doctor, but just holding Mother's hand.

The floor was cold and hard. It hurt her knees, even through the thick wool of her skirt and layer of linen petticoats. The light in the room shifted from pale grey to inky dark as if someone was slowly dripping a fountain pen into the air.

At some point, Meg came in and, seeing the strange scene, curled at Claire's feet. Claire took another throw from the foot of the bed and spread it over them both, having bundled the bloody coverlet with the pillowcase into an amorphous lump in the far corner of the room. It lay there, the bundled shape, as if it contained something once animated, or something that might re-animate without warning. A small gesticulation seen from the corner of her eye every so often… monsters and pookas stirring beneath the folds of cloth.

Under her wool blanket Mother lay, slightly fitful in sleep, her face flushed with fever again. Though Claire couldn't see the tone of her cheeks, from the darkening and glistening of them in the shadows, she knew.

The room grew raw, the fire dying to a feeble glow of embers. It faded away into a half-sleep. Then, Claire woke, still on the floor with her hands on Mother and her forehead on the edge of the mattress. She shifted her legs under Meg's warm weight, pins and needles flaring into her calves.

The wind murmured around the corners of the house, among the eaves, as if someone was speaking in melancholy tones. She glanced around the darkened room, waking fully, and listened to the strange utterance of the wind. As she did, she caught sight of someone standing in the door. The door was open. It wasn't before.

"Father?" Blinking, Claire picked the crust from her eyes. "Who's there?" she whispered.

The figure was a black silhouette, and it moved, taking one step into the room, and that was when Claire saw it was a woman: slight, like Mother, with dark hair spread down her shoulders like the seaweed on the shingle. But where the woman's face should have been, was an oval hollow with scant features, mere shadow where eyes should reside. A mouth-like hole forming a silent O.

Claire tried to speak again, but fear choked her voice. She pressed out a whisper— "Mother...? Mummy?" She stared at the woman, who took another slow step forward. For a confused moment, she thought the woman was her own mother standing in the room, even as she was lying directly next to her in the bed.

Gathering her wits, Claire glanced sideways and looked at her mother in the bed, her hands frantically patting over her. Sleeping, just as she should be. She looked back at the doorway, her heart thrashing in her chest.

But the door was closed, as it had been before. No one was there.

Her heart hammered in her chest and she could hear her own pulse in her head, and a cold prickle of perspiration running along her hairline. She looked at Meg, asleep at her feet, and she placed one hand on Meg's back while holding Mother's arm with the other. A great wave of exhaustion flooded over her, and she lay her head back on the edge of the mattress, and fell into a deep sleep.

Next morning Claire woke to find Mother sleeping peacefully, her breath whistling only slightly. She stood, stretched, and gave a low groan, then bent and placed her own chin on Mother's forehead, which felt cool.

There were chores to do. Breakfast would be gooseberry jam made last summer (one jar left after that, and then what?) and bread that Mr Bolton's housekeeper had baked last week, with the mould cut off. How was it, she suddenly wondered, that she was thirteen and did not know how to bake? What would happen when they finished the last pot of jam? Would Father's prospects come to bear by then?

"Claaaaaire?" Meg yawned and moaned.

There was your answer, she thought, regarding the bread baking. Mother couldn't work everything on the farm, take care of that little one and teach her eldest to cook. At least she had taught Claire to sew and throw together a stew of previous meals' scraps. Proper baking would have to come later when Mother was healthy again. Cream puffs, sweet rolls, they would make them together...

"Go pull water from the well," Claire whispered to Meg, her brain snapping into gear. Boiling water for tea they could both do. "Go on, Meg."

Meg climbed upon the bed, kissed each of Mother's cheeks twice. "That's four-times-kisses," she whispered, nodding at Claire. "Maths are important."

"Good girl. Now, I need to fetch the grain delivered for Stony, so do not wander. Just pull the water, yes? Good."

If, that is, the large sack had been delivered this morning. It was thrown from the cart, on the man's way into St. Allswell, for they could no longer pay the extra to have him bring it up to the shed.

Outside, the sky was pale with a wispy lattice of clouds, and there was a tingle of humidity hovering about the ground. At the far edge of the property the grain sack rested against the hedge, moist but no worse for the wear. Claire lifted it up carefully, tapping the base for leaks.

Walking back, she noticed Will standing at the wall that divided their properties. The wall was in a state of disrepair, ivy and tiny wildflowers growing from the mortar. Where Will stood, the surface flints were dislodged, a soft inner core exposed.

He saw her and waved. His shirtsleeves were rolled, his brown arms exposed. She thought instantly of her little cat on its spool, perched on her nightstand.

She approached with the grain sack on her hip like a baby and, as she neared, she could see he was buttering mortar onto the top of the wall where the cap was missing. "Lazing around, are you?" she mock-scolded.

"Yeah, you know me, always shirking my duties."

"What are you doing?"

"Someone smeared cement over these stones. It's all damp now..." He grimaced as he dislodged another mildewed course and placed it on the ground. "Rotted out. Whole wall is at risk, you can't leave it like this."

"But this wall is ours, isn't it? Father ought to do it."

Will tilted his chin down and smiled, eyebrows raised.

"Oh. Right, then." She pursed her lips. "Don't suppose he knew what he was doing, 'bless him. Here, let me help." She put the feedbag down.

"Help me laze, you mean?"

"Two can loll about quicker than one."

He laughed, took another stone from the wall and set it on the grass.

They talked while they scraped out the crumbling cement and he showed her how to lay the flints back in place, their lime-stained hands grazing against each other across cold, jagged edges, each of them standing on either side of the wall. It was such an ordinary day, an ordinary task. Claire noticed how his hands looked older now he was fifteen, with long but muscular fingers and veins upon the backs and up his forearms.

"Do you have a proper place to store that?" Will indicated the feed. "Storms will come in tonight, or tomorrow morning at the latest—bad ones, that will bring a high tide with the full moon."

"How do you know?"

Will laughed, but his mirth turned contemplative when he realized Claire wasn't joking; when he realized she could read better than he could, but she would not be able to stop her family's farm from going bankrupt. "Store it up off the ground, in the tool-loft. And look to the river sometimes, to see if it's rising. You will see it on the road before it comes over the field."

Claire nodded.

"Did you hear about that man came down from London last week, lost on his way to Exmoor?" Will asked, cheerfully switching topics. When she said she hadn't, he wove a long, slightly convoluted tale involving a carriage taken from the coaching inn, a broken wheel, and a mink top hat floating in a puddle of mud. By midway she was laughing— really laughing—and as he talked, and they put the flints into place like teeth wedged into a gumline, she forgot to worry about how to store grain properly, or whether she understood the tides, or that her mother was still in her room looking ghostly.

"Do you need help with that?" Will looked at the large, heavy sack after they were finished.

Before she could answer, he climbed over the wall to her side and bent down as if to take it. Then, as if changing his mind, he straightened, grasped her by the waist and pulled her against him. His face was close to hers, his chin close to her lips.

He kissed her, his mouth locking softly but purposefully on hers. She closed her eyes quickly, reflexively, and felt her body stiffen, her head whirling with confusion.

But the way he held her close made her feel safe, not afraid, and she returned the kiss. His mouth parted from hers and moved from her mouth down her neck, where he placed another kiss, and she could feel his silky, wavy hair graze her jaw and chin. She could smell the soap he'd washed his hair with and the plaster and sweat on his skin. He kissed the top of her breast just once, above the neckline of her dress, then kissed her once, softly, on her left cheek.

He released her, hoisted the grain bag, and set off toward Allswell.

She stood there, dizzy and stunned.

After a moment, she caught up with him and they walked to the cowshed together without speaking. She was aware of the sound of his breath as he walked. The lace-like clouds moving over their heads.

When they were inside the shed, Will put the bag down with a thump and she took a step toward him. He pulled her into a hug and kissed her again, this time longer. The straw under their feet smelled rich and sweet, and his mouth tasted of salt and warm almond cakes. Claire felt herself melting into him as they kissed until they heard his father calling for him across the fields.

Will smiled at her, looking into her eyes, their noses almost touching. He winked, then darted out, leaving her flushed and leaning against the door of Stony's stall. She could not speak, but a strange, new voice in her head said what she felt. It said: *Take me with you.*

The following day, Mother was sent to hospital. Two weeks later, she was dead.

SIX

1874 ~ Spring
Allswell
St. Allswell, Sussex

Standing on the threshold, Father wore his coat and scarf. With one hand, he held the door open by the knob, letting in the cold, damp air. In his other hand his top hat drooped, barely held by two fingers. He looked as if he did not know whether he had arrived home or at someone's else's home he'd found himself accidentally.

"Do not think of her in the ground surrounded by the others," he said. This was all he said. A single, strange sentence tied to nothing and no one recognizable. His voice was unnaturally quiet for him, his face painted with the jagged brushstrokes of shock.

Just out of the kitchen, Meg and Claire stood apprehensively, having heard him come in. Meg nudged closer to her sister and squeezed Claire's apron into her hand, giving a tug.

Claire's own hands were filled with the glossy wet of a bowl in need of drying. It would have slipped to the floor if she'd actually registered what Father had just said. "I'm sorry...? What others?" she asked.

"Your mother," he said in a small, gasping voice. "Do not think of her there." He closed the door, still hanging onto the knob.

Claire thought about this morning; how she was certain she heard Father say, as he left for the hospital, "Just a short visit, a bit of a hello. I do not know why I even go since she will be home soon."

She stood there with the heavy, wet bowl staring at him. Out of nowhere, she thought she heard someone whisper, *You must have imagined all that.* The voice was close to her ear, taking the form of a cool breath silently whistling words along the tender skin behind her lobe. She looked at Meg. "What did you say?" she asked, and Meg stared back at her, confused.

"It's best we do not remember her in her last hours with this — this terrible disease she could not recover from," Father choked. He leaned back against the door to steady himself as his hat dropped to the ground. "My dearest love... my only wife." His usually deep, confident voice wavered and cracked, the vulnerability of the tone setting the hairs on Claire's neck on-end.

"Is she in Heaven?" Meg asked.

Eerily normal her voice was, and Claire thought she'd be sick from the sound. My God, she realized, Meg thinks it's like the bird she found on the road weeks back. She'd told Meg how the bird was asleep and if they left it, it would fly away to be with the angels. But now she was sorry she had ever said such a stupid thing.

"Heaven?" Father repeated. Disbelief, then anger, took hold of his mouth which rumpled and pursed. "Heaven? We are Practicalists." Quite suddenly, he spoke as if in lucid debate with a panel of theologians. "Our belief is in Life and Nature rather than an invisible realm!"

Claire took Meg's hand from her apron and guided her to the sofa, the bowl still cradled in her other arm like an infant just out of its bath.

"Heaven! What is Heaven? In which realm do we live?" He stared wildly at his daughters, his eyes darting from one face to the other.

Perhaps Father was going mad, now, right in front of them. He would pace round the house lecturing to invisibles on the visible world. Then what? It was Mother who always cooked their meals; Claire only ever washed and dried the dishes. There was supposed to be time to learn all the things Mother knew. Had known.

A terrifying thought came to her: only Mother knew how to soothe him when he was like this.

"I have had three of the finest China Roses planted on her resting place," Father said, tender again. He took a step forward, then another. "One from each of us to bloom crimson, apricot, and amethyst — to always tell the story of her beauty to the living. One always calls roses by their proper names because they are exceptional as they are, and do not need embellishment," he added.

But of course, they'd heard him before on this botanical subject. There were Yellow Hats and Purple Perfume which, Claire thought, might really be daffodils and something else she didn't know the name of but Mother did. But why wasn't Mother coming home to be buried, in the churchyard with Aunt Aileen? *You want to ask this question, except you cannot; your voice is taken from you, is it? Stolen by sylphs and hung out on Aunt Aileen's tree to moan in the wind? Look at you: you are a statue caught in a pose of astonishment.*

"Get up, get up," Father called from the little library, where he had slept since Mother's illness.

When had he gone in there? He was just in here with them, in the sitting room a moment ago. In the room where they'd made their Christmas nest in front of the fire, where the sewing baskets were kept.

"Claire, Meghan!" He called out again, louder. They heard something fall off his desk to the floor. Then he rushed through the sitting room, past them.

He buzzed from room to room like a housefly. He breezed past them into the kitchen again.

"What's happening?" Claire found she could speak, but her legs felt frozen, Meg still leaning into her hip as they sat side-by-side. It was like being in some thick fog she could not find her way out of. She could hear Father opening cupboard doors, rummaging and clanking iron against glass. Yet she could not move.

"Be of help, my darling bairns,"—he popped his head back in— "be of help now, please. We leave before tea."

Meg hiccuped, and swiveled her head to look at Claire, who stared back blankly. "Are we going somewhere for tea? What is Papa doing?"

"Claire!" Father shouted, popping his head into the room. She saw him wipe the tears from his face. New ones appeared immediately after. But his voice was no longer weak and cracking, which meant something important was happening, something serious and necessary required of her.

Taking shallow breaths and trying not to faint, she willed herself to stand. She put the bowl on the floor next to the sofa.

"Go to our room," she said to Meg, looking directly at her. "Lay out two dresses on your bed. I think we are going on holiday." There seemed no other explanation.

"We are going on holiday?"

Claire tried to think but could only hear the pounding of her own heart in her ears. "I think..." she stuttered, "I think we are going to visit Mother's grave." *Or even Mother, herself. For she cannot really be buried already, can she? You will be taken to her, to hold her hand and kiss her cool, white cheek one last time. This is what you are doing. Do not tell Meg, or she will scream with fright.*

"Go, now," Claire ordered. Meg ran upstairs.

Claire was close behind her when she felt Father's hand on her arm.

"Where are you going? Stay with me. Little one, go and gather your things." He directed this last bit at Meg with a weak but encouraging smile, and Meg hopped up the stairs.

Next thing Claire knew, Father was circling her like some bird of prey, saying "put that back" or "that one, there." It all went in a carpet bag, and she wondered what on earth they were going to do with a China figurine and a set of porridge bowls on holiday, or at Mother's graveside. An offering of some kind? Would Father let them honour their mother's family traditions?

Father ran out the back door, calling out "Cellar!" to the wind, like he did the day they first arrived at Allswell.

Dodging him, Claire ran upstairs and found that Meg had made a pile of dolls and dancing bears on the bed and topped it with the paper garland from Christmas.

Escaping to the adjacent room, Claire stopped short at the sight of the bed: the feather and horsehair mattress where her mother's body had lain half-dead, half-living. There was an indent in the linen, where her weight had pressed a curve, a coiled shape of head, torso, and hip. *Why haven't you washed the sheets? Did you think she would return, to fit neatly back into the notch she had carved out?*

Claire felt a lurch in her stomach, vomit hiccupping against the back of her throat. She held onto the bedpost and swallowed hard. The room tilted, then steadied. Her forehead flushed with sweat. Her eyes darted across the wardrobe, the wall, the bedside table: Aunt Aileen's Bible — she grabbed it. Father was in the doorway.

"Put that down."

In the Bible's place, he handed her an ivory box. Usually, it held silver and tortoiseshell hair pins but it felt curiously empty now, and Claire wondered where all the pins had gone. She thought, my cat! in a kind of panic, and she tried to step around Father so she could go back to her room where the figurine was kept.

But Father blocked her path, mumbling something to himself. All was a blur of rushing and double-checking, and Father saying, "No, we have no room for it," and Claire doing what she was told while trying to assess exactly what it was she was supposed to be doing.

Finally, she mustered the courage to ask, "Could I not say good-bye to Will?" She slid a glance to the cat on its spool, sitting on her nightstand.

Father paused at the top of the stairs and looked at her. In that instant, she took his quizzical expression to mean she was not showing proper respect towards Mother.

"I'm sorry, Father I..."

But then he blinked, and she saw that he was only perplexed. He didn't register of whom she spoke. He had no idea she had a friend, a real friend with a name that meant something, at the neighbouring farm. He had no idea that the boy was her playmate all these years. And that the boy had set his lips to hers. She should have told Mother, before she was sent away, for then she might have made Father promise her to Will and she would be headed to his house right now instead of leaving this one. Perhaps Mother had known, maybe even mentioned it to Father?

"Father, about Will Bolton. Do you think when we return...?"

He had headed back into the girls' room, Claire following. "You will only have use for this one, my dear, not these." He stood at their wardrobe, pulling one dress from it and stuffing the others Claire placed on the bed back in. "There will be fine gowns where we are going, the most beautiful and fashionable of frocks for my girls."

"But, Father, that is a summer dress and it's still cold outside. And, Father, I think I should tell you about Will, Mr Bolton's son."

"Do not fret, lass." He paused, put his big hand on her cheek, and she saw the tears forming in his eyes again. His great chest rose and fell in big heaves. He kissed her forehead. She felt the tenor of loss creep up her lungs and breathed it down.

He brushed past her, pulling another dress across the bed. The crinoline of the dress hit the nightstand on its way, sending the little cat into a mass of fabric dumped onto the floor.

Then Meg was crying—wailing, in point of fact—in the doorway. She wanted Mother's hairbrush as a keepsake. It seemed a selfish request, and Claire shushed her and made her stand in the corner of the landing while she fell to her knees and combed through the crinoline for the figurine.

Later, Claire wished she had not yelled at Meg. She wished she had let Meg take the hairbrush or had secreted it for her. She wished she had found her cat, had thrown herself on her belly and felt every inch under the bed. As it was, she had only pocketed one needle lodged into a single spool of real thread, thinking it was her precious present.

But the thread was not blue, but red. And for now, there was Father to think of. Father alone, with one daughter still a child and the other on the verge of a womanhood in which all manner of miseries might transpire. Just look at what's happened, they could almost see him thinking as he pulled the cart, and not their coach, away from the house. His wife had died and left him with two girls. The shock of it, the melancholy, was all over his face.

He snapped the reins against Stony's back and they lurched forward. He waved to the empty pastures, smiling a sad, courageous smile.

"Good-bye to these sorrowful, infertile tracts!" he called out. Then he said to the atmosphere itself more than to his daughters, "A new adventure has begun for us. I promise you, girls, only happy times ahead." His voice cracked again. Eyes red, he patted Claire's cheek as she sat beside him on the bench. He glanced over his shoulder at Meg who sat crying on a low stack of hay next to their carpet back and one small trunk, her sobs monotonous and throbbing.

"It's all right, Father." Claire touched his arm. The cosy brown tweed of his Ulster tugged against his plump frame.

He blinked and sniffed. He snapped the reins again. "I could not go on without you, Claire." He patted her knee. "You will be my sunshine through these dark days."

"I will, Father." She clung to him, though she didn't really understand what he meant.

She looked up at the sky to avoid seeing the Bolton's house as they passed it. She looked up and thought: The sky does as it pleases. The clouds above were dark, thick, and stagnant. Perhaps, she thought, it would rain again, a sign that something somewhere felt so terrible that it would cry as hard as she wanted to.

She didn't realize that a tempest of an altogether different sort was about to rain down upon them. If she had, she might have snatched the reins and whipped the horse into a gallop, heading for Will's as fast as she could.

SEVEN

1874 ~ Spring
Somewhere in Sussex

Mother would have said something about the dark hour of the night and whispered a prayer in the girls' ears to fool the evil spirits, were she with them. But of course, if Mother were with them, they would be home, in their room with the mad chickadees perched on the walls. Or in their cosy arrangement of bedding in the sitting room, the fire blazing. Instead, they were in the flatbed of their cart, parked on a level hillside off the road, with Stony, the only horse they had left, tied to a tree.

Father tucked the saddle blanket around them, then sat on the edge of the cart looking out at the rolling landscape barely illuminated by faintly-glowing clouds. Thoughtful, he lit his pipe and hummed. "We are explorers of a New World, dee-da-dum," he sang. A cloud parted and the moon was revealed. His eyes caught the glint of it with great theatrical effect. He was still wearing his top hat and a brown woolen scarf knotted above his collar. It was the one Mother had made him, woven from her goats' fibers and dyed by her hand.

"We are pioneers," he said, in his storyteller's voice. He spoke in a way that was soothing; he wanted his girls to feel safe and get some sleep after this nightmare of a day. "We are cartographers. Have I told you of the Spotted-Cheetah I kept as a pet, when I was a young man?" His pipe smoke enveloped his head in thick vapors. "'Tis always the countryside—whether Africa, the Pacific, or Fair Britannia—which holds the key to the mysteries of each corner of the world; each geography and its peoples and creatures. Look fast, the moon!" He pointed up. "See how it has peeked out from that malevolent cloud? And now, watch... it disappears again, swallowed up by the vast space the Earth inhabits. Are you afraid, my wee girls?"

"No, Father." Said in unison.

"Good! Now, let me see. The tale of my Spotted-Cheetah. I had, once, the most marvelous pet, which I caught myself on the plains of the Serengeti..."

"This is a good holiday," Meg whispered, and Claire nodded, as if sleeping outside in an open cart was what one naturally did to cure melancholy.

They let the tale of the lithe yellow and black wildcat prance its way around their heads until they slipped into sleep.

Early morning, the sun just below the horizon, the sky neither dark nor light.

Meg's curls frizzed from their plaits as though electricity had struck her in the night, her bright blue eyes shadowed and puffed. Claire felt as she looked: bedraggled and moist. The damp seemed to have worked a dark magic on her limbs and when she awoke, it was with the sense that something had physically invaded her. She felt a foreign, aching twinge throughout her hips and down both legs.

It was grief, Claire told herself, though not in those words, for grief was as alien and unfathomable to her as the constellations. It was a kind of murk, like a cloud that could not be seen but instead was felt. It was a grey, lifeless sadness adhering to everything, even the bones beneath her skin.

They sat atop the bench next to Father as he drove the cart, Meg perched on Claire's lap. He pointed ahead at something. "Do you see the chimney of that inn, the steamy billow rising?"

Ahead of them, a colourless stone bridge, under which ran a pallid dribble, led to a village where lanterns still flickered, and at the top of the sleeping village was a tall, narrow house whose hanging sign bore the face of a ram, its languid expression wagging back and forth in the wind. "At that fine inn we shall have a specialty of the cook's—steamed milk with Swiss chocolate. Would you like that?"

"Yes, please." Meg looked at him hungrily. Claire held her light frame close and kissed her hair, glad to hear some life in her. She inhaled the scent of Meg's damp hair, grateful for her baby scent. But when Meg bounced, the tops of Claire's thighs smarted as if being bruised by sharp blows, Meg turned into a heavy beast.

Father pulled Stony to the post and jumped down to tie his reins. He rapped on the door of The Sleeping Ram. No answer. The girls also jumped down.

"Try the knob," Claire suggested. A frigid gust whipped down the empty street, driving Meg against her. She took a step back and looked up at the windows with their drawn curtains.

The door was swung open by a big, unsmiling woman in a lace sleeping cap and ticking-striped petticoat. "Who the devil are you?" she scoffed.

"Good morning, madam!"

The woman sneered into the early morning wind, looking from left to right along the High Street. With a sniff, she opened the door fully and turned from them.

They followed her inside, down a little entry hall and into a tavern room with empty tables and benches where a fire was just sputtering to life. Not yet five, read a grandfather clock in a corner. Perhaps that was why it was so dim, thought Claire, the sun had still not fully risen. When it did, eventually, it would rise behind a thick sheet of grey as if forever five in the morning.

"Here." The woman slapped two cups of scalded milk before the girls (no chocolate). "Don't waste it," she warned, though Claire could not fathom how that might happen.

At another table, Father made small talk with the owner of the place who had been roused from his bed. He had a day's worth of beard surrounding his rumpled mustache and side-whiskers. His waistcoat askew, his shirt missing its collar, the man slouched over a steaming bowl and nodded as Father spoke, though his eyes had an unsettled, far-off look.

Watching, Claire remembered Mr Bolton; wished him here like a genie from a bottle. *Your little cat. You left it.*

Claire stifled a gag and put her half-drunk cup down on the wood table. She felt in the pocket of her petticoat for her mother's actual spool of thread, which was still there.

After breakfast, they were shown up the narrow stairwell to a third-floor room by their hostess, who announced as she unlocked the door, "Sheets aren't clean."

The hinges squeaked and a garret room swung into view. There was one window and, as they moved inward, Claire could stand up straight in the middle of the room, but not towards the eaves. She looked at the cot piled with tousled bedding that Meg and she were to share, set under the low eave. There was no cot for Father. Claire felt a sudden terror staring at the nebulous clump of linens, as if the room had dropped out from under her. She thought: I'll bolt upright in the middle of the night and bash my head upon the ceiling.

"A fine room for my girls!" Father's sounded in a startling boom.

The innkeeper's wife spun on her heels, huffed at him, and left without taking the old bedding.

"Snug as could be." Father smiled.

"But Father—"

"Ah, just look at her," he said, softer. "A faery she is, a tiny sprite. Do you see?"

Meg was asleep on the cot with her mouth open and her arms tossed wide on either side of her like a bird with broken wings. *My tiny faery.* It was what Mother called her.

Claire took the shawl from her own shoulders and draped it over her sister. She leant down and kissed her freckled cheek, then undid Meg's matted plaits, spreading her hair across the pillow and gently combing it with her fingers. "She is so very tired," she whispered to Father. "She needs to rest."

She looked up, but he was gone.

Near to midnight, a draught blew through the edges of the window and lifted the rough flaxen curtain panel in intervals. Currents of cold air wafted in at each new buffet, further chilling the already cold room. Claire drew the quilt up around Meg, then kicked her own boots off and placed them neatly at the foot of the cot.

"We still live at the farm, don't we Claire?"

"Of course, we do, silly. This is only where we're spending the night." She thought, but didn't say, that they had only strayed — as one does on a walk through an unfamiliar wood — and that they would soon be on the proper path home. Snow White and the Little Sister no one talked about, circling the trees; behind each trunk a different goblin, all the dwarves gone home to hide.

Aching all over, Claire climbed onto the lumpy straw mattress beside Meg and let her head loll onto the musty pillow while listening to the sonorous sound of Father's timbre from the room below. A friend of his was here, Father had explained, guiding him in preparation for a profitable new line of business. There were a few men Claire saw earlier lingering in the stairwell, but she didn't know which was the friend.

It was clear to her, in any event, that their little trip revolved around this business, and knowing this made Claire feel ashamed, and as sad for Father as she was for herself. For, here was Father making it seem like an adventure for them. Without someone to take care of his girls, he had to drag them along, which couldn't be easy or advantageous for him. And the timing of it, with Mother gone so suddenly…

A deep wave of grief rose from Claire's lungs straight up into her head. She held her breath against it. She felt her stomach trip across a scrap of supper, setting off the pain in her hips again.

With a clatter and slosh, the innkeeper's wife had plunked their tin plates down before she swaggered off to jostle mugs of ale, splattering drops the size of eyeballs as she went. They had huddled on a bench by the fire, for all the tables were crammed with men and a few woman at the end of a work day. Claire had stared at her food while Meg gobbled hers. It was May, mind, but May might as well be February in England for all the bitter dank it imparted. Claire's back had continued to ache since that morning, and she felt the indications of a chill—damp between her shoulder blades, shuddering nausea through her throat and bowels. Meg slumped against her after she finished eating, and when their hostess' back turned to serve a table crammed with field workers, Claire took Meg's hand and led her upstairs.

The flimsy curtain in the garret room swelled now, like the heave of a ghost's lungs. A shadow fluttered across the ashen wall and onto the ceiling. Spiders hid in the high corners. They creeped quickly across the ceiling beams once you were asleep and could drop into your open mouth.

Claire felt her eyes grow heavy, her aches and pains settling into a dull throb. The throb became a wave, and the wave became a wind. The wind was harsh and gusted through the trees of a park. A dream…

She was in a large city—she thought it was somewhere she had been, before St. Allswell. Cities were places she thought she had forgotten, where white mansions were scrubbed of soot daily, outside and in, and rookeries were left to blacken. There were formal parks in cities, man-made refuges from the cobbled filth, and in her dream Claire decided to walk with Meg through the gates of one of these to feed the birds.

Suddenly, she found herself with Meg in a high, black coach. The hood was open against the sky as if it was summer, though she was certain it was winter, the atmosphere icy and tight, the trees bare.

It wasn't Stony who pulled the coach, but a horse much larger—black and glossy as the coach itself—and the horse's hoofs clapped on the path like gunshots. The horse galloped faster. He had a will all his own, careening recklessly along a winding route, nearly hitting lampposts, trees. There was a blur of pedestrians hastening out of the way as the carriage sped.

Meg dug her nails into Claire's arm and Claire opened her mouth, trying to force out a shriek, her eyes locking with Meg's. Only, the girl beside Claire was not her little Meg, but Meghan all grown up: a young woman — still petite and fair, but curvaceous, her hair done up in spirals and pins, and wearing cream lace as though a bride — and she screamed, "Do something, Claire!"

Claire tried grabbing the reins. The black horse quickened even more, and she saw his hoofs cracking, thick nail parting like split wood and splattering blood on the path. The animal tore across a bridge that spanned a small lake and she lurched back to onto her seat. At the middle of the bridge, the horse swerved and leapt over the side, taking the whole carriage with him. They plummeted toward the dark, torpid water below, Claire's breath expelled in a long, hollow *whooshhh...*

Claire woke with Meg's forehead mashed against her chin. Meg's little arms were wrapped tightly round her neck. Morning spread across the cobwebs on the ceiling beams. Claire's hair was wet and cold. For a moment, she had no idea where she was. Her legs burned with pain, the sheets damp beneath them. The voice in her head said: *You must have caught a fever after all. You will be joining Mother in no time.*

Without wanting to, she fell back to sleep.

"Come, quickly! Quickly, please, she won't wake up!" Meg's voice was frantic.

"I heard you, I said," said the innkeeper's wife. "I've got work to do, you girls bothering me day an' night an' driving me mad... What's this?"

Meg let out a scream. "She's been stabbed!"

"Don't be daft," scolded the woman. "Go down the street to the tea shop and tell 'em to send up Izzie, you little idiot. Go on, then. Izzie, mind you, no one else."

Claire heard her sister's footsteps hesitate at the door before tearing down the stairs. When she opened her eyes, it was against a weight of pain and sticking wetness. I have got myself ill in the open cold of the cart, she thought. No amount of hot stew could have staved it off.

The innkeeper's wife stared down at her with pursed lips and an exasperated expression.

Claire mumbled, "I cannot leave Father and Meg," because people do, in fact, die of fever. It happened all the time.

The woman looked at her with disbelief, then burst out laughing. "Ain't your mum explained nothing to you?"

"My mother is dead."

That stopped her laughter in its tracks. The woman turned on her heels with fury, but not before yanking the bloody sheet out from under Claire and balling it up in her arms.

Claire heard the door slam as she slipped into the black. Sometime afterwards, the door opened again.

"Father?" Claire's throat was so dry she almost gagged. There was a piercing pain in her temples, the right side worse than the left and making her feel lopsided.

"Look, she is here," said Meg, still panicked.

"Where is your father, little one?" This voice was female, but not the innkeeper's wife.

"I don't know," squeaked Meg. "Look, here is Claire. Look!"

"What d'youmean y'don't know?" Claire directed this at Meg in what she thought was admonishment but was instead a kind of sleepy drawl.

"He is gone, Claire." Meg grabbed hold of her shoulder and hiccuped, mucus dripping from her reddened nose. She tried to shake Claire's shoulder. Her fingers were tiny fire irons poking her. "I've looked all over and our cart is gone and I can't find Stony neither," Meg cried.

"Shh, little one. Do not bother her now." The woman led her away. "Have a seat for me, here. Wipe your face... use this. There's a good girl. Be quiet now. Take this."

"Stop. What're you giving her?"

"You be quiet, too. It is just a bit of lace and a hook, to occupy her. Can you fashion a stitch with that?" she asked Meg. "Poke, wrap, and lift up. Go on and show me, then, while I chat with your sister. Now, on to you," she said, back at Claire's side.

Claire was having trouble focusing on details. The dim light in the room seemed excruciatingly bright. Through her headache, she thought the woman looked plain, an indistinct face and hair pulled back tight so that there was nothing to it. She sounded older than Mother had been, though maybe not very old, and she wore a grey apron. Perhaps it was not grey. Perhaps everything was grey and blurry.

"Are youizzie?" Claire's words were still slurred, a voice unfamiliar to her own ears. Why couldn't she make the words sound faster, sharper? Sound like herself. What was happening to her?

"I am Izzie."

"Man's name."

The woman chuckled. "Short for Isabella. Now, let me see."

The woman folded the blanket down and before Claire could stop her, she pressed her hands into her belly. A midwife or witch, Claire had no idea what she was or what she was about to

68

do to her. Perhaps she was only a helpful neighbour. Or perhaps she was something more terrible.

"Lie still," the woman said in more of a command than a comfort. In two swift motions, she placed her hand on Claire's forehead, then gripped her wrist. "Your pulses," she muttered.

The woman closed her eyes and began to hum in a low, vibrating sound. A frightening sound. She reached into one of the pockets of her apron, and as she leant over again, Claire suddenly thought she was about to do her harm. What had she reached for? A blade? A needle?

"My word," the woman said more gently, "You have had a fright, haven't you?" She gently placed her hand on Claire's shoulder to reassure her.

Claire couldn't tell her she'd seen the physician puncture Mother's arm like the throat of a ram, bleeding her with the hope that what was killing her would be drained away. She felt herself fading in and out of the room, the pain in her head and belly so terrible she could hardly breathe.

Presently, she heard the scrape of a spoon against a cup, and smelled the vapors of something pungent, earthy, and hot... *The scent of Mother's garden when you pull the weeds up, and the wet clumps of hay you must pick out of the cart's hinges. A breakdown of any kind is intolerable. So is a rotted crop...*

Claire waited to be cut, squeezed her eyes shut. Instead, a hand slipped behind her head for support, and the hot and murky liquid was spooned into her mouth.

Then, sleep again.

She woke in underclothes that were not her own: a silk chemise with a tiny bow at each strap, and matching jupon. She touched each of her temples with her finger, then placed her hand on her belly. No pain. On the table were two empty cups and a pouch filled with powder that smells like the waste at the bottom of the cups; a crusted teaspoon stuck to the tabletop. Next to it was her one spool of thread, taken from her old petticoats.

Her body was no longer on fire. Her legs were weak but otherwise without pain, between them a folded square of muslin held in place by yet another ribbon tied at the waist. She was like a crumpled gift no one in their right mind would care to receive.

Claire sat up and scanned the room. Her own shawl was folded at the end of the cot. The carpetbag with their belongings was gone and so, for that matter, was Meg. Draped over the back of the one chair was a myrtle-green tartan walking dress and matching hat; and stays with hooks and laces waiting to stuff her into womanhood. Next to the dress, something glimmered. Claire swung her legs over onto the cold, bare floor, took a few steps and saw a gold chain threaded through an enormous gold ring—a man's ring, with a dark red stone set into it.

Something was not right. About the ring, the dress, the emptiness of the room. She knew that it was all wrong.

She dressed quickly, fumbling with the laces of her new stays. She bolted down the stairs and found Meg on the bench before the fire in a smart red wool traveling coat. A new doll sat on her lap. The doll was the length of her arm and had the face of a dancing bear with the gown of a strumpet. Claire scooped Meg up and hugged her with a relieved gasp.

"Stay here, Meghan, do not move," she commanded, placing Meg back on the bench. "Mind me?" Meg nodded.

She ran back up to the room to grab the pouch next to the cup and saucer. Whatever was in it worked, and she was not about to leave it behind. She stuffed her thread and needle in the hidden pocket of her grown-up tartan dress. She pinned her hair as best she knew how, put the hat on, and headed for the door, then doubled back and snatched the ring still hanging from the chair.

Their sour hostess said, "Out front he is" as she passed her in the hallway.

Claire took Meg's hand, pulled her from the bench.

"There they are! It always takes a bit of time for females to ready themselves for a journey. Ha-ha! Oh, and how beautiful you look," Father said, smiling from the driver's seat of a fashionable little gig parked at the curb, its ornate hood pulled up only half-way against what was amounting to an even colder, wetter day than when they first arrived.

"Where is Stony?" Claire asked, staring up at him from the street, her stomach plummeting as she noticed a large, tan steed hitched to the gig.

"Come-come, girls," he said, waving them up. "Step up into the carriage, we mustn't linger. There are all-manner of things to be done today."

"But, Stony!" Meg cried.

"Climb up, Claire. That's it, settle yourselves. The rug is ermine, from the mountains of Siberia—ermine, as I have promised you! I see you have found my present, Claire. You are old enough, now, to be passed down our family heirloom, or so the delightful wife of our host informs me. 'Twas my father's own ring, and now it is yours. Wear it, my dear, around your neck."

"But where is our bag? Our things?"

"What things? Those old rags? Don't be silly." He snapped the reins and the gig started to roll forward. "My father was a

Squire with three hundred acres of moorland in Scotland on the North Sea, you know," he said over his shoulder. "Have I not told you of him? The ring is meant to be passed down to the eldest son but... ah well, anyway. It is yours now, lass."

Next to her, Claire heard the high-pitched, elongated whistle of Meg's tears begin. "But they were mine!" She meant her dresses and apron, of course, though no doubt the ring made it sting all the more.

"Shhh, there-now. Oh, please be quiet, Meghan," Claire whispered this in her ear. She kissed her wet cheeks, and pressed her face into Meg's neck, into her soft, unruly cloud of curls.

It was then Claire realized that someone—the someone who had dressed them both?—had piled Meg's hair atop her head in a style distinctly sophisticated and adult. It looked exactly as it had been in her terrible dream of the horse. She saw, too, that Father's wide back was clad in black velvet, Mother's scarf exchanged for a smart red tartan one. Claire felt a new jolt of horror wondering where the precious, woven length had gone. "Father? When are we going home?" She raised her voice, tried to make it sound strong. "Father!"

The gig lurched, then gained speed, the wheels pitching over rocks and dips in the road. She gripped Meg tighter as they headed into the unknown, the dreary buildings of the nameless town left in their wake.

EIGHT

1876 ~ Autumn
Bethnal Green, London

When I am the one carrying the sack, thought Claire, I must remember to keep my head in a downward tilt, eyes straight ahead. Make a face like I will bite if someone gets too near. It was a small feat if you were fifteen and pleasant to look at.

"Are you all right with that? It's awfully heavy," remarked their host in a small, sad tone. He was a timid, wiry man sporting a salt-and-pepper beard and a wilting cravat. He saw them off from the entry hall of the London townhouse but offered no real assistance.

"Yes, thank you, sir." Claire stepped down the stoop, then urged Father to do the same. "Come along, Father."

"A very good-night to you, my good man! Many thanks for the fine food and ale, and the very fine company," drawled Father.

"Papa, come."

"And give my thanks to your charming companion who—"

"Father, Meg is falling over with exhaustion." Claire gave the wiry man a quick wave.

Slack-eyed, slightly wobbly with drink himself, the man watched them from the doorway and offered a wave in return. Inside, his dog barked, and his shoulders twitched with the sound. In the window, orpiment light and black shadows flickered as card players rotated their seats in the front parlour. The exterior gas sconce set next to the door hissed and spat as he closed the door and locked it.

Meg's head drooped against Claire's shoulder as they set out along the street lined with similar, middle-class townhouses, all joined together. They walked a block until Meg suddenly angled herself outward and tugged on Claire's arm, as if wanting to take another direction.

"Just a few blocks," Claire encouraged her, fearing she was so tired she might be sleepwalking. She clutched Meg's shoulder and when she did, the sack made a clanking sound she hoped no one would hear.

She leaned hard into Father with her other shoulder, and all three of them turned the corner onto a narrow side-street, separating then knocking against each other as though connected train cars around a bend.

A cab rattled past—coming so close to them Claire felt the cobbles erupting under her feet—and a passenger howled out the window, "How much for the girls, Gov?"

She gritted her teeth. She could feel a last crumb between her molars, what was left of a plate of oat cakes their host's companion had given them for their supper. The woman had been kind but quiet, barely interacting with the girls while flitting gracefully between the kitchen and the parlour with a tray of drinks for the men.

They turned another corner and, on the Broad Street, Claire could see a set of tall iron gates with gilded falcons atop marble posts just to their left. The gates were open, party guests leaving in a steady stream of lacquered wheels and sparkling lanterns. At the other end of the same street—the direction toward which Claire led them—disintegrating houses were all piled like broken packing crates. There were sparsely placed gaslights and reach-me-down dress shops down this way. There were no gates with footmen.

Another block, and Claire felt Father grab her arm and lean on her. "Steady, Father!" But he was trying to alert her: a narrow slip of what one could not in all reason call water had pooled like a lake in the middle of this section of the street. The hue of green tea in daylight, it looked solid as ebony in the dim glow of a lone, dim streetlamp. In the shadows, two men relieved themselves into the liquid ditch. Claire pressed Meg's face into her still-meager bosom. One drop near their face and they'd be done for, the Blue Death ravaging them in a matter of days. Cholera, the plague of a decade prior—boasted by Mayor and Queen to be gone from the city—still festered in this neck of Town.

Claire saw the ramshackle timber house that was their destination, with its painted sign: Goode Rooms. The house should have been torn down ages ago. It was flanked by a newer rooming house on one side and a proper restaurant on the other. That establishment was closing, throwing patrons onto the street and scraps into the side alley where a trio of cats waited.

There was a little crowd gathered in front of the rooming house, and Claire sighed when she saw it. Now they would have to hassle their way to the room she and Meg shared with the proprietess, squeezing between drunk men and loud women.

The proprietess crackled with henna and reeked of perfume with an undertone of whiskey and cigars. She was lively, not entirely unkind, and gave them hair ribbons onto which Claire embroidered tiny flowers and birds and which the woman gave Claire a penny for each, then sold them for four.

Here she was now—Mrs Thompson, or was it Tomasen?— blocking the open door in her Oriental silk chemise and robe, her hair half-undone with the day's activities.

"Good evening, Missus," Claire called (there was no Mister). "My sister is very tired. Can you help us to the—pardon me— can you help us inside, please?"

"You!" the woman screeched, pointing at Father, blood-red nail enamel flashing against ghostly knuckles. "Two weeks you owe me. I warned you, I did, and now you're out on your arse!"

"Father?" Claire looked at him, expecting to hear laughter at the joke. Two street tarts joined the crowd. One had removed Claire's blue shawl and was wrapping it around her own neck, the other had Meg's hat on. It almost fit, since the girl was on the near side of twelve.

"Away with you!" bellowed Father. His arms swung wildly in front of him as he advanced, and the loiterers half-heartedly dispersed. They knocked against Claire, taking her hat, too. On the doorstep sat their open and empty carpetbag, snatched up in seconds by one last brave hand, as they all scattered back into the shadows like rats.

"Stay close," Father whispered, taking the canvas sack from Claire and hoisting it over his broad shoulder.

Meg jumped into Claire's arms and latched her arms around her neck in a fierce strangle. Her dangling legs knocked against

Claire's hips in silent thumps as they walked. It was all Claire could do to keep from screaming: from fear, from exhaustion, from the pain of Meg's kicks. She didn't ask Father where they were headed because she knew her arms would fall off before they got there, dropping to the road in two clunks. *Three: Meg will go next.*

"That's it, Claire, keep pace. Good lass."

The city, for all its lamps and chandeliers and candles inside its homes, was thick with dark. Moonlight was obscured by smog, the cobbles by fog. There were occasional clusters of radiance: haphazard kilns, fires made in metal grates around which the desperate huddled, burning their fingertips on nubs of stale bread and rotted meat.

Crossing over Bethnal Green, they walked up a quiet street where Father flagged a dairy cart. Some words were exchanged, an object drawn from the sack and handed to the carter, and the girls climbed up amongst the milk jugs. Meg lolled against Claire's shoulder again as they passed the shadowy trees and tombstones of Bunhill Fields burial ground. From behind one of the slabs, Claire saw a crouching figure made of shadow. She didn't know what it was doing. She looked away, afraid, and put her arm around Meg protectively.

They passed through Holborn, where the cart made deliveries, and Claire watched the high-brow terraces and their safe, silken interiors retreat into the cold pitch of the hinterlands.

"You'll have to get out here. Can't take you no farther," said the carter, after they crossed the Thames.

"But they are children, sir, have pity."

"Ain't on me route."

They climbed down and Claire strapped Meg to her chest again. They walked on.

They trekked across two miles of parkland where an enormous herd of deer stood motionless in a clearing, watching them. Three were albino, glowing white as though preternatural guards in translucent armor.

In a while, they found themselves on a hedge-lined road where raised fields stretched on either side of them. There was a break in the hedges for a stile, and Father hoisted the sack over, then climbed to the other side and took Meg from Claire. Claire's arms lifted like magic feathers with the removal of Meg's weight, and she steadied herself on the stile before depositing herself onto the squishy ground of the field.

She stopped to get her bearings. All around her was a dense fabric of mist. The air was clean and smelled of hay. The field stretched on and on until it became one with the dark sky. She blinked her eyes, trying to focus on Father's large, black form. "Wait, Father."

"What is it?"

"Just a moment, I—" A sharp spark at the right side of her head.

"A few feet more, my dear, and you may recline on my warm coat."

Father's Chesterfield was thick and dry. But no, it would be damp from the mist and his perspiration. *Damp wool...*

A tattered wool rug draped over a musty sofa of leather upholstery: this is what she saw now. In place of the mist-laden field there was a room, and a weightless feeling telling her that she was not actually standing in it, though it felt as real as if she were. Surrounding the sofa were books and books—hundreds of volumes climbing the walls of shelves—all coated in dust. A beautiful leather-embossed book flaking off in her fingers as she pulled it from the shelves.

And a great bedchamber where someone leans over you. A man growls something, grabs your neck. You open your mouth, and your throat closes in a soundless scream.

NINE

1876 ~ Autumn, dawn
Shepherds Hallow, Surrey

"**S**hh, there-there." Father rushed to her from his position of watchman. "I'm here."

The grey beginnings of morning. Meg was asleep next to her on Father's coat, the grasses flattened hard beneath them. She had no memory of laying down to sleep.

"How are you feeling?"

"Fine."

"And your head-ache?"

She touched her face, checking, pressing her cheekbones and temples. She nodded. She thought, Did I have a head-ache?

He knelt next to her and took her hand. "Forgive this mishap." He spoke softly, so as not to wake Meg. "I—I'd no idea that woman would be so inhospitable. I do not know what came over her. But I should not have had us stay there at all."

She looked at him blankly.

"Well, never mind." He shook his head. He was sad, and guilt ridden. This was obvious.

"I will never again take you to that infernal city, Claire. I will find us a comfortable house, just large enough for the three of us, with a little garden, and there we will settle. I am not unmindful of how difficult our traveling has been on you and your sister. I've tried my best to take care of you, but I know how hard it has been. I do know it."

She tamped her heart down, giving it an admonishing slap as it undertook a leap of hope.

"There, can you see that?" Father pointed across the field. "The road on the other side of this field is the road to Shepherd's Hallow. A good town for business, with lovely little houses removed a bit from the High Street. I cannot think of a better place for us. It's nothing grand. But it is charming. And safe."

She looked across the field but could only see the basic line of the horizon. "Really?"

Father smiled, his eyes lined and puffed, and patted her cheek gently with his big, pudgy hand. "Yes. Yes, really. Let us wake our little one. What say we? A teashop is what we need. Sweety-cakes, yes?"

"But we've no money."

"No money, you say?" He picked up the sack and shook it, smiling. "A sound like bells, is it not?" He scooped Meg up in his arms, bouncing her and kissing her forehead.

Eyes still closed, she muttered, "I want my breakfast."

In the enormous, brown-lacquered Brougham, Meg lounged across Claire's lap, the seat bigger than the whole bed they shared with the Missus T. at her Goode Rooms in London.

"...in that castle on the cliffside," Meg was saying.

Claire looked out the window at the view that slid farther away from the village. The thick, fox fur rug across her lap was frayed and worn on the underside where the hide had rubbed against a hundred legs before. She couldn't shake last night, the dizziness that overcame her when she stood on the field, and the room with its dust-encrusted books, the wool rug over the sofa. *That man leaning down over you...*

"Claire! You never pay attention to me."

Claire guffawed. "As if that's likely." She smoothed the hair from Meg's forehead. "I will have to trim your fringe later. Now tell me, are you going to be a princess, in your castle?"

Meg puckered her face, like a city urchin with sham-sad eyes. "Only little girls want to be princesses."

"You are a little girl."

"You're not playing, Claire. Tell me about your house."

"Mine is not very grand. And yours is the castle today, is it?"

"Yes, that old castle with a real tower and we come upon it on our walk in..." Lately, Meg spoke in long, winding thoughts like Father. "...well it was sometimes sunny, at least not always so rainy, and there was a strand under the cliffs where the sea was, and you said King Arthur lived there once, Father."

"The South Hams!" Father lit up.

"Now I remember," Claire conceded. "The house we lived in was small and pretty. It felt... like someone really lived there."

"We lived there."

No, she thought, we lived along another shoreline; at a farm that belonged to us. It had dragon's eggs and tiny silver fish in tidal pools. It had great chalky cliffs and a cranky old Admiral who lived in a cottage right on the beach. *It had Will.*

Claire quickly corrected her darkened expression and smiled at Meg. "You liked those cakes this morning, didn't you?"

As promised, Father had indeed found a teashop for their breakfast. It was a small but pretty shop, with a window that overlooked the High Street. Only half-done with his tea, Father had suddenly stood up and said, "I'll be not a moment." Claire had gaped as he pulled a handful of shillings from his pocket and threw them on the table. "Order what you like, lasses." And he left them.

The whole time he was gone, Meg stuffed herself with cakes while Claire told her invented stories she thought passed for fairytales. She just had to keep Meg interested until Father returned. She was keenly aware Meg might start a scene, if she became bored or hungry enough.

Claire rose from the table for a moment only to ask for more cream, and it was then that Meg disappeared. Swiveling full circle in the shop, Claire had shouted, "Has anyone seen my sister? Meg? Meghan!" Through the window, she caught a glimpse of Meg outside, on the cobbles, petting a small, shaggy dog. Claire ran out, grabbed her hand and gave it a hard smack. "You cannot just do as you please!" she yelled.

The dog's owner, an old gentleman wearing a bowler hat, shook his head and pulled his dog along.

The owner of the shop, a scowling blonde, narrowed her eyes at them when they sat back down, Meg red-eyed and sniffling.

"Does he always leave you alone?" asked the blonde woman. She plunked the pitcher of cream down. If she smiled, she would have been pretty.

"He'll be back soon," Claire told her.

"Mhmm." She folded her arms across her ample bosom, then returned to the counter where she placed freshly-baked cream puffs onto a platter.

At the next table, an old woman hummed a tune, and she paused to give them a toothless grin from beneath her enormous frilled bonnet.

Claire smiled politely back. The tops of her legs were throbbing again. She'd pulled the pouch of powders from her skirt pocket, taking a pinch and dropping it into her own tea and stirring. Holding the pouch in her palm, she gauged the weight. *It is lighter than last time. You'll run out if you use it too often.*

Out the window, Claire could see the full length of the High Street. Father might be anywhere: butcher, baker, candlestick maker. Mad hatter, murderous meat pie seller. The man in the bowler hat and the dog had crossed the street and was returning the other way. He likely lived in the village. Claire had noticed many cottages near the churchyard and pub.

Just before closing, Father came through the door announcing they would be settled in their new house in time for sweet dreams. He stopped at the counter to place three crowns, stacked neatly, in front of the owner. "For your trouble, my dear."

The woman nodded, and made something like a smile appear on her lips.

"Father, Claire won't play with me," Meg called up to him now as they rattle along the road in their new coach.

"Don't be a damper, Claire," Father said chuckling.

Meg grinned at Claire.

They traveled along main road and then turned onto a winding path. After a stretch of parkland, Father slowed the horses.

What appeared was not a tidy little cottage as promised, but an immense stone manor house through heavy locked gates, a rusted *3* (or *E*) dangling from one. A light colour that once glimmered in sunlight, the stones walls were streaked with centuries of soot. Tall leaded windows filled twin gables. Half-a-dozen chimneys, like spires, poked through the roofline. Truly, it was hard to imagine a more beautiful house. Unless, of course, you meant this one: an abandoned, forlorn version of a once-beautiful house.

Father, brandishing a rusted iron ring with three keys, scraped one key into the latch, pushed the heavy iron gate open, and remounted. As he steered down the drive, the sun beginning to dip behind the chimneys, creating long shadows on the drive. Claire felt an icy flutter in her stomach.

"I don't like this place," Meg whispered to Claire.

The closer they got, the more Claire, too, became afraid. She wondered why on earth Meg was whispering softly, now of all times. Speak up and start whining, she wanted to tell her. Cry, bawl if you have to, so Father will turn around and take us back to town!

"What say you, girls?" Father looked over his shoulder, his eyes wide. "Look at this splendor of glass and stone! The great oaken doors! What mystery is behind them, eh?"

Claire had a terrible sense she already knew. "I think this house is too big for us, Father," she suggested, her voice catching in her throat.

He stopped the carriage, jumped down, and fumbled with the keys again.

"Is it not too large for us?"

"Get down from there, lass."

"We have two horses now?" Claire asked, staying put. She pointed to the one bay, one chestnut, hitched to the carriage. Perhaps if she kept asking questions, he'd forget what he was doing, then rethink the plan when he came to his senses. "Do we really need two horses?"

Meg climbed down onto the drive and looked back at Claire with expectant eyes.

Father opened the door and stepped inside the cavern.

Slowly, Claire climbed from the coach and followed them inside.

The entry was heraldic, with profuse carvings and nauseatingly swirled decoration like a Gothic priory or rooms of Parliament.

"Our horses can play chess on the floor," Meg said, hopping from black to white on the large marble tiles, the heels of her boots clapping in echoes. She pointed through an archway. "Ooh!"

"That is the long gallery, my little one, as all fine country houses must have. Come along, the both of you." Father waved them forward.

As they walked the length of the gallery, Claire smelled the pungent odor of mildew. The ornate ceiling panels dripped cobwebs and spit dust on the carpet in intervals. Faded tapestries of unicorn hunts lined the walls like soiled blankets hung out to dry.

"Father?" Claire asked. "Who lives here?" she slowed her pace again, feeling the urge to run back to the carriage.

"We live here."

"You did not buy this place, did you?"

"In the interest of securing the fairest deal, I am renting this estate until the involved parties will agree to my price. Which, I am certain, they will soon enough. Claire, you must see this — something for you, especially." He stopped before a carved door set into the middle of the gallery, a tarnished brass lion head set into the center of it as a knob. He turned the head and opened the door.

In the center of a high-ceilinged, octagonal room was a lone sofa, a thick wool rug petrified to its soiled leather upholstery. Along the walls were hundreds of books, stacked floor-to-ceiling on dark wood shelves. Volumes of leather embossed with gold lettering on the bindings were coated in dust. *They will crack and flake in your fingertips when you hold them. Go on, try it.*

"Father!" Meg cried.

"What's wrong?" Claire started to ask, but it was Claire herself Meg was pointing at. She couldn't figure out why, until the room spun violently. She fainted into blackness and landed with a thump on the floor.

TEN

1877 ~ Spring
Evensong
Shepherds Hallow, Surrey

"Has he a name, Claire?"

"If he has, I don't know it."

Claire stretched her hand out slowly, with a straight, pointed finger. It was met with a nudge from a wet, black nose. Two azure blue eyes stared at her from a dark chocolate mask on a body of fawn. She recognized him instantly, though she'd never seen one of his kind in real life. A painted lead figurine on a wooden spool wrapped with blue thread. A book of cats with text easy enough to teach Will to read.

"See him! See how friendly he is, Claire!" Meg squeaked.

"Shh, you'll frighten him." She stroked the side of his long, unflinching face. His fur was short and velvety-feeling, his gaze relaxed and steady. It was unlikely he was afraid of anything.

"What is your name, kitty? What are you called?" asked Meg of the cat, excitedly, thrusting her face into his.

"You can ask him all day, but I don't suppose he'll tell you. C'mon then, take the bucket."

Meg groaned dramatically as she stood, and hoisted the water.

"I don't know why you bother complaining, Meg; it is hardly my fault the fixtures cough dust." *That porcelain tub the size of a coach in the kitchen sits parched as a desert. Unusable, like everything else in this house.*

"Girls? Where are you?" Father appeared at the door that led from the kitchen into the neglected garden where the pump sat. "Water for a kettle? No. Tap the ale. The guests will be here soon. What is that thing?"

Trotting behind Claire's ankles was the cat. "I think he lives here," she suggested, smiling down at him.

"Nonsense."

"He likes us!" Meg squealed. "He's following us!" She bounced on her toes, sloshing water, and Father grabbed the bucket from her. "Why do you look at him like that, Father? You look cross."

Without answering, he held the door open with his boot, ushered Meg inside, then followed her. Claire followed him, then hung back a step and let the door close slowly behind her, leaving a crack just wide enough for a slender, feline body to slip through.

On the kitchen table sat a lump of boiled ham and half-wheel of cheese. The recipe: cut bits off and place on Harriet's toast brought from her teashop, finish off with toothpicks Claire decorated with little strips of ribbon.

"My name's Mrs Horner," Harriet had said to them that first day in the shop, "But since my husband's dead and did not have the courtesy to leave me a penny, save this miserable shop, you may as well call me Harriet." Perhaps she had made conversation only to silence the elderly woman who kept trying to sing to them, an act of surprising kindness from someone who had spent a solid hour glaring at the girls. Father had them taking tea there every afternoon since and soon, Harriet had been invited up to Evensong, as their house was known (the dangling *E* was not for nothing). A month in, and she was scrubbing the floors and banging out the drapes, for all the good that did.

Bang. The platter of toast had arrived, along with Harriet. "Little slices," she said to Claire, "we'll have to stretch it. Your Father's invited a mob." Harriet planted a hand on her ample hip, her bosom joggling above her neckline. She was like a giant, pale, Island wench: beautiful and fierce, a character in one of those books in the library Claire had been gobbling up. Except without the dust— nothing settled on Harriet but a flushed sheen. Exertion suited her, though she never stopped claiming she just wanted to "bloody sit down a minute."

The girls often tried making Harriet smile by telling her long, convoluted jokes and surprising her with presents, but Harriet merely shouted at them. It didn't occur to Claire how close in age she was to Harriet, compared with Father.

"They are nearly here." He popped his head in the door, a tweed cap set jauntily on it.

"Well?" Harriet shouted at the room. "Get a move on, then!"

In Claire's bedchamber at Evensong, the coffered ceiling was always shadowed at night. The walls were hung with green brocade paper which peeled at the high corners, the folds creating malevolent clefts where miniscule but terrible things could hide. The great four-poster held an old feather mattress, needle-sticks of quill calamus poking through the linens into her skin.

It was late and Claire could hear the party still alive downstairs as she brushed and plaited her hair. She could also hear, in the room, the scuttling of the mice behind the wardrobe as they began their nightly dance in and out of a hole in the wall.

She climbed into bed and squinted at the underside of the canopy. Stains marred the old silk as though oceans on a map and she had an impulse to trace the lines with needle and bright silk floss, if she could reach the canopy. She now knew the swampy rivers of India and the icy waterways of Norway, though she'd yet to find a map of England or, please God, a novel in that enormous library downstairs. A cartographer was what the former owner must have been, judging by the books. An adventurer, like Father was in his younger days. She longed for Mrs Gatskill, but what the library had in multitudes was *A Detailed Study of Greenland's Neolithic Burial Sites and Pacific Expeditions Ending in Fever and Cannibalism.*

A collective roar from the parlor flared up, a kind of cheer accompanied by an "Ahhh!" Next, the old harpsichord was played, off-key and demented sounding. She giggled at the sound of Father's guests. They were a friendly bunch tonight, who seemed to delight in comic theatrical games Claire and Meg were allowed to watch for a while.

The cat hopped up and settled himself under the covers alongside her ribcage. She smoothed his velvety, fawn-coloured coat, placed a finger on his throat and felt it rumble. He was real, not a toy, not something she could lose. He was hers. She decided to name him Ling, after a character she read in a book about China, where the silk in her room came from. There was a drawing of a little sailing boat at the beginning of the story; a sampan, bobbing and rocking on the Yangtze. "Chapter Nine: Ling called to the ducks and they boarded his sampan one by one. They would all each fish tonight..."

The candle on her bedstand burned out soon after she fell asleep, and the room was dimly illuminated by a half-moon through the dirty leaded windows. It grew icy in the room while she slept, the fire nothing but a pile of cool, black embers.

The sensation of a large, dark shape in the room woke her. Shapes could do that, shadows with matter disturbing the empty air... she knew this. Had seen it in her mother's sick room.

Without moving, Claire let her eyes scan the room, landing on the dark lumps that were chairs and her dress and... this other thing.

The shadow moved again.

She's come to take you.

"Aunt Aileen?" Claire whispered.

The amorphous shape neared. From the shape blew condensation, as though smoke from a slow-moving dragon. Under the covers Ling stiffened, a deep, unearthly growl sounding from his chest.

"Father?" she whispered again. She looked at her dress draped on the chair. But who knew she had sewn four shillings and two-pence into her skirt pocket? Did Father? It was not stealing if he gave her the money for food and she just went without instead of spending it. She didn't know why she even did it; they hadn't gone without food for weeks.

The shadow lunged. It landed with a terrible thud on top of her. The wind was knocked from her lungs in a burst of pain. A callused hand started pulling at the shoulder of her nightdress, and she tried to push the hand away.

"C'mon then, l'il bird." A raspy voice, a breath sour with drink and bile. While the one hand still pulled on her nightdress, his other hand pinned her hip down. "Lay quiet, girl, give us summat for our troubles!" Coarse skin rubbed against hers. He stroked her cheek. "Shhh…" Spit hit her nose and lips.

She twisted, his arms confining her so that she was like prey in a dog's teeth. Engulfed in his stench, she kicked her legs and a wiry beard scraped the side of her face, saliva hitting her ear.

"You're a fierce one, arn't you? Squirm, girl, squirm! Heh-heh… What's this?" The hand squeezing her breast let go and grabbed hold of her ring. He gave a yank, the chain wresting her neck as it held and burned a red line into her skin. "I ain't leaving here with no winnings. Bastard owes me from last time."

Claire kicked again, and screamed, forcing the sound out in a guttural cry. But who could hear her up here, with the rumpus down below?

"Quiet!"—a hand slapped across her mouth—"Quiet, I said!"

She kicked her knee and hit him in the ribs, and he lost his balance, his elbow slipping onto Ling. There was an ear-shattering screech, and an explosion of talons from beneath the covers.

"Jesus Christ!" The man jumped up, holding his cheek, blood streaming from the wound.

Claire scrambled from the bed and raced for the door connecting Meg's room to hers. Faltering for a second, she managed to turn the key in the lock. On the floor, Ling angrily postured and hissed like a viper, the man backing away from him and cursing.

She reached down, grasped Ling by the scruff, and ducked into Meg's room, locking the door behind her. Taking key and cat, she climbed under the musty covers and huddled close to Meg.

"Meg, wake up, wake up. Meg, wake up, please!" She panted, her heart pounding.

It was no use. As usual, Meg slept like the dead.

After this, Claire sneaked nightly through the passage door to Meg's room, with Ling at her heels. She would never again sleep in the green room that was hers.

Claire and Meg never learned to whom Ling once belonged, but both girls thought him the most intelligent cat they'd ever known. Together, they agreed they would keep him, but both girls knew he was really Claire's.

"Off that! Shoo!" Harriet whipped the dishtowel, but the cat escaped from table to top-of-cupboard in one swift leap. "Cheeky bastard."

The front bell sounded in a far-off series of discordant notes.

"I'll go." Claire grabbed Ling before Harriet could and hooked him under her arm where he relaxed into her. As she walked the length of the gallery the bell continued ringing. She could hear the rattle of the doorknob being tried, and an unpleasant metallic scratching sound. "Coming, Father!" she called.

Father had put a new, better, lock on the door when they'd moved in, and the brass plate shone against the old dark wood. She put Ling down on the marble tiles to undo the bolt. "Father, have you forgotten your...?"

She pulled the door open and saw a strange man standing in front of her. With long grey hair and a broad-brimmed hat and breeches, he looked like he'd dropped in from thirty years ago and seemed as startled as if he had done just that. His skin was browned, worn and freckled, as if constantly exposed to the sun.

He was sinewy and gaunt. Yellow Fever? Malaria? *Pacific Expeditions Ending in Fever and Cannibalism.*

"Who—who are you?" the man stammered. In the drive, his horse looked rumpled and windswept and similarly confused.

"Are you looking for my father?"

"Who is your father?"

Claire stared at the man. Gently, he pushed her aside and walked into the house.

Moments later, she was back in the kitchen with Harriet and Meg. The visitor was with Father in the dining hall, and they could hear the man's thin, raspy voice rising in anger from down the corridor.

"Here," said Harriet, sliding a large bowl toward Claire. She had cleaned out the brick oven adjacent to the hearth and lit a pile of sticks.

"Here what?"

"Don't get cheeky with me, young lady. Lard and flour. Rolls?"

"We haven't got any flour," Claire said. "You always bring us rolls from the shop. I thought the oven was stopped up?"

At this, Harriet's cheeks bloomed scarlet. "Right," she said, slamming both her hands on the table, "I have had just about enough of this."

Meg said in a small voice, her lip quivering, "You're always cross with us."

Harriet shook her head, furious. "If you only knew why I'm cross! I never asked for kids. But if I had my own, I'd shout and punish as well as cuddle. I'd teach my girls to spell, and bake, and get someone to teach 'em to play piano and speak French—anything and everything so they'd be useful to someone someday, and someday soon, rather than spend their life as some confidence man's sidekicks!"

Claire touched the little pocket, hidden in her underskirts. I did not steal it, she wanted to explain, I only saved from what I did not eat myself.

"You are steps away from Red Street, the both of you!" Harriet screamed. Her eyes were glinting with tears.

"But we live at Evensong," said Meg, meekly.

"She doesn't mean that," mumbled Claire. "Harriet, Father would never... Harriet, he never — "

"Wouldn't he? You are certain, are you?"

The girls stared silently, not at Harriet but at Father who now stood in the doorway.

"My dears..." he began, his face crestfallen.

"Don't *my dears* me," Harriet turned to him. "Go on then, tell us, who is our lovely visitor? Oh, let us guess: he's just come back from a very long journey and is ever so surprised to find you livin' in his home, and he'll be ever so nice in giving us half-an-hour to get out before he fetches the magistrate?"

"I... my pet, I — "

"You're a liar!" Meg shouted at Harriet. "This is our house!"

"You poor thing," muttered Harriet. She bent down, held Meg's face and kissed her forehead. She stood and turned to Claire, grabbing her hand and squeezing it. "You keep your chamber door locked no matter where you live, do you understand me, Claire?" she said, eyes blazing. She gave her hand another squeeze, then threw her apron on the table and strode out the kitchen door, through the garden and past the pump.

"Leave him, Claire. Put him down."

Claire stood in the drive, feeling the pebbles under the thin soles of her dress boots. She looked up at Father looming on the bench, and thought: I could just walk the other way and let you drive off.

She believed, with a sudden fervor like a religious awakening, that she was, in this moment, about to march straight into town. Harriet would scowl at first when she saw her but if Claire kept quiet, and worked hard, she would keep her. She would keep Ling, too; they'd be an extra hand and a ratter in one neat, little package. She'd think Claire clever for saving Father's change when she went to market. She'd think her clever and frugal, like Mother had been. *It was always Mother who had counted the items in the larder.*

"Put that thing down," said Father. His voice was low-pitched, slow. He stared down at her, steely-eyed. The mild affection was gone from his face, something menacing she'd never seen before replacing it.

"Claire?" Meg looked down at her from inside the carriage. She looked afraid, expectant. She held onto the edge of the door like an exotic pet dressed up in a cage.

Claire looked behind her at the great oak door locked shut, the neglected gardens, the mangled orchard, the stretch of parkland beyond which was the bridle path to town. She squeezed Ling tighter and he gave a soft grunt.

"Claire. Put it down," said Father, his voice so deep and low she could barely hear it.

She placed Ling on the ground, a wave of nausea and terrible regret welling up in her. Her hand lingered on the top of his dark head a moment. Then she forced her legs to move, to step up into the carriage. Her eyes, as if possessing a will of their own, bore into Father's as she did. She thought of her needle, tucked into its spool in the pocket of her petticoat with her coins. *Stab-stab-stab, right into his eyes. Yes!*

She sat down, closed the door. Felt Meg lean into her right away; felt her little hand wrap around her arm.

The carriage jolted, moved.

Ling rose on his lanky, muscular legs and began to walk. He trotted up the drive after her as she rolled away. He followed through the open gate to the road, keeping the carriage in sight. Eventually, he stopped and sat, began to clean one of his paws, looking up every so often to blink his startling blue eyes after her. He would patiently await her return. For, how could she not come back for him? He belonged to her.

ELEVEN

1877 ~ Summer, morning
Wotton Vale, Gloucestershire

Claire looked around the stuffy, dim room as she brushed Meg's knotted hair. The one-room dwelling had low beams garlanded with webs and bent in the middle with the weight of a damp sleeping loft. There were two small, cloudy windows on either side of the low door. There were layers of dust on the wood table and two plain stools, under which a mildewed rush mat stretched along the earthen floor.

Father was on one knee, proposing warmth to the cold hearth. The kindling in the pile flared briefly, then smoked, a whistling sound accompanying each puff of the bellows as he worked. "There might be a hole in this," he mused, looking at the tool.

"Stop moving!" Claire seized Meg's hand and slapped it.

A long whine leaked out of Meg.

"You ought to use her," Claire suggested, "she's full of air." She snatched another lock and brushed it roughly.

Meg howled.

"Meghan my sweet, that sound is an agony. Claire, fetch some more sticks, there's a good girl."

"What would be the point in that? It's as old as Christmas. You'll never get anything to light in it."

"It is not as bad as all that, Claire." Father looked at her, genuinely hurt. "Nothing a broom and cloth won't cure?" Gently, he urged, "Fetch some kindling for me, and we shall have a kettle boiling in no time."

"What about her hair," Claire's tone was flat, unimpressed. "She'll give us lice."

"I haven't got lice." Meg wiped her snotty nose on her apron and turned her reddened eyes to Father.

Claire threw the brush in Meg's lap. "Brush it yourself, you little brat." She stormed out, Father's mouth agape as the doorway.

She stomped through the tall grass that grew around the ramshackle hovel. "Cottage," was what the man had called it, as if it was sparkling with charm instead of some Medieval relic left to rot. They had met the man in a pub in that last large market town. She didn't know the name of the town. She didn't believe the hovel belonged to the man, who told them he'd let it for half the usual price as they were such a nice-looking family with such pretty girls.

She went around the side yard to a paltry woodpile and stared at it briefly before walking through what might have been an old vegetable patch, her cheeks growing hot in the sultry morning haze. She stomped her boots. They were the same fancy ones she'd worn leaving Evensong weeks ago, now dull, and dusty, the soles growing thin.

In a while, she realized she'd walked through a wildflower meadow and then across a common grazing field to a path. She continued, following the path uphill. The path was like a cleared divot in the grasses made by deer or horses. Up the hill she went, until she found herself looking down into the vale where she started and realized how beautiful it was from up here. In the vale, the grass grew on undulating ridges and furrows in waved patterns you could not see when you were amongst them. Far away was what looked like a tiny village made of glowing, golden jewels: the sun bouncing off limestone.

She continued up the path until she was at the level top, breathing hard in the hot sun. Before her was a tended garden and a lone house made of grey stone, its windows opened to the breeze. Inside the house, someone moved about the kitchen. Claire could hear them.

Keeping to the edge of the property, Claire snuck around, her eyes on the house. There were roses growing on the fence, and on a painted shutter of an upstairs window a bird's silhouette was carved into the wood. Pink and blue Cloudies and Purple Flouties were planted along the stone foundation. Claire crouched behind a shrub and looked at the scene. *Magical*.

Claire stayed low and stared up again at the window with the bird carved into its shutter. She saw a flutter of a figure glide across the window. She heard a door opening and she ducked farther down. Peeking over the shrub, she saw a stocky woman leave the kitchen. Middle-aged, in a cap and apron, a basket slung over her pink, bare arm, she walked to the edge of the yard and disappeared down the path by which Claire had just arrived. She might be headed into that village, Claire thought.

She waited behind the shrub. Some rooks cried out, then absconded the roof of the stable to a nearby tree. Inside the stable, a single white horse snorted lazily.

Claire entered the house through the kitchen door. She walked stealthily, her fingers grazing the tabletop where some cream and flour were laid out. She picked a blackberry out of a bowl and popped it into her mouth. Adjacent to the kitchen was a little sitting room. It was decorated with vibrant carpets and narrative ceramic tiles surrounding the fireplace: scenes of little blue people in clogs examining blue windmills. The house was old, but the polished woodwork spoke of ships rather than dreary Gothic domiciles.

Claire sat in an upholstered chair and felt the soft cushion press against her aching back (five nights sleeping on a tavern cot). She smelled the smoky remnants of last night's fire and something else more floral, and clean. She closed her eyes and listened to the quiet of the house. She pretended it was her chair... her house, her garden.

So, said the voice in her head, *you are playing The Game now. Wait til you tell Meg.*

She recognized the voice. She'd heard it once in a while since Mother died, often when she was sewing something, but it did not frighten her. It was a woman's voice: deeper, more self-assured than her own. She decided to answer it. "I'm not playing," she said. "This is real." *Are you certain?*

"I'm not daft, you know."

For a brief moment, Claire thought she heard a creaking of floorboards above her and her eyes bolted open as she listened keenly. The figure in the upper window had perhaps not been the housekeeper, but another woman? She held her breath. Nothing.

A thick, sleepy wave of calm came over her, and after another minute or so, she dozed off, the clean floral scents and the soft feel of the chair enveloping her.

A noise outside. A squeak-clang. The low gate in the kitchen garden, and a real person opening it and stepping through.

Claire roused, her heart beating fast. She stood, tip-toed, and peered in the direction of the kitchen. She saw the doorknob turning. Quickly, she snuck back into the sitting room and over to a set of glass doors behind the chair. She prayed the latch wouldn't squeak as she turned the key extending out of it. But the key was stuck from the humidity and when she finally had managed to turn it, it popped out of the lock and hit the floor with a *ting*.

The woman in the kitchen paused. "Hullo?" she called. "Is someone here?"

Claire levered the handle, pushed the door open, and was blinded by the sun. She gave one last glance back at the room — already spotty with shadows and floating afterimage — and saw the key lying on the threshold. Without thinking, she picked it up and placed it in her apron pocket.

She shut the door and ran.

Out into the garden, past the tall climbing pea stalks, and the mint and rosemary; through the little back gate onto the lawn; darting onto the path and scrambling down its steep course until she was at the bottom, where she had come from.

She ran over the field back to the wood pile, where she grabbed a handful of sticks.

It was three months they stayed in the old hovel. The summer came and went, and the mildew grew along the beams and on the underside of the rush mat. The nights grew very wet, and then very cold.

Around October, they readied to leave for Salisbury — for a festival at which Father would sell pine furnishings he'd bought cheaply from a sale of the contents of a house belonging to a bankrupt dead man. The night before they left, Claire stood at the bottom of the path that led up to the stone house and looked up, clutching a shawl around her shoulders. She could not see the house. She had not seen it since that day, as she hadn't dared to, again. But against the inky night sky where stars scattered across space like fireflies, she could see a warm yellow glow above her. Lanterns and candles, lit inside the house. And a fire, in the fireplace where blue Dutch ladies carried milk across their blue shoulders.

She breathed a sigh, her lungs taking in the cold autumn air. She patted the side of her thigh, where the pocket in her petticoat held the key. She had moved the coins — by now there were four shillings, six pence — to another pocket she'd sewn along her other thigh. She'd used a piece of flax from Meg's old apron and gave Meg hers. She could do without an apron, Father had said, anyway. People would think her his servant, instead of his pretty daughter who was, come to think of it, soon to be of marrying age.

PART II:
A Charming Village

"There were other shadows than those of chasing clouds and wheeling bird flocks over those fields. Ghost stories and stories of witchcraft lingered and were half-believed."

Flora Thompson

ONE

1883 ~ May
Greenmoors Hotel
Tyne, Lancashire

The rush of wind was cold on their cheeks, though they both wore fur stoles round their necks and matching sable muffs encircled their hands.

"Why is the canopy down?" Meg complained.

"It is always down when we do this."

Claire looked at the short-clipped, frosted grass; a low, scrolled iron fence encircling a flowerbed mulched with hay. "Put your hood up," she said. She wondered if Meg would think to do it if she were alone. "But, where did you get those?"

Meg touched the little dangling pearl earrings in her ears. "Peter's sister, of course. She will be my sister now."

"Who?"

The coach sped up. The enormous wheels creaked. Clouds of steam puffed from the horse's wet, black nostrils in a veil of fog. *Huff-huff-huff.* Claire reached for Meg, but her fingers landed in a mound of sable. She tried to regain her balance against the violent rocking, but Meg was further away from her than she was only a moment ago. The coach had grown larger, the seat widening as if Claire was Alice and had eaten the wrong biscuit and was shrinking in her now too-large carriage.

Slowly, Meg turned her head toward Claire, her lips stained with rosy blush, her hair piled in sophisticated knots and curls, a choker of pearls around her womanly neck. "Do something, Claire," she said, her eyes wide and stony.

Claire gulped for air, opening and closing her mouth like some horrid sea animal thrashing on land.

She sat up in bed and gasped. She put her hand to her heaving chest and blinked her eyes rapidly in the dark.

She thought, I am two-and-twenty, the same age I always am in this dream. She did not know, in that moment, what it meant to have reached her dream in her own time. Was its repeated story finally over, or was there more to come? *Or worse, will this dream of yours ever end?*

Next to her, Meg snored softly. Her bridal gown hung on a wood and velvet hanger from the wardrobe door, waiting. Claire lay back in the high featherbed in the hotel. She curled up against Meg and shuddered with anxiety. Their room was called the Blue Room, and indeed the walls looked almost entirely blue at night, because the wallpaper was decorated with large Blue Cloudies: hydrangea, if you were anyone but Father. They did look like clouds, she noted now, the pale blobs chaotically scattered across the wall in some Bedlamite's idea of a pattern.

The Blue Room... were there blue Delft tiles around the fireplace? She forgot to look. She breathed in deeply, slowly, then out even more slowly, one... three...five. *Count in odd numbers, then even, until you calm down... That's it.*

The damask drapes swelled a little in a measured expansion

against the wall, like real lungs breathing. It was only a draught. Or was it? Everyone saw things at night when sleeping in strange places, she knew this. *You tell yourself, I'm just seeing things. How else are you to fall back to sleep after bolting awake, your heart racing?*

"Shhh," she admonished the voice, softly.

Yesterday, Meg had the gall to lecture her on this exact subject. "You know what your problem is Claire? Your imagination is small when you are awake, but it is much too large when you are asleep." Meg was sick of her waking her with cries and grips, she'd said. And Claire had replied, "Are you, now?"

Watching the moonlight change angles, she hugged Meg tighter and focused on anything but her dream. If only it would alter in some way, give her something new to be afraid of. But the dream was the same as ever, like an old bed cap one pulled out of the drawer when settling down for the night. Even the earrings Meg wore now made sense, the repetition of once-meaningless elements sliding into place over time, an aspect of prophecy that made Claire feel worse, not better. She could see one earring, the pair a gift from Peter's older sister Emmeline, glittering in Meg's ear as she slept, a few strawberry-blonde strands of hair knotted through the fastener at the lobe.

Claire realized that, as she held Meg with one arm, she had also been clutching her ring with her other hand. The necklace was meant to soothe or just crown her zenith female, left draped over a chair in that garret room where the stranger had also left her a pouch of crushed leaves and barks. The ruby was the dark colour of blood, joining generations of family. She sometimes wondered if the ring bound her to Father in something like a spell.

It felt so long ago that morning she woke to find the ring. Claire thought Father had maybe given it to her to ward off whatever she'd brought on them that day at the inn. Izzie, that was the strange woman's name. Claire had thought she was going to do her harm when, really, she had saved her. The night before the woman came — the night she fell ill — was the first time she had the dream. Their first night without their mother. Without their real home, which they had not seen again in all these years.

"I don't know why you even complain about my dreams," Claire whispered to Meg now. "You never do wake up."

"If Mother were here…" A questioning sigh in Meg's voice left off the rest of the thought. Fluffed and bustled, she stood in the middle of the room encased in cream silk and lace. Her slightly swollen belly pushed against her bodice like a half-melon in a market sack.

Claire hoped no one else noticed as she buttoned herself into a light summer frock, a trade with a cousin of her brother-in-law-to-be. The heavy curtains had been pulled aside in an exuberant gesture by the chambermaid, and the Blue Cloudies pranced maniacally across the walls in the sunlight.

"If only she were here." Meg's eyes looked glassy, wet.

"You do not even remember her, dearest."

"I do remember her," she muttered back, her mouth curling in a sparkle-eyed grin as she caught a tear with her finger.

"You look like the cat who swallowed the canary, Meg."

"And you look like the sour matron in charge of too many wards."

"I am, you know. Hold still." Claire tightened the laces of the bride's stays.

"Ouch! Too tight. And what do you mean by that? Peter's mate has an eye for you. And Emmeline's husband has a brother who is very handsome? You might stay in Tyne longer and see how it plays out?" All her sentences dispersed at the end, a question-mark floating about the words with an airy nonchalance.

Meg looked hopefully at Claire but not, Claire thought, with any real conviction. Claire wanted to slap her for it. She opened the laces with a loud snap, re-tied them at a slackened point, and Meg breathed, the little dome of her middle relaxing.

"You are mean-spirited this morning, Claire," she sniffed. "It's not my fault you had nightmares again. On the night before my wedding, no less. It will be a bad omen. And you will freeze in that dress! It is still too cold for it? You look like you're going to a Midsommer Fair?"

"You are going to cry again."

"Maybe."

"Never mind, you shall be rid of me soon enough." Claire meant this in jest, but it didn't come out as such. "I did not plan on my nightmares ruining your day, incidentally. I am the worse for the wear on that score, not you."

Meg spun to face Claire, her gown still slipping half-off her shoulders, still unbuttoned at the very top. Her hair, too, was only half-done. She was like an octopus on land, wrapped and unwrapped curls spiraling this way and that. Her dainty but chubby arms, still childlike at seventeen, grabbed hold of Claire, and they embraced.

Claire breathed in Meg's scent as it enveloped her. She was flooded with the realization that after today, it would be weeks before she held her again or even saw her again. Years, maybe.

"Will you give me this, as a wedding present?"

"Stop that, you'll choke me." Claire laughed, prying the ring from Meg's fingers. "Did you think I'd actually give it to you?"

"I would remember you by it."

"I guess you will just have to forget me, then." She gave her a kiss on the cheek. "Your hair looks a fright, dearest."

Half an hour later, Claire lifted the bride's train as they entered the church of St. Stephen And All Angels. Meg's hair had been hastily but perfectly readied by Emmeline. The petals in Claire's basket anxiously awaited flight and her shaking hand remained clamped down on them like a cat's paw on its catch. Craning her neck, she saw the crowd doing the same to look back at her, the Rose Petal Scatterer, the Elder Soon-to-be-Spinster Sister in her Midsommer Attire. Peter stood at the alter looking ecstatic and nerve wrecked. *It is like a show, and you are its reluctant chorus girl.*

Afterwards, she stood on the green, smiling strangers clustered and talking to each other while dabbing at their eyes. She did not cry. She didn't clap her hands excitedly like the others, as Mr and Mrs Peter Dougherty rushed from the church under a shower of rice and petals. Peter's two brothers carried an oak keg to a table set up on the grass, and two other men hauled a roasted lamb. Some children danced around the table, tossing streamers into the air. She watched the rose petals sail to the ground, the streamers spiraling. She could hardly move. She could hardly breathe.

A bright red calash pulled up alongside the churchyard.

"Will you look a' that," a young man next to her said. *Peter's mate: John? Tim?* "That's summat for you. Say, you're not leaving already?" he asked Claire.

"I don't think so."

"Lord save us, that rig's fancy." He had a wide, friendly smile, light brown hair that gleamed from a morning bath. A wry expression about his eyes.

"It is, I guess," she answered. She looked at him directly and he smiled down at her. He was a little taller than her, just enough, so that she could see the weave of his necktie: coarse, perhaps home-woven. His eyes were kind, his lashes dark.

"Claire!" Father called from atop the calash. "Come aboard, my sweet."

"I guess you are leaving." He gave her a shrug. "What a shame."

She stared at him. "I don't know your name."

"Harry."

She nodded. "Nice to have met you, Harry."

"Claire!" Father waved from the bench, then threw kisses at Peter's family, though he should have been throwing coins.

It was a theatrical send-off, climbing a high, brightly-painted vehicle—something the bride herself should have done—and Claire's feet moved mechanically as she performed. Her carpetbag had been packed and stashed for her. The sky returned to its usual grey. A colossal, dark cloud swooped low, threatening to rain on the happy party. No one seemed to care.

Meg stood on the cobbles, one hand hooked on her husband's arm. She reached up for Claire with her free hand, the thin gold band on her finger glimmering. Was her expression hopeful, or desperate? Or something akin to both? Claire couldn't tell. Meg and Claire's fingers folded around each other's but were pulled apart again as the carriage began to roll.

"Meg," Claire said. She had something left to tell her, she could feel it, but she did not know what it was. You stupid girl, was one thing. Or rather, You clever girl. She reached out again, and Meg walked quickly alongside the calash as it moved.

"Meg!" Claire knew her shout was jolting, panicked, and she was filled with shame but, also, a fear she couldn't stifle.

"Good luck and God Bless, young Philemon and Baucis," Father called to the newlyweds. He waved and laughed, and the guests who gathered waved back and cheered as he snapped the reins.

Claire swiveled on the seat, gripped the back of it, and felt her heart pulled from her as Meg grew small, then faded to a tiny pin-prick, and finally was disappeared around a corner of grey stone. She saw, in her mind, her sister's new family enfolding around her in a comforting patchwork of babies, markets, little cottages, vicarages, and constancy. You see, Claire wanted to tell her, I do have an imagination: I am imagining this for you. I hope you know what you are in for.

"Good-bye to these dark, cold Lancashire days," Father said cheerfully, looking up at the sky. "Wretched Tyne, parish of gloomy stone and gloomy faces. We shall have our spring now, Claire, in the south. What do you think? The coast will be our holiday. You love the sea."

"Could we... only, I wonder if..."

"Speak up, my dear. You have been a mouse all day."

"It's only noon," she noted to the back of his blue velvet tailcoat.

"Your voice must be parched from last night's champagne — Ha! Fine bubbly is always best from crystal, but I surmised accurately those Doughertys prefer to gulp from mugs."

"That is because it was ale." The calash bounced over a humped, cobbled bridge that crossed a narrow stretch of river.

"They are not the most celebratory of people."

"The Doughertys?"

"The Doughertys, yes. So serious, they are. I do not know what your sister sees in them."

"Peter plays the fiddle; he's going to play later, he said. The wedding dinner is happening now, without us. They were fetching the bats and wicket as we left."

"I can already feel the air grow milder as we go. Wretched Lancashire. Your throat will clear soon." He shook his head, then chuckled again.

"It is not my throat. Stop saying that." *Be happy: that is what you should have said to Meg.* She pressed her forehead. A headache coming on? This sometimes happened, now, when she heard the voice. Or when she strained her eyes with sewing, as she had this morning getting Meg's dress to fit properly. *A baby. There is a baby growing inside her.*

"Claire, this dreariness is most unlike you. We must not ruminate on departures or arrivals. 'Tis a useless exercise."

"Forgive me, Father."

The rig pitched from side to side. It sped down an embankment, and around a hairpin bend. Dark, open moorland with purple heather crisscrossed with grey stone walls.

She was supposed to enjoy the view and, mainly, to think ahead. But her mind fixated on what she was leaving, turning it over in her head like a marble passed through fingers. She looked behind her, over her shoulder, and wished the edge of the village to reappear, as if wishing herself backwards.

As if willing her entire life to reverse.

TWO

1883 ~ 16th June
Pettypoole, Oxfordshire

But here, in Pettypoole, the landscape was a gorgeous oddity. At one point it was level, then ridged and rolling; climbing at intervals up shallow escarpments to flat plateaus where the view was unparallel. Beechy woodland leaked nightingale song in eerie cacophony. Tracks and lanes wound their way alongside narrow canals. Among the fields, the ancient remains of human bodies were hidden in odd hills called barrows. They appeared as perplexing rings of raised grass—constructed centuries ago by ancient peoples—atop which ewes and lambs now grazed.

The village was clustered around a little river, the center comprised of some shops and a hotel, one public house (a second was on the outskirts of the village), and an array of cottages made from golden limestone. Very pretty it all was—the winding lanes and well-kept gardens, the views of the rolling hillsides—a lovely place to live.

The boy, Davie, loved looking at the village from up here on the barrow. Today, the view was partially obscured by something even prettier, and vastly more exciting. A fairground. Tents pitched: red and blue stripes like sucking candies sprouting from the grass. He thought he must remember to stop on his way home, later and maybe buy a candy floss for his mum and him to share. Not now. Now, he had to rush, or he would be late for Mr Tinsdale. He wasn't even supposed to be walking up here, on the barrow; he should have walked the long way across the field and hopped over the stile to the road. His mother would be angry, if she knew. But he could not resist, on this beautiful spring day.

"Steady, boy!" Father guided them away from a rising canal, the turnpike itself an aqueous mess. "Blasted roads. Steady on!"

"I don't know why we had to go all this way round, only to come back to where we were at the start," Claire said.

"When you hear of such finery only a short distance away, you must adapt your schedule to it."

"That may be, but we were on this road earlier, weren't we?"

She wondered what part of their recent travels had not required immediate adaptation. At Cornwall, fog encased the normally mild coastline as though a swarm of intrusive Welsh ghosts had conspired to ruin an English holiday. At Bournemouth, eight days of rain had met them like some Biblical prophecy, preventing the arrival of their wares.

The pikeman held up a hand and they slowed down enough for Claire to drop a shilling into his palm. His timber shack was soggy, his vegetable garden a pool with stakes like a miniature harbor and pilings. She looked over her shoulder as they rolled through and watched him calmly shovel more gravel into their wake.

A month after Meg's wedding to Peter Dougherty, and it was still hard to fathom how Meg was not with them; how she managed the whole thing in the first place: the falling in love, the swift transfer from one family to the next. Claire had half-expected Meg to appear at the inn where she and Father stayed that first night. "Oh, what have I done!" she would cry miserably. Except she didn't.

"Ho, now. Steady up the bank, boy."

Claire checked their cargo. "All here," she told him. But it was her tea tin she was really worried about, holding not hairpins as Father thought, but her stash of notes and coins, the years of savings condensed into a lighter but more valuable load. At the bottom, under the notes and amongst the coins, was also the latchkey she stole years ago. She hadn't known why she took it. Now it was merely a souvenir, a charm she mostly forgot about but held onto out of habit. She could barely remember the house itself, though she thought she remembered the feel of it, the feel of the soft chair and the sunlight streaming in through the French doors. The taste of the blackberries in the kitchen.

Father slowed the horse and turned sharply onto a cattle path where Claire jumped down and opened the gate. They proceeded across the high grassy field. At the edge of it was a steep little valley where a deteriorating stone abbey stood and where they had parked their cart last night.

Yesterday at dusk, Father had gone to The Lantern, the public house just outside the village, with its long, sticky tables, its fetid odor of puddled ale. Then true night had arrived, and he was still away. With the air in the cart growing stale, Claire had finally climbed out from the tarpaulin and lay down next to their horse, the wind hissing in the tree line. The sky was very dark and full of stars, one or two shooting across in an arc.

They were on the parkland of some lord's manor, as it turned out, but she did not know that yet. She fell asleep, and the quietude of the gelding sleeping next to her turned into the rattle of the black horse, the cracking sound of his hoofs on the path. Then, a far-off shot sounded, and she awoke to a gamekeeper's aim taking hold of some small animal. As a second gunshot echoed, she saw Father walking along a barrow waving a jug of milk at her in the dawn light.

"Here we are." He jumped down now from the cart and led the horse on foot. They had arrived at the fairground, and they hitched the horse to a lone tree.

Claire stroked his neck. He was a sweet boy, with a ruddy coat and a soft disposition. His mane: chocolate brown. *Mink brown. Blue eyes... Horses do not have blue eyes, you silly girl.*

Discomfort crept up her neck, latching on as a distinct pinch at her right temple. For God's sake, she pleaded silently, not now.

"Did you say something, lass?"

"No. Nothing." She grabbed a length of folded velvet, snapped it open and spread it over the floor of the cart. The velvet was cool, soothing to the touch. *Ling, just behind the ears.*

So that was it: her cat, not her black horse. She closed her eyes, counted one... three... five. The image passed.

"Claire, where are you today?" Father smiled warmly at her, put his big hand on her cheek and stroked it. "Are you all right, my sweet?"

She nodded, lips pursed.

"Let us have the porcelain first—leave the silver for now lest your pretty fingertips blacken. Eh?"

She nodded again, and began arranging the porcelain onto the velvet.

Father showed a woman a set of gold-rimmed bowls and matching tea cups. No luck. Claire switched them out for the silver. Another couple looked at a small box with an ivory latch. No luck. Next, came a shrewd-looking man who tapped the side of a silver pitcher and shook his head before moving on to the next stall.

"And they were taken from Versailles, when?" yet another dealer asked about an hour later. Copper-haired, with a coiffed mustache, the man owned a covered van filled with treasures himself, from one of Catherine the Great's tea sets to a palace chest belonging to the Chinese Emperor Ch'ien-lung. He was parked, he pointed, just over there.

"These porridge bowls belonged to Marie-Antoinette's mother," Father explained, with a combination of complaisance and ceremony. "Do you see here, the Austrian maker's stamp? Well, we know what happened to her poor daughter." He shook his head then brightened quickly. "During our tour of the Continent, I came across the set quite by accident. You know how two young ladies will shop."

The copper walrus chuckled at this. "Two daughters? Oh, my." The dealer, identifying himself as a Mr Dean, nodded as he inspected, as if he was looking over the crown jewels. He had the most amazing ginger whiskers Claire had ever seen, and a friendly manner that matched Father's.

Claire handed Father a soup terrine, and Father in turn passed the piece along to him.

"And the sugar bowl... Claire?" Father cleared his throat, held out his hand.

Delivering the bowl, she smiled at their customer. She tried not to stare at his whiskers, the thick, metallic hairs congealed with pomade. His son, a smooth-faced copy of his father, stood apart from them, chipping away at a stick with his knife. Every now and then, he looked up in her direction. No more than fifteen, his eyes held a hint of fear and bewilderment when they caught hers.

Suddenly, it was Will Bolton's face she saw. Will, winking at her from beside his father, then creeping over to sit on the grass and laugh at the farm cat Meg had caught and dressed-up. Will. His warm smile, his dark eyes which unabashedly stared into hers whenever he spoke to her. His embrace... the taste of his lips. *You still miss him. You still miss Allswell.*

"Now, here is a good serving set, but why should a widower like myself need another when I have two more at home that our maid must polish? One is for my eldest daughter's dowry, of course."

"Is she to marry soon?" Mr Dean asked as he smoothed his whiskers and tusks with a webbed paw. Behind the smile was a trace of mistrust, a glint in the eye.

"Sooner than I would like." Father smiled at Claire as if this was true. "My youngest daughter found happiness recently: an Austrian duke met on our trip abroad. What romance it all was! Claire, you look as if you could use a bite." He nodded at her, and handed her two-pence.

Giving a little curtsy to Mr Dean and his son, she slipped away through the festival, her head swimming with counterfeit memories of Meg and Peter sledding in the Alps.

"I'll throw in a roll or two with the jellies, dearie."

"A slab of ham with the wedge? I can give the wedge for half-price!"

Glancing at each stall, she kept quiet, or she'd be harassed right and left before she settled on a crumb. Most people adored these kinds of festivals, she knew. They enjoyed all the exotic and ancient things before returning to their homey comforts.

"Can I help you, gorgeous? One of our delectable pasties?"

"Sorry, no." *Look away, keep moving.*

Dates, cloves and figs, almonds and ginger, carpets, tapestries and soap, taffeta and horses. Claire breathed hard in the thick air, pressing her fingers into her temple. A group of men played cricket on a grassy clearing, some twenty onlookers applauding.

Focus on what is in front of you. Watch the game being played and next to it, the sheep pen. "Cotswolds Lions" the sign read. The man in the pen was sheering one, its long, matted fur and ridiculous wavy forelock making it look like the Prince Regent of yore.

"Are you all right there, sweetheart?" An old man next to her held his cane at a peculiar angle. His nearly white eyes were shielded behind tinted spectacles. "Per'aps you need a sit-down?" he suggested, clearly hearing her laboured breathing.

"Perfectly well, thank you. I'm perfectly well." Her voice sounded like tin. Nearby, the other voice, the one she kept hearing, said: *There is nothing wrong with his hearing, you stupid girl, he knows you are not well. Do not look at his eyes. They will swallow you up into blackness!*

She stepped quickly into the center of the fair and was assaulted by the sickly-sweet odor of plum duff. A juggler put on a show for half-a-dozen small children who teetered on toddlers' legs, clapping and laughing while mothers cooed.

Bending down to the little ones, the man tossed three balls, then six, a bright ring of spinning orbs. Claire kept walking. She heard loud bartering at a table of enormous skeins of wool and smelled an acrid scent of pork fat and cheese. The crowd swarmed. The stench of raw rabbit... a glimpse of a skinned and shiny purple carcass hanging by its feet...

Stop!

Her heart thrashed. Invisible sparks needled at her head.

"Come in, will you? You look like you could use some tea." A woman stood in the entrance to a small, audaciously striped tent. Old, but not ancient, her face sported a strong nose framed by high cheekbones like a Medici portrait. Handsome, you'd call her. Her grey hair cascaded down her shoulders, the top of her head wrapped with a purple scarf woven with iridescent threads. Her rather ordinary light brown eyes were thickly rimmed with kohl, the lids smudged with cinnabar.

"You were here yesterday, too, weren't you?" There was, in her slightly husky voice, no beckoning from a fortune-teller to a potential client, but a relaxed, unaffected greeting instead. Her wrinkled but steady fingers held open the flap.

Claire hesitated, then entered.

Inside the tent was dim and dry. Oddly quiet. It was not a large tent, but neither was it small. There was a low table with lit pillar candles, a glass globe and a deck of ink-tinted tarot cards; and brightly embroidered pillows scattered about the floor. The usual stage set.

"Please, sit." The woman fetched a kettle and two cups from a side table with a single oil burner. "Just one month ago, I was in York, then London, then on to Salisbury. And now here." She let out a sigh as she joined Claire on the floor.

Claire smiled a little and took the cup, the pounding in her chest slowing. She could smell the faint but thick scent of whale oil, she knew it well from when she and Father were a year in Hull, where there was still a trickle of it brought in from Greenland.

The woman shifted on her pillow. "You are too young for all this travel, and I am too old. The knees." She patted them.

"We've had almost the same journey," Claire admitted.

"I know. You were in Salisbury, at the Foxes & Dragons Festival in those dreadful rains. My name is Bella. Feel free to stretch out. I do when no one is around."

"I'm Claire."

"You're a pretty girl, Claire. Do you not remember me? What are you, now, one-and-twenty?"

"Two-and-twenty years, ma'am."

Bella nodded, narrowing her eyes as if waiting for Claire to say something enlightening. "Well. And you do not remember me? That's all right. A pretty girl you are, but not half as noticeable as that." She pointed at Claire's neck. "It catches the eye too quickly. And you have worn it a long time."

"My father gave it to me." She covered the necklace with her hand instinctively, ignoring the remark meant to imply the woman already knew things about her. Which, of course, she did not.

"You misunderstand me, dear." Bella's tone had softened. "What I mean is that you'd better be careful traveling as you do, on the roads."

"Oh. It belonged to my grandfather." Claire leaned in and showed her the ring.

Bella nodded, her eyes squinting like Meg's when she was about to laugh.

"We seldom have trouble when we travel," Claire assured her. But her memory drew up the party guest in her bedchamber at Evensong, and it was as if she could feel him press against her, in the here and now. That man with the foul, fermented breath in the dark... *Can this woman see him, too? Ask her.*

"Are you all right, dear?"

Claire willed her hand to stay around the teacup, though it wanted to rise to her face and press the oncoming pain back into place. It had been years since she felt as off-kilter as she did today at this stifling, stinking fair. Slaughtered rabbit. Whiskey. The stench: that was what she remembered about the man.

"My father has a way of making things work," she said brightly, her voice cutting through the close air of the tent like a murderous scythe. "We've always had good accommodations."

Bella, eyes steadily on hers, sipped her tea. "I met your father yesterday, at the watering tent—my horse was exhausted—and he was helpful finding the blacksmith. He looks like Father Christmas, does he not?"

"He does. He is good at finding opportunities."

"Accommodations are another thing altogether. They are never good when only for a short time."

She looked carefully at Bella. "Can you really read minds?"

"In your case I have no need to. You look as if you haven't had a good night's sleep in months."

"No."

"Perhaps you have set-up camp for now, in your cart...? But the draughty house and lumpy mattress will come soon enough. Have some, you haven't eaten today." She handed Claire a biscuit and two jellies. "A falling-to-pieces house, and then you will leave it. All living things are left in the end, even those that reciprocate affection, of course everyone knows this. But houses, too, are alive with the spirits of their inhabitants—the ones who stay put 'til the end of their days. You must know that." She nodded, as if answering for Claire. "We travelers are always doing the leaving, aren't we? Even when we don't want to."

Claire nodded.

"Do you like cats? I once had a Siamese. Do you know what they are?"

Claire clamped her teeth so as not to drop her jaw. Perhaps Bella really was clairvoyant, as Claire sometimes feared herself to be. "I had a Siamese cat once," she said quietly. It was as though, suddenly, she was incapable of lying. "Ling, I called him."

"They are very intelligent. Descended from the Pharaohs' pets in Ancient Egypt, then cherished by the Kings of Siam. Why Ling?"

"I named him after a character in a book, though the story took place in China, not Siam. There was a library, in one of our houses."

"But I sense he was not your first little cat, yes?"

Claire shook her head no, looked down into her lap quickly. This woman could not possibly know about the little painted lead cat on the wooden spool Will had given her.

"You have been to London again, recently?" Bella asked, as if politely steering away from the real subject matter.

Claire nodded; you didn't have to be a mystic to guess that, she had practically told her a minute before.

"And then there is always Manchester. Or Bristol."

"Yes, but London has the better prices. That's what Father says."

"Indeed." Bella smiled. "What type of wares is your father advertising at the moment?"

She shrugged. "Porcelain. Or it started out porcelain. Mostly silver, now I come to think of it. By the time I get back, he'll have sold it all to that redheaded man."

"With the amazing mustache."

Claire stifled a laugh. "You have seen him, too."

"He's hard to miss. But you must have someone else, Claire, traveling with you? Besides your father. An uncle? A brother?"

She thought of Mr Dean's son by their cart, bored rigid. "Oh, you mustn't worry," she said, "only the silliest things ever happen, and Father is always there. I remember one night in London, years ago, we were walking back to our rooming house. A common enough lane, not far from the High Street."

"Yet one street over from the slums."

Claire nodded.

"This is the way the Great City is, alternating its poverty and wealth like an enormous game board painted with gold-leaf and rubbish. There is always something ghastly to see: frail boys scaling the rooftops in their tatty shoes, their skin black and scabbed from scraping down chimneys; women with rats' nests for hair selling matchbooks, flowers, the raw skin beneath their skirts."

"I suppose so."

"Well, what happened, then?"

"Oh, it was disgustingly funny. It was tidal ditch, with men using it to... well, I had to cover Meg's eyes." Claire suddenly felt the tale has lost its humor.

"Meg is the baby in the family."

"She is. At least, she was before she jumped ship."

"Leaving you to navigate such moments on your own. More jellies? Tell me, what do you dream about?"

"Dream?" Claire glanced around the tent, at the scatter of pillows, the objects of foresight on the table. "I cannot say."

"Dreams I know," said Bella. "Dreams I can do. Go on. No charge." She smiled.

"Are you sure? There is one. I do not know why I always dream it."

Bella took Claire's teacup from her and placed it on the table. Then she took her hand in both of hers, as if feeling its weight. "Now, how might it begin?"

Her touch, the strength of her hands, felt familiar to Claire, and for a second, she wondered if this was what Mother's hands would feel like had she lived to be this old.

"It tries to trick me." Claire's voice was muted, hesitant at first "The beginning is different each time. But soon I'm with Meg, walking in a city."

"Are there other people?"

"No one we know. We decide to make our way through a park. It's winter, but there is no snow on the ground, and we wear coats with fur collars and hats, like two foreigners."

Bella chuckled at this. "Like me?" She looked the part of Romany Gypsy, but her accent was all Somerset. Likely, her name had been Bess or Bertha, once.

Claire told her about the black coach and the enormous black horse, his shoulders rotating and rippling like swells on the sea. She couldn't bring herself to tell Bella about his splitting hoofs, the splattering of blood on the path.

"But what happens next?" Bella urged.

"The horse gallops across a bridge."

"The bridge is wooden?"

"No, stone. He leaps over the side into the lake, and then I wake up."

Bella, brows drawn together, examined the palm of Claire's hand as if mapping the dream on her skin. There was something else, too, about Bella's face: the wit and sparkle that characterized it earlier was gone.

"The Horse is Power," she said. She let go of Claire's hand and picked up her teacup, tilting the remaining liquid and peering at the detritus. "It is an ancient symbol," she said, while still examining the leaves. "But what kind of power does this horse hold over you and your sister? Or perhaps over you only, Claire? And who is driving this horse?"

"No one." Prickling cold crawled across the back of her neck. "But I'm not afraid of horses. Our gelding is very docile."

Bella looked at her with what could only be called alarm. She rubbed her chin with her forefinger, on which was a thick silver latticework ring. "And the park, it is a well-tended park, you say? Or is it wild, like a forest? This is important. You must observe the next time you dream."

"It is grey and bare, just as I've told you." All at once, Claire knew she couldn't stand to have the dream again. She knew she should never reveal herself to a stranger, but she needed to give this woman anything she remembered that might help stop this nightly terror. "The trees are bare," she repeated, "and there are edged beds where flowers would be if it were spring. It's a well-cared for park, with people strolling through it. But I've told you this."

The misgiving on Bella's face deepened. She took a slow breath through her nose. Her voice was a whisper, a veiled dread. "There are many meanings lurking in trees: mysteries, journeys one must travel, fears one must face. And the lake, too, the one you plunge toward: mystics in the East believe that water is a symbol of the innermost path of one's desires and hopes and fears."

"But I always wake up when we drown."

"Ah! But do you drown? Do you actually plunge into the water?" Bella placed her hands over Claire's again. "You know, Claire. What I mean is, your dream knows. It is trying to show you. Maybe you're afraid to discover what it's trying to show you."

Bella poured more tea. The tea was hot, the tent dry; but Claire was chilled to the bone. She would remember this moment, months from now. She would remember it vividly and think of how wrong she was not to listen to Bella.

From the fairgrounds, the cottages in the vale looked like sugar cubes clumped and jammed into a mossy bowl. The journey into the village of sugar cubes was not long—three miles on the Roman Road, in the back of a farmer's dray, now they'd sold Teddy. But just before the entrance to town, they disembarked and took the road on foot.

"The exercise will do us good," Father said. But Claire knew he didn't want anyone seeing him perched on a cartload of turnips.

As the dray pulled ahead, she was aware of Father's strong, purposeful stride, and of her own gait slowing.

She watched Father's back. His Norfolk jacket had been traded at the fair for a good black wool tailcoat: the uniform of a city man of means. She studied the fine black cloth as it rumpled with his step, like the slowly loping shoulders of a horse.

Claire slowed further, and he became smaller as he strode ahead of her. She stopped in the middle of the road and looked back over her shoulder. She saw the winding road as it cut through a vast, high wold, undulating lower fields on either side, thinning until it was just a bit of string stretching out to touch the horizon and the plain world beyond.

THREE

1883 ~ 2nd July
Pettypoole, Oxfordshire

She used to love this time of year. The wheat grown tall, the goats grazing happily, the hedges bursting with berries, the garden's bounty poured into jars or hung to dry. You knew it was all going to be fine, then, in the cold dead months ahead. There was work to do still, in July, but there was a hot sun and a warmer sea. And longer days. There was time for hiding amongst the reeds—muddy, giggling, telling secrets and stories—and for running headlong into the surf: Meg and Claire in their pantaloons and camisoles, Will in his breeches. Diving, splashing, the old Admiral bellowing at them from his garden perch. "Dragged out by the currents, you'll be, little fools! Mark my words!" Met with a "Yes sir, no sir, thank ye, sir" and another dive.

Claire thought Summer would always be that. And Autumn, and Winter, and Spring—each with their own characteristics tied utterly to the land and sea, and the house and farm—each season the same again and again. Always Allswell. *You never quite leave it, do you?*

Their new apartments were in Eldwin Mews, which was once an assembly room for dances and balls, and the sun was harsh and bright as it shined through the tall windows. Eldwin Mews, Pettypoole, Oxfordshire. Father loved the sound of the address.

"Look into this mirror, Claire. See how its ornate carvings frame your lovely face, as if you yourself are a painting." His blue striped nightdress peeked out from beneath a black silk robe swathed in red dragons. He was like an emperor awaiting his royal cuppa.

"Don't be ridiculous, Father."

"What luck of mine that, with so many looking glasses about this place, you are to be the art which graces our walls. *Versailles de Claire.*" He took the cup from her and smiled. "Not a maid in all of England makes a better spot of tea than you."

She gave a little laugh, patted one of the silk dragons perched on his shoulder, and kissed his cheek. "I'm off to market, now. Be good."

The heels of her boots clicked a round of echoes across the marble floor into what was not really a scullery but a tiny closet with, rather mysteriously, a small triangular table and an equally small hearth with a single hanging kettle. On the table was piled the remains of last night's party: Two-in-the-morning, guests slapping cards and rolling dice, devouring what should have been today's dinner. Someone had vomited out the window, leaving a putrid trail on the sill.

Claire looked down at the fire that had gone out again, and at the overflowing triangular table. She put the tray on the floor and headed back to her room, tripping on a bolt of chartreuse along the way. Silk spilled across all their floors in jewel-tones hills. Like the fortuneteller's pillows.

Bella: Claire didn't want to forget her. The copper-whiskered man and his son sprung to mind; from the middle of wool country, Father would now peddle Far East silks, and she wondered if there'd be another Mr Dean gullible enough to take the bolts off their hands when the time came.

In her room, the reflection of yet another looking glass shot back darkened half-moons under her eyes. Reflecting up her neck was the vicious turquoise blue of a dress made from the new silk. At least the style was of recent fashion, which was more than she could say for her old dustcoat and hat; it was a fool's errand to keep up with each Season, magazines announcing the rise and fall of bustle and bustline. She stared at herself in the mirror. She looked like a porcelain doll in the dress, alluring and artificial, like one of Meg's dancing bears.

On the vanity below the mirror sat a stack of folded paper tied with string. They were letters from Meg detailing her growing belly, Peter's little improvements on their cottage, another friend she had made: Oh, Claire ought to have friends like she did, and wouldn't Claire consider coming to visit her, though the journey will be long and costly and did she think Father would let her leave?

Claire set her hair, stabbing pins into the single plaited coil. She fixed the hat—an elaborate purple velvet flowerpot—on a downward tilt, to shade her bruised-looking eyes. She called a last good-bye to Father and headed out for Market Cross.

What happened at the market when one slept-in was this: everything was sold before you got there. Sometimes, with luck, there were scrawny hens to be had, and squashed plums and rubbery carrots. As she approached the poultry seller, she spotted a limp pile of fowl resting on a sawdust-covered table. A tiny old woman was scolding the seller, saying, "Fatty and bony, it was, Tom."

"Fatty *and* bony now, was it?" he countered.

"Don't you speak to me that way, you cheek, I've known you since you were in tailclouts."

The two continued this way, ignoring Claire as she waited for an in, her eyes scanning the nearby empty baker's table, and another holding the remains of some jam and pickled beans.

At the corner of her left eye there was a movement, shadowed and flickering. Then a tall figure appeared next to her. She felt a hint of insight, recognition laced with dread, as she watched a man shift a small pile of books tucked under his arm. His brown linen sacque coat was neat and clean, but not new. A small tear was carefully mended just below the pocket. A tell-tale sign (her own jupon had a two-inch line of stitching just like it near the waistline).

"Have we met...?" He faltered. Awkwardly, he looked down and to the side at some concocted object. Olive-brown skin, dark-hair with equally dark brows, his expression was uncomfortable and grave.

"Beg 'pardon, sir?" Claire said quietly, secretly hoping he had not heard her. There was nothing worse than running into people Father knew. She couldn't keep straight who they were or, more importantly, how they left things.

The old woman continued her tirade against Tom the poulterer, who continued to casually yank feathers out of the goose as though he had all the time in the world.

"I thought perhaps in Bonborough. I have been there on several occasions as a child," said the man, who had heard her after all.

The man looked down at the blood congealed in the sawdust under Claire's feet. A feather floated near her like a snowflake. He scanned her face, her hair where the feather now rested, as if looking for a lost object. He settled on her necklace, but seemed merely bewildered at the large, masculine ring around her neck.

"Bonborough?" She looked at the books he held (Wordsworth, Scott, a volume of Shelley), and at the ink stain on his right index finger, and realized it was she who coveted.

"Bonborough is the market town not twenty miles to the west, past Wotton Vale. Just the small hen there, please," the man instructed Tom over the old woman's head. "And this young lady, I believe is waiting—forgive me, Mrs Easling—yes, that hen there, Tom. Miss?" he said to Claire. "I have his attention now."

"Well? Hurry up then," Tom snapped. "If you are a friend of the schoolmaster?"

"Not a one of us is a friend o' yours, Tom," Mrs Easling glowered.

Claire felt like laughing, but the impulse dissolved as she asked for a miniscule bird to feed herself and Father. Tom handed Claire the chicken by its feet and took her two shillings.

"You're a fool to pay him as much," the old woman coughed at her.

Tom laughed a hearty belly laugh.

Claire smiled blandly and turned to leave, a flush of embarrassment rising up the back of her neck. When she turned, the man—the Schoolmaster—followed suit. She began to walk, and he began to walk. She realized then that he was walking alongside her intentionally.

"My name is Ableton," he said. "James."

She nodded. Cleared her throat but did not look at him directly.

"Did I see you in church last week?"

So that was where she knew him from: Sunday, church. But did she really remember Mr Ableton from then, or from Bonborough...? She couldn't remember where Bonborough was. She looked down: pebbles, millions and millions and older than Christ himself, at her feet. She'd only been in Pettypoole's church once. Father would never have willingly let her go, either, if he hadn't still been asleep after one of his late parties.

"I attend rarely," Mr Ableton went on, "for appearances. That is, for my pupils. Mind you, I do believe in—what I mean is— Forgive me, will you?"

She turned to face him. "Are you a Humanist, Mr Ableton?" There were always a few at Father's parties, quoting Petrarch and speaking of daVinci as if they had known him personally. *Hells bells, he must be one of those.*

They reached Ber St. Eldwyn, the Gothic abbey in question. Pettyton Hall was across the street from it.

"You must forgive me," said Mr Ableton. "This is a small place. A new face stands out amongst the customary."

"No doubt."

"It is a mystery, this building." He pointed to the church. In one of the stained-glass windows Joseph's hand rested on Mary's swollen belly, her face peculiar and groggy as if she couldn't quite believe her luck, or didn't want to. "It casts a dark spell for such a cheerful town. Architecturally speaking."

On the other side of the street stood Pettyton Hall, a former pigeon house. Inside, a handful of constables—nosy, babbling pigeons if ever there were—working clerical duties while a magistrate negotiated arable disputes. They were always half-out of uniform, as there was never any real crime to attend to. Claire kept walking while she stole another glance at her new acquaintance. He wasn't much older than she, despite his sober appearance.

They passed the Hall. "As I was saying, I used to go to Bonborough with my father," said Mr Ableton. "He took me with him on business for the Henry's Stores, where he worked. They are in the High Street if you have not been. But I see you do have a striking dress."

She looked down at the vibrant blue and wished she had not. *Do not think of the hat. Too late.*

Eldwin Mews was just ahead, and she felt like a clumsy train coming into the station, jolting and hesitating and grinding to a halt.

"Here is where I..."

"Will you walk out with me?"

She looked at him, surprised. "What, now?"

She looked around her, a few people running their errands, making squinting faces at the sun. A woman waved to Mr Ableton, and he responded likewise. The baker stepped out of his shop, flicking flour into the air from his apron. "Did you want Mrs Gibson's bread, Ableton?" he called into white clouds.

"I'll be by in a moment to take it for her, Mr McManus, thank you." Then he said to Claire, quickly, "Good-day. I am sure we'll meet again."

"Where?"

"Where? Why at service, I suppose."

"I meant, where did you want to walk?"

"Oh—do you want to? There's a pond next to Grath House, across from the squire's dairy. It's near The Lantern, off the Turnpike Road. Do you know it?"

She looked at the scrawny hen lying in the basket on her arm. The sun was hot on her velvet hat and the inside of her head should have been ablaze with warnings. Anything would do: Meg's peevish whinge, or a silent dream of mildewed manors and threatening hands. But her head did not ache. She did not feel dizzy. She imagined all of Pettypoole's villagers scoffing together in disapproval at her walking out alone with a strange man, but she also thought she should go with this man at all costs. Instinct was often extreme, and perhaps this was why one did not always heed it; common sense told you that nothing so disproportionately unnerving was ever really the outcome of any decision.

Months later, Claire would walk down this very lane, on a blackened, icy version of this bright summer day, and think of her hesitation the day she met him. But by then, it would be too late to reverse the course.

The sun scalded the road, turning packed dust into a baking stone. At each side of the road protruded two sunken markers: once tall columns joined by a massive iron entrance. Claire waited on a nearby stump. She stared at the remains of the old Roman gate. It was thought that the spot was where, at midnight, two long dead but restless centurions stopped strangers from entering Pettypoole. Only a handful had ever seen the men in the years since their living bodies walked the earth but, Claire thought, you had to wonder if that was only because they chose not to make themselves known. If I had phantom guards patrolling my room at night, she now reasoned, I would welcome them; maybe stop sleeping with my hand curled round my ring, fingers aching with cramp in the morning.

From The Lantern voices drew up in a great roar of laughter. Father, likely, treating all to dinner and charming a new lady. Enter Mrs Croome, last week. "There is my dear daughter!" Father had cried. "Did I not tell you she is a beauty, with eyes like a stormy sea?" The men had all whipped their heads toward the doorway where Claire stood, after looking all over the High Street for him. Mrs Croome—stout, shrewd, and still playing unflappable—clearly fancied herself a cut above, though her young companion was more of a conundrum (a niece, Mrs Croome said, visiting, and wouldn't Claire like to show her around and be friends?).

Claire closed her eyes against the sun, obliterating the recent memory in a glow of white. The white dimmed to a warm brown from a shadow, and when she opened her eyes, James Ableton was peering down at her. His eyes were light next to his dark brows and tanned skin, like a fair sky against a mountainous horizon. She had not noticed, before, that his eyes were light, unlike the rest of his countenance.

"I must apologize," he said. "I think this walk of mine might not be exactly—ehrmm—suitable."

"I have no friends here," she countered, feeling immediately stupid.

"I do. And you are most welcome to be introduced to them. My friend Freddy Gibson is like a brother to me, and he has four sisters who are as friendly as he. I will make an introduction to them."

She managed a smile, though in truth she was growing more apprehensive by the second.

"You know, I do not actually know your name." He held out his hand.

"Claire." Did she really forget to tell him her name? At least she left the hat at home, though going hatless in public was another offence altogether. Maybe not in the countryside. She hoped.

"And you were in church last week. But I've said that already, haven't I? Well, it's your distinctive air that made me notice you that day, I am certain." He sighed as he helped her up. "Just as I am certain I cannot keep myself from prattling on like an idiot."

At this she laughed. There was something about him, familiar and welcoming, and warmer than she had first supposed. *Will Bolton, winking and leaning on Allswell's mossy stone wall. Really? Will Bolton again? Don't be pathetic.*

"I think," said Claire, "that it's a lovely day for a walk after all." She walked with Mr Ableton away from the pub, not holding onto his arm but standing closer to him than she had earlier. Three children playing marbles on the road ran past them and one shouted, "Holler or the hounds won't follow! Oh, hullo Schoolmaster." The little girl squealed and waved, then ducked as the taller of the boys lunged for her hair, all three not quite stopping but flailing as they passed.

"Mind your sister now, Andrew," Mr Ableton called. "And you, Thomas, treat your friend's sister as you would your own."

The boys slowed down then, and one took the little girl's hand.

"You must forgive my students," he said to Claire, though she had the feeling he was pleased with them. It hit her, then. The baker, the fowler, a Mrs Gibson and her entire brood, these children: Claire was the stranger here, not James Ableton.

The road curved and nature descended around them in a thick landscape. Strange tree-like bushes dripped with sickly-bright yellow blossoms, bees buzzing around them in drunken reverie. They came off the road and walked a narrow path into a small but lush meadow. The meadow was at the bottom of a hill, atop which sat an old cottage. The remains of a garden wall stood nearby, the bricks jagged as if some giant had taken bites out of it. Lavender grew wild down the hill from the cottage, purple spikes leaning towards the baking sun. There was a little pond, its surface slick and still.

"This is... beautiful. Does someone live here, Mr Ableton?" Claire stood and gawked.

"That is Grath Cottage, lived in by Mr Dewen, an ornery widower. He is the half-brother of Squire Grath who owns the dairy on the other side of the road. He might live anywhere, really, I think the Squire is quite generous with him, but he prefers it here."

"Squire Grath is the primary land-owner in this area?" It was the sort of thing Father would want to know.

"No, that would be Lord Hammpen. Hammpen Manor is back the other way out of town, over the bridge where the Roman Road is. There is high moorland there, and fields, where they let sheep graze and sometimes set up fairs. Do you like fairs?"

"Not really."

He took his coat off and spread it out for her to sit on. He sat on the ground not far from her, but at a comfortable distance. She suddenly wished he would move closer. *Will: nudging you with his shoulder, pushing you into the marsh, wrapping his arm around your neck and messing your hair.*

Dragonflies hovered and darted over the pond. Mr Ableton's students chased each other at the far side of the meadow, the little girl running from one boy to the other and tagging each. She paused to wave, and Claire raised her hand back. The girl's hair was curly, glimmering in the sun, her bow coming undone as she ran, and Claire felt a terrible tug in her heart for Meg.

"'*Once a dream did weave a shade, O'er my Angel-guarded bed, That an Emmet lost its way, where on grass methought I lay.*' That's Blake," Mr Ableton said. "Don't know what made me think of it."

"I like Blake. Angels and fiends. And a Tyger." She drew a **y** in the air with her finger. "There was an enormous library in one of our houses. The room was so dusty it made my lungs ache. It took me weeks to find the poetry, though I was looking for novels I never found. I wanted to take Blake with me when we left." She had wanted to take more than that. She pushed Ling back to his own little dark corner of her mind.

Mr Ableton continued to recite, and she felt herself drifting into his voice.

"'*Pitying, I dropped a tear; But I saw a glow-worm near*'— Hang on, you can read, then?" he exclaimed.

"I have no books of my own."

"But you can read?"

"Of course, I can read." She laughed. "You are joking with me."

"I am not. I suppose I thought... well, I don't know what I thought. I shall have to find you some books. You like novels, you said? Would Collins or Mrs Gateskill do?"

She felt a rush of delight and nodded. "Someone in our flat on Eldwyn Mews once kept travel guides. India is fraught with mosquitoes. But then, I already knew that. China is infested with fever."

"When you say 'one of our houses,' you mean...?"

She picked a single flower from amidst the prickly grasses, perfectly circular petals speckled with purple on a lean stalk. "What is this called?"

"*Ophrys apifera*. A bee orchid. They are very common. Where are you from?" he asked, sounding truly perplexed.

"I wish I had a proper garden. My mother had a garden, but I don't remember it very well. I know nettle, but that only takes one misstep to remember."

"These grow wild as nettle." His finger touched hers as he traced the outline of the petal.

"Why are there never ordinary books where we stay, Mr Ableton?"

"You must call me James if we're to be friends."

She smiled back at him.

"There are odd books in your flat because your landlord's wife collects cheap furnishings and books from distress auctions. She is a magpie. Her husband makes her empty their cupboards once a year, and if the contents do not go to the poor, they land in his tenants' flats." He raised one eyebrow and nodded at her.

"Mmm. 'Tis common enough," she muttered, smiling faintly. "People are forever hoarding and abandoning."

"What is your surname, Claire?"

Why do you keep asking questions of me? she wanted to retort. Instead, she said, "Beitris." BEH-tress, she pronounced it, as she always had.

"Spell it, please."

She did.

"Bee-AYE-tris," he corrected in a teacher's gentle but firm tone. "The Scottish-Gaelic for Beatrice, Dante's blessed love."

"Do you mean to say we have been mispronouncing our own name?"

"No harm done."

"My mother spoke Irish. I think I used to."

"You are Gypsy, then?"

She stared at him, speechless, wondering the same of him. "I don't think so."

"I lost my mother as well, Miss Beitris," he said next, in a low, breathy voice.

She was astounded. "But how did you know that I also had?"

He shrugged. "It is a kind of sadness that one does not lose easily. And, of course, I have only seen you and your Father out and about. I was seven years old when I lost my mother."

"There is a sadness about me?"

He did not answer. He looked out at the pond, as if contemplating it.

"What was it your mother died from, James?"

"Consumption."

"Pleurisy," she said. "I think. Perhaps consumption. I was older than you'd been, when Mother died, but her face is fading in my mind more quickly than I expected. We never had a photograph made, the way you're supposed to. They paint the eyes on their lids and prop them up so they are sitting and alive-looking. I think it's ghastly, don't you? I suppose I should be glad we've no photograph of her like that. Though to have one in which she was in fact alive and smiling..."

"It is a dreadful business, Miss Bietris."

"You are to call me Claire, remember?"

Jaw set tightly, as if he suddenly couldn't bear to speak, he rested his hand on her shoulder and pressed, and she did not mind because it was like they had been friends a long, long time. She felt an unsettling awareness of something existing apart from memory and loss and compensation; a world of the present, of the bee orchid, the old stone cottage on the hill of lavender, the children romping and chasing each other on the other side of the pond.

They talked for a while more, before the heat of the day began to take its toll on her. Things began to fade and waver, in the periphery.

This sun is so very hot, it is beastly. She moved closer to the edge of the pond. Her head felt full of feathers, dappled light dancing in the air before her.

Kneeling by the water's edge, she put her hands into the cool water and patted her face. The water felt wonderful.

But as she looked into the pond, Claire saw, in the stagnant water, an underwater grave, a bottom of unknowable decay; plants and bones, dead things sinking into silt. She blinked and saw only the reflection of the sun atop the water. Then, of a sudden, she saw herself in winter in a quick shift of seasons. Snow coated everything, the grass around her dry and brittle, the pond marbled ice. She saw herself kneeling at the edge of the water, frosty reeds snapping under her knees. She pressed her hands against the surface, thrusting them down, cracking the ice and plummeting into frigid, pulpy silt; the stiff but pliable stalks of plants, the slippery skin of a hibernating frog. *You peer into the gloom, straining to see what lies beneath. A moment longer and you will be overcome with a chill; later there will be a clammy white fever. You walk into the pond and grab hold of a sunken tree trunk to keep yourself from floating back up. You hug the murky depths, and let your lungs fill with water, your body joining the skeletal remains at the bottom...*

Claire opened her eyes with a shock, her heart thrashing, to see James Ableton leaning over her and gently slapping her wrist. She was prone, lying on the ground.

"I think you wilted," he said, calmly but clearly with a little worry.

She was lying on the bank with one arm floating in the cool water. He'd moved his coat and laid her out on it.

"How are you now?"

"Quite all right." She laughed, hoping the sound would cloak the gasping of her breath, the loud pulse in her ears.

"It's been a beastly spring. You must bring your parasol next time. And perhaps," he nodded a little at her dress, "perhaps muslin rather than silk. Helen and Eliza are always on about their muslins in the warmer months."

"Your sisters?"

"No, Freddy's. My friend I spoke of. But as he is like a brother to me, they are also like sisters. You know, I think we have met before. Wait, I am certain of it."

"You're just saying that now." She pressed her temple with her wet finger, nonchalantly, curling her hair around it afterwards as if she just happened to be lying there, relaxing.

But what did it mean, what she just saw? Morbid fancy? Or something more definite? A warning or a moment yet to come? Her heart was still racing with fear.

"Well," James Ableton said dryly, "we should have met."

"We could have met here." She sat up. "Two wild orphans raised by birds." She heard the children running and laughing again. "We could have lived here all our lives without ever leaving."

"Would you like to imagine that?"

"I am." She smiled. She felt calmer, a little embarrassed. She blinked her eyes against the sun, and wiped her forehead with her damp hand.

"The colour is back in your cheeks. You must be tired."

"My bed is not right for sleeping," she admitted, regretting it instantly. Her tongue was never apposite when she needed it to be. The word bed hovered in the air; simple and shocking out of an unmarried woman's mouth, like bug or whore. There was a whole world of sorrow females inflicted, just by opening their mouths and speaking. Surely, a Schoolmaster would know this.

"Then you shall have to make a resting place of leaves and grasses for yourself," James amended easily. "A soft nest is only fitting for a meadow bird." He stood, offered his hand to her, and helped her stand up. He gave her a wry smile, put his coat back on, then hooked her hand over his arm.

As they walked, he stopped at the trunk of a tree stripped smooth by deer, like driftwood washed upon dry land, and with his pocketknife he carved the crude but recognizable silhouettes of two birds, wings open. She traced the craggy outlines of them with her finger. Something stirred in her again, familiar and far away. It was not Will. She did not know what it was.

"Do you believe in signs, Mr Ableton? James, I mean."

"You mean spiritual signs? The Occult? No. Do you?"

She shook her head but couldn't quite manage an outright denial. *Perhaps it's not a lie, if you say nothing.*

On the walk back into Pettypoole they heard a rumbling-slapping noise like a series of thunderclaps breaking the relative quiet. Far-off it sounded at first, but then suddenly it appeared on the road from around the bend. They watched, frozen, as a large coach veered like a curving serpent, heading straight toward them. James grabbed hold of her waist and pulled her to the side. She felt a painful scrape on the back of her hand as she was caught in some low-lying branches, hard buds and thorns snagging her skirt. The recklessly-driven carriage passed, in one astonishing instant.

Claire's heart raced as she unhooked a branch from her cuff, and when James looked at her and asked her if she was all right, there was fear in his face as well. He wrapped his hand around her wrist where blood seeped out of a gash. Then he put his other hand on her other wrist, to stop her moving.

They laughed together. Terror surged through her. They were both covered in laburnum petals.

Still holding her wrists, he took a step closer to her, their bodies nearly touching. Then he kissed her. His mouth was warm. He tasted of plums and felt like velvet, and when the kiss was finished, she let him kiss her again. And again.

FOUR

1883 ~ 2nd September, morning
Pettypoole, Oxfordshire

She sat in the window sewing blue Michaelmas daisies to the hem of her dress, fixing them in a loop onto the flounces like decorations on a cake. She felt she could sit here all day and do this, falling into a trance while stitching a misty Otherworld around herself, ignoring everything, ignoring time itself. Ignoring the fact that it was her own wedding dress she adorned.

"You have no time for that! What a task on your own wedding morning," cried Mrs Croome as she flittered about the apartments. She wore a single ostrich feather in her hair. She said something indecipherable as she passed through the room, and a moment later she rustled back in with a multi-hued hat instead, shouting again. Her gown was a bright green thing with mountains of dyed lace and shoddy tailoring.

Claire took another flower from the basket beside her. She knew they were Michaelmas daisies, as the vicar's wife told her so when Claire admired the prolific plantings outside the rectory last week. "You may take as many as you like," Mrs Snow-Thorpe had offered. And Claire thought immediately to sew them onto her dress.

Claire pushed the needle into a bright yellow pollen center and through the thin cotton of her dress. She thought, I have been welcomed here. She reached her other hand under the fabric, felt for the needle's tip and hit it with a sting, her finger whipping back into her mouth. She withdrew it and looked. A dome of red surfaced quickly at the wound, then spread — one, two, three drops falling on her white gown.

When she was finished sewing, and the rig had arrived, she pulled herself back into the world reluctantly. She didn't look at Father during the short ride meant to show her off (people gawking from the street, from their windows, their shop fronts, waving and clapping). For a moment only she thought, I am glad it is a dapple-grey horse and not a black one.

In Judge Henry's chambers in Pettyton Hall, she looked at James steadily, fixedly, as if climbing into the pale blue pools of light that were his eyes. She didn't think about the spots of blood that she'd hidden beneath an extra blossom at the bottom of her dress, or the little stain left on her undergarments last night.

Freddy Gibson, auburn-haired and freckle-faced, stood next to James. He wrinkled his nose at her, and she returned the gesture. He coughed faintly when the magistrate asked if there was "any reason this couple should not be wed," but no one actually thought Freddy serious. Instead, even the judge laughed.

After the ceremony but before the party, Claire and James were alone together in the room for no more than a minute. But in that minute, they locked eyes silently, feeling as if there was some wild secret between them. As if they had just played some elaborate and wonderful joke on an unsuspecting world. It had only been weeks since they met and walked-out together. But she was sure this was right. She wanted to apologize to Meg, for doubting such things can happen. They could happen. They had happened.

Months later, she would recall the wedding party after the ceremony with vivid clarity. It was like seeing herself from a balcony as Ebenezer Scrooge, fascinated but terrified, viewed his past life. She would look at her own cheeks which were still full above her neck, the ruffles along her soft collarbone framing the blood-red gemstone on its chain. On her finger was a gold band, which she rotated clockwise as if hoping she could move time ahead past this too-warm, too-crowded dining hall. She wanted to wind it forward, but not too far. She wanted to savor this new life, but not this dinner or these guests.

She tried, swiveled the ring around and around. But instead, she moved time backwards and saw herself the night before, giving herself to a man she barely knew...

FIVE

1883 ~ 1st September, late evening
Pettypoole, Oxfordshire

Wind back to the night before...

Father called a sudden fete—a pre-ceremony bash—for the piece workers who wouldn't attend the wedding dinner the next day. Farm labourers, a smithy, some traveling thatchers, they were all friends from The Lantern (if one could rightly call them friends). Round-bellied Father, spreading himself thin, sent her to the Weaver's Wheel to pick from their dregs of the day: dried fruitgums and papery ham, stale pudding, and crumbly cheese. She still didn't know how to cook properly (Harriet slamming her fist down at her fifteen-year-old self: "Right, that does it!").

"I have never had pork as tender as this and will never again now that Claire is leaving me to cook for another man," Father was lamenting. "Taste, McManus, you must, for Claire is a fine cook."

"Ableton, you'll eat well from now on, eh?" smiled the baker through his bushy ginger mustache glistening with fat.

153

Claire's chest tightened. Surely Kyle MacManus knew the loin had been fetched from the pub next to his own teahouse?

She felt as if she'd been thrown into water before she could swim. But what else were you to do when faced with such absurdity? Here's what: refill glasses, clear plates, and dole-out globs of pudding. Arrange things on platters in nice patterns; jam the tap into another keg of ale, empty ashtrays, light pipes.

The room grew loud, and King James' gilded mirrors rattled on the wall. Someone called in a fiddler. Someone else stumbled against Queen Charlotte's ancient porcelain vase, sending it crashing to the floor in a mess of wet petals and razor-sharp shards worth nothing but the new Staffordshire silt from which it was made. By midnight, Claire gave up and let the crumbs and bones pile up like relics in a catacomb. Several people nodded-off, two of them whilst perched on a toppled roll of silk worth more than the forgery mirrors and vase combined. She silently calculated: 7s/6d per standard yard, less 3 standard yards blotched and stained, leaves how much? 4s? Enough to recoup the loss at 20 percent increase in resale?

Kyle's twelve-year-old son Johnny appeared in the door looking confused and exhilarated. Come to fetch his dad, he'd enjoy his first taste of ale instead. A group of people left, their voices carrying down the stairs and out onto the street where they wafted back up through the open windows. Three latecomers took their place, offering as a gift one half-finished bottle of homemade elderflower cordial.

Claire sat on the outer edge of a chair—she couldn't get her back against it with the bustle Mrs Croome insisted she wear—and she wiped her damp forehead. Heaving a sigh, she felt a hand on her shoulder, then fingers stroking the back of her neck.

"I was looking for you," James said.

She looked up at him. His eyes were pink around the irises, his usually serious and alert face lenient and groggy. He kissed her hand, pulled up another chair beside her.

"You're stewed as a boiled owl," she noted.

"Am I? You have it, then." He handed her his glass.

Claire emptied it, then ran her hand down his cheek and up again; first smooth, then rough. She took an inventory of the room and noticed a man in mud-caked wool talking in slurs to Kyle about the state of the fields on the west end of Hammpen Manor. Both men had their boots up on another roll of silk.

"Lord Hammpen won't allow it, Kyle," the man, Jim, said rather too loudly. "He'll never let the land to Barker."

"And why is that? Because his lordship's a stingy bastard."

They guffawed, hilarious over each other. They clanked their glasses together clumsily, a tiny crack sounding in one.

"Nah, Kyle, that's not it—though he is a stingy bastard. Y'ee, he'll not have that witch skulking about," Jim said more seriously. "And you know John Barker would allow her to call on them, as his wife is partial to her."

"You mean the old lady up in the Shirre Wood? Bah! She's no witch. She delivered Lord Edwin, his Lordship's eldest," replied Kyle.

"Not likely!"

"You're just too young to remember, Jim. She's a witch all right until she's needed for one thing and another. Then she's a saint. Ask Barker's wife yourself—the old lady cured her of fever when no one thought she'd live a minute. That's why Barker's all right with her. There always more to the tale, isn't there."

"What about Norris, then?" Jim asked, about Lord Hammpen's brutish gamekeeper. "He's said not to like her, either."

"Ah, well. He won't say anything against her, as some say she's his mum."

"Is she, now?"

"Never mind I told you. Just keep clear of Norris, that's what I say. I'd say the same to his own mother."

They took another swig each of their ale and began discussing the price of wheat.

Claire leaned in a little toward Mrs Croome. "Mrs Croome?" she asked quietly, "is there really a witch in the wood? And is she really Mr Norris' mother at that?"

Mrs Croome coughed. "Don't be daft! Witches? Nonsense." Father snoozed upright on the sofa next to her while she picked the remaining two cheese puffs off a silver platter lined with a stained lace serviette.

James kissed Claire's hand then said, "Do not let her fool you, Mrs Croome. My clever girl knows there are no such things as witches, except in novels and plays."

Claire smiled politely at Mrs Croome whom, she surmised, knew nothing at all about Norris or the woman living in the wood. Nor had she ever seen a play, for that matter. Claire had sussed out that Mrs Croome lived in Pettypoole for no more than four years. Before that, who knew.

Of course, Claire did know there were witches — or apothecaries or midwives, or whatever people called women knowledgeable about medicine. Like the woman at the inn who tended her after Mother died. *Her fingers had pressed into your belly, her bag of powders left on your chair. It's all gone, now, you gobbled up the last morsel ages ago.*

Imagine Norris, she thought to herself, looking over at Kyle and Jim, imagine that man with an exiled midwife for a mum. It would explain the seething face, the resentment etched around his eyes. You didn't want to meet Norris on the wold, as Kyle rightly pointed out—gun slung across one shoulder, the other burdened with drooping pheasants—no one did, except maybe Mr Rollins, Lord Hammpen's stableman. Rollins and Norris skulked and marched about the parkland as if they owned it themselves, rather than their master. Terrorizing birds of all kinds, snapping rabbits' necks, whipping exhausted carthorses. Norris was one of the first men she'd seen, when she and Father had first come to Pettypoole and slept in Lord Hammpen's field near the abandoned abbey crawling with ivy.

Oh, but there was Bella, the fortune-teller at the fair the next morning... now she was another potential witch, if Claire wanted to make a list. Which she decidedly did not.

Mrs Croome began to doze off, a bit of custard stuck to the edge of her thin little mouth. Noticing this, Claire looked at James and held her forefinger to her lips. "Come with me," she mouthed silently. She thought she would go mad if she sat there another minute. She had to get out, get away from the men talking of women; get away from Father and Mrs Croome.

James looked at her curiously, but clearly intrigued, and let her take his hand and lead him out of the apartments into the outer hallway where the stairwell led to another floor of large apartments, and down further to the street.

"Turn around," Claire commanded James as she stepped into a nook in the corridor. She reached under her skirts and untied her bustle. She shimmied it to the floor and left it standing at the top of the stairs like some helpless Mesozoic creature waiting for its skin to be restored. *She sells sea shells... Father hawked some bones to a museum in Brighton, once. Do you remember?*

Claire swallowed against her thoughts, against the voice, and let herself swim back into the haze of her brandied brain. She stepped forward to join James.

Claire and James had to stifle their laughter when they saw the unconscious MacManus boy lying across the middle of the stairs, his head resting on the banister. They stepped carefully over him and went down to the ground floor.

Outside, the night was cool and crisp, the pitch sky speckled with brilliant stars. Claire willed herself not to breathe in the fresh air too deeply because she did not want the giddy nebula in her own head to disperse. She did not want to change her mind.

She walked quickly, her heels clicking on the cobblestones, and pulled James towards Mill's Lane where he lived. He stumbled a little, and she giggled as she pulled him. It was as though he was a boy, not on firm footing in the world, and she too was much younger. They were like two children running headlong into delicious mischief.

Once inside the dark stillness of James' apartments, they stood briefly: he still by the closed door, and she with her back to him looking across the shadowy sitting room to the window where the moon shone.

He stepped forward and wrapped his warm arms around her, his chest against her back, his breath against the nape of her neck. "You will be my wife tomorrow," he whispered, turning her to face him.

He had that new sleepy, happy expression he'd worn most of the evening. She loved it. He cupped his hands around her cheeks. He started to say, "I can wait," but she kissed him before he finished.

She took his hand, laying it against her bodice and pressing his fingers against her breast. He pulled her down to the carpet, and she wrapped her legs around his waist. He hesitated, then pressed against her, his weight heavy, foreign, but also enveloping and sheltering. His hands on her thigh, her breasts, her hips, between her legs. A sensation at her lower back moved forward and through her, until it was as though the very hum of a bee, singing in her head as love, and in her body as lust.

The wedding table, at which only Claire and James sat, held roast goose, sticky ham, and three cakes. There were soufflés collapsed and shriveled, and goblets of too-sweet wine. Grapes that were as warm as the air in the crowded room. Guests sat at smaller round tables, or remained standing and milling about, popping over to the couple's table to pick at food and offer advice and congratulations.

"A reception fit for the Princess Royal," Father had said, beaming, when he told her he had reserved the Golden Lion Hotel for an afternoon dinner. And Claire had answered, "But no one has formal dinners anymore, Father, they have a simple breakfast."

"May I have your attention, please?" Freddy Gibson stood behind the bride and groom and held his glass aloft. He wore his best suit, his well-knotted cravat completely out of place with what Claire thought of as his charmingly disheveled personality. He had managed this look the whole morning, 'bless him.

"Behave yourself, Freddy," Molly ordered her brother from her table across the room. The grown Gibson children were all present and scattered around the party: Molly, the eldest, followed by Robbie, Hugh, the twins Eliza and Helen; then Freddy. "Do not let him do it, Ableton!" Robbie cried.

Freddy and James liked a good prank, and this was shaping up to be one. But Freddy, genuinely elated, continued in earnest. "May the happy couple be as blessed tomorrow as we are, all of us, today. May your pockets and table be full, and your home bursting with children."

A great cheer erupted.

"There," he muttered to James, "You may shower praise on me for my almost dubious self-restraint."

"Dubious, indeed. Though I am suitably impressed with the effect, Freddy."

"Leave him be." Claire smiled. She turned around in her seat and took hold of Freddy's hand. "And how smart he still looks after all of it." She dusted an invisible crumb from his coat, doting.

She didn't want to let go of Freddy's hand. In fact, she had an intense desire at that moment to hide herself between Freddy and James and have them sneak her out of the room.

The party swelled with guests, and it took Claire almost an hour to greet most of them. From her place of display where all attention was on her. Her whole life she was told never to put herself in such a position. She learned this from Father, yet here he was doing just the opposite to her on her wedding day.

Claire watched Freddy and James in their morning suits poke fun at each other and could easily picture them as children. At the same time, this made him feel more of a stranger to her, as each of the guests did. She didn't know James Ableton, not really, not the way James and Freddy knew each other. The way she knew Meg and Father. Dear God, she thought, what was Meg thinking four months ago? Was she overcome with the same terror Claire felt now? "If only Mother were here," was what Meg had said on the morning of her wedding. Then again, maybe Meg had known exactly what she was doing. A bairn in the womb was the cost of a roof over her head and a gentle-mannered husband who would always provide it.

"Do not look now, Claire," James murmured into her ear.

Father was attempting to stand on his chair in the middle of the room. "The Father of the Bride will speak!" his voice boomed. The guests quieted.

Father teetered, nearly toppled, but with the help of two other men, both soused to the eyeballs, he stood. "As The Father, I say this to The Groom: Take good care of my girl. My youngest daughter was ripped from my breast only months ago. But her sister—this daughter here—is a flower growing amongst the rocks, a bright guide in the blackest of nights. I may have lost my Claire, but you have gained her fairly, Ableton." An over-dressed egg on a rickety wall, Father beamed at the groom. "She would not leave me for anyone she did not love more, or at least as equally. And so, I say, Bless You. Bless you both."

The guests clapped and drank. The old wiped their eyes, the young blushed and giggled. Claire smiled demurely, but there was a hollow feeling in the pit of her stomach. She thought, We have just been blessed by Father, and he does not even believe in God.

"Your father is a marvel," laughed Freddy, who had pulled a chair up next to them, viewing the party with great amusement. "He's promised me a story of a spotted wild cat he once owned in Africa. He says you know it?"

"I don't remember."

She turned to James and something in her expression led him to say, "Let Father have his moment. It'll be over soon."

She thought of the night before Meg's wedding—in the blue, early morning hours of dread when a black horse galloped across her heart—and she felt as empty and afraid now as she had in that room. Father would have his moments without her from now on. He would never need her again. *But perhaps it was you all along who took that upon yourself, like a missionary in some dark, hopeless corner of the Earth. Where the Sampan sailor cries Ling, Ling, Ling to his lost pet...*

A wave of dread passed over her. For some reason she didn't completely understand, she said under her breath, "I am free."

As she whispered this, for some other reason she couldn't yet fathom, she knew it to be wholly untrue.

SIX

1883 ~ 15th September
Pettypoole, Oxfordshire

On a display table were columns of cutwork handkerchiefs stacked in two half-moons. It was an arrangement resembling the barrows in the fields, though the folded linens were meant to tempt you into thoughts of romance and adornment.

Claire stood before the odd display, having come to Henry's Stores several weeks after her wedding to finally pick out her trousseau. When she left her and James' apartments, the air outside felt cool now that Summer was ending. But the limestone of the village still looked warm and luminous, as if it knew the trick of keeping the Summers of centuries.

There were a few people going about their day on the streets, some stopping to peer into the large bay window at the displays, some inside the store shopping for whatever it was people shopped for. Women, mostly.

Standing in front of the odd monument-like display of linens, Claire thought about her mother lying under three rose bushes in a hospital churchyard in Sussex; and she suddenly wondered — after all these years — what shape her headstone was. Was there a scroll or wreath of flowers carved along the top? Was there an angel perched on it?

James' parents rested in a more unusual state along with his sister Lydia, forever four years old, all three Abletons interned not in Ber St. Eldwyn's churchyard, but adjacent to it on land owned by the Henry family, his father's employer, the very man who owned this shop. Simple, rectangular headstones etched with six-pointed stars marked the spot, with a fourth stone for the missing body of James' brother, David, drowned at sea on his way home from the Anglo-Afghan War. A great dripping laburnum dangled its flowers over the headstones, depositing yellow pollen and petals onto moss encrusted Yorkstone.

"He'll be pleased to see you in one of these, ma'am." A salesgirl approached, holding an illustration of an emerald-green riding habit. *Miss Taylor*, read her nametag. Eloise, the new girl, James had told Claire. Eloise said, "Thirty velvet buttons down the front, what all the ladies are wearing now. And a slimmer line down the back for your train. No bustle this season."

"Have they come and gone already?" Claire asked, trying not to seem thrown by the lightning change of fashion. "I suppose I need a coat for winter."

"Do you not have a winter coat?" asked the girl, genuinely astonished.

Glancing back at the counter, where a *Miss Pell* kept a critical eye on her *Miss Taylor* and her penny-pinching customer, it occurred to Claire she could get Eloise sacked for the scant sale and, truthfully, Valentine Pell looked as if she might enjoy carrying out the sentence.

"Never you mind, ma'am. Let me take your measurements, and I'll order it made for you."

"Will it arrive by New Year's?"

Eloise was caught off-guard. She obviously had yet to memorize such important information for her customers.

"No matter," Claire said, waving a hand. "And I do not need that." Claire pointed to the ready-made tablecloths Eloise held.

The girl was doing her best, poor thing, nodding her head repeatedly and dashing this way and that, while grabbing more things to show Claire, her smile never wavering, never calling attention to Claire's peculiar inexperience. One minute more of this and Claire would be able to call her a true friend.

Eloise peeled an embroidered gravestone square off the top of the linen barrow. "Aren't they lovely?" She placed the handkerchief in Claire's hand. Her cheeks flushed pink below her cap and neatly pinned black hair.

"They are lovely," Claire said, unfolding the square.

As the embroidery in the middle of the handkerchief touched Claire's skin, there came a spark of pain behind her right eye. She reached up and grimaced. She saw an image of herself as a young girl, sitting at her mother's feet in the sitting room at Allswell.

"Ma'am? Are you all right?"

"Of course." Claire's mouth twitched. There was a terrible lurch of the room, and then...

You are embellishing a chemise with Mother: yours, for your trousseau. The needle punctures the fabric, the strand stretched until it tugs. Too taut! Mother places her hand on yours and with the other loosens the stitch ever so slightly with the dull end of her own needle.

Claire felt—in her mind and her body—another shift of the room, and she saw Mother prone in a bed that was not hers, in a room that was not at Allswell.

Mother, wan and paper-thin, her fingers working satin stitches, a feather on a bird's wing. But how can this be if you are not there to see it?

Mother pricks her finger, the blood surfaces in a tiny dome, then expands and spreads across her finger, surging with the rhythm of her pulse, spilling across her knuckles onto the fabric and obliterating the stitching.

"...and I'll wrap it up, then for you, ma'am?" Eloise's voice ruptured the vision. "Mrs Ableton? Are you sure you're not poorly?"

Claire swayed. "I— I am fine." She grabbed hold of the edge of the table and dropped the handkerchief.

"Ma'am, won't you sit here?"

"I am p-perfectly well. W-will you show me your notions?" She tried to speak as if Eloise's face did not appear in a halo of pulsing light; as if her own face was not cold and white as marble, the bloodless skin stretched tightly over her skull.

Her fingers work a bird's wing, and the thread stains from blue to red with her blood...

"Oh! Have you no thread at all?"

"Thread?" Claire's fingers shook as they pressed her temple. All at once, the pain was gone. "Forgive me. You must forgive me. I don't think I feel well at all."

"Ah, 'bless you, Mrs Ableton!" Eloise whispered brightly, her eyes wide. She guided Claire to a nearby chair and sat her down. "Everyone gets wobbly, they say, then it passes after a few weeks. My sis was just the same with her first. Now: d'you prefer silk or cotton?" She smiled again at Claire.

"Cotton. Some cream, if you have it, and navy and black." Claire felt relief as she realized no one else in the shop seemed to notice she had gone pale and was sat on a chair.

Well, perhaps someone noticed. At the counter, Valentine Pell was glaring through Eloise's back straight into to Claire. Hurry up and finish with that strange new wife of Mr Ableton, her expression clearly said.

In the tea shop, some minutes later, James looked down at the one parcel at her feet. "Is that all?" he asked. They sat together at a little table by the window.

"I was fitted for a winter coat." Claire fixed her purple hat, the very same she wore the day she met James. She knew she was supposed to recount her adventure on the high seas of linens and notions, of woolen domesticity. She ought to have bought a new hat.

"You may have purchased more, Claire," James said, as if reading her mind. "I earn five-hundred pounds yearly, in addition to the income my father left. That is about another five-hundred."

"That is not my business, love." She reached quickly for the sugar bowl. Tiny roses and thorns circled the white porcelain vessel in an unruly fashion.

"Good God, Claire, it is very much your business. Don't tell me you forgot to charge your purchases to my account? It is my wedding gift to you which, I hasten to add, you are weeks behind allowing me to fulfill."

"I did not forget." How could she? It was how Father worked it out.

"Have another cake, you look pale."

"Try these," said Kyle McManus, breezing past with a tray out of the oven. He plunked two miniature sticky buns on her plate. "New brides always get too thin. Time to plump her up again." He added a third.

When the baker returned to the kitchen, James gave her a concerned look, his brows furrowed. "This has all been too swift for you."

"Don't be daft." She tucked an errant lock of hair behind his ear. You could do that all day, if you loved someone: fix their tie, their hair, brush their lapel, any excuse to touch them. She knew this now. "I have some money of my own, you know, James." She dumped a heaping spoonful of sugar into her cup and stirred.

James stared at her. "What on earth do you mean?"

"Father would give me a bob for milk, and if he was feeling generous, he would tell me to spend the rest on myself. But I didn't, you see, or rarely did. After a time, I'd change the coins for notes, and put them into my tea tin. It has a fetching Oriental pattern on it. It's in the bottom of the drawer which holds my underthings if you haven't noticed." She gave him a sly little smile.

His eyes widened. He lowered his voice. "I have not. But did you really? Save all that money?"

She nodded.

"You clever girl. No offense to Father."

"I never told Father." *Like Meg's belly on her wedding night.*

"You must take that money and put it somewhere safe, Claire. A bank, for instance. Where is it now?"

"In the wardrobe, in the bottom drawer as I've just said."

"Just in the drawer?" He sighed gruffly. "Look, are you sure you do not have a head-ache? You really do look peaked."

"I'm perfectly well."

He frowned, then reached across the table and took her hand in his. "Now listen, there is little point in not being sensible, Claire. We must open a proper account for you at Fowler's. One can be sensible, and still enjoy the spontaneous spectacle of life."

For an unnerving moment, Claire thought he was referring to her headache, her near fainting spell in the shop, and the images of Mother assaulting her. Spontaneous spectacles... is that what you'd call them? Then she realized he only meant Father, of course, and all his impulsive amusements.

"We had only the bindweed and lavender for our meals when we were but baby birds," James continued, giving her hand a gentle squeeze, "but there is no need for that now."

She was meant to return his remark with one of her own, referring to the myth they'd created that day in Grath's meadow. But instead, her mind was on Mother again, on the sight of her slender hands working thread onto white linen. *Her fingers work the wings of a bird...* Had she seen her do it, but forgotten until today? It did not feel like memory—at least, not her own memory. It felt more like someone else's memory. A memory clouded in pain and confusion.

Claire shook her head involuntarily, feeling cobwebby and lost.

"Are you certain you're quite well, Claire?"

"I think I preferred meeting you in Bonborough, when we were children traveling with our fathers," she said. "We are not birds after all, are we?"

"I don't think my own father would have been quite so taken in with your father's charms. No offense to Father."

"Mmm." She looked past James' shoulder, out the window where the wind was blowing newly falling leaves down the nearly empty street.

When you are the one carrying your husband's papers —because you see that he's left two of them pinned under his chair like leaves flattened under a boot—you must run out still wearing your apron. You know what it is to be needed, and how to fix things.

Claire hurried across the bridge onto the Roman Road, then turned onto Jacob's Lane, speculating whether she was headed in the right direction. She'd been told, of course, where the Babbage School for Boys was but had yet to see it for herself. She walked a further on and was soon rewarded with the appearance of a relatively new stone and timber building. Simple and sleek, it looked rather like a large, angular butterfly.

Once inside the empty hall, she heard James' voice right away, coming from inside a classroom down the corridor. Locating the room and pushing the door ajar, she found him sprawled on his back on top of his desk, while a boy of nine or ten stood reading from a thick volume.

"Who'is soul still is, uhrm, still prepar-ed for death," the boy stumbled dully.

James made an audible snoring sound. Some of the boys giggled, all of them rapt as they watched him. James sat up, swung his legs over. "'Whose soul is still prepared for death.' Death, my boy, not sleep! Sir Wotton is speaking of a knight — one of the bravest, most honourable men in the kingdom." James hopped down from his desk and knelt before the boy. He closed the book and pressed it against the boy's heart. "Master Thomas, do you feel the honour pulsing through the blood of the knight?"

The boy nodded emphatically.

James ruffled his hair, then directed another student, "Master Gregory, will you continue on page — I say, my wife is here."

The boys erupted in laughter before recovering themselves and standing in rigid formation alongside their chairs. "Good morning, ma'hm," they murmured at her, more or less in unison.

Claire stared at the young students, no older than twelve and some as young as six. They were a true curiosity, most of them awake before dawn to work (the farm, the wheel, the smithy's fire) before wriggling into their uniforms and racing to school ahead of the headmaster's switch. She thought of other children she'd known in her life: small beings denied a childhood and secreted away inside a world of adult peril and abuse. But these children here were bound to each other by an edict of greater good. They were as unusual to her as a sword-swallower was to an audience at the ballet.

She handed James the papers and made her good-byes, then stood just outside the door, listening for a moment to the sound of the children's high voices, and her husband's deeper tones. She smiled to herself.

The school was not large, but it was airy and spacious nevertheless. The empty corridor gleamed. A single unoccupied table stood near the entry, the man attending it first thing in the morning teaching in another classroom at the moment. Where were the dark-paneled ceilings, the dreary walls, the dripping cobwebs? Surely this wasn't considered an "Institution" as other schools were? Or as where Mother had lain.

She had never been to the hospital where Mother was taken — there had not been time — but if she closed her eyes, she might be able to picture it...

Just then, a voice whispered down the corridor. It was like wind through a window which reached her ear in a sharp, icy blast, and it was not in her head. It said, *Her fingers work a bird's wing.*

Claire's eyes shot open.

Cold blew over her as she pressed her back against the wall. She felt her eyes starting to close again in a strange reflex against the cold. A dull throb starting at her right temple. Would there be something to see?

The thread is drawn through. Another pierce. Pull. Pierce. Blue floss... The little cat on his spool? No, a real spool of thread. Real fingers.

She cried out, threw her hand to her chest. Her heart pounded and her breath felt strangled. She ran out of the building. She stood on the road, gasping. This was the second time in a week she had seen the same dream.

It's not a dream, you cow. It is something that has actually happened. Or will happen. But you know this.

"Shut up!" she hissed, her chest heaving as she stood in the sunny road, her hands on her knees as she bent over from nausea.

After a bit, she felt her breathing slow and become deeper. She blinked around her, noting the sheep standing atop the hill next to the road. She stood, counted to seven. Then she quickened her pace back to the village.

"Rushed out the house?" croaked Mrs Easling, as she sidled up to Claire on the lane just over the bridge. She stared at Claire's apron. Next, she stared at her bare head.

"Mr Ableton forgot part of his lesson for today," Claire explained. There was still a flush of perspiration spread across her forehead, and her breathing had not quite returned to normal. She gave Mrs Easling a tight smile and hoped it did not look like a smirk.

"The boys need their lessons, or what's the point in leaving off the farm, eh?" Mrs Easling grimaced back a little. She suddenly coughed, interrupting herself. "But how do you know the lesson was for today?" She lifted her small, oval head so Claire could see her from under her old straw bonnet. Her mostly toothless mouth was smiling, but those watery little eyes were piercing as needles.

"I help Mr Ableton, so I did know which lesson was for today, actually. I have an idea that the girls of the village might do with some lessons," Claire added, trying to be friendly.

"In what? Mending and cooking?" Mrs Easling looked appalled. "That's why they have mothers!"

"Reading, I thought. Actually." *And who says we all have mothers?*

Mrs Easling shook her head, sucked her tongue. "A married woman a teacher? Never heard such a thing. Next time Mr Ableton forgets his papers, Mr Tinsdale shall send Davie in your place." She wagged her finger and clucked.

It was no wonder, Claire thought, that the woman enjoyed fighting with the poulterer. Then she told herself to just smile and nod, smile and nod. "Good day, Mrs Easling. I've the post to get." She hurried away, not waiting for a good-bye.

Inside the shady front room of Clews Cottage, Claire signed for a parcel, which Mrs Fowler handed to her across the counter with an eager expression. Claire wondered if the postwoman opened them at the corner for a peek, or merely accurately deduced the contents by weight and size.

"Came just under an hour ago, Mrs Ableton," Mrs Fowler noted helpfully. One of her two ratting terriers bounced at her heels, while the other slept on a pile of reeds behind the counter. As she worked as Postmistress, Mrs Fowler's thick, reddened hands also wove reeds into baskets with lightning speed. She inspected a spiral now with its unwoven slats pointing hither and thither. As she did, she peered across at Claire's book. "Latest edition, is it?"

"A gift from my sister. Though... of course, I have the previous edition. And how is Mr Fowler today?" Claire looked around as if he might be hiding somewhere in the rafters. Con Fowler was a horse-and-pony dealer. Selling colts or shooting rickety geldings was Claire's guess for today, but mainly, she just wanted his wife to stop looking at her parcel with such interest.

"I'd have thought Annie would be acquainted with all aspects of caring for Mr Ableton's abode by now," quipped Mrs Fowler, about James' former domestic, airily, as if his little apartments were grand. "She's been with him three years, you know. Since she was seventeen."

"She is a daily for Hammpen Manor, now. She only ever came twice-weekly," said Claire.

Mrs Fowler nodded, still looking at her basket as she worked it. "Yes. I know that. Have a lovely day, Mrs Ableton."

"And yourself."

The book under her arm, Claire set back down the lane. Moments later, there was Annie herself, turning the corner with a large crate in her arms. Claire hurried to catch up to her.

"May I help you with that, Annie?"

James' former housekeeper smiled cheerfully. "Ah, hello, Mrs Ableton! It's only her ladyship's Indian teas. They're not very heavy to carry."

"You are well, then, up at the Manor?" Claire hid the title of the book between her arm and ribs.

"Well enough, thanks. If there's anything you need, ma'am, you'll tell me, won't you? I sometimes have a moment at the end of the day, if you should need me for anything." Annie smiled again, her freckles like dappled berries across her cheeks.

Claire nodded politely, and waved good-bye as she turned onto Mills Lane.

The narrow lane where they lived was not long and petered out at a gate which led to a forest path. A line weaver's row cottages sat on just one side, all connected or occasionally separated by a bit of space only a child could slip through. One cottage in the center housed the print shop of Mr Tinsdale, their landlord, and it was above this that their apartments—once James' bachelor rooms—resided. Mr Fritch, the clerk who drew up their marriage contract, lived above them in the snug but bright garret.

James and Claire's sitting room had modern gas lighting, and there was a kitchen with an actual range and a larder. It was almost too comfortable—and normal—for her to trust as her own, and every time she came home from being out, she felt a strange dip of worry in her stomach, then a fluttering of happiness in her chest.

The cottages quickly came into Claire's view as the lane curved. The cottages themselves were set on the curve, the sight of them immediately fanciful and pretty to anyone walking by. Once, men and women had washed and dyed cloth in the stone troughs in front of their front door, when not battling Plague or Invader. Now the troughs rested dry and empty, or flooded over like tubs, depending upon the rains. No one bothered to plant flowers in the troughs, as the lane was charming enough as it was.

She found the front door to the cottage unlocked, a common state of affairs she did not like, but found she could do nothing about except lock the door again (only to find it unlocked when Mr Tinsdale or Mr Fritch, or even James, next entered or left). The whole cottage reeked of oily ink and crisp vellum, and she often wondered if the cottages on either side did, too. Tinsdale and his printer's devil, Davie, were usually smudged black from face to fingers during the day.

Simple and shy as a baby rabbit, Davie's face held something in it that broke Claire's heart every time she saw him. He had a lack of guile too vulnerable for this hard world. He called her Miss-Able, as if he could not wrap his tongue around too many syllables. He had a funny habit of skipping and singing to himself, shy as he was. Claire had heard his mother admonish him not to let his songs distract him from arriving to work on time, but it was clear his mother loved him in her own stern, protective way.

On the landing outside her door, Mr Tinsdale had today left a Cotswolds newspaper, and a Penny Dreadful. On the cover of the latter, a woman in a red dress was stalked by a crazed man with a dagger on a narrow, dark city street. Claire tossed it into the bedroom and plunked the newspaper and her new book on the dining table. It was a guide to housekeeping. "Hells bells," Claire muttered, realizing Mrs Fowler probably knew the book was ordered from London and not sent from Tyne. She likely knew that Claire had never seen an edition in her life.

Claire hung up her dust coat, then sat in her own chair to read. "Scrub with lye caustic, then rinse with boiled water," advised the chapter "Principles of Good Taste in Household Furniture &c. III, Carpets and other Floor Coverings."

Water heated in a bucket, a cloud of lye smoldering the air, Claire dunked the brush and began to move it across the floorboards. Her memories of the houses where she, Meg and Father lived were always of cobwebs, of shedding plaster, of floors caked with eons of bootsteps. Filthy.

As she scrubbed her own floor there came an image of someone having already taught her to do this: a rocking-reaching motion and boar bristles that tore at her knuckles. She had not remembered this until now, and more curiously, the memory was mixed up with one of clenching pain and her monthly bleeding.

Claire stopped mid-scrub, her hand holding the dripping brush. She screwed her mind around the fading recollection, but it slipped fast and was gone. After she was through, she noticed an empty wall which looked all the more empty to her now the room was clean. She hung up her apron and put the brush and bucket on the trough outside the cottage to dry.

In the late afternoon light, she strolled down Mills Lane and back across the bridge into the wide-open air, this time with a tourist's leisure, her lungs filled with relief, smiling with the miracle of an oppressively boring, beautiful day. She walked along the Roman Road again, farther than the school. On Hammpen Manor's parkland, Claire saw red and blue striped points growing out of a field, tents set up in a cluster just as the spring fair had been. She headed toward it.

At this particular Autumn fete were two jugglers and a whole team of acrobats, large displays devoted to pies and jams, crates of apples, and candied fruits in gilded boxes. It was unusual, a fair set up this late in the season, but Autumn had been unusually mild in the whole county, and even Market Cross still had many goods to sell.

As she made her way round the fairgrounds with a kind of heightened anticipation, her pace quickened with hope, and the hope rapidly grew to desperation. Somewhere, tucked between the carpets and sheep pens, was Bella's little tent, she was sure of it. Inside, Bella's warm wrinkled hands would grasp Claire's. She would sit her down and give her tea and tell her what she really knew about the dream of the black horse. Her face would cloud over, that chill of foreboding filling up the tent, and Claire would make her tell her everything and weave some spell of protection to keep her new life safe and stable. To keep the dream from ever coming back.

One small marquee — purple and green lattice print with gold tassels above the entry flap — looked promising. Perhaps the fortune-teller had traded her candy-red stripes out for a more ornate style to match her floor of pillows. Bending down, Claire lifted the flap and peeked in with a smile.

She was met with the sight of a petite man in garish orange silk looking like a Matador, a small, speckled wildcat on a leash by his side.

"May I 'elp you, M'selle? She is much friendly, *venez voir*! You may pet 'er for two shillings."

Claire stood there, staring at the Frenchman in a Spaniard's costume and his exotic cat. She felt a lump in her throat, as if she'd been knocked over by the absence of something not even named. *You can never make anything reappear, just because you want it to. Daft girl.*

She paid two shillings to stroke the little cat's head, then left the tent and bought a jar of blackberry jam before leaving the fair. On her way back to the village, after descending a hill, she stopped to watch a painter who was set up and recreating the scene of the fairgrounds from his vantage point. She bought one of his little works that was already dry and leaning against a tree. Then she returned home.

The painting was of the view the night Father had fixed their dog-cart near Hammpen Manor: the grassland surrounded by barrows, the solitary tree, and the ancient stone bethel crawling with ivy in the divot of the vale. It was strange to think of that night. The painting was all warm and full of sunlight and speckled with sheep, while her memory of the same view was of black shadows, the wraith-like tree limbs and ivy tendrils reaching down for her.

SEVEN

1883 ~ 2nd October
Pettypoole, Oxfordshire

"Claire? What is this?"

"Goodness, James, have you not left yet? You'll be late." Wearing her apron, broom in hand, she joined James in the stairwell where he stood.

"I am leaving, pet. But what is this? Did you buy it?"

"Oh, this?" She laughed when she saw what he meant. "This funny little table appeared yesterday quite out of nowhere. Mrs Magpie must have brought it over. I think I'm supposed to put flowers, or perhaps a pair of those porcelain dogs, on it. But the landing is too narrow for furnishings. Mr Fritch nearly tripped on it last night when he came home from work. I'll tell Mr Tinsdale to take it away."

James nodded. "Yes, but I mean *this*. It was inside the drawer of the table." He handed her something resembling a stiff fishing net rolled to look like a telescope.

Claire knew what it was immediately. Perfectly rigid, the thing looked as if it had been lying in the drawer for ages, as though a long-forgotten shroud left in a crypt. She pried the edge open and unrolled it a little, and two half-skeins of floss fell out. There was stitching in the middle of the mesh where someone had begun making flowers, the kind Mother had taught her to sew.

"It is a needlepoint," she informed him.

Mr Fritch bounded down the garret stairs to where they stood. "Good morning, Ableton," he said, touching his bowler.

"Good morning, sir," said James.

"What is this? Ah! I know, my aunt makes them."

"Does she?" Claire smiled. She held onto the needlepoint, tilted her broom against the doorframe, and followed James and Fritch downstairs where James kissed her good-bye.

"Will you be home for your tea?" she asked their neighbour.

"If you will join me," he said.

Claire nodded. She waved them both farewell. Mr Fritch came to tea once or twice a week, and Claire was happy to have him, giving him a sandwich and a strong cup with cream. They talked of art and books. There was never mention of a potential Mrs Fritch. She knew the type, and she suspected he knew that she knew. They were safe in each other's company in this way. She didn't need to tell him she had once traveled the country like vagabond, sleeping in brothels and cowsheds she only now realized were exactly that.

The din of the printing press filled the entryway. Between the front door and the stairs, was another door that led to the back of the shop from this part of the cottage. It was, she knew, unlocked during the day, and how Mrs Tinsdale popped in to give her husband his tea at one o'clock each day. Claire opened it.

"Mr Tinsdale?" she called over the clacks and swishes. The ceiling was low and, on the beams, were strung lines with newspaper sheets hanging to dry. Everything looked impossibly crowded, but clean and organized. Davie crept up beside her, looking wide-eyed. "No, it's not yet tea, my sweet," she said loudly. "Please tell him I'm here." She smoothed a clutch of matted hair from his eyes, then watched the boy skip across the room and squeeze into a narrow aisle between a press and a table laid-out with type blocks.

Momentarily, Mr Tinsdale joined her in squinting at the mesh which she held up for him to see.

"Looks old, doesn't it?" he said. He peered at it closer, his eyes crinkling beneath his cap. "Now, where did she get that table, I wonder? Davie, enough singing for today, there's a good boy. He's driving me barking mad with that tune. Well, never mind," he handed the object back to Claire. "I don't imagine anyone'll miss it. We'll let our Miss-Able here have it, won't we, Davie? Perhaps she'll make something pretty of it." He waved her away with a smile and restarted the press.

Upstairs, Claire unfolded the mesh entirely, pressing the corners down on the dining table with four large books she took off the shelf. With a pencil she added the outline of more flowers to the few that were there, repeating the pattern in two columns as if the blossoms were reflected back at each other through a looking glass.

She set to needle-pointing with the old skeins of floss until the light in the sky faded. She studied the difference between what she had worked, and what had been created by an unknown hand years before, some disembodied, spectral limb. Her needle was slightly thicker than it should have been, stretching each square of the mesh just a tiny fraction. She would need another needle, a slightly smaller size. She would need more floss, the same weight as the old had been. She would choose other colours to compliment the two already used, as she knew there were not likely to exist the exact same in a newly dyed batch.

Women fussed over knitting booties in this way, and there was her next thought: her irrepressible little sister under the rule of a screaming babe. Was Meg knitting something now, frantically, before the baby and winter's chill arrived together? Would she even know how to knit? Mother only taught Claire to embroider before she died, not even to crochet, and it was Claire who should have instructed Meg all those years they traveled with Father. With a kind of horror filling her chest, her needle poised mid-air, Claire realized this now, years too late.

Lettie Ponting declared, "We could have a steady order of these."

Claire searched the bin for shades of green and rose while holding her half-finished needlepoint against each skein. She thought Mrs Ponting was speaking to someone else. Eloise, for instance, who stacked more handkerchiefs nearby; the columns rebuilt anew as though a post-war restoration.

"Why, that's not your lovely work is it?" Eloise asked Claire.

"It is."

"That will be all, Miss Taylor." Mrs Ponting shooed her away. To Claire she continued, "We sell a few Morris-and-Co fabrics like your pattern here. They're very *OH-cor-AHnt.* Would you fancy making some embroideries in that fashion? Perhaps some crewelwork?"

"Me?" Claire stared at her.

"You."

"Well… I think I could."

"Yes, I think you could. Your own pattern?" Mrs Ponting nodded at the needlepoint.

"Just something I thought pretty."

"Our clients would treat them as custom items created by a talent worthy of a generous tip." She nodded again at Claire while raising her eyebrows, as if to say, *you understand me?*

Claire did not.

"Because you are not the sort of lady who needs payment, Mrs Ableton."

"Oh…?" Then, she got it. Married women did not sew except for their own enjoyment, or to darn their husband's and children's things. She couldn't be seen as a disadvantaged woman, reduced to labour. She wondered if Lettie could imagine a married woman showcasing silver teapots to a Copper Walrus at a fair, a sprig of wilting flowers in her hair.

Lettie's nametag had *Henry's Stores* scrolled in gold thread below *Mrs Ponting*. She was a widow, and past her prime for finding another husband even with a full head of pin-curled black hair, so there was no harm in her being employed. She was also the sister-in-law of the owner of her place of business and was the Lady in Charge of the Department. There were these little loop-holes, if you could find them, and Lettie fit through them all.

"How much might I see, in tips?" Claire thought to ask, nearly biting her own tongue off when she realized she maybe should not have.

Mrs Ponting smiled while deciding whether to ignore her question or address it in good taste. "Do you prefer to have one or two designs at a time to consider?" she posed.

"I don't mind either way." Claire's sing-songy tone of complacent chit-chat rivaled Father's. "'Keeps my hands busy while Mr Ableton reads his paper after supper." She let out a soft, girlish giggle.

That being the ticket, she was sent home with a silk pillow to embroider. It was finished in no time, after which she set about burnishing the kitchen.

PART III

Ice and Scrabbles

"I was called to see a young girl who is stated to be very ill, at King Street, Islington. I found my poor dispensary patient living in an attic… She lay, doubled up in the corner of this bare room, with no bed-linen but a thin patched quilt and a few rags; though bearing marks of having been a very pretty girl."

Dr. William Acton
London, 1870

ONE

1883 ~ 30th October
Pettypoole, Oxfordshire

All will become clear when the dust settles. Such a common proclamation. The problem was, as Claire saw it, that though one's arm made a sweep across a surface, the fragments reconvened and rained down anew. She polished and wiped and next thing she knew everything was coated in dust again. She began to think ahead, to try and avert the inevitable. She began to evaluate the copper pot which soaked their garments as men charted mountain ranges and battles. Twice weekly the floors needed a scour and wax; the rugs and curtains a beating like heretics. Twice monthly the wool mattress cover needed to be combed as thoroughly as Meg's hair at bedtime.

"Twice monthly?" Lettie Ponting scoffed. "That often?" Having come to retrieve an embroidered tablecloth, she looked incredulous as Claire scraped and pulled the comb over the clumped fleece. She leaned against the doorway to the bedchamber and watched in wonder.

"There is a set of matching pillowcases to be embroidered on your dining table," Lettie told Claire, omitting that the gratuity was folded into one of them, tactfully hidden from sight.

"Well, of course not twice monthly!" Claire suddenly laughed when she realized she was being inspected, "I was only joking."

"You make my house look a fright." Lettie smiled at her, but behind the grin lurked something slightly threatening.

Make note: never share house-cleaning rituals with the women at Henry's. And up the combing to thrice-monthly.

"'Macbeth' to start?" Claire knelt before the lesson plan. She had stacked the pages across the berry-red patterns of their Moroccan carpet in numerical order. Onto the seat of her armchair, next to James', she placed seven bound volumes of the play itself.

"It can be surprising what they understand. You must have confidence in them. Here, take these." He sat on the edge of his armchair and leaned across to her.

She placed those sheets onto another stack on the floor.

James stood, poked the fire, and said, "It is so dark so early, now." He glanced at the window.

"I only meant the witches and murder," said Claire.

"What?" he looked at her as if she'd gone mad.

"The play. You say witches aren't real, but I doubt some of the boys' parents agree. Of course, I only ever read about fossils and Marie Antoinette when I was young."

James laughed. "Do you hear yourself? The bones of ancient monsters, and heads lost to the guillotine —yes, those sound like bedtime stories to me. Forget Shakespeare."

"It wasn't my fault, I couldn't help what books we had in the house, could I?" She picked up a small volume of Aristotle sitting near his feet. "'One swallow does not make a summer.' And then I always think after I read it: but two swallows do."

He knelt down on the floor with her, the two of them on their hands and knees in a sea of papers and kissed her. "Do not distract me," he said in a low voice. He put his hand on her cheek.

She kissed him back, wrapping her arms around his neck and pulling him closer. She thought, this is Happiness. This room, our own flat, the fire in the hearth and the sun setting outside.

Then she heard the voice, whispering with dread. By the pricking of my thumbs, something wicked this way comes. *Open locks, whoever knocks.*

"You've only had the one helping, Claire. Have more." James ladled stew into her bowl. A drip landed on her hand as she moved to prevent him.

"I'm not very hungry. Had an early tea at four." What she meant was that she'd eaten a biscuit smaller than her fist for the whole of the day. A sour ache had lately begun to lodge itself in her belly. It was a dull sort of pain, a bit like hunger, though she couldn't rightly say it was hunger.

Why not just tell him?

Claire rubbed her forehead, tamping the voice down.

"Head-ache?"

"Only tired," she said. "A bit."

He playfully grabbed her wrist and pulled her toward him, enveloping her in a kiss that lingered warm and sweet.

When she came up for air, she asked, "James, about the house garden?"

"Ah, that explains it."

"Explains what?"

"The lovely stew, and a new bottle of brandy I see by my chair. You need my help with something."

"Perhaps." She gave his shoulder a teasing flick with her serviette. She had bought the set from Henry's, which she herself had embroidered.

"I'll see to it at the weekend. Eat some more, please."

On Sunday morning, they stood together and surveyed their narrow back garden. There was a single raised bed edged with rotted wood and filled with weeds, snails and beetles, as though a museum display of the grotesque. The outhouse stood at the far end where tall stalks of purple, daisy-like flowers grew along the sides of it. Echinacea, good for tea when you had a cold ("Chapter XIII: Domestic Medicine – The House Garden & Bronchitis, cont.").

They decided on a Plan of Attack. James worked the raised bed by the fence while she pulled weeds from the patch of purple cone flowers after clipping the surviving heads and putting them in a jar for tea.

Grabbing at the subterranean tendrils of the weeds with her nails, Claire tossed the roots and the slimy pests that clung to them into a bucket, furious and determined to get every last thread that might choke her infant seeds. She tried to remember a past feeling of earth under her: Mother had them picking beets at Allswell, had she not? *You must keep the rows tended, just as you must clean clumps of wet hay out of our cart's hinges. A breakdown of any kind is intolerable. So is a rotted crop.*

"Did you say something?" asked James. He plunged the hoe into the edge of the bed now it was clear, where new bricks would be placed.

"I did not," she answered. "Now you've made me forget... Right: Thyme goes with Rosemary." Chamomile, thyme, radish, aubergine (real names, she knew them!). She pressed the seeds into the earth in straight, raised rows. Rows and rows, patterns of flowers and leaves to be embroidered later. *Nature paints for all the world...* Ruskin or Rosetti? Phrases and words, coming to her in an unstoppable manner; perhaps they had taken the place of food in the divot below her ribs, for she was most certainly growing thinner, not rounder as she should have been. Yet there were times when her own words could not seem to find their way out: an object—ash, grate, feathers—that remained lodged in the recesses of her mind and stuck before her tongue.

"You're looking poorly, Claire. Are you sure you have not caught grippe?"

"What a ridiculous thing to say."

"Do you really want to go to all this bother, anyway?"

"What do you mean by that?" She stood up with one hand on her hip, the other holding her encyclopedia-sized volume.

"Never mind."

He set the bricks together into the trench like a miniature wall. He stopped to give her pallor an examination. "You look as if you have a bout of green sickness."

"Thank you very much."

"And, why do you not just go to market? You would have more time to read. I have put Mr Hardy's new one on the shelf for you, if you haven't noticed."

"What kind of a home would we have without a garden? No, on end, please. Twist—no, I mean *turn* it. Yes, like that." She sighed angrily. "Ugh! I am sick of markets," she said, reaching up to press the side of her face. Her cheek and jaw ached. "Markets and fairs, trudging this way and that. Does no one remain stationary anymore? And husbands are not supposed to recommend Mr Hardy, are they? Are they?"

James started to laugh but stopped, as if worried she wasn't joking.

Just then, something flickered in the corner of her sightline. At the far end of the yard where a moment ago there was nothing but the fence and some gravel, now jutted a knee-high marker: grey and worn, a lopsided obelisk. An ancient tomb marker. Behind it, a grassy burial mound began to swell from the gravel. She rubbed her eye with the back of her hand, smearing earth across her eyelid. She blinked again, stupefied. "It is gone now."

James looked at her, his forehead creased.

Something flittered away at the corner of her eye. Something low, bony, crawling quickly and hiding out of sight. A gust of wind kicked up the pile of fallen leaves they had raked, sending them airborne and scattered across the garden.

"There is rain coming," James said, looking away from her and up at the darkening sky. "Claire? Rain."

It's going to rain, soon. You have to look to the river to see if it's coming up, Will had said.

Claire shook her head. "S-s-something," she said. "Something else." She felt a certainty she couldn't explain. More than dreary weather was coming.

Fair is foul, and foul is fair, hover through fog and filthy air... Screw your courage to the sticking place.

TWO

1883 ~ 24th November
Pettypoole, Oxfordshire

The weather was glorious. Peculiar and off-putting, for what November day in any part of England was glorious? In the hot, bright sun, Claire retrieved a letter from Clews Cottage.

"From your sister, is it?" Mrs Fowler asked. She was all pinched dimples as Claire stuffed the letter into her apron pocket.

"Have a nice day, Mrs Fowler."

"An' yourself." Dimples smoothed.

Walking out of the village on the Turnpike Road, Claire entered the hidden path to Grath's meadow, the clearing draped in late autumn gold and burgundy. She didn't know why she had done this, veering from her errands and walking out of town. She supposed it was the warmth of false summer beckoning her.

She saw James' birds, etched months ago into the tree. They were greyed and soft, as if they'd always been part of the bark's patterning. The old house on the hill sat like a statue. A shutter was closed by an invisible hand against the unusual heat of the day and Dewen's dog turned a lazy circle and plunked down on the cool stone threshold.

Sitting by the pond, on the flattened autumn grasses, Claire was perspiring in her wool dress. She fanned her face with her hand, then rolled her stockings down and off her feet, assembling them into two balls on the ground next to her boots. Shimmying closer to the pond's edge, she ran her bare feet along the top of the murky water. She hummed a tune she knew from somewhere: a street performer, a peddler…

An old lady who kept Meg and her company in a tea shop. So long ago that was. They were just children. "Fancy learning it?" the woman had asked with a toothless smile. Harriet clanking cups and plates behind the counter, keeping a suspicious eye on the two girls. Had Father left Meg and Claire alone? He must have, Claire thinks now; how else would we have gone from breakfast to dinner on our own in a strange tea shoppe in a strange town?

Claire hadn't heard from Father since he left Pettypoole, nor had Meg, though they both wondered he should have written by now. She was beginning to miss his jolly laugh and musical voice. She grazed the surface of the pond with her toe and thought of that nonsensical pastime they entertained as children when on long journeys — the game in which they would imagine their future homes. Claire wanted someplace light-filled and dry, overlooking a tranquil view of sea or meadow. She wished for it, as other girls dreamed of dolls and ponies.

Dewen's hound turned another circle on his stoop and yawned loudly enough for her to hear his funny, singing sigh. She looked at him, thinking, I wonder if we ought to have a dog? *You know you prefer cats.*

She reached into her pocket for the letter Mrs Fowler had given her. But the envelope was not a pale-yellow parchment at all; in other words, it was not Meg's letter wrapped in her usual stationery. There must have been two letters in the post, and she'd left Meg's on the counter.

"Damnable," she muttered. The last thing she wanted to do was return to face Mrs Fowler, though how else would she read her sister's news?

She looked down at the letter in her hand, which was written on pale grey stationery, and bore a black wax stamp with the singular monogram S. Something about it — the snake-like curve of the initial, the slippery, black gleam of the hardened wax seal — made her feel queasy.

She allowed a moment's hesitation, then she pried opened the envelope, carefully separating the wax seal from one side of the paper.

Jessups Cottage
Harcourting End
Oxfordshire

17 November, 1883

Dear Mrs Ableton,

My sister read the announcement of your marriage in the Cotswolds Weekly and immediately forwarded it to me. I have enlisted her help in finding you, over the years, and I long told her Bettress was the woman's name.

I was Senior Nurse at the Oliver-St. Andrews Sanatorium at St. Edmundbury, Hallborne, for twenty years, and I tended to a woman who spoke lovingly and longingly of her children.

When I realized they would not be brought to see her, I felt it kinder to be economical with the truth. I told her the doctors thought it best her children stay away. In this, I have always feared I behaved wrongly. I might have sent for the woman's family myself. For this, I shall always feel remorse, and I am haunted by the thought of her never resting eyes on her children one last time.

You might think I would not remember one patient out of hundreds I have cared for, but she was a kind gentlewoman with a family, and she did stand out among some of our more hapless residents. When she succumbed after six months, the doctor attempted notification, but her family had relocated. It did seem unusual, to Dr _____ and myself, that a woman with a family and property would have no remittance for a burial, and we had no choice but to intern her in the hospital's public field.

It is with a full but happy heart that I write to you to tell you that I am in possession of something this woman wished her children to have. Write to me and advise that you have received this letter, so that I may send it.

Yours very truly,
Miss Elsa Searton

Claire looked at the letter. She felt confused. Filled with indescribable pity. She noticed her hand shaking as she held the letter, as if it was someone else's hand, the paper between her fingers vibrating.

She then felt a deep breath fill her lungs, the confusion lifting and filled with the relief of understanding. The letter had been a mistake in landing with her. She was not the girl this woman sought. *Is that what you thought? That the letter was meant for you?*

"No, no. Of course not." There was some pitiful woman, a woman with children—three or five, boys and girls, who knew how many? —who had been confined at the sanatorium where— she looked at the signature again—this Miss Searton served. But this was not even the place where Mother had died.

Claire checked the address again, then re-read the beginning: Bettress. Her name had been Bietris, no matter the pronunciation; the Scottish for Dante's love, James had told her that right here in this meadow, beside this very pond. She let the parchment droop in her fingers as she looked at the sky's reflection in the water. The sun had faded, hazing behind cloud-cover, the water a dull metallic sheet.

There was something terrible about the letter, she still felt that in the pit of her stomach. This was something deeply personal and disturbing which had found its way into the wrong hands. And something else Claire now realized was terrible: the fact that it was *not* Mother this Miss Searton wrote of, and the irony of this. For, to hear, all these years later, some anecdote of Mother—to feel her real and alive again—would have been a comfort she never imagined until now. Instead, Claire now found herself in possession of news some other daughter or son perhaps longed for, a grown child she had no idea how to find. The burden, and her powerlessness in it, was devastating.

She felt a sudden, sharp pain on the left side of her abdomen, followed by another clenching pain lower, in her womb. She felt her back clench next, and she involuntarily thrust forward before the water's edge. She thought, in a fleeting second of clarity, that she would fall into the forbidding murk and then, in another second, she thought, I am no longer expectant. She scrambled to stand, red warmth spilling down her legs.

She hobbled uneasily with her bare feet blistering inside her boots, carrying one stocking hidden tightly in her fist, the other lodged under her skirts between her legs.

At home, she collapsed into bed.

When he called her name, she didn't hear it at first. She became aware of him only when he entered the bedchamber. She could hear her own voice as a low moan, as if she was listening to something apart from herself. The setting sun through clouds cast a dull brown haze across the floor, around which the furniture appeared indistinct and grainy, like subjects in a photograph who forgot to sit still. So silent… No crackle of the range, no hiss of gas. A match struck, snap-snap-shhhh, and the bedside lamp lit in sharp illumination.

James held onto her shoulders, peered into her face, put a cold compress on her forehead, and felt her pulse on her neck, as though these actions were accomplished all at once, though that was quite impossible.

"Are you in pain? Claire?"

She whispered, or thought she whispered, "Something is wrong." The moisture has gone from her mouth, replaced with a sort of bitter chalky texture. The warm damp between her legs remained.

"Stay here, do not move," he commanded, as if she could do otherwise.

One wave of pain was followed by another, and another, the pain getting worse with each wave. She imagined undulating gusts of wind, leaves rising and falling on the bending branches of great trees. She imagined the wind in the trees until she fooled herself into a field with nothing in front of her but a line of trees waving. She wanted to tell someone about the pain, the sharpness of it, but instead she muttered, "Branches." Then that woman Izzie was standing over her, holding her wrist. Izzie said, "You've had quite a fright, haven't you?"

"Yes," Claire answered now, to no one. "I am frightened."

Some time passed. It flickered and stuttered ahead, she knew not how or for how long. The village doctor was a tiny little wire of a man, with the strength of two, and he'd been standing there for some time before Claire had realized it was him. She'd recognized his sharp, confident voice. Then, came an inspection, of her body, and more conversation. "Her complexion is one of green sickness, but there is more to this than that. There is always Hysteria," he noted. "Young women are prone, especially the motherless ones. Or a tumor. Might be a tumor. In any event, she has only had her menses at the moment."

He spoke to James while standing at the foot of the bed, as if she was not present. *You are not really, are you?* He had examined her thoroughly, the wrench and shame of his invasive touch lingering on Claire like grit. She had kept her eyes tightly shut, each prod and plunge another gust of wind causing her trees' branches to crack and break. Now, listening to him drone, she felt like his hands were still inside her.

"Then she's not...?" asked James.

"She is not with-child. At least, it does not seem she was. She could have been. Ah, well, there is always a next time. But she has lost a fair amount of blood. Have you any beef?"

"I do not think," James looked around the bedchamber with some bafflement, "I do not think she purchased anything. There is some lamb in the pot, left over from yesterday."

"It is too late for the butcher," the physician said, pulling out his watch and flipping it open. "Go to The Weaver's Wheel and have them give you a cut of beef. Tell them to sear it only a little, then bring it back here. I shall wait while you do so. And take that necklace off, it will choke her."

"She never takes it off. Forgive me, but did you say a tumor?"

"I should not think it that. Not yet, at any rate."

When James left for the pub, the doctor leaned over Claire, very close, the smile on his face wiped straight. His silver hair smelled of stringent pomade, his skin translucent and speckled as a snail's. "You have only been with your husband?"

Claire looked at him, perplexed. She nodded.

"He may be different than the rest of us, but he is still your husband." A bit of saliva from his mouth reached her cheek, and his breath carried the scent of pipe tobacco and iodine. "Unfaithful wives are afflicted with all kinds of maladies. Remember that. If you do not, God will, and so will I."

He held her arm, and she saw with horror the bowl of steaming water on the nightstand. Before she could pull away, his lancet pierced her forearm, blood draining through steam and staining the white bowl red. "Hold this," he ordered, slapping a cloth over the stinging wound. "Press down."

She slipped into unconsciousness.

When she came-to, James stood beside the bed holding a plate of sliced beef. Blood surrounded it like a mote around a castle. There was a pile of boiled greens, too, soaking in the blood. The bowl with her own blood in it had been taken away. At first, the food smelled good, and she ate some, but it soon made her feel nauseated. She was sore and light-headed. Everything in her body and head hurt.

"You are to take this, love," said James, spooning a bit of bitter syrup into her mouth. *Laudanum.*

She fell back to sleep.

Her mother, wearing a dressing gown as white as her complexion, stood with a nurse in a graveyard. Claire watched them from behind a barren blackberry hedge, where she was crouched. Claire's feet were bare on the winter ground, and she thought to herself that she always had shoes, even before Allswell when they sometimes did not have food. So, where were her shoes now?

She wanted nothing more than to go to Mother, to throw her arms around her. But something held her back.

"Look at her eyes," Father said, suddenly appearing next to her. He was smaller than he was normally, an intensity about him making him seem like a strange goblin imparting a secret she did not want to hear.

Mother's eyes were entirely pale as she stood in the graveyard, her pupils a dull grey. She rotated her head slowly and peered at Claire with vacant desperation. She reached out her hand as if trying to touch her daughter from afar. So bony and long were her fingers… reaching for Claire.

"She can see us," cried Father, "you must come with me quickly or death will follow!"

Claire ran away, running in her cold, bare feet toward where she thought there must be a road. She couldn't breathe. The pebbly ground hurt her bare soles. She looked next to her and realized she'd lost Father. She reached the road and tried to wave down a coach, but it passed her by.

Then she and Meg were in the black carriage together, as they had always been in her dream that she had not had in months and months. There was no city avenue this time, they'd already gone through the park's gate, and the coach was rocking in a wide, leaning undulation as though a ship at sea in a wild storm.

"The Sea is also water," said Bella's voice, but the sight of the black horse's powerful spine as he pulled them faster and faster distracted Claire from thinking about water and its possible meanings. She heard Bella's voice, but she could not see her — it was only Claire and Meg in the carriage. She must tell Bella everything. She must remember everything this time. But all she could do was cry out for her sister, the two of them holding onto each other as they were thrown over the side of the bridge towards the lake below.

THREE

1883 ~ 2nd December
Pettypoole, Oxfordshire

"**B**abbage informs me that my examinations are not challenging enough," Freddy announced at supper. "He complains my pupils' maths scores are too high. Too high, you understand."

There was always this sort of comedic grievance he loved to enact, and Claire did not mind it.

"It is sheer laziness that gets you into this kind of trouble, Freddy," James retorted. "It's true that you must make them work harder or you will not be helping them. Good God, Claire! What's happened?"

She hid her hand, an angry, puckered burn along the outer edge of it, under her apron. "It's nothing." She scoffed. "Do not interrupt Freddy, it's rude."

"That is a nasty burn," Freddy agreed, wrinkling his nose.

She had not meant to do it. Something had come over her before James and Freddy arrived home for supper. Working in the kitchen, she had felt a swooping panic, almost fainted, and knocked a bowl of onions to the floor. Next, voices like rapid sparks had flooded into her head. One said in a continuous rant, *You will no longer hear the sound of his voice, see him smile again, or feel him hold you; your life as you know it will be gone in an instant.* She had felt the room slipping away and reached out to steady herself, her hand hitting the edge of the oven door.

"Claire, how did you get such a burn?"

"Just foolishness. Looks worse than it is."

Freddy tactfully ignored James' tense tone and returned to moaning about himself. "I'll be sacked, you know. Then Mum will throw me out in the street. Have you an extra blanket and pillow, Claire?"

"You will have to sleep over there," she pointed, flouting James' stare at her.

"In the draughty stairwell? Woman, you are cruel." Freddy hid his head in his elbow and pretended to sob.

"No, I mean— there, that— here," she looked at the sitting room, but she couldn't for the life of her think of the word. "*Floor.*"

James shook his head at her again and exhaled through his nose impatiently.

Later, as the three of them sat by the fire playing cards on a folding table, Freddy said, "There is one thing missing from this lovely abode. Wait... I am listening for it." He put his hand to his ear. "Can you guess what it is I'm listening for?"

"Mice?" asked Claire. She slapped a card down.

"The patter of little feet."

"As I said: mice. Oh, I've got an ace and two queens!"

"You know what he's on about, Claire," said James, "and he'll hear it soon enough." He squeezed her knee under the table.

Claire said to Freddy, "Another brandy?" She plunked down an ace: two and two.

Three months since their wedding, and she'd had her courses four times, which was one too many. *Try that for maths, Freddy.*

Then again, it might be perfectly normal after marriage, how was she to know? The starting point — the first time she'd bled — would have been the right moment to ask about these things. But instead of a mother's calm knowledge, she got that innkeeper's wife who looked on her as a nuisance or a source of amusement. For apparently, it was very amusing for a girl to lose her mother and gain her womanhood in one day.

"That's not a queen, Claire, that's a king," Freddy shouted, "and that means I've won, Ha!"

Near ten o'clock, she saw Freddy to the door, following him onto the landing. "Be a dear, will you?" She handed him his hat along with a letter to be posted.

He read the address on the envelope. "In Lancashire, is your sister? Tyne? Hmm.... I think we might have cousins near abouts. I'll ask Mum."

"My sister has grown fond of it, though the weather is unfathomably dreary."

"She's Mrs Peter Dougherty? That is how our cousin would know her?"

"It sounds funny to my ears, but yes, Mrs Peter Dougherty. Meg-as-Missus."

"It must sound funny to her, too, Mrs Ableton," he laughed. "Oh how I hate referring to Helen as 'Mrs Jones.'"

"You never refer to her as Mrs Jones, you only ever call her Helen."

"Do I? She must hate that." Freddy grinned. "But how is your Father? I do not see a letter here for him."

"I've no idea, actually."

"No?" Freddy tucked Meg's letter into his breast pocket. "He's busy on his adventures, no doubt. And when you hear about them, relate them to me, will you? I miss his tales."

"Do you?" she wrapped his scarf about his neck and kissed his cheek. "Stay warm, please. It is winter, finally. It's as though it came upon us by surprise."

"Hang on," he reached back into his pocket, "but there are two letters here, not one."

"Do you mind?"

"Not at all. Is someone ill? Only, it is addressed to — "

"No, no. All is well. It is only an inquiry for a friend."

"Putting James away, are you?" Freddy winked.

"Good-night, silly boy." Claire turned him around to face the stairs as if they were playing blind man's bluff.

She watched as he walked down and out into the night, the two letters pressed against his heart.

In her letter to Meg, she had not written several things she might have. She didn't say how relieved she was Father only owed one month's rent before he left Pettypoole the day after her wedding (instead, he'd left rolls of silk for the landlord who sold them to a dressmaker from Bonborough). She did not tell her of falling ill that warm day by the pond (she was perfectly well, now, so what would be the point?); or about the grey parchment envelope with its oozing black wax seal and sad message meant for another bride. She told her only about the little painting she bought, and her new coat, and the weather changes.

But Claire had in fact made her mind up that she would try to find the proper recipient of the letter about the woman in hospital, and reconcile the sender's distress. Only, how to do so without calling attention to such a strange and horrible quest? To start, she knew she must write the institution in question (the

second letter in Freddy's pocket). What then? "Excuse me, Mrs
Fowler, but might you have, on your postal list, an unfortunate
woman whose mother was left to die in a poorhouse sanitarium?"
Claire would ask, and she'd say, "Why, yes, I've got three at least;
it happens all the time."

"Not really?"

"No," Mrs Fowler would say, her eyes gleaming with mischief,
"not really. And what makes you think anything about our little
village is your business?"

FOUR

1883 ~ 15th December
Pettypoole, Oxfordshire

The sun was a small, curved triangle at the corner of Pettyton Hall's roof. The orange blaze then moved slightly, and slipped behind Ber St. Eldwyn, sending a twilight shadow across the street. The day had ended.

"We will not make it, James," Claire said, her breath clouding before her in the frosty dusk, "the Sabbath has started." A sharp wind caught the hem of her dress and bit at her ankles as she walked quickly, pulling her husband's elbow as she did.

"The bell tower is not the horizon, Claire," James said with a little laugh as the wind helped them down Mills Lane and inside their cottage, slamming the door behind them.

Their cold cheeks flushed back to life in the warmth of their apartments and James unbuttoned her coat and pulled her close to him. They were still breathing hard, their hearts beating in their chests as they hugged. She inhaled the sweet-tangy scent of his neck and kissed it. He took off his own coat and dropped it to the floor. He pressed himself against her, kissing her and walking them both to the bedroom in a tight embrace. He cradled the small of her back as he let her drop down onto the bed, and he lowered himself over her. He raised Claire's skirts and she drew her knees to his hips.

Afterwards, he unbuttoned her dress, unlaced her stays, and stroked her naked spine as if repeating the act in reverse. He whispered something tender and indistinct into her hair.

She clamped her eyes shut with a rush of ferocious love for him, but also against the surprising pain she felt. Pain across her skin where her stays had rubbed her raw, and a deeper pain inside where he had entered her. She imagined wounds closing, throbs subsiding; she willed that to happen. *But why pain at all? Pain when eating, when walking, when bedding your own husband?*

Claire pressed her right temple and willed the voice into silence. She gritted her teeth against an oncoming head-ache. This had happened to her more frequently, each week that went by. *Your honeymoon is well and done. Did you think it would go on forever?*

On Friday last, James had come home to a Yuletide gift of oranges from the Tinsdales which had rolled off the table and scattered across the floor. Sabbath soup boiled over on the stove, and Claire was curled in a huddle on the floor in front of the still-unlit sitting room hearth. The doctor was called, arriving with some Wisdom of the Ages. "Any exertion, whether intellectual or emotional, might stop the flow of her courses, and could be fatal," he'd said to James and not her. "She'll do best to concentrate on dulling the mind."

Apparently, the cure to whatever had come over her was to flush out whatever had caused it, which was to say anything and nothing (congestion, colic, hobgoblins).

"I believe he has actually taken away my novel that was by the bedside," she'd said later that evening when their Village Genius had departed. "Have you seen it?"

"No." James' eyes had darted nervously around the room, avoiding hers.

"He says I cannot allow myself any irritation. It is bad for the liver. Or the spleen. But must I lie here, thinking of nothing? Do you think I am wrought-up? James?"

"I do not think it, Claire."

"But he thinks so. I did think I was actually ill, with an actual illness," she had said angrily. "But I supposed it is a relief that I am merely a wolverine."

In their room together now, James drew the covers around her, the tender flesh between her legs still stinging. The light had grown darker but not completely dark yet. Outside in the lane, she could hear a sound of shuffling feet, and someone whistling a tune. A call of "Good-evening" from one person to another. The wind rattled the pane gently, but it was warm with James.

"This reminds me of Meg, of our chats at night out of Father's earshot," she told him. She wrapped her hand around one of his, entwining their fingers.

"Then tell me how you really are," he said, "as you would tell your sister."

Claire opened her mouth to speak, but nothing came out. What would she say to Meg? She thought of the nurse's letter, hidden at the bottom of her drawer with her tea tin, as if it was calling out to her.

"This week I have some crewelwork on a pair of draperies and some serviettes to be monogramed," she said.

James scowled; she could hear it even if she could not see it. Her head lay on his chest, his chin in her hair. She always used to be able to hear Meg's glower on moonless nights, accompanied by a little snort.

"Your talents, Claire, are inarguable," he said, at length.

"I have saved three pounds in my tin from the work I've done for Lettie. Sorry, not work, *hobbying*."

"For God's sake, Claire, have you still not taken all that money to the bank yet?" He slid her off his chest and looked at her.

"Give it to Mr Fowler? Are you mad?"

"It is a proper bank, you know, backed by Gurneys. Fowler takes deposits twice weekly at Clews Cottage."

"When he's not slaughtering crippled geldings and she's not rifling through other people's mail."

"Claire, really I—"

"Shh, listen. Someone is singing. Do you hear it?"

"What?" He blinked. He listened. "Mhm, I hear it now. Masters in this hall, hear ye news to-day—Nowell, nowell, nowell," he sang along softly.

Claire smiled. "You like caroling."

He nodded. "I do, actually. Freddy sang in the choir when we were at Kings. I loved to hear them practice at Christmastime. Though I can't rightly say my father would have approved of my even listening."

"He approved of you reading at Oxford, I'm sure. Mother always sang at Christmas. Songs in Irish her mother had taught her. And Father used to take us to a party in St. Allswell— someone he knew in town held a ball each year—but he didn't like us celebrating the day itself."

"Your father is an Athiest."

"A Practicalist."

"What is that?"

"It's a—well, it's someone who practices Practicalism, I suppose. But Mother was… different."

Mother says, Dia leat *—God be with you —when she sends you into the field with the goats; and you picture God beside you, helping herd the stragglers, because maybe God is a little like a collie, or maybe He looks like Mr Bolton, with his serious expression.*

"People will always think differently of us," James said quietly, "for what we believe. For whose children we are, and who our children will be."

She placed her hand on his face and kissed him, trying with a single gesture to make him understand that she'd always lived outside looking in.

When they attended Ber St. Eldwyn every so often, the Rev. Mr Snow-Thorpe, his petite wife by his side holding their chubby baby, was always pleasant to them. But his eyes were pleading as he shook their hands as if to say, "Won't you partake of the Holy Eucharist and save your Soul?" And she thought, when he did this, that this was what it meant for James to be different.

Outside the window, the baritone walking down the lane ceased his singing. A cart rolled by. A dog barked, then a different dog barked in answer from another direction. Then nothing. Something outside had changed. Claire couldn't tell what it was, but the lane below the window sounded —no, felt — different somehow. Leaving the bed, she crouched to the side of the window like an intruder in her own home, and pulled the curtains closed. Darkness dropped into the room. From the edge of the curtain, she peeked at the street.

And that was when she saw a woman standing across the lane, perfectly still and looking directly at the cottages. Looking directly up at their window. The place where the woman's face should have been was shadowed, and Claire squinted as she tried to make her out. The woman's dress, straight and starched, was grey under a black cape. She wore a white lace cap tied under her chin, the cape's hood shrouding most of it. A housemaid's dress? *A nurse's uniform.*

The woman tilted her chin up, the lamplight highlighting her cheekbones. Her face —gaunt, and without eyes —was as though a skull floating in a halo of black. Claire opened her mouth to scream but felt paralyzed.

"What are you doing?" James' voice cut across the room, and Claire jumped. He lit the lamp.

"The candles," she gasped. Feeling sick, terrified, she made haste for the kitchen.

"Claire, come back. You are half-naked."

She ran back to him. "We forgot to light the candles. Where is my dressing gown?" *You forgot to keep the dead away.*

"You did not neglect the Sabbath. I did, I dare say," he shrugged, "but you remembered. That will have to be good enough for God for tonight."

He pulled her back into the folds of the duvet and she curled up against him, drawing her knees to her belly and thinking nothing she did was ever good enough. Her necklace felt gelid against her collarbone, and she shivered, half-wanting to check the window again, half-wanting to light the Shabbat candles just to keep the dark away. *You are not imagining what you saw.*

She pressed her cheek further into James' chest and put the edge of the covers over her ear. In a while she dozed off, and soon the black horse was pulling her and Meg closer to the bridge. Over it they rode, snaking perilously towards the lake.

Claire awakened in the middle of the night disoriented and drenched in perspiration. She rolled over, feeling a stiff ache in her lower back. Then she fell back to sleep.

She found herself in a narrow corridor in a house with clean, light walls hung with small paintings of flower fields: one poppy, one lavender, and sunflowers. There were little doorways and she bent down and climbed through, one after the other, each door in a curved frame as in mythic faeiry abodes. Meg's voice said, "You liked that one with the little doorways, even though it was small, because it felt like someone actually lived there."

The doorways eventually led to a narrow, curving stairwell with a tiny window on the landing. The landing and its leaded window made that section of the stairwell look like a nave in a church. Claire sensed she was alone, the only person in the house. She wondered if she was in the hospital where Mother was sent to get better, but all at once she realized it wasn't a hospital but a place she was expected to be.

She went up the stairs and began searching the house for a room she thought she was supposed to go to— a cheerful room with walls the colour of butter, and windows looking out onto a lush and fertile garden filled with flora that changed as you watched it: buds opening and closing, stalks growing taller, then wilting, then shooting up again. She knew this garden, but could not remember how she knew it, or if she had ever even walked in it. She saw the room in her mind she needed to arrive at but could not get to it. She knew there was also a woman somewhere in the house, whom she needed to meet in that room. Claire circled and circled, through doorways and down hallways, desperate but never finding her.

FIVE

1883 ~ 31st December
Pettypoole, Oxfordshire

Breathless and flushed from dancing, Eloise had her hair done up in too-tight curls, in screaming pink ribbons that matched her bright gown. "A very Happy New Year, Missus!" she blurted, exuberant, as Claire and James entered the party.

"How lovely you look, Eloise," Claire replied.

The room was a whirl of sparkle and music. Wassail, stuffed goose, and New Year's cake lined the banquet table; tapers glowed on windowsills in reflecting duplicates. The Henry family's annual fete at The Golden Lion brimmed with excited guests in their best attire, and the enthusiasm of the room was like a flare going off in Claire's chest. For, here was the site of her own wedding dinner of summer, the room looking far more splendid, and this time credibly so.

"Oh, look, you've come!" Molly Gibson embraced Claire as if she'd returned from a year's voyage, her thick black curls bouncing against Claire's cheek. Before Claire knew it, she was surrounded by all the Gibsons with their trademark contrasting raven and ginger heads of hair. Helen — Mrs Jones — was prying James away and pulling him into a dance.

Claire moved further into the room, bid hello to Mr and Mrs Tinsdale. *(pet the little spaniels, note how festive they are in their matching knitted jumpers)*, and made her way to the banquet table.

"Take this. Drink it." Lettie handed her a glass of punch. "The rose in your cheeks has gone."

"It is very cold out," Claire offered. She rubbed her hands together with zeal.

Lettie pursed her lips, unimpressed. "Then you would be flushed, wouldn't you?" She pressed the glass into Claire's hand and watched her take a sip.

"I almost did not recognize Mr Tinsdale, without his leather apron," Claire said, diverting the subject.

Lettie merely glared at her. "Don't just stand there," she suddenly barked at Glynnis Morton, the Henry's new girl, "Mrs Ableton would like some mince pie!" To Claire she said in a low voice, "Have two pieces, your gown is swallowing you up."

Claire pushed at the extra space between her ribs and bodice with her fingertips, trying to flatten the bubbled fabric.

Molly appeared again and introduced Claire to a young Gibson cousin visiting from the Lake District, his clumsiness heightened by his first party. "Will you dance with Edgar, Claire? Do say you will."

"Listen, it's a quadrille," Claire said, encouraging the boy. He was all of fifteen, though tall as a beanstalk. "Do you know it? Never mind. Hold my hand, like this."

They merged onto the dance floor. Claire shouted the steps to Edgar over the music as his feet tripped and bounced. Next, Freddy cut in for a gavotte. Unsurprisingly, he was a singularly good dancer, and Claire thought he must have filled out every girl's card by now. Her neighbour Mr Fritch insisted on a waltz with her after that. Finally, James cut in for a two-step before suggesting they sit down to eat something.

He brought over a plate of cold meats and jellies and Claire took a measly bite before a wave of nausea colder than the meats sluiced her insides. The music grew louder. The room became brighter, noisier, more frenzied. *Like being trapped at a fairgrounds when you wish to be anywhere else.*

Just before midnight, Claire's head began to throb and she felt her heart race against the clapping and stomping of the dancing guests, the vibrations flowing freely from the floor into her body over and over.

"We ought to go home," she said into James' ear, rather desperately.

"Can you not last just five minutes more?" James said back in Claire's ear, even as she shook her head no. But he knew not to push. He had become as swept-up in what the doctor called her "eccentricities" as she was.

The short walk home was interminable. Frigid. Her head reeled. As the church bell tolled the New Year in twelve shattering gongs, she clung to James' arm, teeth chattering. Her boots slipped on a patch of ice and she gripped him harder and hated herself. It was she who had always steadied Father on late nights, her arm wrapped around little Meg.

In the morning, they were expected at the home of Freddy's older brother Robbie and his wife, where the whole Gibson family were to gather. But James went alone, making excuses for her; some joke about drinking and dancing too much last night would have to do. James gave her a solemn little kiss on the cheek good-by.

Left alone in her room, Claire stared at the corner of the pillowcase. She shuddered in intermittent spasms under a pile of blankets. It was as if the night's chill refused to leave her body. *You create these lovely, comforting images of your life (snug as a bug you are, under the covers) but really, they are made from thin air.*

"Shh!" she begged the voice.

But the voice just rambled, *Do you remember that day you broke into the house on the hill and stole its key? What a cosy, cosy room it was. And you just wishing it to be yours.*

After a while, Claire finally sensed true quiet. Only her breathing whispered into the bland afternoon. A robin chirped from a tree branch outside the window. Perhaps she would get some rest after all and would awake renewed. No printing press, no one shouting on the street. No voice. Good. She sank further under the duvet piled with two additional wool throws and drifted into a comfortable sleep.

A loud banging sounded at the main door to the cottage, downstairs. Claire awakened, startled, with the hairs on her arms prickling, her senses sharp.

There was another loud knock. Then two more in succession. *Bang! Bang-bang!*

She pushed the pillow aside, pressed her ear to the mattress, and listened down through the floorboards. Perhaps it was James, left without his key? Or Davie? But it was New Year's Day and James left over an hour ago, or so the clock read.

The knocking sounded again. Three bangs in rapid succession. The sound was deafening, insistent. Something was not right. Claire lay frozen, listening.

By the pricking of my thumbs... Open locks, whoever knocks.

She shut her eyes tightly, but the image of a woman below the window in the dark, now at their door in daylight, came to her.

The woman's eyes were hollow as a skeleton's and framed by the starched lace of a nurse's cap and a cloak's black hood.

Claire covered her ears and rolled onto her back. *You stupid girl, you are not even making sense!* She put her head under the covers as terror boiled behind her ribcage.

Something else occurred to her then, in a swift realization. It was an awareness of something darker at work, something owed and sought. Someone looking for her and Father. Could that be it? *Give us summat for our troubles, l'il bird.*

Claire put her hand to her mouth and stifled a gag.

The knocking stopped.

An hour later, James' footsteps sounded in the corridor. His key turned in the lock. He appeared in the doorway of their room a moment later with a porcelain vase of paper whites, a red tartan bow wrapped around the vase. His face fell when he saw Claire crouched up at the headboard, the pillows stacked in front of her like a wall of sandbags on a battlefield.

"It is from young Master Thomas," he explained awkwardly, "my good and timid student. They are paper whites. Claire? Has something happened?"

The plant, and the note stuck in it, were encased in ice from sitting on the stoop.

SIX

Mrs Peter Dougherty
Park's End Cottages
Tyne, Lancashire

28ᵗʰ January, 1884

Dearest Claire,

I have just received your letter. I beg you do not do as you suggest! You will scoff at advice from me, the reckless one—do not deny it, Claire, I know you think it of me—but believe me when I tell you that I know something of village life now, and nothing good can come of this. I shall be very angry with you if you go through with it, and I will think you have gone quite mad to even consider it.

Oh, Claire, I am an 'old Mama' now, and I realize how like a mother to me you were all these years. I long to see you, but there is another wee babe in me again, and my other little one not even walking yet, and I cannot keep a bite down. Will you not come visit me? Will your husband not let you travel? And what of

Father? Have you not heard a word from him in all this time? Can you tell me a dream you have seen, of him well and happy, and safe?

> *Your Devoted Sister*
> *Always,*
> *Meg*

SEVEN

1884 ~ 27th February
Pettypoole, Oxfordshire

There were bodies inside the barrow, under the mound's steep incline, the plateau's edges softened by the treading of living humans. Forged centuries ago by ancient peoples, the mound was bright green in summer when children loved to slide down it. In milder winters all the barrows turned a darker, dormant shade of green; but this winter they were rigid and pale brown like the bones beneath them. This winter was especially harsh, a northern wind-blown spitefully south. Frost marred the landscape. Sheep died, and cows and pigs. The survivors were kept inside, littering kitchen floors with their excrement, bleating their mournful songs and spreading fleas from mattress to mattress.

Standing at the top of the garden, Claire could hear the snort and snuff of the neighbours' sow inside their kitchen. How long would it be, she wondered, before the wife butchered it not for meat, but merely to shut it up?

Her own garden —separated from the neighbours' by a slatted fence—was half-rotted and reinfested with slugs, the hardy cabbage in the raised patch now dead, the privy sheathed in ice. *Try opening the door when it's like that, as you stand shaking and not knowing whether to go back to the bucket inside, or round back of the privy to vomit on the frozen ground while the sow squeals at you with delight through the window.*

Isadora... Mrs Issington... What had that woman Izzie's full name been? Back so many years ago. If Claire could only remember the town. It was a day's journey from St. Allswell, but in which direction? She could travel there, no matter how long and terrible the trip, if only she could remember where it was. But she could not even remember what the woman looked like, she had been a blurry phantom. Claire needed her pouch of ground herbs, leaves, whatever it was—the thing that made her feel better that she'd used up over two years ago. She would find the woman and demand, "You must remember me! Make me well again!"

Having used the icy privy, back upstairs in the flat Claire felt a sharp, radiating stab below her naval. This was something new, something more intense and in a slightly different location. She stood in the sitting room, one hand on her belly the other leaning against the back of James' chair. She breathed in, then out. *One, two, four, six...*

Meg had recently written that it had been Harriet *(How on earth could you have forgotten that, Claire?)* who advised a hot flannel on the belly for five minutes, then get on your knees and start scrubbing. The floors, she'd meant, as the exercise kept you from having to stand and, also, it directed your face down so as not to belie a pained expression to others. Just keep busy, in other words, and no one will notice. Hide what makes you vulnerable and no one will prey on you.

Downstairs in the print shop, lately Davie had become wary of her. He behaved as if Miss Able was a poltergeist roaming the house, popping out now and then just to frighten him. It cut her heart that he would not ask her for tea.

Mr Fritch, too, had asked Mr Tinsdale if she had a fever. She'd heard them talking from the landing one day. Had she ever been to India? Her neighbour and friend had asked. The Dark Continent? How could they know for certain where she had been before she came to Pettypoole? For she traveled the globe, was what her father had told everyone.

An hour later (scrub brush left in bucket), she made her way to Henry's. *This is how you manage going out into the world: you preen and prepare, you stall and rest between stalling, until you are ready to put your face on; your good face, you hope, the one that does not divulge how you really feel.*

Henry's Stores was crowded with customers, Eloise and Glynnis floating about like dragonflies from table to customer, to rack or shelf.

"Get yourself in order." Lettie's voice was a barely audible snap. She refused to make a scene in front of anyone, let alone paying clientele. Instead, she tallied half of Claire's usual inventory on her little notepad, then said, in more of a command than a comment, "Stop starving yourself. Men don't fancy bony girls. Stuff your cheeks and get yourself in the family way. That's my last bit of advice, so you'd better take it."

Claire curtsied and turned to leave, trying to walk straight as she passed Glynnis Morton bringing linens from the storeroom. "Gypsy whore," Miss Morton said to Claire, not very under her breath.

Pretending not to hear her, Claire stepped back onto the street. She realized she still hadn't eaten breakfast, so she crossed the cobbles to the tea shop. She pushed the door. The bell jingled a little, but the door didn't budge. The curtain was drawn against the panes of both window and door, and she wondered where Kyle was, then wondered nonsensically if it was Sunday and how it had become Sunday just by her crossing the street.

She walked to the Post.

"It's only the two letters there for you, and the book for Mr Ableton." Mrs Fowler slapped the mail down. Her fingers drummed the counter, slowly, like an execution rhythm, as she watched Claire take the batch.

"Thank you, Mrs Fowler." She looked down. There was another letter from Meg, and a second one next to it.

"You don't get much mail, do you? Not a good deal, anyways." One of the terriers batted a dangling stretch of reed from a half-worked basket.

"That depends on what one thinks is a good deal of mail," Claire answered dully. She flipped the other letter over, read the post stamp, put it back in with the others.

"And Mr Ableton?" Mrs Fowler cocked her head and forced a smile. "How is he?"

"He is well, thank you. He'll be pleased his book has arrived. Is the tea shop closed?"

There was a whole width of counter between them, but even so, Mrs Fowler took a step back. She crossed her arms. "And yourself? How is your health?" One of the dogs yipped. She ignored it.

"Quite well, thank you. I asked if the tea shop is closed?"

"I see." She kept her eyes on Claire while shooing the dog back into its bed with her foot.

"May I?" Claire motioned to a stool by the window. The room felt close, and warm from the stove in the corner. She felt lightheaded. She should have eaten something earlier.

"If you must." Mrs Fowler took another step back with her half-finished basket, all the while looking at Claire as her hands plucked and threaded.

Claire opened one of the envelopes and inside was a tintype of Meg with a mass of white lace on her knee, a cherub face staring amazed at the world. Meg's figure was full as the day Claire last saw her. Perhaps she would always be this way now, one babe after the next filling her out with voluptuary beauty. She tucked the photograph back into the envelope and rested it on her knees, the heels of her boots balancing on the stool's spindle. She held the other letter tightly.

The bell over the door sounded and in sauntered Valentine Pell.

"Come for your mail, Miss Pell? On your day off. You've a package today."

"Thank you, Mrs Fowler. Has Mr MacManus returned to us?" she asked with a bit of gleeful dread. "Good gracious, I can see from the look on your face that he has not! His boy is looking everywhere for him. Wife's ready to put his things on the street. Yesterday afternoon it's been, since he was seen at The Lantern."

"So I've heard..." Mrs Fowler's voice dropped, as did Val's, the two of them quietly but furiously chattering.

After a moment, Claire heard Valentine murmur, "She won't make her orders this month."

Now she was on to poor Eloise, Claire thought. But then...

"And if it's one thing a Jew is good with, Mrs Fowler, it's money. Don't suppose her husband is pleased with her now, is he? Don't suppose he regrets ever meeting her...?" Miss Pell slid her eyes to Claire. She peered at Claire harder, her pale-lashed little orbs narrowing and flinching.

Inside her head, Claire boiled. She thought about yanking the iron bells from the door and cracking them over Miss Valentine Pell's head. She stood quickly, awkwardly, the stool tipping over in a clumsy, ridiculous gesture and crashing to the floor. "Good-day, Mrs Fowler!" she called out.

Miss Pell barked with laughter. Perhaps if Claire was lucky (which, clearly, she was not), one of the dogs would bounce up at the sound and bite her in the face. Gathering the letters which had fallen to the floor, Claire strode out the door, tripping again as she did. *You fool! No wonder they laugh at you.*

From outside, she glanced back at the window through which she saw Mrs Fowler racing from behind the counter with a bucket and rag in-hand, scouring every surface had Claire touched.

Crossing back to the opposite side of the street, she turned into the narrow, sheltered alleyway between the Butchers & Butterman's and The Weaver's Wheel, the closed tea shop adjoining. Usually, the alleyway smelled of baking bread and too-sweet puddings; today it smelled of cold, damp stone and the pub's refuse bin. Claire looked at the second letter and read the postmark again—St. Edmundbury, Hallborne—then opened it.

St. Edmundbury Town Hall
St. Edmundbury Parish, Hallborne

10ᵇ February, 1884

Dear Mrs Ableton,

Please be advised that the Oliver-St. Andrews Sanitorium in St. Edmundbury was closed eight years ago under the Hundreds Reform Laws of that year. Though it had hoped to be a beacon of care upon its opening, by its closing it had been deemed one of the most abysmal institutions of its kind. I took the liberty of looking into the matter of Records, but regretfully there are no surviving papers of inmates at Oliver-St. Andrews, on account of a fire in an Easterly wing where such papers were stored. I wish I could be of more help to you in placing your enclosed letter with the proper recipient but, as I cannot, I return it to you now.

Yours Faithfully,
Thomas Kersey, clerk

Claire read the letter again and wondered what the clerk meant by "one of the most abysmal institutions of its kind." Abysmal she knew. But institutions of which kind? A workhouse? A debtor's prison? A madhouse? She tasted the sour burn of sick on the back of her tongue. She pried the opening of the envelope wider and looked at the returned letter from the nurse, Miss Black Wax S.

Standing in the biting wind of the alleyway while looking down at the envelope, a terrible idea began to form in her mind.

Suppose, she thought, the whole story was off? Suppose Miss Searton was not who she said she was (maybe Miss Searton was a former patient, for instance, and not a nurse)? Suppose Oliver-St. Andrews was not the sort of hospital you brought someone to be made well, but rather to intern them indefinitely?

And just suppose, Claire began to think, I'd been contacted not because of any unclaimed gift (because, really, how likely was it anyone would care about a trifle so many years later) but because—as the sender had written—my engagement had been in the newspaper? It was Father who'd placed the announcement, and he would have been mentioned as well. *The proud but not particularly shrewd Father of the Bride.*

And perhaps, Claire thought now (the shadows on the High Street growing long and bold as she hid between the buildings), this was all one of Father's missteps. An investment in some kind of new factory or workhouse, gone belly-up with the closing of the place. Miss S, she realized, could very well be *Mister S*, an investor swindled years ago and very happy indeed to find his swindler mentioned in the Cotswolds Gazette recently.

Claire turned the clerk's envelope over, checked the embossed letterhead at the top—which was all in order, official Town Hall stationery, etc.—and peeked again at the older letter stuffed in with the current one. The grey vellum, the not-quite-matching envelope, that curious black seal that gave one a sense of dread when one touched it...

Claire felt the blood drain from her face. *When one touched it...*

Careful not to break the sealing wax further, she held tightly onto the envelope and ran home.

She ran up the stairs, used one hand to key the latch, and pushed the door to her flat open with her shoulder.

Still in her coat, she held the envelope by the corner and rushed to the kitchen. Opening the stove door, she tossed it in. She added a handful of sticks, struck a match and lit the two nestled letters. Shortly, the flame grew. The paper and melted sealing wax—the red of today's letter, and the broken black of September's—burst into flame, then turned to ash.

Claire threw open the window and placed her coat over the sill. She boiled water, fetched soap, and scrubbed her hands and arms pink while standing barefoot in her pantaloons and stays. Nauseated and weak, she leaned her wet elbows on the edge of the scrubbed table, knowing that likely, it was far too late. But knowing, too, that she had no other choice but to do as Meg had begged her not to do.

EIGHT

1884 ~ 29ᵗʰ February, early morning
Pettypoole, Oxfordshire

The lilac of first light had resolved to a bland, unidentifiable murk. The bridge was treacherous with ice, and under it, thin water tripped over frost-coated rocks.

Last night, the night after she had received and burned the letters, she had fallen ill again. The physician wondered at how Claire managed to perspire and shiver simultaneously whilst not registering a temperature. She was like a magician whose tricks no one could crack. Her body was giving-in to illness, but her brains... Maybe there are just enough of them left to be of help.

This morning, as James slept, Claire crept in stocking feet from the house, holding her boots until she was outside. She was still groggy from the drought she was made to drink last night. Groggy and nauseated, but not in pain. Yet.

The former midwife who delivered two of Lord Hammpen's children until something went wrong with the birthing of the third had been banished to the Shirre Wood. Mrs Norris, if rumors were to be believed. A witch, she was called. Possessing dark and dreaded powers as if, Claire thought, anyone believed such old-fashioned nonsense, which of course they did not. *But oh, how people still love to persecute and bully, don't they?*

And what did Claire care about rumors, anyway? When you suspected you've been poisoned—by a real person, with real mal intent, not by a make-believe character in a child's fairy tale— you didn't dwell on the ifs and maybes, the what-might-happens. You hadn't time to.

Several weeks ago, Claire had obtained from Mrs Fowler more precise details of Lord Edwin and Lady Mina Hammpen's stillborn sibling. "I wonder has that Shirre woman who delivered the poor babe lived her whole life in Pettypoole?" Claire mused aloud and Mrs Fowler had chimed in that no, the woman was not originally from Pettypoole but from somewhere in Sussex. Somewhere in Sussex.

After crossing the bridge, Claire took the Roman Road. After about a mile, she climbed over the stile onto the high wold where ewes stood in the bitter wind, their long fleece caked with frozen mud. As she walked among the herd, she stopped and leaned on one female to catch her breath, the heat of the animal's fat radiating through her thick, matted wool. From here, the grassland sloped into a small deep vale, where the ancient abbey with its long-ago-lost roof stood nestled in repose. In the bland dawn, the abbey's hollowed windows appeared black, as if all inside was filled with dense matter. She had never liked it, not since that night spent near it in the cart.

One of the gamekeepers from the Manor ambled onto the field at the far end with two gun-dogs at his side. She couldn't tell who it was at first; most of the men who worked for his Lordship were sour and brusque though Norris, as everyone knew, was more fearsome due to his being more intelligent.

The man walked toward Claire, rifle and stick of rabbits over his shoulder. The rabbits bounced off the man's back. His eyes stayed straight ahead even though Claire was in his view. Clouds of breath framed his wind-burned face and askew nose. Yes, it was Norris, such was her luck, and here she was off to pay his mum a visit.

Do invite him to come along. Wouldn't that be lovely, you three having tea?

The dull clomp of Norris' boots thudded along the ground. Both dogs suddenly bolted as if on the scent, and for a brief moment she thought they were about to charge her. As he passed by, Norris glanced at Claire for a moment and spat on the ground, then continued on, the rabbits bouncing over his back, their dead, wide-eyed faces gawking at the sky.

Blast it all if something about him—something more than his usual menace—did not gnaw at her now as she watched him. But what, besides common rudeness? She couldn't pinpoint it. *You'd better keep moving, before your courage fails you.*

"Shhh," she admonished the voice softly.

She crossed over the next field, and the wind bit her cheeks raw as she hiked until a huge stone windmill appeared, perched on top of another plateau. The site was a Roman staging camp, though the windmill was built only a hundred years ago and was already abandoned, its blades dismantled. It was a testament to the truly human trait of creating and destroying, then recreating all over again. A steep barrow rimmed the perimeter of the site, and Claire slid down its outer side, the palms of her hands gripping the splintering, frosty grass.

Before her, in a hollow, was the Shirre Wood. The sky could barely be seen through the evergreen canopy above, the floor a moss and needle carpet, though not a welcoming one. A little way in, a cottage stood in a clearing. It had buckled stone and plaster walls and a thatched roof in bad need of repair: a structure not many would occupy with relish. A single, sickly goat was tied to a post in the yard.

Claire hesitated at the blackened pine door. Her heart struck irregular and quick. Inside this hovel was the woman she had contemplated and wished for—her face dim and fogged with fevered memory from what was the worst day of Claire's life: not that first night without Mother sleeping in the open cart, but the day she actually realized Mother was gone forever, and that there would be no comfort or help for her as she herself lay dying with only the sound of her little sister wailing.

This was why Father had brought her to Pettypoole, Claire knew now, because she had always been meant to meet the woman again. For here, too, was where the woman herself ended up. Claire felt a swell of gratitude at Father's silly whims and hair-brained plans, and she almost cried with missing him. He would have been shocked to see her—all bones and sallow skin, a bloodless mouth, a head split-open with pain; he would have burst into tears himself.

Claire knocked on the door. There was shuffling on the other side, and with a low creak the door opened. Shadowed by the dark interior was a mingy woman with soiled white hair plaited into two long, snarled tails. With her whole body came a stench of decay. She examined Claire with clenched pale eyes, up and down, as though wondering if she was the cause of the unpleasant odor.

"Well?"

"I am sorry, I should not have…" Claire began.

The woman waved her in. The woman was rawboned, necessitous, and utterly unfamiliar.

Claire stepped inside.

"And it has been six moons, say you? Six moons?" The old woman spoke with a hoarse crackle, an enunciation Claire associated with a Mediaeval hermit. Martyrs and plagues, burning stakes and boils. She must have been eighty years old, and a good head shorter than Claire.

"It is almost six months since my marriage," Claire told her. The woman was hard-of-hearing but insistent on details. She herded Claire to the open hearth where a small fire burned, and wrapped her in a wool throw, the raw and grainy fibers bristling against Claire's arms. A loom was plunked in a corner of the cramped room, a pile of combed felt in a basket next to it.

"Sit down. Your bleeding—it is at the full moon or the new?"

"It changes. Have you lived here long?"

"What? Born in Pettypoole, down Eldwin Mews. You're not from here, I can see that." The woman furrowed her tangled brows and clucked her tongue, her diminutive figure lost under a shapeless tunic cinched at the waist by a stained calico apron. She approached a long wood table where bowls and bottles were kept near a mortar and pestle. Burlap pouches and glass jars filled with herbs and more ominous-looking things lined a shelf on the uneven wall. The aromas of the barks and oils were, taken together, putrid.

"My sense of scent is magnified," Claire offered, trying not to offend the woman. "I mean generally. The Butcher & Butterman's is bad."

The old woman laughed loudly, then hacked a sharp, phlegmy cough. "The butcher's in Pettypoole has always had a bad stench, that's nothing new! They sellin' summat other than cats now, are they? Ha!"

But when she faced Claire again she was no longer laughing, and Claire felt that same fear creeping over her as earlier, when she saw the black windows of the godless abbey.

"The doctor has not been of much help." That is why I am here, in this squalid place with a raving lunatic, Claire wanted to add, though until this moment she had not equated "useless" with her own death. How stupid I am, Claire then thought, stupid to believe this woman could have been a healer named Izzie who had once cared a minute for her.

"Six months say you, and no babe? And the head-achs. Yes, I know, I know." She waved her hand, dismissively. The tone of the woman's voice deepened as she spoke, like the swooping flap of a raven, grim and cold across Claire's heart. She returned to the table, spoke to the bottles she had placed there as if each was a miniature, cognizant being.

Claire was frightened; the old woman knew this, and Claire knew that she knew this. It was hard to make out other emotions in the room, or the origins of them. Of late, Claire's sharp head-pains had transformed into blinding agony and incongruous scenes even a martyr would not be able to decipher: a sparrow hitting a window pane; Meghan fearfully slamming a door; Claire's hands thrust into the frozen pond; Mother pricking her finger; the butter-coloured dream room with the rapidly-growing garden; Harriet crying in a corner; the son of that copper-haired silver dealer she had all but forgotten also crying, and the dealer himself giving her a menacing wink... on and on the visions blathered, with no other purpose than to drive Claire mad and give her the false hope that all might be put right today.

"My words. Sometimes I cannot find them," she told the woman.

"Your head is muddled."

"Yes. Sometimes. Look, am I poisoned? I think I've been poisoned. I received a letter. The paper—the wax seal—they can be doused with poisons, can't they?"

The woman laughed again. "Who do you think you are, the Queen? Why would anyone want you dead? Anyway, 'tisn't the first time you've been poorly. Agreed?"

"Once, when I was young. But—"

She waved at Claire, dismissively.

"Fine, then," Claire quipped. "What do I do about it?"

"It's what I can do. You do not have that kind of power... Though," she squinted at Claire, tilted her head. "Though you have some power, yes?" she asked slowly, more quietly. "You see things."

"No," she lied, "I see nothing." Claire felt deathly afraid. *It was wrong to come. Meg was right.*

The woman spooned some paste into a small glass jar, and what looked like crushed leaves into a little box.

"Give me your wrist again." She grabbed hold of Claire's wrist. "The pulses... the pulses... This metal," she grasped Claire's necklace before she could stop her. "The ring is too heavy. You should not wear it so close to your throat."

Claire held onto the ring, squeezing the woman's fingers off of it, her leathery skin sliding against the tiny sharp bones of her joints. She worried she could break her finger. She wanted to break her finger.

"So keep it," the woman smirked, "it's your neck. Anyway, your spleen's got trouble. Bile gathering in the wrong place. Listen to me," she announced. "You take this with a wooden spoon, yes?" She held up the jar. "And this one, drink with milk in the afternoon; and this one with whiskey at nightfall." She pursed her pruned lips confidently. "You'll be fine."

But as Claire rose with her stash tied up in a bit of calico, the woman took her hand again and squeezed hard. She put her face close, her pale eyes mere inches from hers. "Do not tell anyone about what you see. Your visions— never tell!"

Claire yanked her hand back. She threw off the wool blanket and put some coins on the table, afraid to touch the woman again.

As she walked away from the hovel, the old midwife called out to her and Claire turned reluctantly. "What is it?"

"You must make your cycle happen with the full moon!"

"But I'm on the new," Claire called back against the lifting wind, "and not always then."

"No, no, canna be on the new. Must be the full moon or it won't work. Take the powders, then pray every night for the full moon." She waved and shut the door.

Claire stood alone in the glen, the wind fierce and biting through her long, thick coat. Thirty buttons all down the front, Eloise had said. What all the ladies are wearing now.

NINE

1884, 29th February, that afternoon
Pettypoole, Oxfordshire

On the walk home, Claire's hand began its involuntary stretch to her eyes. Next, her fingers made their way to the back of her neck as if on their own accord, trying to locate the source of the pain before the rest of her body recognized it. It was more sudden than usual, this head-ach, and the trek in the cold had not helped any.

She rounded the corner of Mills Lane and could hear the printing press through the closed windows of the storefront, could already feel the vibrations in the pebbles under her feet. She opened the door into the entryway of the cottage.

One flight up, and you will be there, and just thank God James did not rent the garret.

Clack-clack-clack went the press, filling the hall with its workings.

Just keep moving, one foot in front of the other.

Up a step, then the next. But half-way up, there was a movement, another sound, that forced her to stop.

"Davie?" She blinked in case it wasn't him but someone else; some phantom image from the migraine fluttering at the corners of her eyes.

But it was Davie. The boy, mud-smeared and shivering, stared up at her from the threshold of the open door with hollow eyes. He must have been just behind her when she came in, but she had no awareness of him following her.

"Close that, dear." She gestured to the door. but suddenly it was abruptly clear to her there was a much greater problem at hand than the draught. "Davie? What is it?" She held her skirts and stepped back down the stairs toward him, gingerly, slowly. Like a stray cat, he fixed his eyes on her and stiffened. "Davie? Are you alright?" Her head felt like it was splitting open and her lids fluttered. There was a rage of pain but also the boy, who seemed in more trouble than she, both predicaments filling the space between them.

Finally, she thought to call out. "Mr Tinsdale!"

The mud-covered boy took a step back.

"No, no," Claire whispered to him. "Shhh... stay right there, Davie dear."

She shouted again in the direction of the shop door—a real scream this time against the hum and clack of the press, and she hoped to God her voice wouldn't scare Davie off. There was a slowing down of the machinery, and then quiet.

"Hullo, Mrs Ableton?" Her landlord popped his head into the corridor.

She gestured to Davie, whose palms, she noticed, were also coated in mud; one with a jagged gash. He hadn't just been out collecting wood: there was an alarming and sinister quality to his whole appearance.

"What's this all about, lad?" Mr Tinsdale, also uneasy, approached the boy and held him gently by the shoulders. "I thought you were late in coming." He put a hand on Davie's earth-streaked cheeks and tried to wipe the dried earth. "What's happened, then? Can you tell us?"

Snapping out of her own fug, Claire came down the remaining stairs and slammed the still open front door against another vindictive gust.

"Help me sit him down in the shop, Mrs Ableton. We'll get to the bottom of this."

The print shop was miraculously warm and dry, as if the sheets of vellum had absorbed all moisture, all trace of mildew and damp. In a moment, Claire had the kettle to a boil.

"There," she said, handing Davie the cup.

He let her stroke him gently on the back, and her heart soared for the trust he imparted to her, his terrifying banshee. For a moment, she felt everything would be all right. Then she looked at the boy again, examining his face and clothes, and felt an awful gloom descend upon them.

"Now, son, slowly tell." Mr Tinsdale nodded. He stood in front of the boy and put a hand on his shoulder. "Go on, then."

"Mum says the old Celts bur-bur-buried them," Davie stuttered. "The manner'd made 'em go under."

Mr Tinsdale glanced at Claire, quizzically. "Alright, now. That's good. That's a start. Your mam's been telling you stories, has she? In the manner of the Celts, fairy tales and the like?"

Davie shook his head. "The manner made 'em go under," a scooping motion with his hand, as if diving down, "su-supposed to be under."

"The barrows," Claire said, a lamp inside her head turning up. "The long-barrows at Hammpen Manor is where they buried their dead, long ago." She thought of Aunt Aileen's tree, of Mother's stories and songs.

Mr Tinsdale's eyes widened. Then he nodded. "I wouldn't have gotten all that." He gave an uneasy chuckle; it was clear she was not supposed to have gotten all that.

Davie looked up at Claire and stirred in his chair as if it was heating up beneath him. "Did you take him up, Miss Able? D-did you?"

"Calm down, lad. Be calm now," soothed Mr Tinsdale. "Mrs Ableton is our friend. She is here to help, as am I."

"Did I take who up, dear?" Now it was Claire who felt uneasy. *Beannaigh an bhiotáille de na crainn… Her spirit is still in the blessed tree.*

"The man, the man! He shouldn'a be up!" Davie shouted, wriggling in his seat, his bulging eyes darting from Claire to Mr Tinsdale and back to Claire. "The man—th-the mud man, all full o' blood an' mud, an' I was jus' walking over 'em, jus' a sk-sk-skip, an' I did trip 'cos Mum always says, 'Davie, watch your step on the heath' b-but I didna an' I fell." He cried hard, sobbing, streaks of tears revealing pink skin beneath the earthen mask.

"You do not think this has to do with Mr MacManus?" Claire asked Mr Tinsdale with a lowered voice.

"To do with Kyle?"

"He's gone missing."

"Has he?" Mr Tinsdale was startled at the news.

"Never mind," she said, "I must have heard wrong."

"All right now, take some of this lovely tea Mrs Ableton has made," he told Davie. "That's it. Let's start again, shall we? You said you fell, yes?" He wiped Davie's cheeks and nose with a cloth stained with ink, a Dalmatian patterned remnant. "Now, think Davie, up at Hammpen Manor— did his Lordship's man see you? Rollins—did you run into him? You know he's not much brighter than you, 'bless your little soul. He wouldn't mean you too much harm—though he's a big man, Rollins, isn't he, Mrs Ableton?"

She felt a sag of relief within her before she quickly became incensed. "No. It is Norris, Mr Tinsdale, not Rollins. Surely, that must be it. He's a nasty man, Mr Tinsdale. He is, very."

Mr Tinsdale grimaced, nodding furiously. "Yes. Yes, that's it, of course that's it. It's got to be Norris. All right, Davie, you listen to me — just pay him no mind. Pay him no mind at all. And you're to stay off Lord Hammpen's estate on your way home, you know that, so never do it again. Understand me? Never! You take the road proper from your mum's house. Come now, you're all right—he's not pushed you down too hard, eh? That Norris," he turned to Claire. "I've never liked him. No one does, you know."

"He was quite rude to me earlier."

"You've seen him today, have you?"

Mashing his fist into his eye, Davie hiccupped. "Doctor has 'im now. Constable took 'im away."

Mr Tinsdale and Claire looked at each other again. "A row?" he suggested to her. "Had a real row with Davie here?" He chuckled, a little smile on his face. "I wouldn't have thought Norris could be hurt all that badly by our little Davie, would you, Mrs Ableton?"

"No, indeed," she agreed, smiling, though all she could think of was Doctor. Yellowy pools of light had begun circling her periphery. The pain in her head was a tunnel she was falling back into quickly. "I will go see about it now," she said.

And before Mr Tinsdale could stop her swift resolve to straighten out a situation she had no business being part of, she was out the door and back into the binding damp.

A moment later, she regretted the lack of her muffler and hat — both left in the press room — but the regret was like the mist moving across the River Poole: disobliging and fleeting.

Ber St. Eldwyn's bell tower sounded out the afternoon, its resonance reverberating through the streets.

As she neared the gates, the vicar called out to her. He had just locked the double doors to the church and hurried up the path. "Mrs Ableton... Mrs Ableton, just a moment." He opened the gate and took a step toward her.

"Mr Snow-Thorpe, hullo." *Twist your mouth, make a smile, keep walking.*

"I do not think ladies should be out and about just now." His normally mild face was etched with misgivings. He quickly wrapped his scarf around his neck and began buttoning his overcoat. "I have just locked the chapel doors, which I do not care to do but think I must."

"Excuse me, Vicar?" she slowed but did not stop walking completely.

"I've told my wife to return to the rectory with the baby. She was out in the garden, in a sheltered spot but one that is perhaps too remote for me to hear her. Have you no bonnet, Mrs Ableton? It is very windy and cold. Nevermind."

They were now, she and the Vicar, almost facing each other. She paused, then took a step or two again.

"Mrs Ableton, listen to me. I advise you go back home until this matter is resolved. Please." He reached out his hand, making that grasping gesture he was so good at.

Still on the move, her arm brushed against his hand. "I am sorry. But I must," she said to him over her shoulder.

"Mrs Ableton, you must not..." but his voice was lost on the wind as she quickened her pace.

Doctor, was all her ears kept hearing, from inside her own head. The Village Idiot, she and James called him, though he was also the only one who had the syringe from which drops entered her veins and coated her sharpened brain in sweet syrup.

Try to remember to ask about Norris. For Davie, poor thing, try to remember it for Davie.

"Poor thing," she heard herself mutter. "Dear God," she prayed aloud, "just get me past Henry's without running into anyone else."

The lamps in Pettyton Hall were turned up brightly against the stormy dusk, as if furious labour was about to commence just in time for supper. Voices were at full volume as always, but there was hardly a laugh to punctuate the din. Something was indeed amiss.

You are. Your head: it is falling off your body.

She passed the dry winter fountain in the square and realized that there was no one else about on the High Street. Finally, she reached the physician's place of work and residence.

The bell over the door clanged vociferously when Claire entered the cottage, her eyelids cracking like delicate porcelain against the sound. Inside, miserable Victorian splendor welcomed the ailing. The waiting parlor was dismal with drapery and pillows, with demure stuffed velvet armchairs. At the back of the house, the kitchen was cold, the nurse-come-housemaid nowhere to be seen. For a moment, she thought no one was here and that she should not have entered at all.

Claire pressed her clammy hand against the bridge of her nose, closing her eyes against torment and steeling herself to take just a few more steps forward.

"Who's there? Stop!" shouted a voice from behind one of two doors off the parlor.

"What is it, Constable? Who's there?" asked another voice from inside the same room.

The door opened a crack and the doctor's face popped into the doorframe of his surgery, decapitated and livid. "Lord save us, here is Mrs Greengills."

"You are not to come in here." Mr Fritch, her friend, squeezed his own head into the crack in the door above the doctor's. They were stacked dwarves in a fairy tale, alarmed at the uninvited; they were enormous rabbits defending their burrow. One after another they appeared: next was a constable toad. For a moment, she thought she was seeing the wrong people in the wrong place, the wrong characters in the wrong story.

Mr Fritch had his spectacles on, his notepad in hand, as if at his office at Pettyton Hall. She was used to him at her dining table having tea with her, relaxed and himself. He pressed past the doctor, stepped out of the surgery and moved toward Claire, then stopped before he found himself within contamination limits.

"We're finished for now, Mr Fritch." The constable brushed past Fritch. "Nothing else can be done 'til the magistrate returns with the Detective Inspector from Bonborough Town."

"Then I will head back to the Halls and wait for Judge Henry," Mr Fritch said as he put his coat on. He nodded politely but anxiously at Claire and followed the constable out.

"Now," began the doctor, "what exactly can I do for you this time, Mrs Ableton?"

"My head," she started. But her words slipped away, as did her balance, and she slid to the floor.

She woke, having been arranged on one of two tables in the surgery. The floorboards under her were stained with years' worth of attempts at rescue and salvage. She tested opening one eye. The light was exceptionally dim, and she was glad of it, but she hoped her physician could see what he was doing.

"Eaten today?" he asked.

Claire nodded, though she couldn't in effect remember eating breakfast.

"Another of your head-achs again, so soon?" A sigh. "I am understaffed, you know. My nurse has chosen today of all days to abandon post for her errands in Oxford." He yanked her sleeve up irritably, tapped around for a vein with his little hammer fingers.

Claire couldn't imagine why he was angry at his nurse for embarking on a scheduled run for supplies. Should the nurse have foreseen Claire's state? If only she herself had, she would never have left the house this morning. Was it this morning she was at Henrys? No, not Henry's. The forest— she had made her way home after seeing the old woman, was half-way up the landing, and then... Davie. His mud-caked face and hands, his terror-swelled eyes.

"Doctor, there is something I—"

A prick... a pulling sensation... then the sting. "There we are." He leaned close and examined her face with his monocle and something like worry. He pursed his lips, crumpled his forehead. "I would, normally, not let you remain here, but I've no other place for you just now. We can't have you fainting across a chair in waiting, can we?" He managed a little smile. "Just close your eyes and you shall feel better soon. Close your eyes, Mrs Ableton. Whatever you do, do not open your eyes."

She did as he said. She already felt like she was beginning to swim. She was wading into a calm sea. The water, warm and iridescent, lapped at her waist, soothing her ribs. The sea, with its Mediterranean colour. Slipping her hand into Meg's as they waded out together. The water rose up her chest, her neck, her chin. It was washing over her head. Suddenly, she was not in the wide open sea with the white cliffs behind her. There was no clear turquoise water. She was in a black, bottomless pond. A freezing pond.

She gasped, gulped for air.

Don't be a fool, you're not drowning. You are only in morphia. See how your imagination blooms and thrives with the needle. You must tell Meg you still have it, your visions and dreams, your creativity swimming round your brain.

Time passed—she did not know how much time—and there was eventually an ebbing of pain from her head. She could look around the room more easily. Could see the ceiling beams, the edge where the wall met the plaster (the wall with its faded rosebud wallpaper in cheap cream and pale oxblood holding all manner of stains). Who would think to paper a surgery rather than use a clean lime-wash each spring? The abandoning nurse. The dead wife. At least the rosebuds gave one something to look at, though it was all in-and-out of focus.

Except, this was what she was not supposed to do. She was not supposed to open her eyes and look.

Too late.

She was not alone in the room. She never had been.

A form—a long, irregular mound—lay on the table next to her; the table that was the twin of hers with a narrow aisle between them. When Claire turned her head, there was not enough clarity in her to scream. She felt her mouth widen into a gape, a silent *ohhhh*.

On the table was the body of a man, though not a very recognizable one. He was not young but not very elderly either, perhaps a few years younger than Father. He was tall, perhaps thin—or maybe just festered and hollowing—with high cheekbones and a bushy mustache. His legs were slightly splayed, one ankle turned entirely wrong. Everywhere his clothing was matted in a dark crust. It was hard to tell exactly what colour his hair was, though she thought she saw copper-red peeking from beneath the earthen encasement.

She realized the crust was not all mud—it was gelled and brown in places, a brown that was more rufous than common soil. The man's coat, a black Ulster, had patches of dripping ice stuck to the elbows. It was torn at the shoulder and the tear showed a peek of palest, whitest skin. Beneath the Ulster, his fawn-coloured flannel waistcoat was seeped with burgundy stain, fragments shredded out from a wound like the remnants of a butcher's grinder. His insides had been pulled from his body through the wound, and they reeked of sulphurous cabbage as they thawed.

He was no Celtic tale from eons past, this corpse, this once-living thing. And he was not Norris the gamekeeper, nor Rollins either. But he was surely what Davie fell upon as he skipped blithely across the barrows earlier that day.

She thought, I have never seen him out of his baking apron, without his tweed cap, his wide smile. But she knew it could only be Kyle MacManus.

Sick welled up in her throat, along with grief. With disbelief.

A jangle of bells sounded out front and a door slammed. Men's voices. One was the doctor's and there were two additional voices, a younger male, and a gruff older gentleman. Also, she heard Fritch again.

"Back here. Wait, I've a patient."

"A patient?" It was Fritch's voice.

"Only Mrs Greengills."

"You cannot mean...? Dear God."

"Never mind, she's unconscious."

The door to the room opened as Claire's eyes shut in a reflex. Fear hid behind her ribs, her heart knocking through the slow, fleecy waves of opium. She saw the calm sea again, opened her arms to the mercurial stretch. But she also heard voices next to her as she waded into the water alone. The sea turned into the pond again. The pond began to freeze. A bird in a nearby tree said, "Is that him?"

"I — Oh, God." It was a young male voice in the room. Kyle's son, Johnny, though his tone sounded gruff and unlike himself.

"Steady yourself, lad. Look carefully — I'm sorry I must ask it of you. Turn the lamps up, would you be so kind, Doctor?"

The sun, previously behind clouds hovering across Claire's imaginary view, peeked out in a haze behind her eyelids as the lamps were turned up.

"That's him, that's my Dad! Oh, Christ, what's happened?"

"And you last saw him when?"

"This young man reported him missing almost a week ago, Mr Fritch. I took the report myself."

"Yes, Detective Inspector. But how did he get to Pettypoole? And when?"

" 'Tis not so very far."

ERICA-LYNN HUBERTY

"More than a half-day's journey in winter, with the roads gone to ice. Far enough."

"He'd said he was meetin' someone, a business acquaintance. He was meetin' him at, erhm... The Lamb, I think he said."

"Yes, I see. The Lantern," corrected Mr Fritch. His pen scratched in his notebook.

"He was sold some bad goods, y'see. Looked real enough, but it was all tin underneath the shine." His voice cracked and whimpered. "I told him, 'Don't bother about it, Dad. It's not worth it.' But my Dad wanted it sorted out. We'd lost a lot of money, y'see, because of the deal. The man had such a friendly manner."

"Confidence game men always do," sighed Fritch in a sympathetic tone.

"Dad thought he'd just work it out with him over a pint. But he never came home. Oh, Jesus and Mary, what's happened to him? Why does he look like this?"

"There, now, son. We shall get to the bottom of it," said the Detective Inspector. "Could you give us a description? Of the man that knew your father?"

"I think so."

"Good. Judge Henry, our magistrate, should have returned by now. His office is the better place for this. Thank you, Doctor."

"But of course, Detective Inspector. Mr Fritch."

"Alright then, son, follow us."

"I am sorry for your loss," said the doctor.

"Don't touch him," said the young man fiercely, sniffling. "I don't want him torn apart no more!"

250

"There'll be no need for that. I can see the bullet holes. An Enfield, I'd say. He has been beaten about the head as well. The left leg looks broken."

"That's from shoving him into the grave," noted the constable, eagerly.

"I will let you know, Doctor, when to send for the undertaker."

The voices followed each other out into the hall. The doctor, still in the room, halted the mantel clock's arm with his finger, freezing the hour of identification and the commencement of official mourning. There was the scratch of his pen on paper before his footsteps followed the voices out. The possibility of a meal brought from The Gold Lion to Pettyton Hall was then discussed, as it was nearing suppertime and it would be a late night of work for all. The bells over the door sounded again, followed by a yawn of frost that barreled down the hall and into the open doorway of the surgery.

It was, Claire thought, the breath of an enormous, sharp-toothed beast swallowing everything up. Swallowing her up.

TEN

1884 ~ 1ˢᵗ March
Pettypoole, Oxfordshire

The room—her own sitting room—was sharply focused when she opened her eyes. It was very early morning, the sky still dark. A lamp on the mantel was lit and logs burned in the hearth.

"Have I spent the night on the sofa?"

"I thought you would be warmer by the fire. Mr Tinsdale told me about Davie. He said you were a great help to him."

"Davie wasn't imagining ghosts, poor thing."

James nodded. He pulled his chair closer to her. "He found a man, on the grounds of Hammpen Manor. The body had been buried in a barrow, in an attempt to hide it. The grave was badly done, apparently, and too shallow to last."

"I thought so."

"Yes, Mr Tinsdale said you were quite clever about it." James said this uneasily. "Claire look, you are not to speak to anyone about this, do you understand? You are not to be so clever with other people as you are with me."

"It was a guess, about the barrow. *Burgh* the word is, in Irish. My mother used to tell us about faeries burying their kin. I didn't know there was an actual body, until I was in the surgery. I only meant to rid myself of my head-ach."

"He never should have let you in the surgery. Mr Fritch was shocked. Some Detective Inspector from Bonborough was there as well, and one of our incompetent boy-constables."

"Poor Mr Fritch. It is nice of him to have worried for me. I'll have some tea, please."

James brought her the tray.

"James," she remembered something. Something to do with shock and grief. "Oh, James... Kyle MacManus!"

He shook his head. "No, no. It was not Kyle, though you are not the only one to think it might have been."

She wiped her cheek and shuddered. "Oh, my graces... I did think..."

"It's all right, Kyle has been found, at his sister's no less. A visit planned but forgotten by his wife."

Claire screwed her face up. *How daft do you have to be, with a kid and all? Any dimwit is allowed to be in charge of raising children; yet where is your chance?*

"Is it your head again?" He leaned in, put his hand on her forehead. "Look, Mrs Fowler is going round saying you weren't quite right the other day."

She laughed. "Naturally. My head was splitting open. And wouldn't you like to know what she and Val Pell were saying about you."

"Do not joke about what anyone in this village says."

"They will say anything to amuse themselves. It's not likely I'd be able to stop them." *You cannot even stop the physician from calling you Mrs Greengills.*

"Let me fetch the post for a while, Claire. Keep away from Mrs Fowler."

"Wait, stop talking a moment." She put her fingers over his lips. "There is something," her eyes narrowed against a nagging but dim memory. "There's something about that man. He is not Kyle, you said? But he keeps whiskers as Kyle does. Such thick and drooping red whiskers, almost like a..."

"Listen to me, my love. Those women—sorry, but it's true—are the worst of your kind."

"I could tell you something about the worst of your kind," she countered.

"Those two shop girls, Miss Pell and Miss Morton, they waggle their tongues over dust and fleas as if they are really mountains and wolves. You have not been well, that is true, but there's no reason they must see you unwell with their own beady little eyes."

"Shhhh."

"What? The dead man again? Claire, I've told you—"

"Shh, be quiet. I thought you liked me clever. It's just that I thought I remembered... oh, never mind. It's up and gone again. I am tired, I think." She leaned her head back against the pillows and inhaled the sweet chamomile aroma of her tea. She closed her eyes, the teacup steaming in her hands and coating her chin in condensation.

"Have your tea, then have another lie-down. The man's son is being taken care of. Judge Henry has put him up for the night. There is nothing for you to worry about, Claire."

"Has he no other family? What a shame." She opened her eyes, a real remembrance surfacing. "No, there is something, James, I knew there was. The son. His name. Did I hear them say Daniels?"

"Daniels. Yes, I think that's it. No, wait. It's Dean."

A glint of ginger hair streaked with white beneath the muddy shroud, the waxed mustache set awry. With his waistcoat on, his bright hair combed, his high cheekbones pinched in a smile...

Two daughters, oh my! the Copper Walrus had chuckled, colluding in Father's ruse. *My daughter,* Father had told him, *has a softness in her heart for the poorer of the children in our village.* He had nodded, Mr Dean, inspecting the pieces carefully as a jeweler might a diamond.

"Claire? What is it?"

She gave him the cup before it could spill. Hand over her mouth, she ran for the kitchen and vomited a mouthful of tea into the basin. She returned to the sofa, lied down with her back to him, and closed her eyes. "You are right, I do need to rest," she said into the cushion.

"Of course."

She waited until she heard him leave the room, then opened her eyes. She counted the tiny thistles she'd embroidered onto the cushion. One, two, four, six, eight...

ELEVEN

1884 ~ 2nd March, morning
Pettypoole, Oxfordshire

Downstairs the latch on the door to the cottage was scraped, the handle jiggled. There was a brief burst of wind, and then a slam. From bed she could hear all this. Shoving the pillow aside, Claire pressed her ear to the mattress and heard footsteps pause briefly at the shop door, their person assessing the silence, then the footfall resuming up the first flight of stairs. She sat up, seized her nightcap and shawl, and ran to her own door.

"Mr Fritch, forgive me. Hullo?"

Three steps up toward the garret the tall, lanky clerk stopped, startled by her. "Mrs Ableton? I... I hope you are feeling better today."

"Quite well," she lied, "and yourself?"

"I'm on a short break." Under his arm was a briefcase, brimming with evidence.

"Come in and I will give you your tea, Mr Fritch. Philip." She smiled leaning on the doorframe, the door to her flat half-opened.

"That is very kind, but I am home for a moment only before returning to the Halls." He adjusted his spectacles with one long finger.

"Yes of course. That is, have they sorted out yesterday?"

Fritch grimaced slightly. "There are some unanswered questions."

"Oh?"

"Beg your pardon, Mrs Ableton."

"Claire."

He nodded but did not speak her Christian name as he ought to. He started up the stairs but appeared to change his mind. He stepped backward a few paces with his hand still on the rail. "I should have mentioned it sooner, but... Well, I did not think you would mind my locking up for you."

She shook her head, puzzled. "I'm sorry?"

"The day before last?" he prompted. "You must have left it open."

"I am terribly confused, Philip, you must forgive me. I've been somewhat tired lately."

"Sorry. I mean your door."

"My door?"

"Yes, I found it ajar when I returned Sunday. I saw you in church of course, but you and Mr Ableton must have had your dinner out after we parted, and since I did not think it impudent, I went ahead and shut your door and locked it. I keep the key to your apartments for Mr Tinsdale, you see. In case of emergency."

"Oh, oh yes," she stammered. "Excuse me... Yes, we are very grateful to you!" She laughed, a little too loud. "Forgive me, I cannot imagine how we could have done such a stupid thing, leaving the door open! Yesterday, you say?"

"I am sorry for the confusion. Sunday, actually. The day before yesterday. No matter, we've all done it. And as I had the key, and you were not home—and now I am glad I did, of course, given what happened near Hammpen Manor."

"Quite right, Philip. Mr Fritch. You're very thoughtful. Thank you." She began to close the door.

"Claire?"

"Yes?" She looked up through the narrowing lintel while gripping the knob.

"You may wish to consider—that is, I have an idea that a holiday by the sea would further your health. I'm sure Mr Ableton would be pleased to join you."

"What a pleasant thought. But it's only just March and Mr Ableton must teach until end of term when Easter comes. That is some weeks away I think."

"The south is temperate, is it not? The Isle of Wight would feel nearly tropical to here." He glanced up the stairwell at his door, then down through the hollow of the stairwell in the direction of the entryway as if checking for anyone's presence. There was only the two of them, alone. "Perhaps Headmaster Babbage would give your husband leave. A week or two. Three weeks at most, plus an extra on the end for Easter half-term. Why, how nicely that works out. Do you like the sea?"

"The sea?"

"Good. A little holiday, then. Away from the gloom."

Away from this village.

"I do not find the Cotswolds gloomy, Mr Fritch."

"Oh, but you must try the South Downs, Mrs Ableton. I took a holiday there myself, once. The chalky cliffsides are magnificent."

Yes, you must try the South Downs. St. Allswell is a particularly charming place. Dragon's eggs, faerie's nests, marshy grasses...

"I fear," he continued, "that the coming weeks may not bring you sufficient rest, and I can see — forgive me for saying so — that you are in need of recuperation."

Claire was silent. After some seconds she said, "I thank you for your concern."

His gaze lingered on her a moment. He looked at her as he used to. As if they were friends. Then he sprinted up to his rooms.

The thoughts in her head were too numerous to sort. They banged to get out, little hammers and pickaxes scrabbling at her temples. *No, stop! Calm yourself. Mrs Greengills cannot go back to the surgery. Not today. Not ever.*

Claire locked the door and chased her thoughts about her head until they rested on two questions: Why did Philip Fritch want her to leave Pettypoole, and who was in their apartments on Sunday, leaving the door unlocked and open? And a third: If there was a murderer running about the village, why would he take cover in their apartments? That question was answered by the voice whose creeping presence grew more insistent: *Because you left the door open, you silly goose.*

She had left the door open. Just an accident. As she pulled it shut behind them it must have not clicked into place. They were lucky not to have been home, she and James. She thinks of the letter from the supposed nurse, the vindictive parchment she burned. Anyone would tell you where someone lived when searching these little villages, you only had to ask around.

Another possibility dawned on her, one less malevolent but no less complicated. One that made her go to the kitchen, start the morning fire and put the kettle on the range, deliberately and carefully. She took a deep breath, cleared her mind, then confronted the idea again.

She returned to the front door and stood with her back against it as if she was entering the apartments herself from the outer corridor. As if she was a stranger just come in.

To her right: James' easy chair before the hearth. A narrow bookcase built along one side of the mantel was stocked with books. To the left, James' writing desk and chair was against the wall nearest the door. Close by was the little sofa and her own chair.

She sat down at the desk as James might, and opened each of the two drawers, grabbing at notebooks and scraps of paper, then pulling the drawers out and dumping their contents onto the desk. The kettle on the hob began its low rattle. She searched under the desk, spilling the rubbish pail and sifting through the crumpled scrapheap. She stood again, her eyes scanning the wall and cataloging: a mirror, a framed etching, a brass sconce, the mantelshelf, the bookcase again...

There: resting along the top of a row of books on the third shelf was a piece of her own stationery, a folded edge jutting from the line of bindings. She snatched it.

Claire

How I am sorly disapointed to have missed my dear dotter! Come meet me at our favrute Lantern for a sup. As I see yor skoolmaster takes good care of you, I did not think yod object to my borowing a bit of chink. Theres an eksellent investment awating me in Manchester and I will send yor bit and more when it comes.

yor loving Father

Claire read the note twice. She bent to the hearth and threw it on the coals. Just as it started to curl, she reached in and retrieved it, singing the tip of her finger. She blew on the blackened edge of the note, folded it and slipped it into her pocket.

She ran to the kitchen to turn off the kettle, then bolted for the bedroom. She opened the wardrobe. In the bottom drawer, the normally pristine linens were unfolded and crammed haphazardly back into place.

"No... no," she gasped, pushing her pantaloons and camisoles aside. She reached farther in and found her old tea tin. It was light as a feather.

The top, askew, fell off. Looking into the metal hollow, the empty casket where a near-lifetime of money had been scrounged, was like peering into the skeletal frame of a room where your most beloved belongings were once housed.

Is that how Allswell appeared, after you'd left? The house picked clean by vagrants and thieves, by debt collectors and clerks, leaving only an empty shell? The empty shell of your family's hard-earned home?

"No, no, no!"

Claire turned the tin upside down as if some hidden compartment might suddenly give way. She shook it with an angry, anguished snarl. Even the latchkey from the house she had snuck into that summer's day years ago—the souvenir that meant nothing to anyone but her—was gone.

Collapsing on her knees, she covered her face with her hands and shook her head over and over as she wept.

Collecting herself, sniffling and wiping her face, she returned to the kitchen. She opened the oven door and placed the tin on the glowing coals and watched it crumple and melt into a molten heap. She did not know why she did this. Perhaps it was because she couldn't stand the sight of it, though she once loved its Chinoiserie patterns, its bold enamel and curled lettering heralding the jasmine leaves it used to hold. Just as she had loved the curved shapes of the latchkey, the fantastical little curlicue loop at the top and the long straight bar with two different-sized teeth.

Claire dressed. She plaited and coiled her hair. She poured her tea. She sat at the table and attempted to drink it. Her arms quaked and the cup jostled, hot liquid splashing her hand.

Be calm. Think carefully so you can decipher what is actually happening, not what you imagine to be happening. You are overreacting. No one gives a toss about your clown of a father showing up unannounced.

"But he will interject himself, make himself important," she said softly. "He will..."

He will disturb your peace?

She did not care that there was someone talking to her, someone not in the room, but in her head. She'd lived with the voice long enough. There were greater things to worry about now.

She pushed her tea away and put her coat on. She tied her new olive-drab velvet hat and adjusted the pleated velvet flower at the narrow brim. She made her boots sound as light as slippers on the stairs and, at the bottom, she gently tried the side door to the print shop. It was, as she suspected, locked.

Mr Tinsdale, she thought, must be paying a concerned visit to little Davie and his mother. Then he would go home and moan to his wife about what was to be done with his tenants: the Jew with the wife suffering from Hysteria or Infectious Fever, and did you hear that her father, the lurid tavern-hero, came to stay with them? In our cottage we own? We'd all thought we were

262

done with him, at least. 'Well, you'd better go over to the Halls, then,' Mrs Tinsdale would say, 'and tell them about that woman's too-quick explanation of buried bodies. Not that we think she's anything to do with it, but a little insinuation wouldn't hurt, would it? We'll fetch twice what we do from Mr Ableton, in rent, when you kick them out.'

Claire left the cottage and walked quickly up Mills Lane. She crossed the bridge. She walked the Roman Road and paused at Jacob's Lane, which led to the school and to James. She must go to him, get her head straight, have him use his tender logic on her. It was why she loved him, why she married him. He was her way out of chaos, her way into normality.

Straight ahead, at about two hundred yards, stood a constable's parked gig and a large brougham, their horses' breaths pulsing like steam from a waiting train. She stood there, not moving, not turning into the lane to the school, but instead contemplating something else altogether. A thought that perhaps, after all, honesty would be best. Is that what normal people did, tell the truth?

Yes, she could do it. She could approach the constables directly. *Look, there is their gig, they are surely nearby.* She could tell them she once met Mr Dean, and that he was a pleasant but not altogether decent man. She would point to the center of the vale and describe the fair, and how the man had been cheerful and talkative, but concluded his business rather too quickly. For this would be the best tactic to avoid any misconstruing about her or Father's relationship to the man. Just get it done with and come clean about having met him.

She thought about seeing Norris the other morning and — hang on a moment, where was Norris, anyway? Had anyone asked him who he was drinking with at The Lantern a few nights back? Had anyone seen him recently?

You have.

She climbed the stile onto the craggy, frozen wold. Farther ahead, on the adjacent field, stood the herd of ewes. One lifted her head and peered in Claire's direction. Soon, the beast would notify the others and they would begin their lumbering walk toward her, their bells clanging softly and calling attention to Claire. The abbey, roofless, was still obscured by neglected yews and ivy that were too plentiful to have died back in this hard frost. It was a perfect spot.

Quickly, Claire made her way along the hedgerow that divided the grazing field from the rougher moor. Peeking over the top of the hedge, she could see the windmill with its tall stone archways. In one of the convexities stood four men. They were talking and pointing, looking like tiny mechanical dolls maneuvering around a large cuckoo clock.

She snuck her way down to the abbey and from there she watched the men while still concealed in the horrid, close dampness of mossy stone. The men spoke to each other, but she couldn't hear what they were saying. She could see a police inspector pacing restlessly while another detective-constable type stood still, arms folded across his chest like a boorish wrestler assessing an opponent. The Chief Constable of Pettypoole blathered on while pointing at the ground, then pointing at the road, with Mr Fritch furiously taking notes and pointing to what looked like a churned-up little hill.

The fragrance of moss, of decay, was lush even in the bitter wind, and it seeped off the stones of the abbey, up from the ground below her feet. This had never been an untroubled spot, the Church plundered and burnt through and through by

Cromwell, the first (*Reformation & Theological Tradition*, third-right shelf in Evensong's library). Father had somehow thought this a good place to sleep, and she would never understand why he did. Mother would have told them to stay away, there were surely evil spirits about. On the other side of Pettypoole, reclusive old Dewen lived with his sleepy dog and sweet meadow, but it was this way Claire had been led: toward butchery and mad witches with their sickening cures that did not cure, their sons full of rage and revenge; it was always toward the hills of the dead she was dragged.

The men were finishing up but she had already decided she would not speak to them. Something had changed in her. Perhaps it was only the knowledge that they would wonder what kind of woman would admit to knowing a murder victim no one else was acquainted with. A man met through a not very above-board sale of not very authentic goods.

Not the sort of woman you'd want in your little village.

"Exactly," Claire agreed, with only the creeping ivy listening.

And yet, you could do some good, couldn't you? Help that poor boy who has lost his father? You should.

"Nonsense," she quietly murmured. "What good can I do?"

The men made a few last comments to each other, their breath like Christmas pudding steaming into the arctic air. They made their way back to their vehicles. When Claire was certain they were gone, she walked to the site of the crime.

Atop the barrow near the old windmill the impromptu grave looked two feet deep at most, a pathetic attempt at concealing an adult body. The constables would have found it difficult to imagine how the frozen ground was hacked away at in the first place, thinking it would have taken a strong man to do so.

Claire looked at the clumps of frozen earth stained the colour of rusted iron. Her mind lurched not backwards, but sideways. Because perhaps it could be reframed as not murder at all, not cold-blooded murder. Perhaps there could be another, more subtle explanation. Could murder be subtle? Death could be accidental, of course, one did not need to be extremely stupid to die stupidly. Stepping into traffic, brawling in a pub, not changing your wet boots; it happened all the time. Father, for instance, had never been one for common sense. Claire always had to remind him to dry his boots out, to eat and sleep. *He might be quite thin by now, come to think of it, without your care.*

She gritted her teeth and balled up her fists and wished she was not so angry at him, at her tin ransacked and her door left open. As she beheld the revolting grave, Claire tried to imagine Father in a moment of True Action—an act of rage or revenge, of heroism or courage—that would bring about spilled blood. That would create this terrible crime scene.

Go on, imagine it. You could point a clue in his direction and punish him for snatching your cash.

She shook her head. "Ridiculous." Not even in self-defense had Father ever laid a finger on anyone. She knew this better than most. There was something almost disappointing in it. Occasionally, there would be a shove or two by some great oaf against Father, but he would always smile and joke, talk the threat down or shout for Claire and Meg to run for it. The sad thing was, Claire knew just what sort of person Father really was: the sort who only ever ran away.

Now, imagine Norris and Rollins. Yes, *there* was a situation one could easily believe. The two of them at The Lantern (heads bowed over foam, wondering how long they could keep their tabs going and Norris telling the stupider Rollins, "Just let me do the talking, will you?"), when in walked Father, pockets full and eyes smiling. Sometime later Mr Dean must have entered the pub.

"What a marvelous coincidence to see you again! Come join us," Father would have exclaimed. Next you know, more ale was poured, and poured again, and then Rollins said with his big, nearly-toothless smile, "Come up to the gamer's cottage wit' Norris an' me, men, an' we'll throw some dice," and all four could have left together, fate bestowing its haphazard charms. Only much later was one of four drunken men brought to a mindset where all-in-good-fun goes south. Father would have ran for it of course, having lost all of Claire's money. But men like Norris and Rollins were not runners. One or both may have been hiding out even now, biding their time and plotting before they slipped away unnoticed or rejoined their lives as if nothing had happened. How far would Lord Hammpen go to keep this on the down-low, if only to save his family's good name?

Claire peered at the ground. Were those the marks of a shovel, or bare hands? The mess of earth and blood scrabbled by Davie, and combed over by constables, was a pandemonium of indecipherable evidence. Scratches and dents, boot marks and knife marks.

A strong gust rattled through the trees at the edge of the wood like a supernatural breath. They might still be here, Norris and Rollins, hiding in the dark mould of the pines. A few nights of cover in the old crone's cottage was worth a pair of hands around her throat, even if she was your own mother. "Go and warn her," Claire whispered to herself, aloud, "Do not be a coward."

Oh, but you are a coward.

And in that instant, she knew it would be her fault if anything happened to that woman. Or to Father. Claire knew he would come back, asking for more money. *He'd have never found himself in such a brainless muddle in the first place if you had not married James and stayed in Pettypoole.*

Oh, why didn't he just write her in the first place? She would have sent him something, the fool! She would have willingly given him half the contents of the tin if he had asked! He must really have needed the money, must have needed a warm bed. And where was she when he came to her? In church, praying to a Messiah neither he nor her husband believe in.

Cold battered through Claire's coat, and her head began to pound. She wondered how Dean's son had not recognized her lying on the surgery table. Shock, perhaps. That, or she was so altered not even Meg and Father would recognize her. *Nor Mother. Nor Will. Not even your proud little cat would know you...*

Claire knelt at the empty grave and pressed the palms of her hands together, saying a prayer in Mother's tongue for the dead man's soul. She did not know enough of James' prayer for the dead, as women were not supposed to say it. Kaddish, it was called.

When she opened her eyes, the light in the sky was faded and she could just make out the edge of the wood where the trees were clustered in shadow. Time had passed by quickly, she did not know how. This was not the first instance this had happened—time stalling, then lurching ahead and leaving a blind spot. It happened just the other day, after she left the wood and the old woman. One moment she was saying to the old witch, "But it's on the New Moon, and not always then," and the next she was turning the key in the lock at home.

How did you get home that day? And what did you do on the way? You don't remember, do you?

She swayed, feeling the hill tilt, and slipped. She caught herself as she fell forward onto the ground. Her hand touched something solid and cold, and she recoiled, forgetting for a moment that the corpse had been moved. She rubbed her knee, then righted herself.

She stood, unsure. Squinted down at the ground. She leaned over in the dusky half-light and looked closer at the place on the ground where she had fallen and touched the something. She picked up the object of interest. A latchkey—burnished, cold, made of iron and encrusted with blood. She shoved it into her pocket. She looked left, right, behind her. She was alone. She went down the side of the barrow.

She knew she must make haste before the road was filled with carts and men on horseback; with children walking in twos and threes, throwing sticks and stones, and calling out names: Ollie, ollie, oxen free; Poor dog bright, Ran off with all his might.

TWELVE

1884 ~ 2nd March, evening
Pettypoole, Oxfordshire

Claire tilted the blue glass bottle, pinching her neck into an arch. Only one swallow was left, hardly enough to accomplish a faint delirium. Standing before the tub, she peeled her chemise from her sweat-salty skin.

When she had arrived home, there were some flowers in a jelly jar left in front of the door, Freddy's signature scrawled on a card. She had a vague feeling of having hauled several pots of water from the range; of rolling off her wool stockings and crumpling her mud-encrusted overskirts into a ball and shoving them all under the bed. A cloudy remembrance of scrubbing the hem of her coat with James' shoe brush, then washing the brush and putting it back on its hook.

Stepping into the tin tub now, she let the water burn her skin as she sat. She slid down and a small cloud of blood surfaced. She thought immediately her monthlies had begun. Clots floating as though marbleized particles of duckweed on a sluggish pond. But the source was her left knee. She must have gashed herself. She would have to check her stockings, repair the hole or throw them on the fire. Around her swirled oxblood red, the colour of the ring on her necklace. She lay still and watched the water.

The sound of James' key in the lock, of his footsteps on the threshold, abraded her into focus. He dropped his briefcase near his desk with a thump, hung his coat with a rustle.

"James?"

He did not answer.

Claire dried herself; pressed her knee with an edge of the bath sheet, then balled up the stained cloth and hid it under the bed with her clothes.

"I did not hear your good evening to me, my love," she said, crossing the sitting room in an old Lindsay-frock.

"You did not." He sat at his desk, head bowed, still wearing his boots. He looked up briefly but did not meet her eyes. "Is there no supper? What are you wearing?"

"There is some leftover..." she made for the kitchen "...but where is Freddy?" She glanced at the desk. Had she put everything back properly, the way it was before? His back was to her, blocking the view. "I thought Freddy was supposed to come for supper."

"He has declined to join us."

"He came earlier today with a group of — a bouquet, I mean — of flowers that he left at the door. I don't know why he did not knock."

"Perhaps you were not home to receive him."

Claire's mouth opened, then shut. "I was here. Of course, I was here."

His pen rasped the paper.

In the kitchen, she busied her hands.

At supper, they did not speak. James' fork scraped against the plate. He chewed methodically. She was keenly aware of details: the reheated, days-old roast lamb growing congealed on the platter, the ticking of the mantel clock, the heaviness of the ring below her collarbone. There was a crackle in the range, the sound of a piece of coal falling into place.

"Perhaps Freddy has tired of our meals together," she said softly. "Or perhaps you have."

"Where were you today? Do not lie to me," he added tightly.

"I don't know what you mean."

James slowly put his fork down and silently rested his hand on her shoulder, not to comfort, but as if to steady himself.

"Have you tired of me, James?" Her voice was small, pathetic.

He rose suddenly, his chair knocking backwards to the floor. "If you ever ask me that again, I will —"

She flinched reflexively, thinking he might strike her. "But you have been thinking it, have you not?" she asked. She began to cry, in earnest. She had voiced the bottomless fear all women walk with, and she could not take it back now. "To whom have you been writing? A solicitor? An asylum? A lover?"

He paced from the sitting-room to the kitchen and back, then stopped at the table. Grabbing the edge, he leaned over her, raging and saying through clenched teeth, "Babbage called me in today. Have you any idea why, Claire?"

"Do not say my name like it is a curse, I beg you," she sobbed.

"You would like to know why Freddy does not come to dine? Why Mrs Fowler thinks you are mad? I will tell you. Because you appear to be mad. Because you are withering away and were seen traipsing up to the wood to see that old madwoman. And because you fabricate tales as if it is second nature."

"No, no, no that's not true!" Even as she lied, she felt sick with shame, with remorse for not being able to feel the difference between lying and merely protecting herself.

"Headmaster Babbage called me into his office today because there have been complaints from parents who are fearful of my influence over their good Christian children. 'Your father was a respected man, one could hardly tell he was of a different sort,' he said to me. 'But Missus Ableton—no one knew anything about her, did they, until she married you?' And you know, Claire, I thought to myself that even I barely know you."

"But y-y-your family," she stammered, wide-eyed. "You have lived here all your life. S-surely he knows this."

"And your family, Claire?"

"My family?" Her grandfather, with his seaside estate and ruby ring, evaporated into thin air. *And your mother? What really happened to her?*

"Imagine the expression on the face of my headmaster as I paid your father's tab for The Lantern. The owner did not have a stitch of diplomacy to send a bill through the post—he came directly to school yesterday."

"What?" She paled further. "B-but why did you not tell me this? He came to your place of employment?" she gasped. "What propriety is that?"

"You might want to ask, Claire, why your father had the tab at all. It was not from September, when he still lived here, but more recently." A plum-toned flush broke out along James' forehead and neck. "My employer suggested it might be better if we take up residence elsewhere," he continued, "in London, where there is a larger community of *my* sort of people; where I can teach the children of the dispossessed, which is perhaps my 'real calling.' We are to live in Whitechapel, now!" He clutched her shoulders, his face almost touching hers. "Would you like that? Living in a swampy gyre, amongst the petty thieves and whores, the more disenfranchised of us Jews? Where some murderous fiend will slash what's left of you?

"I h-have. I have lived in that horrid place. You're hurting me!"

"Oh, you have lived there, have you?" he squeezed harder, "During one of your exciting journeys around our fair country, I'll wager."

"I have never lied to you."

"You just did."

"James, wait—"

"Unlike you, I have never lied to anyone about myself." His voice quieted, his grip loosened. "I am respectful of them and their God, but I am not a liar. And in this, I have been very fortunate indeed."

"I have brought you misfortune," she rasped.

"No. Not yet." He released her and turned his back. Pressed his eyes into the crook of his arm. His shoulders began to shake. He stumbled to the door, grabbing his coat as he went, so she would not see him weep.

Alone in their bedchamber, she closed her eyes and fell into a fitful half-sleep. She found herself in a near-empty room, her cheek pressed against a barred window. Behind her, in other rooms, half-dressed women wailed on beds of straw, pulling on the little tufts of hair left from the wig-maker's shears. Seeing through time, backwards, she stood before the judge as she and James signed the annulment: there were no children to prove a proper union. Or, perhaps, there was no need to go before the courts at all—he had signed the papers alone; she was declared incompetent.

The glint of her future ended, and she was catapulted deep below the street, behind bars again but this time surrounded by men. The dripping stone cell faced a darkened corridor. There were no windows. A boy wheezed and coughed; he'd caught his death down here for stealing sugar. A man moaned, faking injury or fever; he was adept at deception (last week he slit a man's throat after stealing his wallet). An inebriate in the next cell bawled at her, "Let's see you without your knickers."

Then she was standing in a field in the middle of the night. It was freezing cold, and the mist was thick and low to the ground. She looked for Father. He had shaved his tell-tale beard. She did not know what he looked like without it. She was lost without him.

James' cool hand on her forehead woke her.

She sat up and saw that his eyes were heavy and miserable.

She hid her face in her chapped hands that looked like two paper maché models of someone else's limbs. "What have I done to us?" She felt her mouth twisting horribly as she spoke. She cried loudly, with great heaving sobs. The white sclera of her eyes were vivid crimson, the surrounding skin a lack-luster violet; the rest of her face was white as salt.

"Don't look at me," she commanded him from behind her hands. "There is something terribly wrong with me, James." *You have no control over anything when you are like this, not even your own expression or the sounds you make.*

He nudged her gently off the bed and they knelt on the floor together. He whispered in Hebrew, "Bring complete healing for all our sicknesses, for You, God, are our faithful and compassionate Healer." He added, in English, "Forgive me, Claire."

She couldn't speak, but forgiveness spilled from her torn heart.

"The Lord's Prayer. Say it for us."

"You know it as well as I," she said.

"It is not my prayer. It may be better heard from you."

She hesitated. If she reminded James she had not been raised in any formal religion, and God heard her say it aloud, it might be another strike against them. There was Mother's God, her spirits, saints and faeries; were they Claire's? She knew the Vicar Snow-Thorpe didn't think any higher of that peculiar mix of pagan idolatry and Catholic superstition than he did of the enigmatic Hebrews.

"...hallowed be Thy name..." As Claire stumbled through the prayer, there was an invisible tugging at her faith: it was Father yanking and dragging, the jolly force of Practicalism. Half of her—the part that lived with Father and knew his ideals to be sensible—thought it ridiculous to believe in anything other than the nose on her face. Yet, how to explain the other half? How to explain how she loved and believed in both James' faith and Mother's?

After she finished speaking, they sat on the floor, in the dark, leaning their elbows on the windowsill and looking out at the icy street together. The stars glimmered sharply against the impossibly black sky. One streetlamp burned dully. A nightingale trilled a wish for spring. An owl answered in a low and dangerous bay.

"When I first laid eyes on you," James said, "I thought you delicate, but with a strong, calm gaze. A quiet, intelligent beauty."

"All that at first glance?" she asked, sardonically. She had been a healthy, child-bearing aged girl, then. He must have thought this; all men do.

He said, "Or art not thou A man like me? For I dance And drink & sing, 'Til some blind hand Shall brush my wing."

The words were Blake's, as when they'd first walked out together. The words were as sharp as the stars, but they made her think that perhaps he did not regret her just yet. *It is time to tell him.*

"James, there is a letter I received, several months ago. From a nurse. Or someone impersonating a nurse. If you want to know the truth about my life before I met you, I will tell you: the roads are hard, the world a cold and unfriendly place. There are people who took from us, but I'm not such a fool as to think we were always the victims, that Father was always honourable. How could he have been? A widower, with two young girls to care for, and an ever-altering profession? He must have made someone very angry, and this is their revenge. Perhaps they thought he lived with us, that I would show him the letter and it would be he who would fall ill from the poison that lined it. I think they may have followed him here, to our apartments, looking for him."

He looked at her squarely. "Where is the letter now, the one from the woman?"

"I burned it. So that it would not poison you, too."

"And you are certain it was poisoned?"

"I've remembered the name of the hospital where Mother was sent. It was Jessups Infirmary. 'Twas a proper hospital, near St. Allswell, not this other place. Anyway, I wrote to them, of course I did, but they have been closed for years. Look, this letter has haunted me on the chance that it's real and meant for some poor soul. But, in the end, I do not think it real at all."

You are leaving things out again. You have seen Miss Searton in Pettypoole right outside this window, on your street; in a pew behind you in St. Eldwyn's; at Market Cross. You have burned the letter, but that does not mean you are safe.

She sighed with aggression, gave her head a quick shake. "I have not been a good daughter to him, James. Father is alone in the world. That open grave haunts me. It could have been Father, murdered. It could have easily been him."

"So that is where you were, when Freddy came?"

"I wanted to see for myself."

"But why?"

"You forget that man was lying in the surgery, as close to me as you are now."

James grimaced. "Damn that fool doctor… What did you see, out on the barrow?"

"Blood frozen in the earth, like someone had shot a fox. Norris, spilling a man's blood—it's just like him, you know that. Everyone knows it, for God's sake. He and Rollins, they are always at The Lantern swigging past their tab. Norris' temper and marksmanship is why his Lordship keeps him on when no one else can stand the sight of him."

"You know, his father—the late Mr Norris—worked for his Lordship's father. There is history between them, Hammpen and Norris. Claire, you said there is still blood on the ground?"

She nodded. " 'Yet who would have thought the old man to have had so much blood in him.' You see, I do like Shakespeare's witches. It's not just the postmistress who thinks I cavort with them, incidentally. The men do, too. Our good doctor has a funny little name for me: Mrs Greengills."

"Never mind him. You mustn't step foot on Lord Hammpen's parkland anymore. You mustn't act like you have anything to do with this disaster."

"Yes, but..."

"What is it?"

"It's nothing. It's only that Father and I once met the man."

James flinched. "You knew him?"

"No. Father sold him some wares, ages ago. I didn't remember it until yesterday when I asked you the man's name. We were one of a hundred people who must have had dealings with him, you understand. But his son, if he mentions me or Father—the police will get the wrong idea, without a shred of evidence." *The shreds of organ and flesh oozing from that corpse.*

"You are not his keeper, Claire. You never were." He looked as if he had just thought of something.

"Say'ist you," she answered dully. "Of course, Father would have left town before Mr Dean met his end. You see, he left the door open, on his way out of town, so I know he wasn't here that day, and Mr Fritch saw it, too, though he did not see Father—"

"Shh."

"Now what?"

"Shh!" James held a finger up and listened. Softly, he said, "We must keep our voices down. It may be good if someone heard us arguing earlier but does not hear anything now."

It was the kind of thing Father would have said, manipulating facts into a different truth. She felt a knot in her chest, a twisted ribbon she tossed away before she began to like the feel of it. The sky began to lighten, and the deeper cold of a new day imparted its punishment. She shuddered.

"Here." He pulled the quilt off the bed and over her shoulders.

"No use, I'm done for. Head is pounding again."

279

"I shall find you a new physician," James said. He helped her to the bed, then sat at his desk. "Inquiries, do you see?" he called back to her, "We need to find a more learned doctor, for surely there must be one in a place larger than Pettypoole. Oxford is not too far a journey."

"You can hope one exists. I do not."

"But I do hope."

Her eyes fluttered and half-closed. "You only get that sort of information from eavesdropping, you know," she murmured, talking to her pillow. "People will say almost anything, at an inn."

James' face, poking into the doorway, lit up. "You are too clever, Claire, really. Leave it to me."

"Fritch wants us to go to the Isle of Wight for a holiday," she continued, barely listening to James. "He's not a bad sort, Philip Fritch. I believe he really is concerned about my health. I hope we are still friends."

"We will make you well."

She nodded, just to give her head something to do. She wondered who "we" were.

"Stay home today. Do not go anywhere."

The advice was not difficult to acquiesce. She watched as he put his coat and hat on. She forgot to remind him to take his scarf. She watched him from the window walking down the street, hurrying in the opposite direction from the village square. He was going to take the long way round to the Turnpike Road, she thought, through old Dewen's meadow.

She thought of summer. Of sunlight glinting on the pond, the *sssip* of dragonfly wings. Of how she had allowed herself to hope for all the possibilities of home that never came to be.

PART IV

Home

"Since her eyes fell last upon it she had learnt that the serpent hisses where the sweet birds sing, and her views of life had been totally changed…"

Thomas Hardy

ONE

1884, 3rd March
Pettypoole, Oxfordshire

"Get your things."

Claire stirred. Reached her hand and felt the empty spot on the mattress.

"Claire! Get your things."

She rolled over, rubbed her eyes. *Where is Ling? You have no carrier for him! Quick, find Meg's doll for her, or she will cry too loudly.*

He, James, snuffed the lamp in the sitting room and lit a feeble candle by the bed. "Now!" he ordered, jerking the covers off her.

She had spent the morning watching daylight spread across the frosted lane, and with this had come to her a sense of calm. She heard the print shop open as usual, the gears rotating. Mr Fritch had left the garret at his usual time and did not return. She had pulled her muddied dress from under the bed and located the knee-high tear, edged with her own dried blood, on the front of the skirt. She repaired the tear, then embroidered a floral motif over the stitches and continued the embroidery down the front panel in a fashionable cascade. Then she brushed and mopped the dirt from the fabric and draped the dress over her chair before the fire. After a supper of bread and jam, she had climbed back into bed. She didn't leave the house, exactly as she'd promised James.

The little mantel clock in their room now struck four in the morning. Four earsplitting little chimes as if the bells in Ber St. Eldwyn's tower had been moved into their cottage. James lunged at the clock, stopping the hand before the last strike.

"What is the matter?" Claire whispered, sitting up. "Have you only just returned?"

"Get your coat, and your carpet bag. Quickly and quietly."

The village felt as desolate as an abandoned war post as they left the cottage, taking the stairs in their stockinged feet and putting their boots on just outside the door. The stores were all shut and dark on the High Streeet. The lanterns of Pettyton Hall still burned, however, seeking to catch sight of anyone daring to walk the streets at this bleak hour. As they passed the building, James threw an arm out and gathered her behind him into the shadows.

We are fleeing, Claire thought. She tried pretending they were finally going on their long-awaited honeymoon. But the thought was too ridiculous.

The fact was it was she who handed Mr Dean inferior silver and porcelain. In her mud-splattered muslin and flowers in her neat hair, Claire had smiled demurely and let Father run-on about a French queen's cutlery. James had denied how that could possibly matter. "How do we know," he reminded her last night, "that someone else did not do the same at the next fair?" And Claire had thought, But that is not all there is.

As they walked, James said in a low voice, "I have found a doctor who will help you."

"What do you mean?"

"A physician, in another town."

"But I thought we are running away?"

"From what?"

"I—"

"You need care. Good care. He is a renowned physician."

A renowned physician—what a ring of importance that has. Touché, Father!

'That man has nothing at all to do with our departure,' Father says as you pull away from Evensong with Ling sitting in the road, 'For we have always hated that mouldy old house, and a telegram from a friend just yesterday of a new investment would have us leave only a day sooner than planned.'

"Shh!" Claire rubbed her head.

"Did you say something?"

She did not answer.

Through the closed-up High Street they stole, passing the fountain, and the doctor's cottage, until they were through the old Roman gate markers. There, at the crossroads between the Village and the outer world, lurked the sentry ghosts. What might they do to James for leaving the place where he was born? *A curse, a curse...*

Once on the Turnpike Road, thick, packed snow muffled their footsteps. The trees on either side were covered with frost which glinted white from the light of a full moon. Limbs and torsos emerged from the dark, gaunt bodies frozen in desperate stances as though some horrid figures from Grimm. The anomaly—the snow's patterns against nature's objects—could be beautiful, Claire knew. Downy tufts of feathers, faery's glitter, lace cakes. She told herself to see things that way, but it was impossible.

And this was when it occurred to her. She thought, I should rid him of me.

Yes, you can do it. You can turn and leap into the thicket and run far away from him; because with you, he will never be free to return to the contented life in the village he was born into.

"Stay with me, Claire, and keep pace," James urged.

She was supposed to focus on the road, keep her eyes peeled for the public coach. She used to be good at this.

"James?" she whispered, "did you not see the constables, still in the Halls? They have been there since this afternoon." A glance behind her proved the village had indeed disappeared behind a bend. Still, the distance between them and the Halls was not great enough if the coach was late.

A frosted clump of earth caught her heel. She stumbled and sucked in her breath, recalling the pressure to her temples and the back of her neck. Would she see something useful, something to get them out of this?

There was a stirring, a rustle in the hedge next to her. She looked too quickly, and the hedge spun. With a loud flap a quail flew out of the thicket, and she did something she did not mean to do: she called for Father. She said his name softly, wishing him in a whisper to come out from the bramble and put his arms around her as though she was still a child. "Father... J-James?"

"Hush." He stopped and faced her, his hand up. "The coach will come before the police do. Do not panic."

"But—"

"I will not have us hiding in the brush like animals. Keep pace with me."

You do not understand, she wanted to say, you can tear into the wood or across a field and lay low until they pass you by. Without doubt you can. I have done it many times.

"Listen..." James stopped walking again. "It's coming."

285

The public coach was the very last thing she wanted to climb into. It was cheap and direct, but the whole of it swayed precariously, wobbly wheels clattering against drops in the road as though an ill-navigated ferry through unexpected chop. Men crammed atop the upper benches behind the driver and straddled luggage. Inside, the coach was warm, and one was less apt to fall off onto the road, but that was about all you could say for it.

James positioned himself between Claire and a new housemaid from Hammpen Manor, on an errand for her Ladyship that was purely a test of wits and fortitude she was expected to fail. Directly facing Claire sat a man in worn canvas trousers and tweed cap, though his fingernails were scrubbed clean. Next to him was a messenger boy with scant whiskers and a too-big, hand-me-down uniform, a bulky mailsack wedged between his feet. Incongruously, a woman wearing a fine dark blue coat and veiled hat sat at the other window. Her hem was ruffled silk, her cuffs were dyed ermine.

The dawn sky turned from lilac grey to oyster pink and the view out the window moved jerkily by. Claire slid her eyes to the woman in the expensive dress and coat, her face eerily hidden behind her veil, and she began to fixate on the woman as if she was a forbidden object. A gentlewoman like this should have had a coach of her own. Had she embarked at Pettypoole without Claire noticing? Her gloves were the finest kid, no nurse could afford them... but still.

After an hour, the coach stopped at The Broad. It was the public house at a busy intersection where James had heard yesterday about the physician they were to see. The driver let two men down from the top benches. Two others climbed up in their place. The boy handed some letters through the window to a waiting postman, then handed the man in the tweed cap a newspaper he asked to borrow.

The vehicle continued onward. Just over ten miles from Pettypoole, there were twenty more to go before they reached Bonborough, where this new doctor awaited their arrival tomorrow.

"Have we met? I thought, perhaps, in Bonborough," James had said to her that lazy, hot summer day. But whimsy could quickly turn to horror when you realized you were, in fact, heading directly into the lion's den: the last home and resting place of John Dean.

Body Revealed As One John Dean read the headline on the front page of the newspaper. The man sitting across from them read The Bonborough Standard with interest, having pushed his glasses down to the end of his nose. It was from Bonborough that Mr Dean had traveled a day's journey, perhaps on this very coach, and met his bloody end. His son had gone home after identifying the body and it would not be long before, through his grief and rage, his search for vengeance, he would remember Claire as she remembered him, both of them once traveling similar vertiginous mazes with their showman fathers.

Do not think of mazes, or of circles. Do not think of the spinning wheels beneath. Do not look at the headline or attempt to read the article.

With each stretch of road, Claire felt the skin on her neck grow hotter. The coach rocked and pitched. An acerbic odor emanated from the man in the tweed cap, whose knees knocked against hers with an irregular rhythm. He snapped the paper full open, folded it back onto itself, and resumed reading. His face was covered with an advertisement for lavender soap: pen-and-ink doe eyes and waterfall curls staring out at Claire knowingly.

287

"That is exquisite work." The woman in ermine was speaking to her.

Claire looked at her, startled.

The woman indicated Claire's skirt. "Silk floss, or cotton?"

Claire's mouth was dry. If she spoke, she would be sick. And there was a new kind of pain inside her abdomen, a short pinching like a pulse that was quickly turning into the clamp of a dog's teeth.

"Thank you, m'am," James replied for her. "My wife has a talent for needlework."

The woman nodded. "Indeed."

"Claire?" James asked, in her ear. "Are you alright?"

"I am unwell."

A hot wave—of blood, of other fluids—rose from her ribs to her face. She wrenched the olive-drab hat off her head, one of the ribbons tearing. She opened the window, leaned out and expelled last night's bread and jam.

"Driver!" James called up. "Driver!"

"No stop 'til Halleford," the driver yelled down.

"Can you hang on?" James asked her. "Can you just hang on a bit longer?"

"Can't stay. Must be on—no, *off*. G-g-get *off!*"

She beat the door with her hand, pressed her cheek against the cold frame as the wind blew in from the open window.

Are we certain you must see this particular doctor? Will he really know any more than anyone else? Unless of course there is some other reason for getting you to Bonborough...?

"Shut the bleedin' window," snapped the man from behind the paper.

"What's wrong with her?" The maid was all of fifteen and spoke in horrified squeaks. "I don't want to sit near her!" She probably heard about Claire from James' old housemaid. *Competent, cheerful Annie, James ought to have married her instead.*

Her eyes shut tight, her breath panting, Claire felt James shut the window, locking out the air. "Do not think of it like that," he advised softly in her ear. He knew she felt trapped. He touched her back gently.

He does not want any harm to come to me, she told herself, he does not want me put away. *Are you certain of that?*

"Do not think of the time. It will pass," he whispered in her ear. "Say one of the Sonnets to yourself, then repeat the lines when you are through. You know this one, Claire: *Why didst thou promise such a beauteous day.* Yes?"

She nodded.

The coach plodded on with the team of tired old horses straining to trot, yet it felt to her as if the coach was actually increasing its speed.

> *Why didst thou promise such a beauteous day,*
> *And make me travel forth without my cloak,*
> *To let base clouds o'ertake me in my way,*
> *Hiding thy bravery in their rotten smoke?*

The slamming of the horse's hooves sounded faster, and more unified.

> *Why didst thou promise such a beauteous day,*
> *And make me travel forth without my cloak*

The team of aged horses became as though one giant, strong animal, a black steed pulling them all to their deaths.

> *Why didst thou promise such a beauteous day, and*

"Stop! Let me down!" Claire tried standing but was jostled back.

The tweedy man rammed his knee against hers, with purpose this time. A passenger on the upper bench peered through the window, his face upside-down like a carnival fool. Claire recognized him instantly from The Lantern.

"Got any goods to sell?" he cackled. "I hear you know all about that!" The other men sitting up with him laughed. One said, "Have pity, Colin, her father left her with only a dowery of tin and the pillow between her legs." A snarl of glee followed.

"We cannot walk," said James to Claire. "It is too far. Sit down."

"What's wrong with her?" the Post Boy asked. "She's got Fever, does she, sir?"

The little maid blubbered and sniffled. "Lady Hammpen says…"

"—Don't be stupid, child!" the well-dressed woman chided her. From her cuff, she flicked her handkerchief in the maid's face before handing it to Claire. To James she said, "There's a sort of inn, not far from here, owned by a friend of mine."

She lifted her veil, revealing her face. She was beautiful, about fifty years, with powdered skin, and flax-blonde hair streaked with snowy white. "Stop, driver," she ordered. She knocked her fist on the ceiling of the coach.

The vehicle came to a halt, the horses snorting and stomping. Passengers groaned. The tweedy man said, nastily, "I've got to get to bloody Stranton by tomorrow."

"What's the problem?" someone above inquired. "Ah, nothin', that Judy's just knapped," answered someone else, meaning Claire, the pregnant prostitute.

"It is that way," continued the woman to James, ignoring everyone around her like a duchess dropped into a snake pit. She pointed toward a narrow lane they had just passed. "Walk east on the Silk Road and you'll see it. Ask for Miss Campion. Tell her Lady Jandits sent you. Rest there, and go on tomorrow to...?"

"Bonborough," said James.

She nodded. "My friend will lend you a trap. You shall be well-rested by then," she told Claire. "It will be an easy journey."

They descended and were handed their belongings from the top and, as James reached for their case, a man shoved it at him, and it knocked him to the ground. The man who threw the case hung over the railing, cackling, the others egging him on.

James stood up in one headlong, clumsy movement, his soles slipping on the ice. He grabbed hold of the lantern on the side of the coach—for support, it seemed—but then hoisted himself up to the railing. Before the laughing half-wit noticed, James had wrapped one arm around the back of the man's neck. He withdrew his clenched fist and thrusted it into his teeth. The man reeled back, blood spraying from his mouth.

As the coach pitched forward, James released the rail and landed on two feet. He shook his hand out, put his hat back on and walked toward Claire, his face set with no expression. He withdrew his handkerchief. "Here."

Shocked, open-mouthed, she took it and wiped the tears from her face as the coach teetered away.

"Come on." James marched past her.

They turned off the Turnpike Road and found the narrow Silk Road lined with a canopy of trees. Branches, covered in ice, reached overhead and met like pensive fingers. They glowed extravagantly with sunlight, as though buoyant versions of last night's frost-laden ghouls.

"There's been little traffic," James said. He noted a singular set of blade marks, like an inspector in one of Mr Tinsdale's penny dreadfuls.

She let his composed tone expunge the rage she had witnessed. The image of him hanging from that foul man's body, the blow of his fist into the snickering, then bloody, face. She listened to her judicious schoolmaster as he explained how this tree was a beech, at least three hundred years old, and that elm lost a limb in a storm many years ago; and, by the way, did she remember the great Christmas Snow of 1875? Or the fairy tale of *The Sparrow and The Oak* from when she was a child? Because he was certain his mother, in fact, had made that one up to entertain him and his brother David.

And all at once Claire realized that his talk was all useless chatter. Just enough to keep her calm and moving, like some broken ox you needed to haul out of a ditch so you could slit its throat.

"She used to tell me stories I later learned were not written down anywhere," James continued. He almost added how sorry he was that Claire would never know his mother, but he held his tongue just before he finished the thought. Instead, it came out, "What a shame…" the words trailing off into clouds of condensation. Claire understood what he meant.

He seemed, to Claire, nearly desperate to get her to Bonborough. But why must he rush her there by tomorrow? Perhaps he did, indeed, think her mad. A doctor would confirm this.

Anyway, you will never survive the walk to the gallows unless a doctor makes you well.

292

"My head does not ache so much as it has," Claire announced.

"Yes, love." He walked on.

"Then why do we pursue this?"

"Not long now. I can see the chimneys up ahead."

"You are not listening to me. I do not like it. I will try harder, James. I will be... more myself again."

ames paused, looked at her sadly. He tilted her olive-velvet hat back from her eyes and tucked the one dangling ribbon behind her ear. "Why did you only get yourself the one hat, for winter?" he softly scolded. "You could have had two." Unfurling her clenched hand for her, he withdrew his handkerchief, a squashed and crumpled mess, and dabbed at her face. "You are bleeding. You've bitten your lip."

"I'm cracked to bits." She meant her skin, which was dry as a cornhusk, though anyone would think she meant otherwise.

They walked on and reached the end of the lane. At the head of a half-circular pebble drive stood a house and a modest stable. The house was covered on one side with dormant vines, which James pointed to and stated: "Wisteria sinensis." Now he was a horticulturalist giving a lecture. Just stop, she wanted to tell him, there's no point in continuing this prattle.

A cob was tethered to the fence, saddled up, and his hot breath formed clouds around his dozy face like a man smoking a pipe in a favourite easy chair. As she leaned against the muscular bulk of the horse's shoulder, his whiskers grazed Claire's chin, and the bristle nudged her from her stupor and caused her to notice the details of the house and garden. The roses at the fence, in a formation more French than English, the soft, grey Normandie stone of the house, and the sturdy stone chimney, with shutters at the windows painted the periwinkle blue of an early-morning sky...

And that was when she saw it.

"James," she whispered, "the bird. Like the ones you made in the tree." A single silhouette—wings open—was carved into a panel of an upper shutter.

He held the gate open. "Only a few more steps, my love."

"No, look," she pointed up.

"Claire, please."

"I could see you coming up the drive," a woman called from the open doorway.

"We are looking for Miss Campion?" James asked.

"I am Georgina Campion." Her auburn hair, shocked only at the temples with thin whisps of white, was pulled back in a tight chignon. She wore a simple but fine navy silk dress, and an apron of oilcloth smeared with a haphazard mix of colours.

"Lady Jandits," Claire began, her voice light and hollow. *Indigo, cadmium, emerald. Look at the paint on her apron.*

As Claire stepped inside, Miss Campion drew nearer to her and scanned her face with intense eyes. "You are poorly, I can see that."

A man in a sable top hat passed through the entry. The horse's master.

"Mr Perret, will you be returning next week?" Miss Campion asked.

"In a fortnight. I have business that will keep me in Guilford for a time. Here," he reached into his pocket. "From my wife. She has been sorting through her late uncle's articles and found these." He handed her two little tubes.

Miss Campion smiled. "Cobalt and veronica. Thank her for me. Good-day."

The man bowed to James, his eyes pausing on Claire uncomfortably before he left and mounted his horse.

"I have an elderly lady and her niece here," Miss Campion explained, "And I shall put you down the hall from them, where it's quiet."

She led the way up a staircase lined with portraits, pairs of eyes all staring off at an indeterminable presence. They were not grand, the paintings, not the kind of large-scale thing Claire had lived amongst in those imposing bastions of the gentry Father installed her and Meg into, but they were stern and watchful.

Their room sat at the end of a hall and its walls were butter-yellow and illuminated with a flood of light from tall windows. That was what Claire noticed right away: the colour of butter. *Vermilion, cadmium, butter-yellow.* She couldn't stop thinking in colour, as if a foreign language had expropriated her own familiar vocabulary.

James and their hostess were a vague and static whir as they drew the curtains, took her coat, and buzzed about the room like synchronized bees. She felt softness beneath her, the crispness of clean of linen, the warmth of a hearth. Out the tall window was a garden and rolling hills far below. *The room is bright, the colour of butter, with windows looking out onto a lush garden with flora that changes as you watch...*

It was her dream of the house with its little elfin doorways, the garden that grew faster than was possible, and the woman she had to meet in the room. And there something else, something even more familiar.

Familiar? But this house has no elfin doorways, and a dream is only a dream. Isn't it? Ah, yes... You have seen this view before.

Well, then. If she was not cracked entirely yet, she had certainly begun the descent. For, if I recognize this house, Claire thought, it must also recognize me.

TWO

1884 ~ 3rd March
Silk House
Silk Road, Oxfordshire

"I hope it wasn't me who woke you." Round, with raven black hair and freckled cheeks, the housemaid stood at the side of the bed. "Go easy now, there we are, mustn't sit up too fast, that's it." She spoke quickly and in rambling sentences.

"What is the time?" Claire asked her. A quince-blossom sun blazed low through the curtains.

"Half-past four, ma'am, and Mrs Matthews serves supper at six-thirty, at least this time of year, and I've sewn your ribbon for you as it was lodged inside your collar." She held Claire's hat out to her like a child showing off a new kitten. "You don't have anything to worry about as for a chill, because this is a dry house and you've a good fire in here, as you can see."

"Thank you." Her hands still under the covers, Claire touched the smooth, soft wool of her overskirt, the newly sewn embroidery along the front panel. They had not undressed her.

Good. She prodded through the overskirt to her jupon, relieved at finding the folded paper and metallic lump beneath the fabric.

"You'll sleep well here tonight, as do most of our guests." The housemaid smiled in a manner that seemed forced, dimples cutting into her smooth, doughy skin. Her eyes darted over to the window. "You'll be plenty warm in this room. Plenty warm."

"Thank you — ?"

"Ruthie." She seemed offended, though Claire could not make out why.

"I am Claire. That is, I'm Mrs Ableton." *You never do get all the proper social graces down when you are not born into them; why one even tries is a mystery.*

"I keep the rooms clean and warm, always. But if you should hear anything... Well, come out the bed now and you can join your husband downstairs."

"Hear anything? What do you mean?"

"Beg 'pardon, ma'am?" Ruthie's face performed an odd, twitch-like gesture followed by an unnatural little laugh.

As Claire swung her feet onto the carpeted floor, Ruthie placed a shawl over her shoulders. It was woven paisley and not Claire's. "Thank you, Ruthie."

"If you will follow me, please, ma'am."

The corridor was lined with small, vibrant paintings in the new en plein air manner. "This house has been in Miss Campion's family for three generations — down these stairs, please... Her great-uncle, Captain Mayle, built it for his wife, Lady Bridget. Then Miss Campion's uncle, the Admiral, lived here. Miss Campion and her sister were born in this house." Ruthie pointed to the portraits like a museum docent who was in a terrible rush, the eyes of the dead glancing at Claire only when she looked away.

"You are awake," James greeted her in the sitting room. "Take some tea, will you?"

"Have a walk, actually."

"Are you sure?"

He grabbed a tartan rug and placed it over the paisley Kashmir, making her feel like an absurd notion of some ancient Warrior Queen. She was struck, as she looked around the room, at the familiarity of it, though of course she must have been in hundreds of sitting rooms over the years. Drawing rooms, galleries... *Moldy libraries, gaming rooms.*

They set out through glass doors into the gardens, her arm linked in his.

"These are miniature roses. See how small the thorns are?"

"I do know that dearest, roses are obvious even when they're not in bloom." Claire pointed to a tall, wide bush with long, flat leaves and closed buds. "'Tree Faeries,' that is how I know these. Father likes to see them in my hair."

"Rhododendron. They are as ordinary as roses. And will bloom as early as next month. Tree Faeries, huh?"

"He made up the names: Bushy Pinks, Scraggly Hedge-Hearts. Queen Anne's Lacey Hat."

"Yes, I know. I just mean... nevermind."

"Perhaps he did it to amuse us. He was wonderful that way. But sometimes I feel as if I'm still learning the most basic things. And losing words I already know. Before I met you, all I knew came from books."

"Myself, as well."

"But my books were all the wrong ones, James. I can tell you how a Raj prince rides an Elephant, and I've never left England. This shawl—" she lifted the edge of it and showed him, "I know it is from the Punjab, but what use is that, except to tell me our hostess has traveled or knows someone who has? The fireplace tiles come from Holland, by the way," she added as they continued walking. "And I might as well have been to Africa, for all Mr Fritch knows, because I am more versed in Rhodesian malaria than I am Cotswold sheep. I can tell you how to abandon a house without leaving a smidge of personal belongings—you should have asked me, last night—and I know how to seem as if I'm an expert on gold-rimmed porcelain vases and sable rugs. But I cannot tell you how to sow a proper garden, or if rain is coming and that garden will flood. I do not speak French or play piano. My education was by obscure travel log and drinking songs, of stories my father embellished. I have only known of things I should not have."

"You have shown me how to care for things." He took her hand and held it firmly. "Look, there is your kitchen garden." He indicated rows of tiny green shoots mulched with hay. "I will help you with that when we return, I promise."

She did not respond. She knew Mr Tinsdale had likely already posted eviction papers on their door. Their clothes were in a crate with her little painting of Hammpen Manor. No doubt the late Mrs Ableton's tea set, and Sabbath lace and silver candlesticks, would be hawked at Market Cross next week.

At the end of the garden, short blades of early flowers were pushing up through snow. The property was on a high ridge looking down on a vale covered in white, where the windows of a lone nearby cottage glowed amber in the indigo dusk. To their left, dug into the garden, was a little pond, surrounded by tall, dried reeds. The vale was vast and white and nondescript, though still beautiful in an empty way. It could have been any landscape, in any place, in winter.

"There is something you do very well," said James. "You could sew this whole scene before us if I gave you silk. A tapestry from sky to earth as beautiful as the real thing."

"It would take much white, cream, and silver-grey thread, with darker greys for those long shadows. It would be a startling picture."

She looked out across the landscape. Barely visible, near the horizon, were a cluster of buildings and a tall church spire. A place they once called home.

"He was an Admiral," Georgina Campion related, of her uncle who left her the house. "He knew the excitement of the sea, as did his father, Captain Mayle. I, myself, have been to Australia and India by steamer."

The two other guests, Mrs Collbert and her niece Juliette, whose room was down the hall from theirs, dined with them. Stoic and silent was the old aunt, like a relic, while Juliette was bright-eyed and seemed starved for the company of the living.

"I understand the house has a history?" Claire asked.

Miss Campion offered her a sardonic smile. "Ruthie has been chatting away to you."

"The bird, carved into the upstairs shutter," said Claire. "I wondered about it."

"The Admiral carved it, for his wife. It is said he meant to carve another on the companion shutter but after she died, he refused to. I would not put much stock in this tale, though, as there is likely a more mundane reason lost to time."

Claire nodded, feeling more questions rising inside her. "I had wondered about some of the paintings—yours, I believe? Has your family always lived here, or was the house perhaps let out at one time?"

"There are stories about this house and its former occupants," said Miss Campion, "and Ruthie does love to tell them, but do not pay her too much attention. She is still fond of Mrs Radcliffe and will attribute anything to the supernatural if it amuses her."

"She's told me a story about your room, Mrs Ableton," Juliette declared. "Makes my skin crawl."

"What a remarkable necklace," noted Miss Campion, gently cutting Juliette off. "It is quite Baroque."

Claire touched her ring. It had been months since she'd been around strange eyes fixing on it; she had almost forgotten what that felt like.

"She never takes it off," said James.

"And you have lived here your whole life?" Claire asked their hostess again.

"I left for a time to study painting in Paris at the *Académie*, but the house is mine, as is a fine little house in Paris that I let to my cousin."

"My wife makes embroideries as detailed as paintings," said James. "Your friend Lady Jandits remarked upon the flora she has stitched on her dress."

Claire thought of her orders for Henry's, the ones piling up at home. *Lady Hammpen will be placing a new order: a runner with the east view of her fields, the barrows to be stitched in Blood Red, an Ivory bone protruding from the spill.*

"We say that men put their hearts into their work," Miss Campion said to Claire, "but the same is true for women."

"Oh, but you are putting the house up for sale, Miss Campion!" Juliette said. "So that she can live abroad and paint," she explained to Claire and James. "The estate agents will be descending upon her by mid-week."

"It's true. I am returning to France. My cousin no longer needs my house there, and I no longer want the responsibility of this one."

"But surely, Miss Campion, you are not?"

"I will miss this house—for it has a history and a lovely feeling about it. But Paris is where I spent my happiest years. Lady Jandits will be joining me."

"And who is this Mystery Lady of the public coach?" asked James.

"She is an accomplished sculptress— Ambrose Osborne, to the world. Perhaps you've heard of 'him'?"

A smile spread across his face. "The Black Horse series. I saw several of those marvelous busts when I was at Oxford, on display in the King's College Gallery. My goodness, I'd no idea Osborne was Lady Jandits."

"Black horse series?" Claire was aghast.

"Those are particularly magnificent, Mr Ableton, are they not?" Miss Campion had grown excited. "They are made of Egyptian black limestone, Mrs Ableton. Each bust is twice the size of a common friesian's head, carved by her own hands. Lady Jandits was on her way back to Halleford Hill this morning, from London," Miss Campion explained, "She is quite amusing, taking the coach whilst her own is filled with marble and canvas by artists whom she patronizes—Mrs Matthews will you please bring our pudding to the sitting room?—She gave me the moody little painting above my desk, made by a woman who lived in near-poverty because her family disowned her for her undignified profession."

"Good heavens," Mrs Collbert quipped.

James helped Claire out of her seat. In her ear he whispered, "You have glazed over."

"Will you not be joining us for pudding?" asked Juliette.

"I think not," said James, smiling politely and hooking Claire's arm into his. "We bid you good-night."

He helped her upstairs and into their room. He unlaced her while she held onto the back of a chair, her gaze half-focused on the tall, dark window. The garden she could not see.

In bed, James kissed Claire's hand, perfunctorily, then extinguished the lamp. His eyes, half-open, glimmered with the glow of the fireplace. "It's a pity," he mused sleepily. "I wonder what will happen now. To the house, I mean."

Claire closed her eyes against the clean, soft bedlinen, but her mind refused to sleep. The sanctuary this house had given her would soon be lost. The house would be emptied, renters coming and going, wearing down what was so carefully crafted. Or some speculator would tear it up, adding useless columns and turrets, putting stone where wood should be. Or worse, the home would be abandoned altogether, sagging under its own weight, broken panes letting in the rain, the hearths forever cold.

'My dear girl,' Father always says, 'it's not as bad as all that; nothing a broom and cloth won't cure.' A scrape or two, then a screech, the great squawking gates swing open...

THREE

1884 ~ 4th March, morning
Silk Road
Wotton Vale to Bonborough, Gloucesteshire

Overnight it had snowed. A shimmering carpet, like glass shavings flung across the garden, had buried everything that had begun to sprout anew. It was a sign of thwarted assurance. One could hardly remember another winter like this one.

Last night, after James had unlaced her, she had insisted on sleeping in her underskirts. Feigning a chill, she did not chance removing them and exposing where, when embroidering the overskirt, she had sewn the flat pocket onto the jupon, placing the paper and object into it and closing it up with stitching so that the whole was buried under the layers of her skirts. *Only if you press down on it, you will feel it against your thigh, reminding you what you have done.*

Ruthie helped her into her stays, and as she hitched up her train and looped it, Claire felt as though she was being readied for a terrible commemoration at which she was the sacrifice. One moment you were taking refuge at a strange but lovely house on the way to Bonborough, where the police have been dispatched to investigate the body found on the barrow near your own village... *Next, you are being dressed for slaughter yourself.*

"Be quiet!" Claire wanted to scream back. Instead, she bit her lip and grunted, pretending Ruthie was lacing her in too tight.

"There, now." Ruthie placed the hat on her head, her chignon fitting perfectly into the dome of the crown.

"Thank you. It was kind of you to mend it for me." Claire spoke with soft gentility and gave Ruthie a little smile. *A lady's maid: what Father always wanted for you.*

Downstairs, she found Miss Campion at her desk. She looked up and said, "Your husband is with Matthews. My dapple-grey needs a new shoe before you leave."

Nerves began to seize Claire's voice, so she merely nodded. She felt a swell of nausea.

"You will need an extra rug, for it's an open rig. Ruthie has them upstairs."

Claire went back and, finding the rugs herself, took them downstairs to the kitchen instead of to the drive. The room was unchanged from her memory of it. For, overnight, her memory had finally grown strong enough to realize.

Heart racing, perspiration beading at her forehead, she dropped the rugs in a chair near the range, then walked out into the cold air and steadied herself.

She looked right, where the path that led into the vale, tamped down by years of Mrs Matthews going to market, was hidden under snow. She walked to the ridge and turned left down a shallow slope to the little pond. Once there, she crouched in the reeds and tried to slow her breathing. She had to think. *We need to think.*

Her fingers were numb with cold. The chain on her waist, holding her watch, a pair of tiny folding scissors and a silver needle case, swung over the surface of the water like a pendulum. Tick, tick, tick. Her ring, close against her collarbone, swayed only a little. The iced-over water was snow blown and had drifts at its banks. It waited for her.

She couldn't muster anything resembling the cunning she needed to get herself out of this mess. Instead, she was flooded with hopelessness. It was time to leave for Bonborough, but that town was the last place she ought to be seen, of that she was certain. From here, she could see the drive and stables. She could see James, walking around the trap, inspecting it, talking to the stable boy. James trusted her, but the truth was that she was a coward, and he shouldn't trust her. And she often wondered if she should trust him. He once had a good life. Before her, he had known acceptance and made an honourable living. His life might yet go back to the way it was. *Without you.*

She peered at the surface of the frozen pond and saw herself at Dewen's pond months ago. That day, through the stagnant water, she had seen an underwater grave, a bottom of unknowable decay; plants and bones, dead things sinking into silt. She had seen herself in winter, the grass around her dry and brittle; the water marbled and frosted. She had seen herself kneel at the edge of this very pond, pressing her hands into the surface, cracking the ice and plummeting into frigid, pulpy silt. She had felt the stiff but pliable stalks of plants, the slippery skin of a hibernating frog, the slow flutter of a fish.

You peer into the gloom, straining to see what lies beneath. You walk into this water and grab hold of a sunken tree trunk to keep yourself from floating back up. You hug the murky depths, and let your lungs fill with water, your body joining the skeletal remains at the bottom...

A quarter of an hour later, still dry but cold, Claire appeared on the drive with the two rugs folded over her arm. She was composed. Her face showed no emotion, betraying nothing she had done or thought. Her gloves hid her damp, raw-pink hands. James would suspect nothing.

The trap, fitted with blades, slid away from house, and turned onto the Silk Road. The canopy of trees glistened with the new snow, the sky splintered with intermittent sunlight. The ride was swift, and the air rushed at their faces as the dapple-grey horse trotted evenly. James reached his hand out to touch Claire's arm and she wished he would not touch her at all. She smoothed the rug on her lap in a repeated motion, combing the fur with her fingers. She willed herself not to think of her own feather mattress back in Pettypoole, the wool overlay she prized and combed with vigilance.

Because it is then that you will remember Lettie's expression when she came that day and found you combing. Glaring wide-eyed at my clean house and at my threads and floss neatly sorted in baskets, Claire thought, my needles in so many sizes (all gone now and thrown out the doorstep or snatched up by other women — Lettie, for instance, or that bitch Valentine). Pray Eloise will get some of it, at least, and perhaps stab Valentine with a long, sharp upholstery needle when her back is turned. Or the sturdy whalebone knitting needle, a number eight right in the eyes. There were so many weapons one could use, it did not have to be a gun.

"Are you alright?" James folded his hand over hers to stop the repeated, fidgety motion of her fingers.

The public coach was at their rear now, fitted today with rusty blades. More traffic joined the Turnpike Road and the vehicles slowed and merged through the entrance to town like thread through the eye of a needle.

Bonborough was an average town of commerce, bustling and larger than Pettypoole but not as large as Oxford. Claire strained to remember it from her past, but the memories were clouded by the camouflage of snow, and by the stark fact that this was where young Master Dean resided, his father now interned in the public fields; for what churchyard would agree to house a penniless con artist who met his end unnaturally?

"Stop. Turn around. I'm boiling up."

"Impossible, it's freezing. Put that back on." James jerked her coat back over her shoulders.

"Go back to Miss Campion's. Go back."

"Don't be ridiculous. Bloody drover—move them aside!" James shouted as a flock of sheep weaved chaotically in front of their horse. The dapple-grey whinnied and stomped, jerking the rig.

"Wait, James, please, I—"

"Damn it, Claire, *sit down!*"

James' arm, tight round her shoulders, kept her from standing, and he steered the horse away from the drover and his flock with three sharp tugs. He maneuvered down a narrow lane, then back onto the High Street. He slowed the horse, made another turn into a side lane, and steered the trap straight.

"You are peaked, Claire. I shall have them give you brandy when we arrive."

"I am always peaked. It's my talent." I've got loads of tricks up my sleeve, she almost added. She tried not to smile, her mouth twitching like a limb with a life of its own because, in fact, she did not think any of this funny at all.

They passed a washwoman and a tiny girl of no more than eight helping her wring out a sheet into a tub, the steam rising from it like fumes from a cauldron. The small painted shingle over the door read Levy's Laundry. Claire had not realized there would be other Jews, away from the big cities. When James first told her about his family, she had tried to reconcile this with images from her childhood: of men with long beards walking to their synagogue, heckled by factory workers coming out of the pub on a Friday evening; of mothers calling to their children in German and Russian whilst exerting themselves over pots of cabbage and bones; of the orphanage where a single Star of David above the door meant the children within would never have a proper home. *James Ableton, respected schoolmaster at the Babbage School for Boys, see him how others really do. Just try it, and then you will know what you are really in for.*

She shuddered, clutching the rug. "It is too cold today. We'll catch our death in this open trap."

"I thought you were boiling up."

"I—"

"We're almost there."

"You know the way?"

He looked at her curiously. "I have been to Bonborough many times, remember? With my father, on Henry's Stores business."

She nodded. "I think I remember it, too, James. I mean, really remember it. I really think I was h-h-here once." A pub, after hours, and a man Father had met who gave them the key to a cottage because his girls were so pretty. But the cottage had been an ancient hovel for herders, rundown and not lived in for decades. They could not even get a fire going in the hearth. "I think we lived not far from here, once."

He did not respond to her. Perhaps he had stopped believing anything she said. *Two can play at that game. Ignore him, as he ignores you. Play his game.*

"...and you know what I say is true," James was saying. "Claire, are you listening? I said you know we must see him, this physician."

"But why m-must I?"

"You are stuttering again. Are you in pain?"

"I have never b-been arrested before."

Now he stared at her, his eyes wider. Clenching his jaw, he snapped the reins.

You have never been arrested before, though perhaps you should have been.

She felt a horrific giddiness creeping up her chest that felt like ghastly little fingers. She felt lost, untethered. She thought she may have just lost time again, half-a-minute vanished into thin, cold air.

"We are almost there," he said.

Do not let them blood-let you!

The trap's blades scraped as they inched past another bakery, a butcher shop, and a draper. A single streetlamp, forgotten by the lamplighter, spit into the morning.

Claire silently noted the shops as they went by. A pub, a milliner's workshop. On a corner stood a bobby, taking a smoke, and she saw the building behind him: Divisional Station, Gloucestershire Constabulary.

"James, they will wonder why we took the public coach."

"Who will?"

"The police will say we were escaping."

"The police? We are not *escaping*, Claire, we only came to Bonborough to make you well."

"There's a difference, is there, in escaping and 'trying to leave'? They will say we took the public coach to Bonborough because t-that is where the man is from," Claire tried to explain. "And they will say we were g-g-going to do away with the son."

"But we did not stay on that bus, did we? We never actually disembarked at Bonborough—Jesus, Claire, *do away* with him? What on earth are you talking about?"

"But now we're here, and we should not be. We should never have left Miss Campion's."

"Enough. I am past my limit. If you lose your bearings now, all will be lost."

You fool of a husband, she thought, all was lost long ago.

Next to the Constabulary was a bakery, and next to that a pawnbroker's shop named Fortuna, in whose window was crammed all manner of objects and jewelry. They stopped in front of it for a group of school children to cross the street. Chaperoned by nuns, the children's mouths were set in mock-solemnity as they marched in their uniforms. The sight of the little girls, of their fine hair and soft cheeks and little hats with ribbons, cut into Claire's heart; a torment wrapped up in sadness, envy, and physical pain.

A half-block later, they came to a brick house with drapery pulled conspicuously shut across the tall windows. James turned into the drive. A stable hand took their horse and they jumped down from the trap.

As they crossed the little courtyard and approached the back door, the hum of a violin could be heard from some nearby window. A voice, loud and friendly, sounded from another window in one of four houses that shared the courtyard.

The door swung open. The housekeeper stood looking bored with fatigue, as if there was little by way of infirmities she had not seen. She led them to an anteroom, her pristine uniform rustling with starch. Her hands were red with constant washing. Her back was straight. Her face dispassionate.

Silence hovered in the waiting room like a stale cloud. There were innocuous lime-washed walls, a settee and armchairs upholstered in a vague hue with faded fringe. A curio shelf was crammed with collectibles, all of them porcelain and white as the walls. The one window which faced the courtyard was shrouded in white lace.

James and Claire sat side-by-side in the waxen space. The room, though its intention was tranquility, was a bloodless haven for tricks of the eye. Soon, some ivory flowers in a painting on the wall appeared to Claire to be frayed and blurred, like torn segments of mildewed parchment; the trinkets on the shelf appeared as shrunken people. *"Chapter Thirteen: A Samoan Voyage. They shrink the heads on a bed of embers, palm leaves stuffed inside the hollowed skull."*

Is that why the real owner of Evensong, when he finally arrived home, wore such a startled and soulless expression? Had he not been warned, by the myriad volumes of perilous ocean journeys recounted in his own library, of what he might see and experience? Had he not read them as carefully as Claire had?

She heard the doorknob turning, and an elderly man entered the waiting room. He made his way slowly with a cane, shuffling one foot forward and then the other. A round man he was, with bright eyes and a ready smile.

"Good morning, madam," he said. "Good morning, sir."

"Good morning to you, sir," James replied.

The man leaned back into a chair, winced a little, and closed his eyes. His cheeks had a too-rosy pallor, his mouth a naturally contented cast. His white sideburns were bushy and gleaming.

The more Claire watched him, the more she thought she knew him, not in the way she had recognized James' face when she met him because she had wanted to, but because this man here bore a striking resemblance to Father.

James's head was bowed to a newspaper. Claire wanted to poke him in the arm. Did he not see the resemblance?

She felt the beginnings of pinching pain in her lower ribs, and also of a head-ache; and a heat swelling to her neck and cheeks. The heat, growing stronger, eventually lodged itself as two coals in the inner corners of her eyes. This sensation was something else altogether. She had never felt it before.

"It is not you who is ill?" The man's face, already embedded in Claire's mind as Father's, altered to a gentle-mannered old man she didn't know. "Oh, but I see it is you," he said. "You are too young to look like you do. 'I had fainted, unless I had believed to see the goodness of the Lord in the land of the living,'" he then quoted from Scripture. "The land of the living. What a land it is, eh?" He gave a sad, short laugh. He looked with empathy at Claire.

"Indeed, sir." She noted the grimace he made as he shifted in his chair.

"This leg here," he patted his right thigh, "it's gone, I think."

"I'm sorry for your ills."

He waved a hand. "Eh, no matter. It is only a leg. I myself am not crippled, on the whole. My wife and my children are worried, so I've come here for them. But who cares about a leg? A body is only a house after all, empty but for the soul that lives in it."

She nodded.

"You're too young," the man repeated. "You have life in you yet." He reached out to her, and she placed her hand in his as if they'd always known each other. He patted the top of her hand a few times.

They sat like that for a while. His eyes closed. Her hand slipped from his. As she felt the warmth leave her skin, she remembered holding her mother's hand as she fell into a feverish sleep. *The door is open, the corridor and stairwell black with shadows. She is here, in the doorway. Aunt Aileen, come to see if Mother is ready.*

Claire turned to James. There was something hazy but pressing, just coming to light. Something to do with that vicious heat lodged in the inner corners of her eyes.

Something about Mother.

"James? James." She touched him on the shoulder and as she did, the door opened.

"Mrs Ableton? Come with me, please."

Claire shook her head no.

"Claire. You must go with her."

"Why?"

Confusion crossed her husband's face, followed by doubt and then annoyance. "Claire, do not disobey me."

"Disobey you?" Her eyes widened as she felt a kind of horror wash through her.

"The doctor is waiting, ma'am," said the nurse.

Claire stood, a frilled sofa pillow falling to the floor. If she followed the housemaid into the examination room, she would never leave the way she came in. She would leave in the madhouse wagon. James writing at his desk... suddenly finding this physician... forcing her to come here... it was all too calculated. Perhaps he did mean her well, but perhaps he did not. She could not take that chance.

Claire looked at James. "I am sorry. I wish I could be different for you." She took a step back from him and rushed forward at the housekeeper.

"Claire!" James reached for her, but his hand slid along her coat.

The old man tried to stand, saying, "Oh dear, is she alright?"

Claire shoved the housekeeper hard against the doorframe and tore past her.

She ran through the scullery, where a girl was washing beakers and bottles, and out through the back door into the courtyard. The stable hand, smoking, watched her disinterestedly, and she could hear James panting several yards behind her, and the housekeeper shouting at the scullery maid. She ducked through a side garden and ran along a narrow length of alleyway between buildings — stone scratching at her wool-lined arms — until she found herself on the street. She hurried, seeing the park across the road, and the parish school now empty of children. Ahead, at the far end of the street, was the police station. As she neared it, she slowed to a stroll. She was a teacher from the school, sent on an errand; she was the wife of an accountant off to her dressmaker's. She was anyone but Claire Ableton.

A bobby was standing outside the constabulary talking to a clerk who was having a smoke. The clerk said something, and the bobby laughed. The men looked in her direction and she tilted her head down, tugging on the brim of her hat. She ducked into a shared entryway between two shops. The smell of baked goods rushed from the bakery on one side as she walked through the adjacent door into Fortuna, the pawnbroker's place of business, setting off a little bell.

"My dear girl," the shop woman behind the counter exclaimed, her large, light-brown eyes devoid of kohl powder. Her dress was a fashionable Continental style, a deep, royal blue against her Medici face. Her grey hair, curled tightly, was piled high in a flattering style. "Just look at you, hiding beneath that bonnet!"

Claire's heart leapt with astonishment. With elation.

"Come to me!" cried Bella.

Claire rushed to her.

The two women embraced.

"How are your travels?" Bella's face fell as she removed Claire's hat, her eyes scanning Claire's. She turned the sign around in the window to *Closed*. Then she ushered Claire into the back of the shop. "Come, my dear. Tell me about that old black horse of yours."

FOUR

1884 ~ 4th March
Fortuna Pawn-Broker's Shoppe
Bonborough, Gloucestershire

"How pale you are." Bella took Claire's hand and halted her bony, searching fingers at her wedding band. She nodded, as if in confirmation of something she had already suspected. "You must tell me everything."

They sat on proper chairs with seat cushions. There was a round, lacquered folding table holding the tea set. "I keep a few of my fanciful pillows at my cottage," Bella told her, though Claire hadn't asked. "Two of the pretty velvet ones, and two of the blue silk. They are from Persia—did I ever tell you?—and I keep them on the sofa now, as I don't sit on the floor anymore. At least, not unless I am alone." She smiled mischievously.

"Have you actually travelled to the East?"

"Of course, I have. Maybe some day you'll travel again, too. But," she shook her head, "I do not think soon."

"I'm not good at traveling anymore."

"And I have done enough journeying to last me several lifetimes. So, there you have it: we are two nomads settling down."

"I went looking for you, months ago," Claire told her. "There was another fair set up in the same field. You were replaced with a Frenchman and a tiny—a cat thing— *leopard*. My words..."

"You lose them when you are rattled. You cannot remember the names of the simplest objects. But never mind, you and I would have found each other eventually. My cottage is just up the street. It's small, but flooded with sunlight, and it has a garden." Bella smiled proudly. "I have neighbours who mind their own business, a gentleman friend who takes me to a hotel restaurant for roast beef and pudding on Thursday evenings; and my mattress is thick with goose down. Yours?"

She nodded. "I spend too much of my time on it."

"And yet, there is someone else to keep it warm now. Not your sister, I mean." She took Claire's teacup and peered at the grunge of leaves at the bottom. "Ah. There it is." She put the cup down, took Claire's hand again and turned it over to examine her palm.

"Bella, I did not know you were here. I came into the shop for another reason entirely. Can you believe that?"

"Mmm," she murmured nonchalantly, while examining the lines on Claire's skin. "I said I knew I'd see you again, my dear. Lies are not my strong suit."

"Yes, I know that now."

"Then you also must know that we were always meant to be friends. Do you not remember me? Even after all these years?"

"But of course, I remember you. We met at the... But you asked me that same question in your tent. Surely...?" Claire parted the curled fringe off Bella's forehead and squinted, creating a more unfocused, slightly shadowed image of her face.

"You had just lost your mother," Bella said. "Your sister—the little thing with the ginger-blonde curls—told me this when she came to fetch me. She said you were going away to be with her mama if I didn't come quickly."

"Bella... is for Isabella."

"Izzie, they used to call me, in that provincial little place. Bishops Market, about ten miles north of St. Allswell. Bishops my foot, more like sniveling little vicar."

Claire could hardly believe what she was hearing. "I've wondered for so long where you were—where we had been, what village it was we stayed. The Sleeping Ram was the name of the inn, I think. But that's all I knew."

"We have crossed paths more than once. I told you I saw you at the Foxes & Dragons Festival."

"I thought you were just saying that."

"There was a gaming house in London, too—not that I gambled, mind you, but my companion at the time loved to run games. Your father made off with good loot that night. I played backgammon in the kitchen with you and your sister. But that was then. Look here," she stroked Claire's palm, "your lifeline is not short. Neither is the line for love. And your health, there, see it? Good health."

"But that cannot be right. I told you."

"Yes, I know, you are always telling me. But are you listening?"

The ordinariness of Bella's eyes without makeup made Claire's sting and a lump swelled in her throat. Bella could have been anyone's mother or grandmother. She could have been Claire's.

"The powders you made helped me. Can you make them again?"

"The right flowers and herbs can ease any number of symptoms. There are other women I have known who suffer as you do. It is a condition of the womb that reaches, like tentacles, to other regions of the body, bringing with it pain and affecting how one digests sustenance, how one moves, or even breathes. A baby in the womb can be a cure of sorts, if the tendrils allow the babe to stick where it must grow."

Claire, dumbfounded, shook her head, then nodded in agreement—neither motion feeling like the proper conveyance of the true understanding she felt. The true validation of what was real. "There is a doctor I was meant to see, here in town. But I ran. I think my husband wants to put me away."

"Would he do such a thing?"

"When someone is desperate enough, they will do anything."

"Desperate for what?"

"A better life."

Bella laughed. "How do you know his life with you is not the better life? Do you know what his was like before you came into it?"

"I have never been anyone's better life."

"Claire, there is something I need you to understand," Bella said, tapping her palm. "You may have merely traded one misery for another without meaning to. This line on your hand—the one that rules your head—it says there are momentous decisions to make yet. And your fate— do you see how it starts at the base of your thumb and crosses over your lifeline? That means you do have assistance in making these decisions. Ask yourself: are you sustained and assisted by the people around you— your husband, perhaps?—or by the spirits of your departed kin?"

"I don't understand what you mean."

"My dear, you of all people know what Nature is capable of, so feigning ignorance won't work with me! You have your own gift for seeing, and it's served you well, though you hardly admit to it. You ran away from someone you needed to be clear of, that is true. But now you have also run from the one person you need to keep close. He has dark hair, creamed-coffee skin as men do in the Middle East, with eyes as light as a summer sky. Yes?"

Claire clutched Bella's hand. She placed her head on Bella's lap like a child and cried. *Just when you think you are all dried up. They never end, these tears, they drown you first.*

"Come now, this won't help any." Bella stroked her back, then lifted her up again. "Look what a thumb you have. That marvelous callus! You have an artistic gift?"

Claire smiled, her cheeks wet and salty as if she'd dived into the sea. "I make beautiful things."

"And you are happy making them. Who wouldn't be if they had your gift? More tea? Here, let me. And your work makes other people happy, too. Pillows or hangings?"

"Both, anything." She wiped her face. Hiccupped. "Linens, tapestries, serviettes. The little cushioned tops of boxes. As long as I can create it with thread. Bella?" she looked down at her own hands, "Do you really believe all this?"

"I believe what I see: that you are miserable but should not be. No lines could tell me otherwise."

"But do I have *your* assistance?"

"Don't be daft. I would not have left our meeting to chance, you know," Bella added, deadly serious.

"I think I may be in danger."

"Yes, I know. Not from your hands, mind you, I read the papers."

Claire sighed with relief. "So, you do know."

"Well of course I know. What do you need from me?"

"I need to do something, but I don't know if I'm even capable of it, or if it is the right thing to do. I see things, in my head, and hear things that I can't make head or tails of. But I believe they mean something important. Something terrible." *What you do not say: Sometimes I forget what I have done and where I have been.*

Bella closed her eyes and rotated her head slowly as if exploring another world only she could see. "A man alone, eluding a chase... darkness deeper than your reckless horse fills his soul. He travels north, with purpose." Her eyes shot open. "Is there someone who would shelter him?"

Claire whispered a name close to Bella's ear.

"Listen to me," Bella said fiercely. "Momentous decisions have yet to be made. Something has been left unsolved, a mystery lurking under the surface."

"I think I saw pieces of it in the pond this morning, and just now in the physician's anteroom," Claire said. She felt the same unnerving sensation as when she had been waiting for the doctor. That sensation of calm, the stillness of the air nearly suffocating, the heat between her eyes and a certainty of a truth coming to light, a moment from the past that had been trapped for years under a painted veil, one decorated with clandestine skill. A gruesome *trompe l'oeil.*

This is about Mother. Her pearl bracelet, her ivory brush, which Meg wants merely because it is Mother's. A silver candlestick and creamer, a pillbox...

Coming into herself again, Bella pulled Claire close and kissed both her cheeks.

"Isabella," said Claire, "I want you to do something for me."

FIVE

1884 ~ 4th March, evening
Silk House
Silk Road, Oxfordshire

"You will want a pretty penny for this place. You must not be impetuous, Miss Campion, for there is income to be had, from lodgers." A meticulous mustache belonging to Mr Winston sat above invisible lips and a long, rectangular chin. Counseling came between shovels of beef loin. "I have dealt with several transactions in this area. I am this week," he boasted to James, "on my way to Richmond for an immensely complicated estate case."

"I cannot wait for someone who will take lodgers, Mr Winston, and there is only Ruthie's little room for living-in," replied Georgina Campion. "This is a family house, not a grand house."

At this, the solicitor became irritable. "But what I shall do now, Miss Campion? What shall any of us do! The Broad is not the place for me, nor is that abruptly-run hotel in pitiful Pettypoole. Forgive me, Mr and Mrs Ableton."

"You cannot mean the Golden Lion," James jested dryly.

"Nothing could be worse, save The Lantern! You have no idea what it's like, Mrs Ableton, to yearn, as we traveling men do, for a real bed and meal. To yearn for home."

Claire looked at James. They had barely spoken since this afternoon. His expression was unreadable as he returned her gaze.

"It's too late in the day to journey the whole way to Pettypoole," she had told him earlier, when she had found him waiting in the doctor's courtyard with the stableboy. "Shall we return Miss Campion's trap to her, and stay another night?" And he had answered, "I'm not certain we should return home at all." She had not known what he was thinking by this remark, and they rode in silence back to the house. He did not seem angry. He did not seem anything, which somehow felt worse.

"Mrs Ableton," Mr Winston said, "I will tell you what you cannot possibly understand."

"Oh?"

"What one must consider when traveling is safety. One's personal safety, Mrs Ableton, must be considered. You have all heard about the grisly murder on Lord Hammpen's parkland? On the grounds of Hammpen Manor itself. Can you imagine?"

Juliette gasped and her old aunt chirped, "We have not had the occasion to hear of such terrors as we ladies do not read the newspapers."

"They believe the suspect has an accomplice, and there is a rumor come through Pettyton Hall that the accomplice is a woman. Ha, what nonsense!" Mr Winston barked.

"It will be the murderer's lover, no doubt," Juliette said, her eyes wide, "as in one of Mr Hardy's novels."

"There, you see?" Mr Winston nearly shouted. "There is the path which leads to women and the Vote, I tell you! You glare at me, Miss Campion, but I can see Mrs Collbert is in complete agreement with me."

Georgina Campion guffawed. "Mr Winston, how absurd you are. By your reasoning, I am a murderer twice over. I'm certain there is more to this macabre tale than the papers make out. Mrs Matthews, you have something for our pudding, I hope?"

The cook stood in the doorway. "Queen cake, ma'am."

Claire offered her arm to Mrs Collbert. "Let us sit nearest the fire?" she suggested sweetly, and she led her from the table.

In the sitting-room, rum-soaked pudding on the side table, Miss Campion asked Juliette, "You are off to Cornwall day after tomorrow?"

"If weather permits," answered the aunt.

"Do not travel if the sky is not perfectly clear," implored Mr Winston. "Your rheumatism will not thank you for it."

There was a detailed conversation about the frost and its effect on the roads as well as the bones, the spring that was so oddly late in coming. Juliette and James embarked on a game of backgammon. There was the clicking of the marble disks, some cheerful banter and applause; there was the continued, pompous advice the solicitor imparted to anyone who would listen. Claire observed all of it carefully. The alarm raised at supper had waned, but there was no knowing what tomorrow would bring, what the next day and the day after that looked like. You could only hope to continue to slip by unnoticed. *You have traded one misery for another.*

"Old Babbage," Mr Winston remarked to James as he slapped a card down between them, James having lost at backgammon. "How is he, anyway? He was always a good egg. We were at Eton together."

Claire didn't know what kind of an egg Babbage really was: hardboiled, with the hatemongering he had directed at her husband; but Winston didn't know anything that had recently transpired between James and Babbage. The Abletons were assumed to be the loveliest couple Winston had ever met and, because he was a self-righteous buffoon, if he thought present company lay in friendly circles he would likely stick to that notion 'til the sheep came home no matter what anyone told him later.

This is what we do when we are in the thick of it: noting people's habits and foibles, seeing where we might fit in and what might, at some point, be useful to us. You have not forgotten how to do this.

Later in the evening, James and Claire retired, saturated with cake and cordials. They paused at one of the portraits in the stairwell — a man with dark hair and light eyes in a uniform from the Napoleonic Wars — and she noted, "Grave and dour this soldier is. Like you this afternoon, on the ride back."

"Did you think I wouldn't speak to the physician myself, after you bolted?"

"I... Did you speak to him?"

"There are medicines, Claire, that will help your pain."

"But no cure."

"Your pain is real, he said as much."

"You believed otherwise?"

"There are other women who suffer as you do."

And do they hear and see what no one else does?

She tilted her head against his shoulder affectionately. "You have been angry with me all evening."

They both looked at the soldier.

"They are like portals, these portraits," she told him. "They are breaches to the Other Side."

"I don't believe in that sort of thing."

Claire was silent. She knew there existed a marginal space that could, at any time, overlie the Living World. She knew it was Aunt Aileen who came to visit Mother in her sickbed, perhaps thinking she was ready to join her that very night; or perhaps she had come to warn Claire that Mother would soon be taken from Allswell, that she would die away from her home. But how was Claire to have stopped that?

"This looks like you." James pointed to a painting of a woman with dark, elaborately-plaited hair and a green gown.

"It is."

He looked at her, about to laugh, then his mouth fell straight at her hardened, eerie expression. Claire winked, pinched his arm, and ran up the stairs with a little shriek. He took the steps two at a time, laughing, and they stumbled together in an embrace as their door slammed behind them.

He kissed her cheek, put his hand on the back of her neck and kissed her just below her ear.

"I had an aunt, you know, who could see things others could not," she whispered as he kissed her again and again. "Aileen, my mother's beloved sister."

"I did not know, my love. What else will you tell me?" His mouth lingered on her throat.

"I will tell you all," she said, "in the morning." She placed her hands on his cheeks and kissed him on the mouth, and he pulled the shawl from her shoulders.

His hand stopped at her bare collarbone, astonished. Before he could say a word, she embraced him and pulled him down onto the bed.

There were always these episodes: occurring within dreams, within memories that were hers and not hers, in the many houses she lived in that possessed other people's memories. When she was younger, Claire told herself her mind had merely conjured these images accidentally, that she was a victim of tricks of the eye. Mostly, she kept quiet, never putting words to what she beheld. Only occasionally would she whisper to Meg about something she'd seen, and Meg would listen, never contradicting but never breathing a word of it afterwards.

This house that was more French than English, this home for displaced strangers, was dark and still on this night. It had been quiet, too, that day she had snuck in through the kitchen door when she was young. The sun had been bright. She had been a resentful girl, then, ready to commit a crime to avoid spending another minute in that ramshackle shed down the hill.

Silk House had been empty, except for Mrs Matthews, she now realizes. But even that was not quite true. Whilst in the sitting room, Claire had heard, above her head, the creak of footsteps; she had moments before seen a figure move across the upper window from where she had crouched in the garden. Then the cook had left with her basket on her arm, but too soon for her to have been the woman upstairs. The garden had been thick, green, and vibrating with bees, all the windows open to the heat of that strange, long-ago day. And Claire had walked in and fallen asleep in the sitting-room as if it was hers. Claire had been overcome, even in her anxious, angry state, with a deep sense of peace and tranquility and belonging.

Claire had not been sure it was the same house even yesterday, when she saw the bird carved into the upper shutter. It was years ago she'd been here, and she had been blinded by fury and rebellion, as well as by sunshine, then. But this morning, when she left the pond and retrieved the rugs from the kitchen, she doubled-back around the house to where the French doors led to the cosy sitting-room with the Delft tiles around the fireplace.

Certain no one was watching, Claire lifted the front of her dress, and, with the scissors from her chatelaine, she snipped at a square of fabric sewn into the gauzy jupon. Carefully pulling only an inch of stitches, she reached into the hidden pocket where a folded piece of parchment lay flattened. She dug further and produced an iron key with a decorative curl at the top. She turned it over in her fingers, the metal already growing frigid in the cold air. She slipped it into the latch and turned it, but the key did not move. She tried again. The lock hesitated, then released. The door swung open.

The key was back in her pocket now, the patch re-stitched, her dress and underclothes draped over a chair in the corner of the room. She fell asleep with her legs wrapped over James'.

It was for no apparent reason that Claire awoke in the middle of the night. She knew with certainty that she was looking at the wall closest to James' side of the bed, that the windows were at her back, and that patterns of shadow and moonlight were swimming across the painted plaster like marble under water. She was too sleepy to reflect on what this meant, but she knew the sight was real. They must have left the curtains open.

Presently, a different set of shadows formed: from a tree bowing in the wind, or someone walking past the window. *Except the room is not at ground-level, is it?*

Claire rolled onto her back, turned her head to look at the casement. What looked like faint clouds of white smoke gathered between the curtains. The patterns on the walls swirled and churned until it seemed as though only she and the furniture in the room were actually still, while all around her the walls moved and shifted. She willed herself not to blink—she was afraid of missing something. And she feared whatever it was she thought she saw would disappear. But her eyes began to water, her sight unfocused, so that she finally did have to blink and after which she saw the clear shape of a figure standing by the window, inside the room.

Claire started to sit up, then lay back again. "Mrs Matthews?" she whispered, "is that you?"

But she knew it was not Mrs Matthews. It was the woman she had seen crossing the window—this window—all those years ago.

The woman, bathed in shadowy murk, glided toward Claire, her skirts rustling softly as she approached. With a wide width of silk, under-layers shaped like the rounded tiers of a cake, her gown was not of current fashion. She stood alongside the bed, her face still undefined, and bent over Claire.

She placed her hand on Claire's forehead the way a mother might check a sick child, then slid it down between Claire's ribs and rested it on her abdomen. Claire stiffened against the cool, smooth touch; she could feel it through the thin fabric of her chemise as surely as if the touch was human. Withdrawing her hand, the woman turned and retreated in one fluid movement to the window. Then, she was gone, evaporated like a lifting mist.

The room returned to its dim, ordinary existence. The walls were still.

Claire felt like a deer caught off-guard in a thicket. If I move, she thought, I'll discover that I am really asleep—or that I am really awake—and I do not know which is more terrifying.

She reached up and touched her own forehead. She was very much awake, she knew. The caress of the ghostly hand was embedded on her face and body.

Though she knew that the woman was not Mother, her touch had brought Mother back to Claire with vehemence. The memory of Mother's smell, her touch, her voice, surged over Claire now, and she had to hold her hand over her mouth to stop herself from crying out and waking James. So, she lay still, listening to her own quick, shallow breathing; feeling silent tears run down her cheeks into her hair. And after a few minutes, she was asleep again.

Just before dawn, it rained. The droplets sounded slowly at first, like fingers drumming on a tabletop, and built to a crackle like burning wood. Then, the crinkling of tissue paper and, finally, a deep breath of aqueous wind rushing and receding. Breathing with the house.

SIX

1884 ~ 5th March, ten o'clock a.m.
Silk House
Silk Road, Oxfordshire

Morning sounds: the bell-like chink of dishes and teacups, the breathy bellows puffing up the fires. And scents: of boiled eggs and ham, smoky odors wafting around the house, as though an unseen hand was sliding under each door and releasing them.

"We can make the exchange later."

"No." Claire counted off the notes. "That's the whole of it." She fixed her eyes out the window as she held out the bundle.

"You seem anxious," Georgina Campion noted.

"Not at all." She forced a smile. The pre-dawn rain had washed away all but a few patches of snow. The raw ground was drenched and ductile. Her hair, not yet coiled and pinned, was uncharacteristically unkempt; wavy tendrils stretching down her shoulders, spilling over Georgina's paisley shawl, which she had made a present of to Claire.

"You are anxious." Georgina lowered her voice. "Yet I wonder why you would have reason to be. What is it?"

Claire's eyes caught hers, then darted back to the pound notes.

"I shall send for my solicitor after breakfast. If you do not mind my asking... Claire — this is a substantial amount of money, procured in a short amount of time. And your husband is a primary school teacher?"

"I have a small savings." She stared at the little painting of the nude figure above the desk made by the banished creature Lady Jandits had tried to rescue. The girl had starved anyway, in the end.

Georgina leaned in and displaced the shawl from Claire's bare neck, in a bold and intimate gesture.

The sight of Bella, behind the counter in her shop, came to Claire. Bella's arms had opened, and she had rushed into them like a child. "What can you do with this?" Claire asked. She had unclasped the necklace and the sound of the heavy ring hitting the scale was like the final, reverberating bass note of a long and complex symphony. The gold and ruby turned out to be genuine, as did her fortune teller: they were, both, legitimate items in a lifetime of shams.

"Please, take this now." Claire pressed the notes into Georgina's hands and Georgina nodded and began drafting a simple contract.

"Put Mr Winston on your list for lodgers. He is a dogmatist, but he causes little trouble." Georgina dipped her pen into an inkwell. "When he wakes, I will have him notarize this. Sign here... and now I shall, here... Mr Pirret comes only occasionally, but always bears a gift. Do not tax yourself with too many guests."

"Yes, I have thought of them both."

But will you really see either of them again?

James will, she thought. And also... but she couldn't think about that; she had no idea if what Ruthie imparted to her earlier will come to pass; she could not believe in something so tentative and fragile.

"I want the big house we saw with the enormous pillars," Meg once sang, during one of their interminable travel games.

"Columns," Claire had corrected, ever the peevish schoolmarm, imposing a description from a book found in some forgotten, crumbling house.

Meg bumped against her, tiny and immature even for eleven, the two of them jostling in the back of a cart with feed bags for cushions. Father spoke to the driver, cajoling him to let them spend the night and take them as far as three towns over the next day, where they might take the rail west.

"I saw a house, once," Claire said to her, "with a lovely garden at the top of a hill. I went inside, but no one knew."

"You shall have the white room and Father shall have the blue," said Meg, paying no attention. "I shall plant a thousand Gangly Hedge-Hearts and Blue Cloudies in my garden. A thousand of each."

"We can't be together, you know, if you have one house and I have another."

"That's not true. As long as our houses stay put," Meg explained, as if houses could just walk themselves away. "We shall always know where the other one is, and we may always visit. Plait my hair, Claire. Not like that. In two pieces curled 'round my ears. It's all the fashion again."

Claire had huffed, taking a piece of Meg's hair in her fingers.

"In two plaits, I said. Like Mother used to."

"You do not remember Mother very well, dearest."

"Do you?"

"Yes."

James appeared in the doorway, dispelling her memory. He would tell Claire, later, that she had a look of mystery, and of satisfaction, about her. In mere seconds, that expression changed.

"Claire." The one word was like ice on his tongue. You could know in an instant, just by the tone of your name being said, what was meant by it.

His eyes flickered to Miss Campion, then back to Claire. He said, "They are in the entry."

"We need to see the master of the house," said the more brusque and imposing of the two men. Both wore suits, woolly tweed, neither being a common street bobby, though the burly Detective Constable should have been in uniform. They stood in the entry hall, the now-closed front door at their backs.

"Are you a guest here, sir?" the smaller, older man asked James, with an agreeable tenor the first did not possess. He was the Inspector in charge, clearly. His hair was sandy-grey and neatly trimmed, his face weathered with full, grey side whiskers; but it was his voice Claire recognized. He had been nearer to her than this, his breath grazing her forehead as he leaned over her to peer at the corpse. And she had been the comatose patient with closed, swollen eyes, neatly piled hair, and felted blanket pulled up to her chin: a mummy in a museum, when he saw her in Pettypoole's surgery.

"I am a guest here," James said.

Claire could feel his hand, hot as coal tongs, grip the fabric of her dress at the small of her back.

Mr Winston appeared from the kitchen, wiping his mustache with a serviette. Now they were a group, all off them standing in the entry, looking at each other.

"An' the master of the house?" the Detective Constable asked. His eyes were deep-set in his rectangular, ruddy face, his scarred scalp visible beneath a close crop of hair.

"It is mistress, rather," noted the Inspector as he checked his notepad.

Georgina's shoulders were straight as a ballerina's, her expression pleasant and impassive.

Claire felt the tightening of James' fist as she stepped forward. She heard him whisper a frantic, barely audible "No."

"Sirs. I am the owner of the house."

The two men looked at Claire.

"Excuse me, but…?" Mr Winston tried to interject.

Georgina Campion remained mute, expressionless.

"Ma'am?" asked Ruthie meekly, but it was impossible to guess to whom she was speaking.

Removing his hat, the older man nodded to Claire. "I am Detective Inspector Lewes. This is Detective Constable Marley. My apologies for disturbing your guests."

"It's quite all right," Claire heard herself say.

"We are following a lead," Lewes continued, "involving a gamekeeper from Pettypoole, and a woman by the name of Betriss."

"She was on the coach to Bonborough," added Marley. His pin eyes darted about the hall, impaling any invisible bubbles of deceit.

"A lady with a gamekeeper? What does she look like?" demanded Mr Winston with his usual bombast, "and why on earth would you think she was here? Forgive me, but you police never seem to be on the right path. I should know," he chuckled to Georgina, who smiled blandly back at him.

"She was seen wearing a velvet bonnet," said Marley. "One of those things sits high on the head, her hair pulled back under it, so there's no agreement what colour, and a very large ring she wore."

"That is not a description of a criminal, that is a fashion item from a magazine," snorted Winston, "written by one of Judge Henry's incompetent clerks in Pettyton Hall."

"You'll pardon me, Solicitor," said Lewes tightly, "but I must ask you do not intervene. For the moment." The two were clearly acquainted with each other, the Inspector countering snobbery with civility to no avail.

"What colour hat is your mystery woman wearing?" Georgina asked.

The two men exchanged a bewildered glance. "Olive drab, ma'am. With a pine velvet ribbon," Marley informed her.

Ruthie sounded a tiny hiccup.

Georgina nodded. "What's this all about, Inspector? Stolen jewels?"

No, ma'am. Murder."

Georgina broke into a loud and unseemly laugh. "You must be joking!" she guffawed.

"Now, Lewes," said Winston, "you and I both know the papers have the man heading north as of last night's edition. He was spotted at an inn in Shropshire, am I correct? Could he not have gotten off the coach at The Broad? Really, it's a waste of time to impose on these good ladies—and scaring the wits out of them needlessly—though I suppose you are paid, either way."

Lewes crossed his arms. "When I want rumors and hearsay, Solicitor, I'll ask for them. Otherwise, I prefer to act on the facts."

"This woman you are looking for," interjected Georgina, "she is herself a murderess?" She smiled sweetly, as if listening to a fable told by silly children.

"We suspect the woman has aided in the plot of a rather gruesome crime, with her husband, the gaming man."

"Do you mean a game warden? Or a gambling man?"

Lewes checked his notebook. "Excuse me, ma'am, but are you a guest here?"

"I am indeed."

Mr Winston coughed, "My word, Georgi—"

"Forgive me," interrupted Claire, "but I do not believe you have presented your identification." Her voice had dipped two octaves, to the deepest caverns of her throat, the only way she could keep it from quavering. Her hair was still an undone mane (*so unlike you, one can hardly think of why you have come down in such a state*), and a lock of it fell across her eye, which had begun to twitch.

The fierce-looking Constable swiped his badge from his pocket while the Detective Inspector withdrew his notepad again, flipped open the black leather cover, and held a single finger up to invoke silence. "Just a moment, all of you..." His lips moved soundlessly as he turned the pages of the little book. "You are the owner?" He looked at Claire.

She nodded.

"And you, Madam," Lewes asked Georgina, "Did you travel from Pettypoole yesterday morning?"

"I did not."

"Is this true?" Lewes asked Claire.

"She has been here," Claire replied, "for quite some time." Her heart pounded in her ears, blood sloshing loudly with each beat. "Have you finished, Detective Inspector? I have much to do this morning."

Marley leaned close to Lewes. "Are we sure about that ring, Gov?"

Lewes' eyes made one last sweep of the faces before him. "I am sorry," he said, "but I insist you come with us." He jabbed his hand forward and caught Claire's wrist.

"Wait!" James lurched forward.

Too late, Lewes held her securely, opening the front door and wrenching her through it.

Marley threw his wide back in front of James. A picture on the wall swung and scraped. The clock was knocked into, the pendulum clanging off-time while an edge of wood bit into the wall. The two men formed shackles on either side of her, forcing her over the threshold to the outside.

"Stop," shouted Ruthie, "please stop! Let her go!"

The men hauled her onto the front path. One yanked Claire's arm abruptly in one direction while the other wielded round to look at Ruthie, and at this moment Claire thought she would be torn in two.

James shouted and tried grabbing at the Inspector, but Winston held him back. "Leave it," he said to James. "I will follow you to town," Winston called out, to whom Claire was unsure. It was as if an entire building was collapsing behind her, people running and hollering.

As they dragged her, she tripped, and was lifted entirely off her feet for a moment by their firm grip.

"Keep moving! Get her in."

She felt the jab of a knee in her back, and a hand pushed her head down and into the back of the black police wagon.

"Stop!" Ruthie, arms waving, ran toward the drive. She was frantic to a nonsensical degree, disproportionate to her relationship with a woman she barely knew.

"Ruthie, please, you will make it worse for her," called Georgina.

Make what worse? Claire thought. Then she realized with horror: If these men were insulted, they would beat her inside and out. Or worse.

"Listen to me," Ruthie continued arguing, "it's not only her life you'll endanger!"

The door to the wagon slammed shut, and in the sealed compartment Claire felt a narrow wood bench beneath her. Through the tiny, barred window, she saw James break free of Mr Winston. The Black Maria leaned, then righted, as the men hoisted themselves to the driver's bench. The whip sounded, and the wagon pulled away.

Still on the drive, Ruthie became smaller, but Claire could see James grab her by the shoulders. He shouted, his face in hers, "What the bloody hell do you mean it's not just *her* life?"

 SEVEN

1884 ~ 5th March, two hours previously
Silk House
Silk Road, Oxfordshire

She hadn't pinned her hair only because she feared waking James with her fussing. It was more important to find Georgina first thing, to draw the agreement and secure the house.

"Ma'am?" Ruthie was standing in the hall at the top of the stairs, a basket of linen in her arms. "I couldn't help but wonder—"

"Is Miss Campion awake?"

"Yes, ma'am. But what I wondered is if you'll be staying again tonight?"

"Why do you ask?"

"You rested well, did you?"

"I did." Her hand on the newel post, she paused. "Actually... Have you ever passed a night in that room, Ruthie?"

"No. It was Miss Campion's great-aunt and uncle's room." She was back to being the museum docent.

"The Captain's wife, yes?" Claire asked impatiently. She took a step down.

"Lady Bridget, that's right, and Captain Mayle. She was never very well," Ruthie continued. "Beautiful, and kind—this is how she's remembered—but very poorly. She passed on twenty years before her husband. He never remarried, the Captain."

"He had their children to comfort him, I am sure." Claire continued down, then paused and looked back up at Ruthie, a thought crossing her mind that she was not sure she should have.

"No, ma'am. There were no children. It was Lady Bridget's nephew the Admiral, you remember, who came to live with the Captain after she died."

"No children?" A woozy sensation scaled up her legs. "It is all very confusing, these relatives of Miss Campion's."

"It was Miss Campion's nephew on Lady Bridget's side who inherited the house, you see. It passed down through the female line of the family—unusual though that is—but that is how it worked out. And then it was empty for a while, when Miss Campion was away in France, though Mrs Matthews did stay on to keep things up. Oh, you do look pale, ma'am! You'd better sit down."

The stairwell tilted. "I did not sleep well."

Ruthie knelt next to Claire. "Sit here. On the step. That's right." She dabbed Claire's brow with a linen from the basket. "Tell me, were you awakened?" There was conspiracy in her voice.

"What?"

"It's just that every so often," she lowered her voice to almost a whisper, "she sometimes pays a visit." She dabbed Claire's glistening neck. Her eyes were steady and intense. She was a gargoyle, crouching close and keeping guard.

"Bridget," Claire said, "she appears in the room?"

"She won't harm a soul, mind you, she'd never do that. Lord, how pale you are, Mrs Ableton. Ladies, in particular, tend to see her."

"But I did not see her, when I first came here."

"Have you stayed with us before?"

"I mean — no. What I mean is: Do women see her? Women who are like her? Who are ill and will never bear children; who will die before their time?" Claire heard her voice pitch higher. She had given up the thought of death too soon; it had come to get her, after all.

Ruthie, puzzled, shook her head. "I don't think you understand. Every once in a while, some lady's seen her and been touched by her like this," she put her fingers on Claire's forehead, sparking pins and needles across her scalp. "And it's as if she knew before they did. They were all with-child, you see. That's the only way anyone sees her." She whispered, "the only way *you* might have seen her."

EIGHT

1884 ~ 6th March, three o'clock, a.m.
Bonborough Station, Gloucestershire Constabulary
Bonborough, Gloucestershire

The air was frigid. There was little light, other than the faint glow of the lantern in the windowless corridor where a man sat at a tiny wooden table that posed as a desk. Her cot, too, was wood. Everything else was iron or stone.

With her fists balled, moisture erupted from her warm lungs, her vibrating shoulders clattering the slats of the cot. She no longer thought of herself as being at-one with her own body. She was like the remnant of a dying spirit trapped in a decrepit encasement. She was glad James was not here to see her.

It must be the middle of the night. *If he has not left, he will still be in the station entry.* The entry's walls were tapestried with police-notices, one of them a photograph of a Wanted House-Breaker, another boasting a Ten Guinea Reward for A Debtor Carrying a Knife. A sergeant in uniform sat up on his dock writing things. In the entry, James would not have a place to sit because the one bench would be crammed with men in handcuffs.

You worry about him when, really, you should be worried about them coming in to measure your neck. No gallows can be weighted for someone as tiny as you have become; you'll kick as you swing, you know.

The voice had not left her alone for hours.

They'll have to let me go soon, she thought, I only must wait it out.

Not likely.

"Shut up," she hissed.

Do you really think they will believe a housemaid's ridiculous fairy-tale? You don't even believe it.

She lodged her tongue between her teeth and curled-up tighter on the cot. It was just like riding in the cart, she told herself, think of it that way. Imagine a layer of hay beneath you, Stony's blanket placed over you and Meg, the two of you huddled together, giggling...

She remembered lying under an open sky, her arms around Meg. Out of the hundreds of nights they'd slept in all manner of places, it was this one—the first without Mother—which came back to her so clearly. She had not been as frightened that night as she was now in this cell. Confused, perhaps, and shocked. There had been a beautiful, pearl-white moon peeking in and out of pewter clouds. There had been Father's stories of his Spotted Cheetah-cat to entertain them. It smelled lovely, too: of boggy fields and newly-sprouted grass.

But it had been very cold, she had to admit, and damp. And the damp had eventually worked its way into her grieving heart and inside her bones so that, in the morning, she had awakened a different person altogether.

The sound of boots pounded down the stone steps. She raised her head, blinked against the dark, and saw it permeated by a single blinding flame fractured into a pulsing star. The celestial glow swung and next sounded a key scraping in the enormous iron lock, and the cell door yawning.

Figures stood in the opening of her cell. Two men were multiplied by dehydration into a small infantry. "You're going up," one said.

Claire retched and leaned over the side of the cot. Nothing came, but as her hand shot down to catch herself, her fingers grazed matted fur. A scurry across the floor. *Scurrying and busying themselves, looking for crumbs. Soon, they'll discover there are none; there is only your flesh to be had. You won't know they've touched you until you feel their bite.*

Claire had given up wishing the voice would stop. At least now it was trying to be helpful.

They kept you down here over-night, you realize, to make you talk, the voice offered. The men, not the rats.

"But I've been ready to tell them all along," she whispers, so as not to draw her gaolers' attention.

Have you now? it counters. *You are sure of that?*

The constable stepped forward and lunged at her—or so she thought—and she pitched herself back against the weepy, dank stone wall. He screwed his face up with bewilderment, reached a hand under her arm, and tugged her to standing.

As they walked her past the other cells, two of the prisoners approached the bars to gape at her. A boy who stole sugar was lying motionless on his cot, eyes wide and glistening. He made a clicking sound in his throat to stop himself from crying. Claire had been able to see him more clearly than the others when they first brought her down yesterday, though she could not see the colour of his hair or eyes; whether he resembled Davie... or Will, forever a boy, though he was likely a father himself by now.

The bobbies had walked her along this same narrow corridor formed by the wall on one side and four cells on the other. The same constable sat at a small table jammed into the corridor with a ledger and inkwell, framed by the glow of a single lantern that also partially illuminated the boy.

"In for stealing a pound of sugar out of a delivery cart," he'd mentioned to the bobbies attached to each of her arms. Both in navy, high-necked coat with a single row of brass buttons, the bobbies were not much older than the boy in question.

As they continued walking her down the row Claire heard, in the shadows, someone mumbling in one cell. A consumptive cough from the next. There was a dark, shapeless form in the corner of one chamber, with another hunched on what must have been a stool. Men they all were, except the boy.

At the sight of the boy, she had gone limp and let the bobbies hold her up, her boots scraping. She would let the floor tear the leather from her feet, her skin from her bones, before she walked into that cell willingly.

"Keep moving," said the bobby on her left now. Younger than she was, Claire could hear in his voice that he was not accustomed to being cruel to a woman. He almost added, "ma'am," before he swallowed the word.

Up the narrow stairwell they took her. Then, she was led into a bright corridor and the shuffling of the station. A clerk stood with a ledger and some drunkard in a checked waistcoat slurred, "Teddyteddyteddy," whilst the arresting officer laughed his head off. There was a door in the middle of the corridor, wedged open by another clerk, and as she was guided clear of it, she could see through to the main entry. At the dock, the sergeant consulted paperwork and barked orders to no one in particular; two doxies in the cage looked sullen; and there, on the bench, elbows on knees, exhausted...

"James!"

The grip on her arms tightened, her shoulders were hoisted to her ears. "Keep moving."

She thought she heard her name returned as they moved her forward past the door.

A room at the very end of the gallery: Marley was inside, now in uniform, and Lewes still sporting his brown tweed. The walls were made of thick, jagged stone, a once pale hue mottled with dark drips and stained with years of sick, of beatings. Rain sprayed against a small, high window, a portion of sky glazed black. Time was unspecific. Perhaps it was still the middle of the night, perhaps nearly dawn.

They sat her in a hard chair at a table. She clutched a portion of the hem of her skirts. The two-inch diameter hole sat below a swath of flora she embroidered three days ago over the other, much larger, tear. She ran her fingertip gently along the edge of the rip and thought of her folding scissors and needle-case she usually wore around her waist like appendages she couldn't live without. They had been confiscated, and she wondered now if they would be returned to her. She told herself they would be. Then she told herself she'd be let go very shortly.

Not likely, said the voice.

"Shut up," she hissed.

The truth of it is —let us face it, shall we?—you are a coward. (She agrees.) Maybe that is the real problem: you have always been weak-willed.

She took a deep breath and gagged from the stench in the air. She realized she was being watched closely by the two men, her movements examined and catalogued.

She rested her hands in her lap and willed herself into stillness. Her hands were raw, fingertips marred with little calluses and splits from all the needlework. There was a particularly ugly spot where a callus had peeled away in the damp cell to tender new skin on the inside of her right thumb. Her dark brown hair hung wild and clumped around her gaunt, sallow face.

She never wore her hair down except at night, with James. Each morning she plaited it, spiraling the plait atop the crown of her head in a neat chignon. When she and Father traveled together he often, magician-like, produced floral sprigs and she would weave them into the chignon. He would say, for instance, that Bruised Lilies set off her grey-green eyes, which he said were the colour of the sea. Other people would say so, too, when they met her. Now people said, "What a shame, she was nice to look at, once. A pretty Gypsy girl." She knew she now had the wan appearance of a Whitechapel street urchin: whoring at ten years old, dead at twenty of consumption or by strangulation in a dark passage. She could have gone that route, at one point.

Perhaps you should have.

She wondered if James ever thought about her appearance last summer, when he'd fallen in love with her. It was hot and sunny the day they met. He was all height and solemn expression, with thick dark hair and browned skin, and clear, light eyes. He held an armful of books she would have traded her supper for.

"What's a Jew doing in Pettypoole?" That was one of the first things Lewes had asked yesterday, about James.

Without letting her answer, Marley had jumped in, "What's this roller here doing in Pettypoole? And why, if she's such an innocent missus, is she on the run from us?"

Lewes returned, "I should like to know that myself."

Back and forth they went, a dance-hall comedy show. They ought to sell tickets, she thought now.

Marley set a plate with a wedge of bread in front of her, then took a step back and watched.

Mr Winston, she thought, was putting the pressure on. Claire felt herself groping for hope the way a drowning person flails at a nearby buoy. *The hope: that you will be able to talk your way out of this.*

Marley leaned in. "Eat."

The most familiar of human tasks—the consuming of food—had been nearly absent from her life for months. Her life had become one elongated day into night into day, with mere bites of sustenance speckled about. A coward's escape, slow and lazy, from the punishment she knew she deserved. They were bound to catch up, she thought. You can't really live as someone else the rest of your life without being found out.

If you tell them the truth...

The truth is something different than what can be said, she thought back to the voice. Similar, maybe, but not the same.

That is only because you believe the actual truth will make things worse for you. You are losing your words again, by the way.

"It will certainly make things w-worse for me." This might have been said aloud.

All right, then, go on and lie, that should be easy enough—you are an expert at lying—but which lie to tell? And how long will the story stick if you are weak, exhausted, not in the right state of mind to think swiftly?

She had no answer. Instead, she thought, how instantly things change when it comes to murder: in a single moment a boy's innocence is ripped from him, and a tranquil storybook village becomes an ill-omened corner of an already bleak world; one moment a man is walking and speaking, sharing a pint with his mates, the next he is mangled in the ground.

One moment you are going about your bucolic little life in Pettypoole, and the next, you are in a cell in Bonborough.

"Won't eat? Feeling poorly again, are we? Don't know how she does it, Gov, being sick on command. Always been able to do it?" Marley asked in earnest.

"Not always," she said, plucking a crumb off the crust.

Marley let out a roar of laughter.

"Is that funny, sir?"

"You know what I'll find ever so amusing, love? When you hang. You see," he noted dryly, "I don't care if you're a sorceress or a leper, or a common whore—whatever it is they say you are, be my guest—I only care that a man has been murdered and your name is all over him."

Her expression, in return, was vacant.

He sprung forward and slapped her across the face with a swift and painful crack.

Lewes put his hand on Marley's shoulder. "None of that or Winston will hear of it." Calmly, he asked Claire, "How is it a schoolteacher's wife has employment? For the Henry's Stores, yes?"

"I-I-I make needlepoints and embroideries in my spare time." Her cheek throbbed and stung.

"In your spare time, Dutchess? Ain't that lovely," said Marley.

"One Mrs Lettie Ponting says you were employed by her," continued Lewes.

Claire shook her head no. Oh, how stupid people are, she thought, there is just no end to it; it was Lettie who had set her straight about married women working for money, and now she'd violated her own code. It looked badly for Henry's as well, did it not?

"So, you do not have employment—except that you do. And we see you are also a great letter writer. And receiver of letters." Lewes unfolded a piece of parchment, *Mrs Peter Doughterty* engraved at the top.

Claire did not have to see it up close to know the letter spelled out the route she took through Lord Hammpen's fields, and who she went to see (Norris' mother, the shunned midwife, who likely also met her end by now), with Meg begging her not to do precisely that.

Carefully, Claire said, "Mrs Dougherty knows nothing of the matter you're concerned with."

"Oh?" Lewes' face brightened a little, in a manner more alarming than friendly. "And yet she writes, 'nothing good can come of this plan, and I'll be very angry with you if you go on with it.'"

"What she means, it's not what you're thinking, but..." she stopped herself.

"Well?" Marley pressed.

"You must understand." *You must be calm. Cooperative.*

"Go on."

"I'd only ever known—"

"Known the dead man?"

"Let her speak."

"You'd only ever known who?" Marley probed, ignoring Lewes.

"What," Lewes suggested. "You have only ever known what, Mrs Ableton? Claire. Claire Bietris." Pronounced correctly. "You've only ever known the life with your father, is that it? You had no choice." His bland suit and sad bright eyes said: I've seen it all so not even you can surprise me.

Marley regaled, "Is that why John Dean's lying in the morgue, his guts all blown out?"

She shook her head. She couldn't speak.

"Had his way with you once before, did he, as per Dad's arrangement? But this time things are different. You're a married woman now—albeit to a Jew. And you know what? I think maybe there's another body out there, and it's going to turn out to be your father's."

She heard herself laugh a big, loud guffaw, and as soon as she did, she knew she was doomed. But she couldn't stop herself and fell into a fit of laughing. She put her hand over her mouth as if it belonged to someone else. The voice said: *You never should have waited this long.* Claire laughed until she was crying.

"She's cracked, this one." Marley snorted.

But Lewes' stoic face had begun to grow a thin film of doubt, like moss developing on a forest floor. The shift was ever so slight. Could she use it? Work her way in, like slipping into a crack and widening it?

"Fuck all," Marley barked. "She's useless. Throw her back downstairs."

"Just a moment." Lewes bent down so his face was next to hers and he placed his hands on the back of her chair, on either side of her shoulders. He was so close she could smell the rosemary and lard soap he used that morning. He spoke softly, with crisp clarity. "I am going to tell you something, Mrs Ableton. You are wondering where your husband is, and I will tell you. As I speak, he is under this very roof being questioned by my superior who, I am sorry to tell you, is not as sympathetic to your husband's sort as you might wish him to be."

She willed herself not to show any reaction.

"You can read. Is this true?"

"Yes."

Looking grim, he sat down in the chair across from her and folded his hands neatly on the table. "Do you know what the law says about murder? About aiding and abetting?"

"I'm very cold."

"Do you understand why you are here?"

"I have never been arrested before."

"Though perhaps you should have been?"

She felt that appalling giddiness again creeping up her lungs.

He placed the letter in front of her. Tapped it. "You can read this?"

They have rummaged through your things to find them all, nestled amongst your stays and chemises. All the letters but two: both burned in the grate. Ah, but you did not burn them both, did you?

"This was written to you last month," Lewes said. "What does Mrs Dougherty mean when she writes, 'nothing good can come of this plan'? I am waiting." Again, he tapped the letter, looked directly at her.

You always hold Meg's eyes with your own when you speak to her, or she'll never do what she's told: Get Stony's harness; Take the water from the well; Go fetch the doctor, Mother is poorly; Do not tell anyone.

"Your sister has been in Tyne since when, exactly?"

"She has been there since the time before."

"The time before when?"

"Since—since she was there... since she was married. In Tyne."

"You hesitated. You are making this up?"

She shook her head. "I lose my words. You think Meg knew him—Mr Dean—but she c-can't have known him."

"Your sister is married to Peter Dougherty, orchardman for Lord Whitlock."

She hated hearing they knew her brother-in-law's employ. "I came to Pettypoole, as I said, not for any reason."

"After the wedding, yes, I've got all that."

"—and you say you were not running away on the coach," Marley interjected, "yet you came to Bonborough anyway, to find that poor lad, John Dean's son, and silence him before he remembered you."

"No," she said. "Is he alright? The boy? It's Norris he wants. Why hasn't he been brought in?"

"Who says he hasn't?"

"But then…?"

"She thinks she's clever."

"When Davie came in looking like he did," she began.

"Who the bloody hell is Davie?"

Lewes shot his hand up to silence Marley. "The printer's devil. Go on, Mrs Ableton, tell us."

"He's a simple boy—you m-must know that if you spoke to him or to M-Mr Tinsdale—and always taking the wrong way into town, which Rollins and Norris don't like as it scares the game away. I w-was going to the doctor, you see, because my head ached and I said to Mr Tinsdale, 'I'll find out what this is all about,' because we both thought Norris had fought with Davie."

"Hang on. That was you, on the surgeon's table? You are the woman I saw?" said Lewes.

She nodded.

"But you knew this man, John Dean."

"It was you who robbed him blind with the goods, you and your father," Marley added.

This is madness! Tell them!

"No, no!" She pounded the side of her head with her fist. "People seek him out, without encouragement, because he is amiable and g-generous. You cannot imagine..." She wiped her face, smearing tears and soot across her cheeks, and stared ferociously at Lewes.

And Lewes fastened his fingers before him as if praying. He pressed his mouth to his fingertips and watched her across the table, not so much with accusation, but with intense concentration.

Several minutes passed. The gas lamps sizzled. Rain, rushing against the window, seeped between the pane and the stone, sliding down the walls and forming a shallow puddle on the floor.

Lewes glanced at the window where the black sky had lightened to a dull, charcoal grey. He said, "You are running out of time."

He looked at her hands, held firmly in her lap. "What is that you are doing? Your fingers make a motion as though pulling thread. Are you mad, Mrs Ableton?" There was no unkindness meant. "I've been told that you are mad, but I'm not certain I believe it. You are unusual, perhaps even extraordinary, as artists or lady novelists sometimes are, hmm? And in my experience that means holding oneself with a kind of superior intelligence that puts others on edge. Perhaps that's all you've done: put people on edge."

She kept her eyes down as her fingers picked at the embroidery running along her skirts.

"You call attention to yourself without meaning to," Lewes continued. "I do not think that constitutes actual madness but tell that to him." He indicated Marley.

The precipice neared. At the edge, she must jump, then fly or plummet. She couldn't keep the truth from them any longer, but she couldn't bring herself to betray someone whose entire being was eternally linked with hers. The weight of devotion was as though an ancient boulder pinning her to the sand, the tide coming in quickly to drown her. If only she could hold her breath long enough for the tide to slip back out.

The door opened and a clerk entered with a file, which he handed to Marley.

In the seconds when the door was opened, she saw who was on the other side, standing in the corridor: two women quarreling with a bobby; in this split-second Claire saw two women, she was sure of it.

"Mrs Ableton, did you hear me?"

"The ladies in the corridor."

"Never mind them."

"Do not hurt them."

"Concerned about them, are you? The old one especially?" Marley waited. "I thought as much." A look of satisfaction.

"We took the public coach from Pettypoole to Bonborough," Claire said.

"When?" asked Lewes.

"Friday."

"But you did not stay on it, did you? You never actually got to Bonborough."

"No. Not on the day we planned."

"You're a lying little bunter, you know that?" Marley again. "You tell us you are the owner of this house, Silk House, which really belongs to this Miss Camperie."

"Campion," corrected Lewes.

"But I do own the house."

Marley lunged forward across his superior and grabbed her by the hair, wrenching her head back.

"Stop, please!" Her scalp was peeling. "Stop, or I'll never give it to you!"

He let go and gave a long, deep belly laugh. "She's going to give herself to me, now." Bending over at the knees, he wiped an eye. "Priceless, she is."

"That's not what she means. And I told you to bloody stop it!" Lewes' expression was of all one emotion, now: *regret*. "I am listening, Claire."

"I don't know why I took it. I never stole a thing in all my life. Father did. And I helped him, with my s-smile, the flowers in my hair." Her hand gripped her skirt.

"What did you steal?"

"It is only a latchkey. A key to my own house. Only, it wasn't my house, then, and it was wrong of me, very wrong." She asked him, in a whisper, "Do you think I will go to Hell for taking it?"

"No."

"Will he?"

"I do not know. Mrs Ableton, tell me you have something that will release you from this nightmare. What is it? Where is it?... What are you doing?"

She lifted the finely embroidered wool skirt up over her knee, to the white jupon beneath. Exposed, her legs were bruised, and nearly blue with cold, her stocking torn and sagging below the knee that was swollen and red with a jagged gash.

"Stop, please, do not disgrace yourself..."

She flipped the underskirt up, revealing a square of barely noticeable stitches. With her fingernails, she tried tearing at the stitches, then she bent over and gnawed at them with her teeth, ripping the little pocket open.

A clink sounded on the stone floor: a latchkey, spotted with browned, dried blood. Next to it, a folded note, the edge burned but the rest of it still intact.

She said: "There is no other way it could have found its way so far from my tin."

Lewes turned to Marley. "What are you waiting for?" he barked. "Get the Chief. Now."

NINE

That night, after she was released from the gaol, she dreamed. An exhalation of wind and rain became one of snow falling on the streets of a familiar city. This time, the city was Bonborough. She thought to herself, in her dream: *it will always be Bonborough from now on.*

She walked against the blustering flakes until she saw Meghan—her pale, ginger hair, her pink, lightly freckled cheeks and bright eyes—waiting for her under a streetlamp. How Claire had missed her!

Before they could embrace, they seated in the carriage at the gates of the park. This time, Claire tried to angle forward in the pitching vehicle. Standing, her hand holding the door for balance, she tried as hard as she could to grab hold of the driver's bench with her other hand.

There is no driver.

"Stop!" Claire shouted at the horse, but the animal was already headed on his terrible path, and the bridge neared.

Meg pulled Claire back onto the seat and latched onto her arm.

Yes, it is your sister who holds you back, and so tightly. How could you have not noticed it before?

But, surely, Meg didn't need Claire anymore, so why cling? "Listen to me, Meghan, you are married," Claire told her. "You are a mother yourself now. We must get down from this!"

Meg's nails squeezed into Claire's arm. "I tried for years to stop him, but you did nothing but shut me up!" Her eyes bulged monstrously. She was not Meg. She was a *bean sí*, one of Mother's terrible faeries. "It's *you* who should have stopped him!" She bared yellowed, sharp teeth. She was a horrifying specimen brought back from an explorer's trip to Hell.

Claire wrangled herself from her sister's macabre grasp and pitched herself forward across the bench. She reached for the horse again. His muscular back was wide, his coat shiny and black. He turned his great head to look at her and his expression, for a fleeting moment, appeared dozy and content. But before she could make eye contact or try to communicate with him, he was crossing the bridge.

There was a sharp lurch. Claire was thrown back onto the seat with Meg. The carriage jumped the side of the bridge and the horse leaped out over the lake.

They were falling, fast, and with great force. Claire's heart stopped as her hips were levered off the seat. She sucked her breath in a great flash of terror. The carriage hit the water with a violent strike.

The lake: its murky chill, its long, oily strands of grass. *But do you actually plunge into the water?* She felt the cold shock of the water, felt her boots touch a spongy bottom. She pushed off toward the surface. Her sopping dress and winter coat were sandbags meant to sink her. Struggling, she surfaced and looked for Meg.

Swimming hard beside her, Meg was her plucky and good sister again, the *bean sí* gone. They paddled and gasped and coughed up water. They began to help each other toward the banks of the lake. Meg's pale curls were flat and greenish against her head, her eyes wide and wet. "Help us, help us, someone!"

Claire wanted to tell her not to waste her breath, but she couldn't ingest enough air to speak. Walking along the embankment were people, normal people: a boy holding his father's hand while eating a steaming potato wrapped in newspaper, a woman pushing a pram, an old man tapping his cane. No one looked at the sisters as they struggled in the water.

Meg was first to reach the side, an edge of cobbled stone. She hoisted herself up onto the bank and knelt, leaning towards Claire. "Now you—quickly, quickly!" With Meg's help, Claire pulled herself out of the water, and the two of them, arms wrapped around each other, fell back onto the frozen grass.

At first Claire could not believe they survived the fall. Then she remembered the horse. They jumped to their feet and peered hesitantly together over the edge of the embankment, their collective breath as white clouds puffing from their purple lips, their cheeks flushed red with cold.

The black horse, a warped shadow at the bottom of the lake, lay still and dead, his white, cataracted eyes glinting skyward.

She awakened, knowing it was over.

Almost over.

PART V

A Parting Blessing

"I had no right to see it: all this was too sacred for any eyes but her own, and she had done well to keep it from me."

Anne Brontë

ONE

1884, 8ᵗʰ March
Halleford-on-Marsh to St. Andrews Parrish
Gloucestershire

"**Y**ou have traded one misery for another, Claire," Bella had said
when Claire took refuge in the Fortuna Pawn-Broker's Shoppe.
She had taken Claire into the back room, given her tea and
traced the lines of her palm. "I shall tell you why you are
miserable, Claire. Your unhappiness originates from an old
wound which festers beneath an artifice created to obscure it
long ago."

"An old wound?"

"It is a wound that's like a puzzle, and it is the same puzzle as
existed when I first met you, years ago when you were a girl who
had just lost her mother. And later, when you had become a
mother to your own sister, Meg's head tilting sleepily onto your
shoulder in my gentleman friend's house, the both of you so tired
I almost offered up my bed to you. The riddle festered, unsolved.
You could not reconcile the sudden change in your life anymore
than an honest merchant can reconcile plated tin for silver."

"Because Mother was departed. Gone forever."

"Not just departed—for we all lose our mothers, some sooner than later. She was dead, yes, but how? And *when?* Whatever you believed that story to be, it was only that—a story."

Claire spun the conversation over in her mind now, then tucked it carefully behind her heart so that she could get through this day without faltering. Without backing away and running from it. She stared out the window and watched the rail platform shift away. She glanced at Bella, composed and thoughtful-looking on the seat across from her. Three stops, and they would be there.

Bella had traveled by cab from town and met her at the station at Halleford-on-Marsh, where James brought Claire in Georgina's little trap. He said to Bella, "Take care of her. Do not let her tire." Only five miles from the Broad, the station was. Then four stops on the rail. An easy journey if one was well enough.

But how long was the journey from St. Allswell, by the coaching routes, if one was seriously ill? A week? Too long. A rail carriage could be arranged, so one could remain prone and carried by stretcher. *So, then: coach for a bit, then rail, Brighton to Swindon would do it.*

But Bella already knew this, didn't she? "Let us go and see for ourselves," Bella had urged gently, "and face Nurse Searton's story, whatever it may be."

The train stopped at the first station and their compartment companions, two elderly sisters, exited. A university student came aboard, sat next to Claire and promptly hid himself behind a large volume of *Principals Of Geology,* the round lenses of his spectacles reflecting the flickering scenery out the window. The train passed a cluster of cow sheds and a piggery with willow fencing, a miniscule village, then a large farm and two arched stone bridges. The train slowed and stopped at the next station. And the next.

After another little village and another bridge stretched large tracts of grain fields. The train slowed again.

"We are here," announced Bella. "This is St. Andrews." She stood and took Claire's hand to ensure she followed.

The ticket seller inside the station house was exact in his directions To Oliver-St. Andrews, or what had once been Oliver-St. Andrews.

Overhearing the conversation, a farmer offered to take them from the station. Claire placed Bella next to the driver on the bench. She sat on the back of the cart bed, her legs dangling comfortably like she had done this a thousand times because, of course, she had.

The sun came and went behind fair-weather clouds, and the countryside was as pretty as Pettypoole's, though slightly less hilly and rambling. There was a light but cold breeze. The farmer said nothing to them as he guided the horse on.

After a while, he stopped the cart at an old double-gate that sat frozen open, one side off its hinges and leaning on the stone gatepost. A mass of vines grew up each post. A large beech bent like an old man's spine, its budding branches lightly shading the gravel path between the gates. From the gravel grew tufts of weeds, and some early buttercups looking hopefully toward the sun.

The man who had not spoken during the ride spoke now. "My uncle was in there, for a time." He looked ahead at the road as he said this. When Bella climbed down and joined Claire, he shook the reins and wordlessly moved his cart forward.

There was a brass plaque on one of the gateposts, half-covered in vines, and Bella peeled the vines aside and silently read the tarnished engraved words, then looked at Claire to make sure she, too, read them:

The Oliver-St. Andrews Lunatic Asylum for the Poor ~ Est. 1853

Claire walked through the gates.

The drive was long and straight, no vehicle had driven down it in years. A rabbit hopped across the drive from tall grass on one side and into equally tall grass on the other. Sparrows jumped about, picking at worms and dried-up seed husks. At the end, the drive curved around in a half-circle and joined back up with itself. And at the head of the half-circle, rising up out of what had long ago been open moorland, was the asylum.

The cluster of rooflines were in fact one connected building, arms bent angularly off of a central main hall. One wing looked much like the next: York stone, dull even in sunlight, with little artifice or ornamentation; a single, stubby tower placed incongruously at the end of one wing. All the wings had straight facades and triangular rooflines, as if someone had asked dull, unimportant businessmen with pointed hats to line up, face different directions and stare disinterested at a bucolic countryside they bared no part in.

The parkland around the asylum was overgrown, exhausted with long grasses, nettle, and weeds that fluttered in the wind. A few malnourished beech had been planted with great hope but never maintained. There was, once, a sizable garden meant to supply human beings with nutrition and industry, to focus them away from their ills.

In this garden sit four patients cutting potatoes for seed, singing to themselves, and in the wash-house are many who would be tearing their own clothes to pieces were there not the prodigious array of linen to be folded. On the second story of the west wing are coteries of basket-makers,

369

*and embroiderers among the women, and saddlers and tailors among the
men. There is a good deal of senseless chatter in these rooms; but look:*
our patients are orderly, sociable, busy, and useful! When the
dinner-bell rings, what cheerful smiles run round, accompanied
by the feeling, perhaps, that whatever little is left of their inner
selves, they all know what the dinner-bell means. There is not a
chain to be found (except on one lower floor; but let us not
discuss that); those who might, in a moment, be provoked to
howl and yell are lying quietly in bed talking to themselves. We
make sure of this. A few who are not to be trusted with the use
of their hands, but who are better in society than alone, are
walking about their ward with their arms gently confined, *such a
blessing is this humane internment...*

Bella pointed to the chapel—nearby but unattached to the
main building—and drew Claire's attention back to the present.
The little chapel had a plain façade, with two round windows like
beady eyes, a mawing arched mouth for a door, and pointed little
hat for a roof on its dumbfounded head. Behind it, was a fence
surrounding an acreage of sharp blades and stinging nettle.
Claire, her arm looped into Bella's, walked toward it.

The women thrusted forward together through the nettle, their
skirts as though enormous silk sickles flattening grain. Claire felt
a sting on her wrist as a stalk snapped back before giving way.
They continued moving into the field.

After about ten feet, the plot consisted mainly of long, fine
weeds. Nestled in the green were several hundred markers: iron
discs about the size of Claire's hand, plunged into the ground by
an attached stake. Each disc bore a number: **83. 114. 22. 147.**
They looked sprouted, a field of stunted brown vegetables all
petrified and uniform and entirely impersonal.

Claire stared at the markers with great confusion and said, "But how will I know which one is hers?"

Bella gasped once, as if strangled, but composed herself quickly and stared fiercely ahead. Their arms were knotted together, the two women like porcelain dolls about to be swung into view on a clock; they were stiff as pilings against a hurricane's wave of sorrow and horror. They were all things inhuman, so as to remain standing.

Claire felt an odd sensation of calm, of stillness, and the certainty that something was coming to the surface. The painted veil decorated by her own father with blood and clandestine skill was parting. From the stillness now came a dry, hot rage rising in her chest.

"How could he?"

"How indeed," Bella whispered. "Your Mother was not departed. At least, not when you thought she was."

"No, she was not."

Mother is not dead, but he tells you she is, and makes you leave your home. For, he could not have come all this way to see her in such a short time; he has only gone to Bishop's Market to begin the deal he will finish one night later. He rushes about the house, grabbing things you do not think are useful but that you will later realize have monetary value...

"A set of silver candlesticks," Claire recounted.

"What else?" Bella urged.

"Mother's pearl bracelet, her ivory-handle brush, which Meg wants desperately. A silver creamer, a pillbox..." Claire closed her eyes and moved through time.

Father takes each item and hands it to Claire, and she places it in the carpet bag because she has to; because they have always — even Mother — done what he tells them to do. He orders, "Pack quickly, my dears," as if their ship is leaving, the one that will take them on a luxurious holiday to Venice or Athens. But there is no holiday, and he has just told them Mother is already gone, so what's the rush?

They scramble like rats, little Meg and young Claire, as Father trades their dowry to pay off his debts (for it is they who own Allswell, thanks to their clever, dead Aunt Aileen and her entail, though how can they know this at their age?). It's a sprint to avoid the Debtor's Prison. To avoid the solicitor who will read the will and hand the whole lot over to the girls when their mother, eventually, passes over into the next world. It is a mad dash to abandon Mother, not to forget her passing.

Because she is not actually dead. She is here, in this place.

For months, Mother will ask for them and wonder where they are. "He has promised they will be joining me," she tells Nurse Searton. A four-day journey she had endured because he said she would be in the best care, and won't the girls love a holiday in Oxfordshire? Who wouldn't at springtime? "Mr Bolton is leasing our land," he'd assured her, "and when we all return there will be enough money for a new herd, a new start, my love."

But no one comes. No letters are answered. She grows weaker, heart-broken, surrounded by the shrill chatter and outbursts of other women less sane but more hopeful than she. Her pale fingers stitch book covers for wealthy ladies, and when she can no longer sit upright in a chair, she stitches onto torn sheets from her bed, sewing her daughters a message with the only form of communication she can devise.

After months of this, she dies with a gurgle in her throat, alone, in the middle of the night, her eyes fixed on the ceiling, thinking, *Please, not yet.* Her withered body is placed in a rough elm box with a trap opening at the head. The box is loaded onto the grave-digger's cart. Half-a-dozen like coffins are piled together, and the cart rattles from the east wing around the front of the building to the church yard, a potter's field cloaked in a pretense of propriety.

"The ones y' see in the pit are some of the lot from last Tuesday," the gravedigger says to the driver, gesturing toward the gaping hole in the ground. Oblong lumps shrouded in white gauze are slipped ingeniously out the coffin's trap lid. *Thump, thump... thump.* A hill of bodies in powdery lye at the bottom. "Wot would be the sense in digging a hole big enough to hold so many if you shut it up before it's full, eh? Eh?" He laughs, slapping the driver on the back.

The vicar arrives, his handkerchief pressed to his nose. The young nurse, Miss Searton, is with him. She has only just heard that her patient will be interned with this batch of bodies today (an unexpected influenza sweeping through the upper floor of the south wing taking many of her charges). Her cape is hastily thrown on over her uniform. Her cheeks are blown raw by sleet-infested gusts.

The vicar says a prayer meant not for one person known and loved in life, but for any soul who is left to this end. He calls out, "Have pity, Christ in Heaven," raising his voice above the moaning wind.

There is no one else except the gravedigger, the cart driver, and the nurse. She stares tearfully. She is shocked and angry. The Vicar thinks, Does she not know this is what happens when no one claims them?

There is no one else to stand by Mother's earthly body; not even a distant cousin or friend to drop earth on the shroud that slips out of the box's trap door into the ground with that hollow thump, the coffin later reused. The vicar will never know her story, or why this should be the last chapter of it. He will never know, as he recites his psalm and the grave digger shovels his lye down into the basin of tangled bodies, that she has a home with hallowed ground waiting for her. That she has loved ones to mourn her.

He will never know that she was your mother, and that you cannot get her back.

But Miss Searton begins to wonder immediately. To question. She herself begins to age, almost over night, from self-imposed guilt and regret, and she dedicates years to search for the daughters of an anonymous woman who lies in a pauper's grave. To give them the message the woman had painstakingly sewn for them which she has taken from the woman's bedstand and kept carefully all these years.

Claire came back into the present as Bella also opened her eyes and returned to herself, the two of them having been linked to Mother's memories.

Claire blinked, looked out at the field of markers, at where Mother lay below her feet. Somewhere. She took a deep breath and realized that while one hand had been linked with Bella's all this time, the other had begun hugging her own belly, protectively.

"I have done the right thing, Bella."

"Yes," said Bella, "you have done the right thing."

TWO

1884, 9th March
Tyne, Lancashire

The sprawling moors, dark purple in the pre-dawn, were swathed in mist. A winding clutter of flint and tumbled walls led to a flinty village, and to the little cottage and bedchamber of the orchardman Peter Dougherty and his pregnant wife. Their toddler was asleep between them while gripping mummy's hair in his fist.

Tyne, with its grey stone and stormy skies, had an altogether different air to it than Pettypoole: something more stringent and defensive, a layer of chilling wariness cultivated over centuries that suited Meg.

But not far from Tyne was Manchester, a city as complete in its Metropolitan operations as London. Dominated by its ash-spitting textile factories, it was a city large enough to lose oneself in, but also more compact than London and owning a police force considerable enough to be able to retrace steps a person of interest may leave behind. A city which, Father had scribbled to

Claire in his hasty note the day he stole her life's savings, held the prospect of an excellent investment.

In her bed, her son tucked between herself and Peter, Meg dreamed that her as yet unborn new babe was turning playful summersaults in her womb before hammering its fists against her belly.

Bang, bang, bang! It was a rapping at her actual door that woke her.

Still in her bedcap and own, a shawl hastily thrown over her shoulders,, Mrs Dougherty swung the front door open and frowned at two constables and a Chief Inspector from Manchester. She'd cultivated a bit of the north in her speech and used it to her advantage when necessary. "What're you getting' at, knocking my door off its hinges?" she scolded, seeming immensely offended by the intrusion. "An' at this hour?"

"What's all this racket, luv?" Bewildered Peter nudged himself alongside her, holding bawling little Petey whose pink hand had been mercilessly wrenched from Mummy's hair. Behind them, a few embers still glowed faintly in the grate, a long chestnut table Peter built was stacked with half-folded laundry and a loaf of bread.

Meg's hand rested on her swollen belly, the other gripped her hip. Her expression was annoyed but otherwise unrevealing.

Her eyes, however, were focused behind the men, knowing there could only be one person they would be looking for at this hour: *Father.* For she was not so stupid as anyone supposed (nor did she really spare herself the newspapers, as she made out to gossipy villagers). I always could take care of myself, she thought proudly, only Claire never gave me the chance. Maybe Claire is finally giving me the chance now, she then thought, in the form of that telegram warning me of Father's path. Maybe she does believe in me after all.

The constables ran through their inquiry: "Has a man of about sixty years called on you, or been seen in the neighbourhood? Is this man a relation of yours? We've got a warrant to look round your shed and through the house." She fixed her eyes beyond their steely mouths, their spotless uniforms, and examined each cottage on her street, each shadowed portico and doorway. She sent a dark message through her eyes, as if telling Father with just her searing gaze, *If you're hiding nearby, see them. See them at my door, and never come near me again. I won't lie for you. I'll never lie for you again.*

Miles away, Claire imagined Meg's disdainful scowl as she stared down the Chief Inspector. Meg would let the constables peek into every room and wardrobe in the cottage, and along the back garden, but she would not tell him or the constables a thing, because she knew nothing more than they did — Claire made sure of that. But Claire also knew Father would meet his match if he dared disrupt Meg's carefully constructed peace. Like him, Meg had always been the free spirit; but there was something of Mother's core in her, too, something moral and grounded and fiercely protective of the family she'd created for herself.

"Like you, Claire," James remarked, later, after reading Meg's letter informing Claire the coppers had dropped in, and that they already had a lead in Manchester city.

"Not like me," she corrected. She took the letter from James and threw it on the fire. She knew it was fear in her core, fear that enforced her to do good. That, and the desire to use her heart wisely where others might not. She aspired to this, anyway. It was all any of us could do in the end.

THREE

1884, Late-Spring
Birdswing House, Silk Road
Wotton Vale, Gloucestershire

She could see the moisture lingering along the waxy leaves of her budding roses, tiny magnifying bubbles reflecting the morning light. The roses wound around a newly forged iron B set into the scrollwork of the front gate. Every house should have a name and Silk House, for her, conjured only merchandise. *Birdswing House* evoked both flight and nesting, as well as other things she held dear.

She would remember for the rest of her life the moment she was freed into this splendor. When the constables walked alongside her—no dragging this time, no digging fingers into her already-bruised arms. Lewes showed her into the police station entry, and it was like the room, with its wobbly stacks of paperwork and the tap-tap-tapping of the telegraph machine, and the young bobby-clerk in his uniform with brass buttons down the front, all came into focus with extraordinary clarity. All around her was suddenly shouting and pointing and shoving—the cacophony so clear, a thousand bells ringing out different notes at once. A court artist scribbled her likeness with charcoal in his large sketchbook and two newsman shouted different questions at her simultaneously. Georgina stood near the dock with Bella, the two signing paperwork and reclaiming the bail they had posted that a clerk now remitted to them: a full purse of notes and one large ruby ring. Mr Winston was berating the Chief Constable and somewhere behind her Marley's gruff voice said in a disappointed tone, "Drop the charges, she's free." Her earrings, wedding band, scissors and needle case were returned, and she wrapped the Punjab wool around her filthy dress, cloaking its ripped and ruined seams, its torn embroidery. She felt the room swell with chaos and then she felt James' arm around her shoulders and watched his other arm extend forward, palm out toward the crowd, forging the way forward.

James, his leather apron smudged with preparations for Georgina's coach, stood close to Claire now just outside the gate. He leaned against her hip; another point of bone that had rounded with flesh in the weeks since the house was made theirs. Her arms were already softer where her shoulder and back met. She'd let out the seams on all her dresses.

"Freddy will be staying, tomorrow night." James had a note of mock-irritation in his voice.

"I have to chase him out of the kitchen from breakfast to supper, you know, he drives Mrs Matthews barking mad asking after her puddings. Sorry, I meant to tell you Bella is coming through later this week, on her way to an estate sale. Skeins of floss for me, I hope."

"Have her look for some writing tablets, too, will you? And some chalk pencils for the children."

"Has the other trunk been mounted yet, sir?" Ruthie asked from the open front door. She looked like a washwoman at the end of her shift. Claire felt not far behind on that score. They'd both been buzzing about since daybreak, trying to fit a few more of Georgina's things into the bulk of her belongings: a music box had just been wrapped in a petticoat and tucked between two books. Claire also attempted, in vain, to wrap one of the smaller portraits lining the stairwell.

"Don't be ridiculous!" Georgina exclaimed when she caught Claire taking it down from the wall. "These faces live here. It is their home. You and I shall never rest if we displace them." It was the first time Claire heard Georgina admit to the house's unseen inhabitants, and she wondered how much humor, if any, was behind the remark.

"Bring me the rug off the chair in Miss Campion's bedroom," Claire told Ruthie, as she marched back up the path toward her. "She will need it on the Channel crossing. Ruthie?" She shooed her from the doorway. "Go on, then, move along. The rug? Thank you."

In the kitchen, Claire reached for the hamper before Mrs Matthews closed it up. Two loaves buttered, a jar of marmalade, a pint of ale, a slice of pork. "This one is too thin," she handed it back. "Give her the whole cut if you must. Not you!" she reprimanded the kitten.

"He's had a yen for it all morning, ma'am."

Claire picked up Ling, kissed his dark muzzle and carried him out of the kitchen.

"The master can have the smaller slice for his tea," Mrs Matthews suggested.

"Wait —" Claire returned, handed Ling to Mrs Matthews, and tied a bunch of hyacinths to the top of the basket.

"She'll always remember the garden," said the cook, her eyes welling up.

Claire gave her a reassuring pat on the back and took Ling, his blue eyes blinking mischievously at the cook over Claire's shoulder.

She circled went into her sitting room, the kitten's purr loud in her ear, and stopped to take a breather in this one room that was void of activity. Near the open French doors, she saw a fourteen-year-old girl with dark hair and a tattered, too-small wool dress dozing in a comfortable chair. *It had always been your comfortable chair. Your doors opening onto your garden. Lady Bridget knew this.*

She felt Ling tugging and chewing on the hair at the nape of her neck as she took one more deep breath before walking through the French doors and around to the front drive.

Outside, Georgina vaguely counted her bundles. "Please don't worry about my things," she said.

The roof of the coupé was stacked with two trunks, a chair, crates of books and art. James, Claire, and Ruthie stood together as the send-off party.

"If I remember something," said Georgina, "I shall have you send it. Or better yet, you will bring it to me—you will love Paris. And," she touched Claire's arm, "if I do not remember something I have left, consider it yours. I've felt like a welcomed guest these last weeks, as if on a lovely holiday. Thank you for that."

Claire kissed her on both cheeks.

"Help me up, man," Georgina ordered James blithely. "You and Matthews have done fine work on the stables." The hay loft, she meant, half of which they'd altered into a schoolroom, for four children who walked up from Squire Grath's tenant hovels in the vale to learn their letters and numbers. One child was a girl, and Claire was teaching her to read.

Claire passed the hamper through the window of the carriage, and Georgina sniffed the blooms on top of the basket. "My hyacinths are the most vivid and pungent in all the Cotswolds! Try showing them at the fairs and you will see: a medal for each hybrid."

"I've sent notice with the removers to the Rose & Crown at Rudgewick, about your staying the night," James informed her. "They will be ahead of you by then."

"The Rose & Crown is excellent accommodation. Your wife's idea, I'm sure. Do not let her spoil you," Georgina warned. She winked, but it was Claire's hand she held firmly, her comfort she spoke of.

Their fingers were pulled apart; the coupé began to move.

"Good travels," Claire called, as the coach rolled away. She waved with a little sadness, but not with apprehension. She was learning to see good-byes differently: a farewell, for instance, could be replaced with a greeting.

She wondered how much she had missed of life without this clarity. How many people have I trusted when I should not have, she thought, and how many could have been trusted had I only realized their true nature? Meg had known that Peter was good almost instantly when Claire did not. And Claire had trusted Father. James and Bella coming into her life seemed like mere luck, when looked at from this perspective.

James rested his hand around her waist while she fanned the neckline of her dress; the linen sticking to her flushed skin. "Are you quite well?" he asked.

She smiled, a little wave of queasiness rising up her middle, then dropping back down again. "It passes, you know, by midday."

"By then you're asleep at your sewing table."

"A small price," she said. "It feels different, you know, from before. From my illness.. There is no fear in this."

James nodded.

"By the way," she said, "Mr Fritch will come for tea tomorrow, instead of Tuesday."

"Fine. Does he have more papers for me to sign, about my school?"

"Yes. But I think he just likes getting out of town for a bit."

"You make him feel welcomed. He can be himself with you."

Placing his hand on her middle, James glanced behind them where a hired man was putting a fresh coat of paint on the shutters. James himself had carved another bird into the shutter on their bedroom window, the old silhouette on the front shutter no longer an orphan.

There was another pair of wings in her sewing room. Beautifully embroidered house finches: a square each for Meg and Claire to quilt onto something larger. The little squares arrived carefully wrapped in tissue, the package bearing Miss Searton's black wax seal, the seal seeming more elegant than ominous now.

The matching birds were crewelworked in indigo wool onto plain white linen torn from the sheets of the asylum's infirmary. An *M* curled from the wing of one bird, a *C* from the other, each wing outstretched and reaching for freedom.

And where was Father now? A vagrant, his once smart waistcoat was now torn and filthy, his hat stolen or toppled into a ditch. He was sneaking through woods and over moors, sleeping under barn eaves as he made his way to nowhere in particular. He was traveling his spiral routes around England, working his charm; or he was holed-up, still, in some shadowed slum of Manchester. Perhaps he was under a barrow himself, having finally met up with someone more clever, and ruthless, than he. Claire would let Mr Fritch tell her if he ever got wind of the ending to that tale.

She watched the back of Georgina's carriage on the drive and waved again. It is true, she thought, I have little use now for sadness, even if its messengers pay me unexpected visits. Life will offer up what it wants whether I like it or not, and it is nonsense to pretend otherwise. *Such is life*, she sometimes heard the voice say. *But now you are living it.*

She watched as the coach receded, as it shrank to the size of a toy then vanished down the lane altogether. In a fortnight, another carriage would grow larger as it neared. Claire would be standing right here at the gate when it pulled up. Her sister would step down: belly-first and proud, descending like a petite empress expecting the next-in-line. Peter would emerge with his cheerful, ruddy face. He would hand Petey to Claire, his little hands outstretched toward his auntie.

She was still thin enough, just now, for him to wrap his arms around her, as she held him close saying, "Welcome home, my love."

AUTHOR'S NOTES

Many of the locations in this book are fictitious, including St. Allswell, Shepherd's Hallow, Pettypoole, Tyne, Halleford-on-Marsh, St. Andrews, and Bonborough, though I have based them somewhat on real locations in Sussex, York, Surrey, Oxfordshire and Gloucestershire respectively. Much of the description of London from 1870-84 is taken from first-person accounts of the time recorded in public records.

A History of Private Life, vol. IV edited by Michelle Perrot has been very helpful to me, as have *The Victorian Dictionary: A Guide to the Social History of Victorian London* by Lee Jackson, *Cassell's Household Guide (Edition, c. 1880)*, *Bibury: A Cotswold Village* by Joanna E. Dee, *Open Fields & Carthorses* by Peter Stayt, *English Style and Decoration* by Stafford Cliff, *William Morris and Morris & Co.* by Lucia van der Post, the various and numerous descriptions of Victorian England in Charles Dickens' essays; also useful were my own travels and experiences throughout England.

Some of the dated medical jargon in the story came from William Buchan's section on "Diseases of Women" in his 1849 book *Domestic Medicine.* The description of tidal ditches and of London's sewage system in the 19th century was lifted in part from the testimony of Henry Mayhew, in the Morning Chronicle, 24th September 1849. Though the city sewage system was improved by the 1870s, when Claire Bietris lived in London as a teenager, much of it was merely forced underground, draining it into the Thames to settle in front of Parliament, and the fear of illness from Cholera remained until the very late 19th Century; proper modern sewage systems were not in place in London until the beginning of the 20th century, and East London as we know it today was not fully existent until after World War II.

Some portions of the description of the fictional Oliver-St. Andrews Asylum were paraphrased from the article "The Hanwell Lunatic Asylum" by Harriet Martineau, in Tait's Edinburgh Magazine, 1834. "The Character of a Happy Life" by Sir Henry Wotton, is excerpted in Chapter Four ("Whose passions not his masters..."), as is William Morris via John Ruskin ("art is the expression..."). Several lines of *The Tragedy of Macbeth* by William Shakespeare are quoted throughout, as well as his *Sonnet XXXIV*; several lines of "Early Spring," by Alfred, Lord Tennyson, are also quoted.

Epigraphs are, in order: Part One: E.M. Forester, *Howard's End*; Part Two: Flora Thompson, *Over to Candleford*; Part Three: "Medical Journal of Dr. William Acton"; Part Four: Thomas Hardy, *Tess of the D'Urberbilles*; Part Five: Anne Brontë, *The Tenant of Wildfell Hall*.

The complex illness that afflicts Claire in this novel was identified in the early part of the 20th Century, and it's only during more recent years of our current century that it is better understood. In explanation of it, I would direct the reader to the following passage of the Bantum Medical Dictionary, Sixth Edition:

Endometriosis, n.: the presence of fragments of endometrial tissue (the mucus membrane lining the uterus) at sites in the pelvis outside the uterus... symptoms vary, but typically include, pelvic pain, severe dysmenorrhea, dyspareunia, infertility, and a pelvic mass (or any combination of these)

And to the literature provided by the Endometriosis SHE Trust of the United Kingdom:

Commonly reported symptoms of Endometriosis include: loss of large clots, migraines, bowel problems... lethargy, mood-swings, swollen abdomen. There is no cure for Endometriosis.

Claire Ableton's story is inspired in part by my own experience, and that of millions of women who, due to societal and medical ignorance, suffered with this disease in previous centuries, many of whom were diagnosed with mental illness or "depravity" and sent to appalling institutions for the mentally ill; and to the one out of every ten women currently living with Endometriosis, many of them also chronically misdiagnosed. An additional thank you to Dr. Caroline Fierro, Dr. Maria Bowling. and Dr. Ilona Polak, for their careful treatment of my own condition.

ACKNOWLEDGEMENTS

Thank yous after all these years are great and start with my family: my children and husband, sister and mother. As always, I thank Ann Hood and Kathryn Tarlow Sears, for absolutely everything.

In addition, I owe a debt of gratitude to Jane Goodrich, Charlotte Rogan, Gabrielle Selz, Heather Harpham, Erin O'Donnell, Emily Amber Faust, Rosalind Woolcott, and Missy Griffiths for their reading and comments, as well as their friendship. Thank you to Matt Connors and Rosie Schaap for support in ways hard to describe, including the gifting of two books that changed my life. Love and thanks to Tim Buggs, J. Stoner Blackwell, Sara Licastro, Ron e Shavers, Mohammed Naseehu Ali, Anna Mazzola, Liz Bertsch and Roger Rosenblatt who have all, at times, offered their time, advice, and support. Special thanks to Hilary Thayer Hamann, who has been a great reader, friend, and provider of various desks and chairs in her home when I needed them most.

I hold dearly in my heart the immensely kind and wise Hilary Mantel, whom I miss more than I can say, and whose reading and notes were vital to the final draft of this novel. Hilary, I hope

I have given the reader the smooth yet still winding path you knew Claire's journey needed.

A huge thank you to Jaclyn Baer at Briar Press, the most supportive and insightful editor and friend a writer could hope for. Thank you to everyone at Briar Press, including Aeven O'Donnell, Chloe Sears and Jen VanArsdale, for helping to make this book a gorgeous object, and shepherding it into the world.

ERICA-LYNN HUBERTY holds a Masters in literature & art from Bennington College. Her essays have been published in The Washington Post, Providence Journal, The New York Times, and many other outlets. Her short story collection, *Dog Boy and Other Harrowing Tales*, was shortlisted for several literary prizes. She is also an internationally acclaimed fiber artist.

A NOTE ABOUT THE TYPE

The text of this book is set in Cochin typeface. It was originally produced in 1912 by Georges Peignot for the Paris foundry G. Peignot et Fils and was based on the copperplate engravings of 18th century French artist Charles-Nicolas Cochin.